Angélique and the Sultan

In the years after her first husband, Joffrey de Peyrac, was sentenced to death by burning, beautiful, emerald-eyed Angélique lived many lives: she was cast penniless into the Paris underworld; she became the mistress of great wealth and married again; she held King Louis XIV's heart in thrall. But she could never forget the scarred nobleman whom she knew as the gentlest and wisest of lovers, and, when the King reveals that Joffrey was spared execution and later escaped his guards, she knows that she will make any sacrifice to find him.

Angélique embarks upon a voyage of discovery which takes her to the wildest coasts of the Mediter-ranean Sea. The clues lead her from Marseilles to Candia, blood-soaked centre of the slave-trade, to Algiers and the fabled harems of Morocco. Ship-wrecked, sold to Rescator, masked prince of the pirates, given to the Grand Eunuch of the Sultan Mulai Ismail, cruellest and most fanatical of the sons of Mohammed, Angélique is sustained only by her great love and by the devotion she inspires in men as diverse as the courtly Admiral de Vivonne and the rough, proud slave, Colin Paturel.

SERGEANNE GOLON

Angélique and the Sultan

TRANSLATED FROM THE FRENCH

BY

MONROE STEARNS

HEINEMANN : LONDON

William Heinemann Ltd

LONDON MELBOURNE TORONTO

JOHANNESBURG AUCKLAND

Published in France by Editions de Trévise 1960
First published in Great Britain 1961
Reprinted 1962, 1964, 1969

434 30104 3

Printed Offset Litho in Great Britain
by Cox & Wyman Ltd,
London, Fakenham and Reading

CONTENTS

CAST OF CHARACTERS

The action of this novel covers less than a year's time and commences in the early 1670's.

Following is a list of the principal characters, including those who play a small part or are merely mentioned in this novel, but who figured in previous episodes of Angélique's life. Those marked with an asterisk are known more or less prominently to history.

Angélique. Born Angélique de Sancé de Monteloup, of a family of the minor nobility in Poitou, she first married Comte Joffrey de Peyrac of Toulouse, Prince of Aquitaine, of the Palace of Gay Learning. Joffrey, a remarkably brilliant and powerful man, was condemned to the stake by Louis XIV on a trumped-up charge of sorcery, and was supposedly executed in February 1661. Reduced to extreme poverty, Angélique became a member of the Paris underworld, the rendezvous of which was the Court of Miracles in the Saint-Denis quarter of Paris. Later, under the name of Madame Morens, she opened a chocolate shop with David Chaillou, whereby she made a great deal of money which she invested shrewdly, becoming extremley rich, and a member of the literary society of Paris. Having been in love with her cousin Philippe, Marquis du Plessis-Bellière, since they were both adolescents, she more or less blackmailed him into marrying her, thus gaining a position in the high nobility of France. She became a shrewd adviser and trusted confidante of Louis XIV and his Minister of Finance, Colbert, and one of the leading members of Louis's brilliant Court at Versailles. The King's attentions to her involved her in a fierce rivalry with his mistress, Madame de Montespan. Louis XIV was deeply in love with Angélique, but she resisted his advances and fled the Court, thus incurring the King's grave displeasure.

Cantor. Angélique's younger son by her first husband, Joffrey de Peyrac. He went as a page on the expedition of the Duc de Vivonne to Sicily, where he disappeared in the pirate Rescator's attack on the French fleet off Cape Passero.

Charles-Henri. Angélique's son by Philippe du Plessis-Bellière.

*Daisy-Valina.** The English-born queen of Mulai Ismail, Sultan of Morocco.

David (Chaillou). Angélique's partner in her chocolate shop business.

Desgrez, François. Lieutenant of the Paris police. He had acted as defence attorney for Joffrey de Peyrac, and had been much in love with Angélique during her days of poverty.

Escrainville, Marquis d'. The younger son of an impoverished family of the minor nobility, who had his career as a young diplomat ruined by amorous intrigue, and turned pirate.

Fatima-Mirelia. A woman from Marseilles who had been captured in her youth by Moorish pirates, and after many years of slavery now served Angélique as a companion and waiting woman.

Flipot. Angélique's lackey. A friend from her Court of Miracles days.

Florimond. Angélique's elder son by Joffrey de Peyrac. A page in the household of Monsieur, brother of King Louis XIV, at Saint-Cloud.

Great Coesre. A legless, loathsome cripple who reigned as King of the Paris underworld in the Court of Miracles, and was once a protector of Angélique, who subsequently stabbed him.

Gutter Poet. A vagabond ballad-singer whom Angélique knew in the Court of Miracles.

Javotte. Angélique's maid. One of her friends from her Court of Miracles days.

Joffrey de Peyrac. Comte de Toulouse and Prince of Aquitaine, Angélique's first husband.

Leïla Aisheh. The chief wife of Mulai Ismail, Sultan of Morocco.

Lesdiguières, Abbé de. A young priest employed by Angélique as tutor for her son Florimond.

*Louis XIV** (1638-1715), King of France from 1643, when his father, Louis XIII, died, leaving the government in the hands of his widow Anne of Austria and Cardinal Mazarin. In 1660 he married Marie-Thérèse of Spain, and after the death of Mazarin early the following year took the reins of government into his own hands. He became something of a despot, but raised France from anarchy to a world power through his skilful employment of ministers and militarists wiser than he. His Court was so brilliant, and he stimulated art and literature to such a degree that he ranks among the greatest monarchs of history and probably deserved the title of 'Sun King'. His character is best expressed in his famous remark: '*L'état, c'est moi*' (I am the State).

Malbrant. Fencing-master of Angélique's sons. An elderly man, he was nicknamed 'Swordthrust' because of his preoccupation with all kinds of swordplay.

*Mezzo-Morte** (d. 1698). A pirate from Calabria, Italy, who became Lord High Admiral of Algiers. In 1683 Louis XIV sent a special expedition against him under the command of Admiral Duquesne, who captured him. Mezzo-Morte promised that he would no longer oppose the French if he were liberated, but as soon as he had regained his freedom, he seized the Dey of Algiers and became ruler of the country under the name of Raj Husain. When the French sent another expedition against him, he fired their envoy-missionary Father Levacher out of a cannon at the attacking ships, but soon thereafter met his own end in the ensuing engagement.

*Monsieur** (Philippe, Duc d'Orléans) (1640-1701), brother of Louis XIV and founder of the existing House of Orléans. He was married to Henriette d'Angleterre, sister of Charles II of England, whom he possibly poisoned and whom he greatly abused owing to his profligate and degenerate way of life.

*Montespan**, *Athénaïs de* (1641-1707). Born a Rochechouart de Mortemart of Poitou, she married a minor Gascon noble, Pardaillan de Montespan. In 1668 she became Louis XIV's mistress, succeeding Louise de la Vallière, and ruled as uncrowned queen of France. Historians and biographers still debate whether she was actually involved in the 'affair of the poisons', which removed many courtiers, or practised the Black Mass with the sorcerers of Paris. She bore the King several children, and befriended Françoise Scarron, later Madame de Maintenon and the unofficial wife of Louis XIV.

*Mulai Ismail** (1647-1727). Sultan of Morocco (1672-1727) and the counterpart in many respects of Louis XIV, he was the greatest of the Filali (or Hasanid) dynasty and a brilliant though cruel ruler. He maintained diplomatic relations with France and England, and once sent an embassy to Louis XIV to ask for the hand of the Princesse de Conti, which makes an amazing incident in history. His love of building was equal to that of Louis XIV, and he made a magnificent city out of his capital of Meknès. He cleverly unified his large empire by a system of roads and forts and, by establishing agricultural communities throughout it, redeemed it from the barren mountains and desert of which it consisted. His only major failure was his inability to recapture the outposts of Christian nations in Morocco, such as Ceuta, which he besieged for many years. He is said to have begotten 528 sons and as many daughters on his numerous wives and concubines, and to have held as many as twenty-five thousand Christian captives at one time, whom he set to work at his buildings and gardens.

Nicholas (*Calembredaine*). First attracted to Angélique when he was a shepherd boy on her family estate in Poitou, he became her lover after he had turned robber and met her again in the Court of Miracles.

Osman Faraji. The Grand Eunuch of the Sultan of Morocco, Mulai Ismail.

Paturel, Colin. A Norman sailor and sometime pirate who, after being captured by the Moors, became the leader of the Christian slaves in Morocco.

Philippe, Marquis du Plessis-Bellière, Angélique's second husband, was one of the great nobles of France, dearly beloved by Louis XIV, whose Master of the Hunt he was, as well as a Marshal of France. He was killed at the siege of a town in Franche-Comté.

Rakoczy. An Hungarian prince and revolutionary with whom Angélique had a brief affair while he was an exile in France. His character and career are modelled on those of Francis Rakoczy II (1676-1735).

Rescator. A mysterious trader in contraband silver, the richest and possibly the most powerful freebooter in the Mediterranean.

Reynie. The Chief of Police of Paris.

Rochat. Angélique's deputy at Candia in Crete. Angélique had won the office of 'Consul of Candia' from another French noblewoman in a game of cards. This meant that she was entitled to a certain percentage of the duties collected in the port, but the office required no administration on her part.

Rodogone the Egyptian. One of the vagabonds of the Court of Miracles.

Savary. A little old apothecary and alchemist whom Angélique had known at Versailles and who had assisted her in her diplomatic mission for Louis XIV to Bakhtiari Bey, the ambassador of the Shah of Persia.

Sévigné*, Madame de (1626-96). A famous wit of the reign of Louis XIV, whose brilliant, charming letters, written principally to her daughter who lived in Provence, are an invaluable source of information on the life of the Court and the social history of the seventeenth century in France.

Vivonne*, Louis Victor de Rochechouart, Duc de Mortemart et de (1636-88), the brother of Madame de Montespan. After brilliant military service under Louis XIV in his campaigns in Holland and the Rhenish Palatinate, he was made Admiral of the Fleet, in 1669, and Marshal of France in 1675. He conducted many successful campaigns in the Mediterranean. Well educated, generous, and a patron of literature, he was famous also for his wit as a writer and conversationalist. His character, however, was not universally admired by his contemporaries, largely because of his association with Monsieur's extremely dissipated household. Madame de Sévigné despised him; the Duc de Saint-Simon praised him.

PART ONE

Departure

The coach of Police Lieutenant François Desgrez swung out of the *porte-cochère* of his hotel and slowly turned on to the pudding-shaped cobblestones of the Rue de la Commanderie in the Faubourg Saint-Germain. It was hardly a sumptuous vehicle, but it was substantial. Made of dark wood, enough golden tassels dangled from its window curtains, which were usually kept tightly drawn, to render it comparable to the equipage kept by a respectable public servant richer than he wished to appear. Two piebald horses drew it, and it sported a coachman and a footman.

The only thing Desgrez's associates held against him was his bachelorhood. Such a good-looking man, at home in the best society, ought to have by his side the daughter of some judicious, honest, frugal merchant. There were plenty of them, trained for just such a marriage by strict mothers and severe fathers, right in the very homes he was passing on his way through the Faubourg Saint-Germain. But Desgrez, charming in a stiff conventional way, seemed in no hurry to change his status. Too many bedizened women and too many suspicious characters shared his waiting-room with the highest born and most loftily titled grandees of the realm.

The coach wheels grated across the ruts to the middle of the street, and the horses' hooves struck sparks from the stones as the coachman reined them into a straight course. The numerous pedestrians idling in the hot dusk flattened themselves servilely against the walls of the buildings – all but one masked woman, who seemed to be waiting for the coach to catch up to her. As it drew near, she leaned into its window, wide open because of the heat.

'Lieutenant Desgrez,' she said coquettishly, 'let me ride beside you and chat for a few minutes.'

The policeman, startled out of his brooding over the outcome of a recent investigation, turned to her with anger in his face. There was no need for him to ask her to raise her visor. He had already recognised Angélique.

'You again?' he growled. 'Don't you understand plain language? I thought I had told you I never want to see you again.'

'I understood,' she said, 'but this is very, *very* important and you are the only person who can help me. I didn't want to do this, and I thought a long time before I did. But I couldn't think of another

3

person in the whole world who could help me but you.'

'I told you I did not want to see you again,' Desgrez repeated through clenched teeth.

Such an outburst was unusual for him. Usually he disguised his feelings in a dry, cold impassivity, which now deserted him.

Angélique had not expected such an explosion on his part. She had thought he might begin by brushing her off, for she had broken her agreement not to bother him again; but she had decided that what she had learned from the King was extraordinary enough to touch Desgrez's hard heart if he were still in love with her. She did need him. Still she was not surprised to find that he was 'not at home' on the two occasions she had called at his hôtel, and that there was little chance he would ever receive her. Hence she had waited for a propitious moment like this to approach him directly. She was convinced he would listen to her and eventually oblige her.

'It's terribly important, Desgrez,' she wheedled. 'My husband is alive. . . .'

'I told you I did not wish to see you,' Desgrez said for the third time. 'You have enough lovers to keep you busy, whether your husband is alive or dead. Now, let go of the door. The horses are about to move on.'

'I won't let go,' Angélique insisted. 'The horses can drag me over the stones before I'll let you go without listening to me.'

'Let go of the door!'

Desgrez's voice was sinister. Seizing the walking-stick beside him, he brought its pommel down hard on Angélique's fingers as they grasped the window-sill. She screamed with pain. The coach jerked forward.

Angélique had fallen on her knees. A water vendor who had been goggling at the entire incident came up to her as she struggled to her feet and began dusting off her dress.

'It's just not your night, dearie,' he said, 'so make the best of it. You can't always catch the big fish. But they do say he likes pretty girls, so you've still got a chance. You just chose the wrong time. How about a cup of water to pull yourself together? A storm's coming up and that always makes people thirsty. My water is fresh and pure. Only six *sols* a cup.'

Angélique walked away without answering. Desgrez's uncompromising behaviour had deeply pained her. 'It's unbelievable,' she said to herself, 'how selfish men can be.' Obviously he wanted to torture himself by consigning his love for her to total oblivion, but still he could have made one more little effort especially when she was so desperate

4

for someone to turn to, someone to help her out of her dilemma.

And Desgrez was the only one who could help her. He had known her since the time of Peyrac's trial; in fact, had been closely involved in it. His policeman's turn of mind could help her sort facts from fancies, find some theory to work on for further investigation. Perhaps he even knew something about this extraordinary turn of events. There were certainly plenty of mysteries and secrets carefully stowed away in the depths of his memory or filed in his locked cabinets. Furthermore, though she did not admit it to herself, she needed Desgrez to free her from the terrible burden of the secret she carried so that she would not be so wholly alone with her possibly insane hopes – flickering raptures that could easily be extinguished by the icy wind of doubt. If only she could talk with him about the past, and about the future which loomed before her like a whirlpool in which, perhaps, lurked the crowning happiness of her life.

'You know perfectly well there is something waiting for you on the horizon of your life. You are not going to stop seeking it. . . .'

That was what Desgrez had told her long ago. Yet now he had just cruelly renounced her. Her mouth twisted in disappointment.

She was walking rapidly, for she had borrowed Javotte's skirt and summer shawl so as to be unnoticed in the crowd while she waited for Desgrez to leave his house. For three long hours she had stood waiting, and now – for what!

Night was falling and the streets were emptying. As she crossed the Pont-Neuf, Angélique turned around apprehensively. Two men she had noticed hanging about her house the last few days were following her. Perhaps it was merely a coincidence, but she could not understand why that red-faced loiterer who had been staring so continuously at Beautreillis should have chosen this particular hour of the day for a stroll through the Faubourg Saint-Germain and over the Pont-Neuf.

Probably some admirer, she thought. But it worried her. If he kept on manoeuvring that way any longer, she would instruct Swordthrust Malbrant to persuade him to try his luck elsewhere.

Near the Palais de Justice she hired a sedan chair and a linkboy to bring her to within a few steps of the little door to her orchard on the Quai des Célestins. She walked along its paths, fragrant with the scent of the still green fruit that hung from the branches of the silver-potted trees, past the gothic well-head with its gargoyles, and stole up the staircase.

A single lamp was burning near the ebony and mother-of-pearl secretary in her sitting-room. With a sigh of fatigue she sank into a chair and kicked the slippers off her aching, burning feet. She had grown quite unused to walking over uneven pavements, and to the hot thick leather of the shoes she had borrowed from her maid.

'I haven't the endurance I used to have,' she reflected, 'but if I'm going to have to travel under difficult conditions . . .'

She was plagued by this notion of setting forth, seeing herself on rough roads, poor and barefoot, as she pursued her pilgrimage of love in search of the happiness she had lost. I must go, she said to herself. But where to?

Then her thoughts returned to the documents the King had entrusted to her – those few sheets of time-stained paper, scabbed with seals and scrawled over with signatures. There lay the only concrete proof of the incredible story he had revealed to her. Whenever she thought she might have dreamed it all, she read over again their record of how Maître Arnaud de Calistère, lieutenant of the King's musketeers, had been charged by the King himself with a mission he solemnly swore to keep secret. It named the six musketeers selected to assist him – all known for their loyalty to the King and for their uncommunicative dispositions. Hence it would not be necessary to cut their tongues out as was done in olden times.

Another page, conscientiously itemised by Maître Calistère, listed the expenses incurred on his mission:

> 20 *livres* for hiring the Blue Grape wineshop on the morning of the execution.
>
> 30 *livres* to pay the owner, Maître Gilbert, to keep the secret.
>
> 10 *livres* to buy a corpse from the morgue for burning instead of the condemned man.
>
> 20 *livres* to silence the men who delivered the corpse.
>
> 50 *livres* for the tumbril and for silence.
>
> 10 *livres* for the hay-covered barge to carry the prisoner from Saint-Landry gate to beyond Paris.
>
> 10 *livres* to stop the mouths of the boatmen.
>
> 5 *livres* to hire bloodhounds to track down the prisoner after his escape. (Here Angélique's heart began to beat wildly.)
>
> 10 *livres* to silence the farmers who rented the hounds and helped drag the river.

Total   165 *livres*

Angélique laid aside Arnaud de Calistère's meticulous accounting and scrutinised the report he had so scrupulously compiled.

6

'. . . Toward midnight, below Mantes, the barge on which we were transporting the prisoner stopped and tied up on the steep river bank. Each of us took a little rest. I left a guard by the prisoner, who had given no sign of life since the moment we received him from the hands of the executioner. We had had to carry him the entire length of the tunnel from the cellar of the Blue Grape to the water's edge. Since he was lying under the hay, hardly breathing . . .'

Angélique could picture his huge tortured body wrapped in the shroud-like white robe of a condemned man.

'Before dropping off to sleep I asked if he needed anything. He did not seem to hear me.'

As a matter of fact, while Maître Calistère was wrapping himself in his cloak to 'drop off to sleep', he expected to find his prisoner more dead than alive the next day. But that is not at all the way he did find him.

Angélique burst out laughing. The picture of a defeated, dying or dead Joffrey de Peyrac was incongruous to her. She would never be able to imagine him like that. Rather she kept seeing him as he must have been right up to the very end, every fibre of his senses on the alert even though his body was exhausted, every morsel of his spirit refusing to yield to death, resolved to play the game boldly till the last moment of existence. He was a miracle of will-power. She had known him to be quite capable of that, and more.

In the morning they had found only the deep impression his mighty body had made in the pile of hay. She pitied the guard who must have had to confess that watching a dying man did not require the utmost in vigilance and who, at the urging of physical exhaustion, must have yielded to the entreaties of the goddess of slumber.

'The disappearance of the prisoner is entirely inexplicable. How could a man, without enough strength to open his eyes, have slipped off a boat without attracting attention? And what could have become of him afterwards? Even if he could have managed to drag himself off the barge, how could he have escaped discovery, half-naked and in the state of exhaustion he was?'

They had immediately scoured the countryside for him, alerted the peasants, hired hounds to track him up and down the riverbank. Eventually they had concluded the prisoner had by some superhuman means slid off the barge but had been carried away by the current and, too weak to struggle against it, had drowned.

Later, however, a peasant complained that his skiff had been stolen from its moorings the night before. The lieutenant of the musketeers did not fail to investigate this piece of evidence. The skiff had been found near Porcheville. They combed the whole district, questioned all the inhabitants as to whether any of them had seen a thin, limping man wandering about. Some said yes, and took the musketeers to a little monastery sequestered in the poplars whose abbot a few days previously had sheltered one of the lepers one still found wandering about the countryside – a pathetic creature covered with sores, his disease-ravaged face partially concealed with filthy rags. Was the leper a big man? they asked. Did he have a limp? Yes, perhaps – the monk's memory was vague. Did he have a cultivated voice, unusual for a vagrant? No, the man was dumb, his only sound being the hoarse warning call of a leper. The abbot had reminded him of his duty to seek out the nearest lazaret, and the man did not refuse. He had climbed into the work-wagon with the abbot, but had found a way to give him the slip as they were going through some woods.

They found him again near Saint-Denis on the outskirts of Paris. But was it the same leper or another? At the instigation of Arnaud de Calistère, whom the King had given extraordinary authority, all the police of Paris were alerted. For three weeks after the disappearance of the lieutenant's prisoner, the gates of Paris permitted no wagon to enter the city before its layers of hay had been prodded and poked, and no one on foot or on horseback before he had been carefully measured and examined.

The dossier Angélique was leafing through was full of reports compiled by some painstakingly literal-minded sergeant of the guard testifying that on such and such a day he had detained 'an old man with a lame leg, but who was thickset and not handsome, but not ill-favoured either . . .' or a masked nobleman, 'who turned out to be disguised because he was bent on some amatory errand and was not lame either'. Et cetera, et cetera.

The wandering leper had not been recognised, yet all Paris knew who he was and was in fear of him. He looked like the Devil. His face was especially frightful since he always wore a shroud or a kind of monk's cowl. A policeman caught him late one night, but had not the courage to lift that cowl, and the apparition vanished before he could call the soldiers of the watch.

Then the speculations as to the wandering leper suddenly came to an end. In the rushes by the river below Mantes, at Gassicourt, was found the body of a man who had been drowned at least a month. The corpse was in an advanced state of decay, and all that could be determined was that it was a large man.

Heaving a sigh of relief, Lieutenant Calistère remarked in a letter to the King that he had already foreseen this ending to the story, as it was the only possible one. By escaping, the man had failed to appreciate the mercy of the King who had snatched him from the flames of the stake at the last moment. God had punished him for his arrogance by condemning him to the icy waters of the river. All was, as ever, for the best.

'No! No!' protested Angélique. 'It can't be true!'

Horrified, she refused to acknowledge this painful epilogue to the story, preferring to fasten her hopes to the few lines added to it by the Bailiff of Gassicourt who had conducted the inquest on the body: 'A few shreds of a black cassock still clung to its shoulders.'

When he escaped from the barge, the prisoner was wearing only his white shroud. But Arnaud de Calistère had underlined the words in his own handwriting: 'The description of the drowned man tallies exactly with that of our prisoner. . . .'

'But what about the white shroud?' Angélique said aloud.

She sprang to the defence of her feeble hopes against these shadows of doubt. Then fear crept over her. Perhaps the soldiers had changed the prisoner's white garment for a black cassock before hauling him through the tunnel to the boat that was to carry him out of Paris.

'If only I could locate that Arnaud de Calistère or one of his men, and question him!' she said.

She searched her memory, but she had never heard his name mentioned while she was at Court. Still, it would be relatively easy to find out what had become of a former lieutenant of the King's musketeers. Fourteen years had gone by since these events. Fourteen years! How short a time it seemed, and yet since then she had lived so many lives! She had gone from the depths of poverty to the heights of wealth. She had married again. She had held the King's heart in thrall. Now all that had vanished as a dream.

A letter from Madame de Sévigné lay open on the writing-shelf of her secretary:

'For almost two weeks, my dear, we have not seen you at Versailles, and people are beginning to ask questions. No one knows what to think. The King is gloomy. What is going on? . . .'

Angélique shrugged her shoulders. True, she had left Versailles. She was never going back. Never! Phantoms swirled around her, but she ignored them, concentrating all her thoughts on her reconstruction of

9

a heavy barge beside the icy bank of a river on a winter's night long ago.

Thus she returned to life. She forgot her body, possessed by so many; her face, the triumph of the cosmetician's art, which could cause the King to weaken; all the marks that harsh destiny had branded upon her. She felt miraculously purified, restored to all the untrammelled innocence she had possessed at twenty – a completely new woman with eyes of emerald green, captivatingly tender and turning to *him*. . . .

'A man is asking for you.'

The white head of Swordthrust Malbrant was suddenly before her eyes.

'A man is asking for you,' he repeated.

She hesitated a moment out of surprise, suddenly aware that she must have dropped off to sleep as she sat on her footstool, her hands around her knees. By opening the little door behind the tapestries the old man must have roused her. She passed her hand over her forehead.

'What? Oh! Yes . . . a man . . . What man? What time is it?'

'Three o'clock in the morning.'

'And yet you say a man is asking for me?'

'Yes, Madame.'

'Did the gatekeeper let him in at this hour?'

'The gatekeeper had nothing to do with it. He did not come in by the door, but by a window. Sometimes I leave my window open, and this fellow came through it by way of the rain trough.'

'You're making fun of me, Malbrant. If it were a burglar, you would have taken care of him.'

'As a matter of fact, it was the other way round. This gentleman "took care" of me. Then he assured me you were expecting him, and I let myself believe him. He is surely some friend of yours, Madame. He gave me plenty of evidence to prove it.'

Angélique frowned. Here was another wild story. Then she remembered the man who had seemed to be following her the past week.

'What does he look like? Small or big? Red-faced?'

'No indeed! He seems quite a gentleman. But it's hard to say what he looks like because he's wearing a mask. His hat's pulled down over his brows and his cloak muffled up to his nose. But if you want my opinion, Madame, he is someone important.'

'And if so, why does he steal into a person's house by way of the roof! Well, go fetch him, Malbrant, but be ready to sound the alarm.'

Curious in spite of herself, she waited until the figure appeared in the doorway. Then she had no trouble recognising him.

CHAPTER TWO

'You!'

'Yes, it's I,' answered the voice of Desgrez.

Angélique gestured to the old man. 'You may leave us.'

Desgrez pushed back his hat, and took off his mask and his cloak. 'Whew!' he said. He took the hand she offered him and gently kissed the tips of her fingers. 'That is by way of apology for my brutality a while back. I hope I didn't hurt you too much.'

'You almost broke my fingers with that stick of yours, you naughty man. I must say I don't understand your behaviour, Monsieur Desgrez.'

'Yours is not much more understandable – or agreeable,' the officer answered. He pulled up a chair and sat astride it. He was not wearing his formal wig or his highly conventional clothes. Clad in the shabby greatcoat he wore on all his secret expeditions, and with his unkempt hair, he looked the image of a policeman.

Angélique, too, was in the garments of a poor woman, her bare feet crossed in front of her. 'Did you really have to come to see me at this hour of the night?' she asked.

'Yes, I did.'

'So you thought over your unjustified hostility to me, and couldn't wait till daylight to make amends?'

'No, that's not it at all. But since you kept saying over and over again that you needed to see me so badly, I couldn't wait till daylight.' He made a fatalistic gesture. 'Since you do not wish to understand that I have had enough of you and that I do not want even to hear your name again, I had all the more reason for coming.'

'It's terribly important, Desgrez.'

'Of course, it's important. I know you. Nothing would make you bother the police for a joke. With you, it's always something important – you're about to be murdered, or else commit suicide, or perhaps you've decided to involve the Royal Family in some fiendish scandal, or disobey the Pope. How should I know?'

'Desgrez, you have never caught me out of my depth.'

'That's what I resent. You never get involved in the farcical situations self-respecting women do. With you there's always drama afoot, but never drama on a grand scale. In your case no one has to do anything but pray he won't arrive too late. So, you see, here I am – and in time too.'

'Desgrez, can you possibly help me one more time?'

'We shall see,' he said darkly. 'First tell me what it's all about.'

'Why did you come in through the window?'

'Now don't tell me you don't know why. Haven't you noticed that you've been followed by the police for a week?'

'Followed by the police? I?'

'Yes indeed. An accurate record has to be kept of all the comings and goings of Madame du Plessis-Bellière. There's not a cranny of Paris you've visited that you haven't been followed by two or three guardian angels. Not a letter you've written that hasn't been stolen and read with great care before being sent on to its destination. A network of guards has been woven just for you at every gate of the city. No matter what direction you choose to take, you can't go a hundred yards without being accompanied. A very high officer has to answer personally for your presence in the capital.'

'Who is it?'

'Monsieur de la Reynie's own lieutenant, a certain Desgrez. You've heard of him perhaps?'

Angélique was astonished. 'You mean *you* have been instructed to spy on me and keep me from leaving the city?'

'Exactly so. Now you may understand why in such circumstances it's been impossible for me to receive you openly. I could hardly carry you off in my coach right under the very eyes of those I had put on your trail.'

'Who gave you this undignified assignment?'

'The King.'

'The King? Why?'

'His Majesty did not take me into his confidence, but you must have some idea of why, haven't you? I know only one thing, which is that the King does not want you to leave Paris. I have made my plans accordingly. Aside from that, what can I do for you? What commands do you have for your faithful servant?'

Angélique twisted her hands nervously in her lap. So, the King did not trust her! He was not admitting she had disobeyed him, but was just keeping her near him by force until – until she did what he wanted. But that she would never do!

As Desgrez kept looking at her he was thinking that in these simple clothes of hers and her bare feet she was like a wild bird anxiously darting its eyes in every direction to find some means of escape from its captors. Already the gilded cage that imprisoned her with luxurious appointments seemed no fit place for this woman who had laid aside her usual sumptuous raiment. Indeed she had even rid herself of her worldly mannerisms and she seemed a stranger in the atmosphere she had now created around her. Suddenly she was like a lonely little barefoot shepherdess so far away that she touched Desgrez's heart. He brushed aside a thought that occurred to him, that she had never been made for this kind of world, everything was a mistake.

'Well, what's the matter? What do you want of your servant?' he said aloud.

In the soft light Angélique's stare wavered. 'Do you want to help me?' she repeated.

'Yes, on condition that you make your eyes behave and keep your distance. Stay where you are,' he ordered her as she started toward him. 'This is no time for pleasure. Don't tantalise me, you little devil!' Desgrez took out his pipe and dug it into his tobacco pouch. 'Go on, my dear, tell me the whole story.'

She liked his way of speaking, as if he were her confessor. It made things easier for her.

'My husband is alive,' she said.

He did not even flicker an eyelid. 'Which one? You had two, I believe, and both seem to be quite dead. One was burned at the stake, the other's head was blown off in a battle. Has there been a third?'

Angélique shook her head. 'Don't pretend not to know what I'm talking about, Desgrez. My husband is alive. He was not burned in the Place de Grève as he was condemned to be. At the last moment the King pardoned him and had him spirited away. The King himself told me so. My husband, the Comte de Peyrac, was saved from the pyre but was still considered dangerous to the safety of the kingdom, and so had to be taken secretly to a prison outside Paris. But he escaped. Look, here are the papers to prove it.'

The police officer was applying his tinder box to the bowl of his pipe. He puffed a while, then carefully put the box away before casually waving aside the dossier she was holding out to him.

'No need for me to look at it. I know what's in it.'

'You know?' Angélique echoed in bewilderment. 'Have you already been through all these papers?'

'Yes.'

'When, for heaven's sake?'

'Some years ago now. Yes, I got a little curious. I had just bought my commission as a police officer, and I thought it wise to forget a few things. No one remembered any longer that "unattractive lawyer" who had been so stupid as to get mixed up in the defence of a sorcerer con-

13

demned before trial. The whole affair was buried, but sometimes it would pop into my mind again. People let a few things drop. I searched. I slunk off. A policeman has ways of getting into almost any place, you know. In the end I discovered this. I read it.'

'And you never told me!' she murmured.

'No.'

As he stared at her through the haze of blue smoke he kept exhaling, she began to hate him and his loathsome way of prying into things like a sly cat. He could not be still in love with her. There was no such weakness in him. He would always be stronger than she.

'You remember, my dear,' he said at last, 'the evening when you said good-bye to me in your chocolate shop? You had just informed me you were going to marry the Marquis du Plessis-Bellière. In one of those strange intimacies that women manage you said: "Isn't it funny, Desgrez, that I can never get out of my head the hope of seeing him again some day? There are some who say it wasn't he who was burned in the Place de Grève." '

'That's the time you should have told me,' she exclaimed.

'What good would it have done? You were just on the point of gathering all the fruits of your superhuman efforts. To harvest them you had spared yourself neither hard work, nor courage, nor the lowest kinds of intrigue, nor even your own virtue. You had thrown everything into the scale to balance your ambition. You were on the brink of triumph. If I had said anything, I would have destroyed it all for you and left you with only a phantom.'

She was hardly listening to him. 'You should have told me,' she repeated. 'Think of the mortal sin you let me commit by marrying another man while my husband was still alive.'

Desgrez shrugged. 'Alive? There was always the chance he was the corpse they fished out of the river at Gassicourt. Dead by burning or dead by drowning, what difference did it make to you?'

'No!' she shouted jumping up. 'No, it's impossible!'

'What would you have done if I had told you?' Desgrez said coldly. 'You would have wrecked everything just as you are about to do now. You would have thrown away all your trump cards, all your chances, your destiny and your children's too. You would have gone off like a crazy woman in search of a shadow, a phantom, just as you are about to do now. Admit it,' he said threateningly, 'That's what you have in mind – to go searching for this husband of yours who vanished away some fourteen years ago.' He rose and stood before her. 'Where is he? How? And *why?*'

She jumped up at his last word. 'Why?'

The police officer gave her a look that pierced her soul. 'He was the Comte de Toulouse,' he said. 'But the Comte de Toulouse no longer exists. He reigned in a palace. Now he has no palace. He was the richest lord of the whole realm. He is no more the richest lord of the kingdom. His wealth has been confiscated. He was a scholar known throughout the entire world. Now he is unknown. Where could he practise his craft? What would be left of all you loved him for?'

'Desgrez, you cannot understand the love a man like him could kindle.'

'Perhaps, but I think I understand how he could enchant a woman's heart. But now that those spells of his are no more . . .'

'Don't make me think you're naïve about these things, Desgrez. You know nothing about the way a woman loves.'

'I know a little about you, though.' He put his hands on her shoulders and pivoted her around until she could see herself in the tall, gold-framed oval mirror. 'You've added years to yourself – your skin, your eyes, your soul, your body. Such a life as you've lived! All those lovers you've given yourself to . . .'

She broke away from him, her cheeks flaming, and looked him square in the face. 'Yes, I know. But that has nothing to do with the love I bear him . . . that I shall always have for him. Between us, dear Monsieur Desgrez, what would you think of a woman so blessed by nature as I who kept living alone, abandoned by everyone and in the depths of distress, who did not try to get herself out of such a state of affairs? You would say she was a moron, and you would be right. Perhaps I seem like a cynic to you, but if I had to today, I would not hesitate one instant to use my power over men to get what I want. What did any of the men – all the men – who came after him really mean to me? Nothing, absolutely nothing!' She kept staring at him boldly and wickedly. 'Nothing, you hear. Even now I feel toward them only something very close to hatred. Toward *all* of them!'

Desgrez was contemplating his fingernails. 'I am not entirely convinced by your cynicism,' he said. A deep sigh escaped him. 'I recall a certain little Gutter-Poet . . . And as for the handsome Marquis Philippe du Plessis-Bellière, wasn't there a little tenderness on your part somewhere there . . . a rather warm affection?'

She shook her head so violently her hair flew. 'Ah, Desgrez, you can't understand. A woman has to have her illusions. She has to try to live. A woman needs so desperately to love and to be loved. The memory of him has always stayed with me like a piercing sorrow.' She glanced down at her hand. 'In the cathedral at Toulouse he slipped a golden ring on my finger. Perhaps it is the only thing left of our life together, but it binds me to him. I am his wife, and he is my husband. I will always be his, and he mine. That's why I shall search for him. The world is wide, but if he still lives in some corner of it I will find him if I have to tramp the rest of my life.'

Her voice caught in her throat as she saw herself plodding along a broiling hot road, old and despairing.

Desgrez took her in his arms. 'There, there,' he soothed. 'I've been too hard on you, my darling, but you've been hard on me too.' He pressed her to him until she cried out. Then he released her and began to puff on his pipe again abstractedly.

'Good!' he said after a moment. 'Since you've made up your mind to indulge in this foolishness, to destroy your fortune and perhaps your very life, and since no one can stop you, what are you planning to do?'

'*I don't know,*' said Angélique. Then she thought for a bit. 'I had thought,' she said, 'I would try to find that Calistère, the former lieutenant of the musketeers. He is the only one, if he has any memory left, who could help us eliminate the doubt hovering over the drowned man of Gassicourt.'

'It's been done,' Desgrez said brusquely. 'I located that officer, gave him a good meal and found ways to refresh his memory. Finally he acknowledged that the affair of the drowned man of Gassicourt had reached a point where it was advantageous for him to bring to an end an investigation that was putting him in a bad light. But he admitted there were only very vague points of resemblance between the corpse and the escaped prisoner.'

'Oh, yes!' Angélique gasped hopefully. 'Then the trail of the wandering leper would be a good one to follow.'

'Who can say?'

'We must go to Pontoise and question the monks of the little abbey where he was seen.'

'That has been done.'

'How so?'

'Well, in a manner of speaking, I took advantage of an inquest that brought me into that region to ring the bell at the abbey.'

'Desgrez, you are an astonishing man!'

'Stay where you are,' he said rudely. 'My visit did not shed much light on the case. The abbot could not tell me much more than he had told the soldiers when they questioned him. But a lay brother, the monastery physician, remembered a detail or two when I found him grubbing in his herb garden. He had pitied the poor wretch enough to want to put some salve on his sores, and had gone to the barn where the exhausted vagrant seemed so sound asleep he thought him dead. "He was not a leper," the doctor told me. "I lifted the rags from his face and found it not eaten away but merely badly scarred." '

'So it was he, then, wasn't it? It was he! But what was he doing at Pontoise? Wouldn't he have come back to Paris? How stupid!'

'The same kind of stupidity a man like him was capable of committing for a woman like you.'

'But they lost track of him at the city gates.' Angélique riffled through the papers feverishly. 'Still, they say he was recognised in Paris.'

'That seems impossible to me. He could not have got in. For three weeks after his escape the strictest orders were given to watch all the gates. Then the discovery of the corpse at Gassicourt and Arnaud de Calistère's investigations put an end to the excitement. The dossier was closed. To make absolutely sure, I rummaged around a little in the archives afterward. Nothing about the affair appeared again.'

A heavy silence fell upon them.

'Is that all you know, Desgrez?'

The police officer paced the floor for a while before he replied: 'No.'

He kept gnawing the stem of his pipe as he stared at her. 'No!' he growled between his teeth.

'What is it? Tell me!'

'Well, here it is . . . three years or so ago I had a visitor, a young priest with leaden eyes sunk in a waxen face, like those fellows who haven't the slightest inspiration yet are determined to reform the world. He wanted to know whether I might be the same person as the Desgrez who in 1661 had been appointed defence attorney in the trial of the Comte de Peyrac. He had searched for me in vain among my colleagues in the Palais de Justice, and he had had considerable difficulty recognising me in the cast-off clothes of a dreary jailer. After I had assured him I was the same Desgrez he was looking for, he told me he was Father Antoine and belonged to the Order founded by Monsieur Vincent. He had been the prison chaplain, and in that capacity had accompanied the Comte de Peyrac to the stake.'

Suddenly Angélique saw before her eyes again the outlines of the priest who sat hunched before the executioner's blaze like a half-frozen cricket.

'In a roundabout way he asked me if I knew what had become of the

Comte de Peyrac's wife. I said I did, but that I would like to know who was so interested in a woman whose name everyone had forgotten. In some embarrassment he said it was he himself. He had often thought of how sad and forlorn she must be, and had prayed for her. He hoped life had been merciful to her at last. I don't know why, but there was something in his protestations of interest that sounded false. In my business you can often detect a touch of insincerity in such embarrassment. Still, I told him what I knew.'

'What did you tell him, Desgrez?'

'The truth. That you had indeed been relieved of hardship, that you had married the Marquis du Plessis-Bellière, and that you were then one of the most envied women in the Court of France. Curiously enough, instead of pleasing him, this information seemed to alarm him. Perhaps he thought you were doomed to perdition, for I let him understand you were about to supplant Madame de Montespan in the King's affections.'

In despair Angélique exclaimed: 'Oh, why did you have to tell him that? You're a monster!'

'It was the truth, wasn't it? Your second husband was then quite alive, and your star was soaring in the eyes of the world. Then he asked me what had become of your sons. I told him they were in good health and were also doing well at Court in the Dauphin's household. Then, as he was about to leave, I said to him point-blank: "You must remember that execution very vividly. Such sleight of hand doesn't happen very often." He jumped. "What do you mean?" he said. "I mean," I replied, "that the condemned man bowed himself out at the last minute while you were blessing some anonymous cadaver. You must have been rather upset when you noticed the substitution." "I swear I never noticed it then. . . ." he said. Then I thrust my face right into his. "And when you *did* notice it, Father . . . ?"

'He turned as white as his hands. "I don't know what you're getting at," he said, trying to get out of the trap. "Yes, you do know," I said. "You know as well as I that the Comte de Peyrac did not die at the stake. And that hardly anyone else knows it. No one paid you to hold your tongue. You weren't in on the plot. But you know. Who told you?"

'He continued to play dumb. Then he left.'

'And you let him go? You shouldn't have, Desgrez! You should have forced him to talk. You should have threatened him, tortured him, compelled him to reveal who had told him and who had sent him. Who was it? Who?'

'How would that have changed things?' said Desgrez. 'You were already Madame du Plessis-Bellière, weren't you?'

Angélique put her hands to her head. Desgrez would not have told her of this incident if he had not thought it important. Desgrez was thinking the same thing she was: somewhere behind the unexpected appearance of this prison chaplain lurked the presence of Angélique's first husband. What was the hiding place from which he had dispatched this messenger? How had he got in touch with him?

'We must follow the trail of this priest,' she said. 'It will be easy enough.'

Desgrez smiled. 'You would make a fine policeman,' he said. 'I will spare you the trouble. For several years now he has been the chaplain in the galleys at Marseilles.'

It would be easy for her to find this Father Antoine again, she thought. The priest would certainly confide in her the name of the mysterious person who had sent him to Desgrez to inquire the fate of Madame de Peyrac. Perhaps he would even know where this unknown character was. Her eyes glistened, and she kept biting her lip as plans raced through her mind.

Desgrez surveyed her with an ironic glance. 'Providing you can get out of Paris,' he said in answer to the thoughts he could read so easily on her face.

'You wouldn't stop me, would you, Desgrez?'

'My dear child, it is my duty to stop you. Don't you know that when I accept an assignment I am like a dog with a criminal's coat-tails in its teeth? I am prepared to give you all the information that may interest you, but don't count on me to give you a key to the open fields.'

Angélique whirled around to face the police officer, her face suffused with tender pleading. 'Desgrez! My old friend!'

His youthful face grew hard. 'The King himself pledged me to keep an eye on you. I don't take such responsibilities lightly.'

'Yet you say you are my friend.'

'In so far as that does not interfere with my duty to the King.'

The realisation of his duplicity swept over Angélique like a burning wave. She began to hate Desgrez again as she had always hated him. She knew he was so scrupulously single-minded as far as his work was concerned that he could erect impenetrable barriers in her way. Once he had snared his prey, he always ended by destroying it. He could confine her like a jailor. No one escaped from him.

'How could you accept this revolting assignment when you knew it was directed against me? I will never forgive you!'

'I admit it rather pleased me to be able to prevent you from doing something foolish.'

'Don't intrude into my life,' she shouted. 'Oh, how I loathe you and all your kind! You make me vomit, you and all the rest like you – spies, torturers, lackeys fawning on any master who'll throw you a bone to gnaw!'

Desgrez relaxed and began to laugh. He never liked her so much as when rage exhumed from the deep tomb of luxurious living in which she had buried that secret episode of her life when she was the Marquise of the Angels, the character she had first shown him in the Paris under-world.

'Listen, my dear . . .' He took her by the chin and raised her face to his. 'I could have refused that assignment, even though the King entrusted me with it because of my reputation. He was not unaware that if you took it into your head to flee, the whole Paris police force would have to be mobilised to stop you. I could have refused, but he spoke to me with such concern about you, so much anxiety, as man to man. . . . And, as I just told you, I decided to accept because I could keep you from once again destroying your whole existence.' His features softened, and he gazed tenderly at the face he held between his hands. 'Poor dear foolish little thing,' he murmured, 'don't hold it against your old friend Desgrez. I want to spare you this disastrous, dangerous undertaking. You risk losing everything and gaining nothing. And the King's anger will know no bounds; you can defy him just so long. Listen to me, Angélique, poor little Angélique. . . .'

Never before had he spoken to her with such gentleness, as if she were a child he was preventing from harming itself. She would have liked to hide her face on his shoulder and weep there quietly.

'Promise me,' he said, 'promise me not to do anything rash, and in turn I will promise you to start things moving that may help you in your search. Just promise me.'

She shook her head. She wanted to comply, but she distrusted the King and she distrusted Desgrez. They would always be trying to restrain her, imprison her. How they would have liked her to forget and agree. She distrusted herself, too. Some day she would get tired of fighting and yield to cowardice and say to herself: What's the use? The King would entreat her favours again. She was so alone in the face of all these forces allied against her to prevent her from finding her true love.

'Promise me,' Desgrez kept insisting.

Again she shook her head.

'Stubborn as a mule!' he said with a sigh. 'Well, from here on, it's a test of which of us is the stronger. So, good luck, Marquise of the Angels!'

Angélique tried to get to sleep in spite of the dawn which was whitening the windows, but she could not drift completely off and remained in a state of suspended animation, her body relaxed but her mind racing. She was trying to trace the mysterious wanderings of the leper, conjuring up the personality of her husband behind that solitary soul and thinking with horror that she herself might have seen him plodding over the roads of the Île-de-France on his way to Paris. It was this last detail that, so far as she was concerned, spoiled the illusion. How could an escaped prisoner, knowing he was being pursued and that every detail about him was known, have been so bold as to return to the wasps' nest that was Paris? Joffrey de Peyrac would not have been so stupid as to do a silly thing like that.

Yet he might, Angélique reflected; it would be like him. She tried to guess what would have been in his mind. Would he have come back to Paris to look for her? No, that was too foolish. In Paris, the huge city that had condemned him, he would find no friend, no place of refuge. His house in Saint-Paul, the beautiful mansion he had built in honour of Angélique, had been confiscated. She remembered the many trips he had made from Aquitaine to the capital to supervise the workmen himself. Would Joffrey de Peyrac, with a price on his head, have conceived of taking refuge in that house? Stripped of everything, he might have intended to search for gold and jewels he had possibly hidden away in places known only to him.

The more she pondered this, the more likely it seemed to her. Joffrey de Peyrac was quite capable of risking everything to get possession of his wealth again. With all that money he could protect himself, whereas naked and in dire want he would have to wander helplessly. The peasants would throw rocks at him and some day one would betray him. But with a handful of gold he could gain his freedom. He knew where to put his hands on that gold in his Hôtel de Beautreillis, every nook and cranny of which he loved.

As she followed this line of reasoning Angélique persuaded herself that it was probable. She recalled his often repeated, rather scornful, maxim: 'Gold can do everything.' The young King's ambition had proved an exception to that rule, but it still held. With a little gold the wretch would cease to be defenceless. He must have come back to

Paris, she was sure now, must have come here. At that time the King had not yet laid his heavy hand on everything, had not yet offered the house to the Prince de Condé. It stood empty like an accursed dwelling, with great wax seals stuck on the doors, watched over only by a terror-stricken gatekeeper and an old Basque lackey who had not known where to flee to.

Angélique's heart began to thump wildly. Suddenly she was on the track of certainty.

'I've seen him myself. . . . Yes, I have seen him again in the lower gallery. . . . I have seen him. It was one night after the execution. I heard the noise in the gallery and recognised his footsteps. . . .'

So the old Basque lackey had said one evening as he leaned on the rim of the medieval well-head at the bottom of the garden when she encountered him just after she had regained possession of the Hôtel de Beautreillis.

'Who wouldn't recognise his footsteps? The footsteps of the Great Crippie of Languedoc! I lit my lantern, and when I came to the turn in the gallery, there he was, leaning against the chapel door. He turned towards me. . . . I recognised him the way a dog recognises its master, but I did not see his face. He was wearing a mask. Suddenly he vanished into the wall, and I did not see him again. . . .'

Angélique had fled in terror, refusing to listen to the prattle of this almost senile creature who thought he had seen a ghost.

She sat up in bed and jangled the bell violently. Janine appeared, the affected redhead who had taken Thérèse's place. She sniffed suspiciously and disdainfully at the fumes of tobacco Desgrez had left behind him, and inquired what Madame wished.

'Go get that old lackey right away . . . what's his name? . . . Oh, yes, Pascalou . . . Grandpa Pascalou.'

The maid raised her eyebrows.

'You know him perfectly well,' Angélique said. 'A very old man who draws the well water and brings in the firewood.'

Janine looked at her with the resigned expression of one who does not understand but who is going to do her duty. A few minutes later she returned to say that Grandpa Pascalou had been dead for two years.

'Dead?' echoed Angélique. 'Dead! Oh lord, how awful!'

Janine could not understand how her mistress could be so upset at learning of an event which two years before she had completely ignored. Angélique kept Janine to help her dress. She got into her clothes abstractedly. So the poor old man had died and taken his secret with him. She was at Court in those days and had not even been present to hold the hand of her faithful servant on his deathbed. Now she was paying dearly for neglecting that duty. His words were etched into her memory with letters of fire: 'He was leaning against the chapel door. . . .'

Hurrying down the stairs, she sped along under the graceful arches of the gallery tinged with the pale reflections of the stained-glass windows, and opened the chapel door. It was a sort of oratory, with two Cordovan leather faldstools, and a little green marble altar topped with a splendid painting by a Spanish artist. The place reeked of incense and candle grease. Angélique remembered that when the Abbé de Lesdiguières was in Paris he said Mass there. She knelt down.

'Oh God,' she said aloud, 'I have committed many sins, but I beseech you, oh God, I entreat you . . .'

She could not find anything else to say.

He had come there one night. But how could he have got into the hôtel? How, for that matter, could he have got into Paris? What could he have been looking for in that oratory?

Angélique let her eyes roam around the little sanctuary. All the furnishings dated from the time of the Comte de Peyrac. The Prince de Condé had not disturbed a thing. Apart from the Abbé de Lesdiguières and a little page who served him as altar boy, few persons had ever been inside it.

If there were a hiding place in that oratory, the secret could have been kept well enough. Angélique got to her feet and began to search diligently. She ran her finger into every crevice of the carved altar in the hope of locating some hidden spring. She studied every detail of the bas-relief, tapped every enamelled tile of the floor, then the wood panelling that covered the walls. Her patience was ultimately rewarded. Towards the end of the morning it seemed to her that a place on the wall behind the altar gave a hollow sound. She lit a candle and scrutinised it in the light of the flame. Cleverly disguised in a carved moulding were the outlines of a keyhole. It was there!

Feverishly she strove to find the trick of opening it, but she had to give up. With the help of a knife and a key which she wore on a chain at her waist, however, she managed to crack the woodwork. A hole appeared. She thrust her hand into it and found a casket that she yanked into the light. Since there was no point in trying to unlock it, she prised the lid open. The casket was empty.

Angélique clutched the dusty little box to her bosom. 'He did come! He took the gold and the jewels. God was watching over him. God has preserved him!'

But then what? Enriched by the fortune he had recovered at the peril of his life, what had become of the Comte de Peyrac?

CHAPTER THREE

When Angélique decided to go to Saint-Cloud to fetch Florimond, she discovered that Desgrez's warnings were in earnest. As she got into her coach she gave scant attention to the 'admirer' whose ruddy face had glowed under her windows for some three days, and she paid no heed to the two gentlemen who emerged from a neighbouring wineshop to dog her heels as she drove through the streets. But she had hardly passed the Saint-Honoré gate than a squadron of armed guardsmen surrounded her carriage and a young officer politely requested her to return to Paris.

'The King's orders, Madame.'

When she objected, he showed her a writ countersigned by La Reynie, the Prefect of Police, instructing them not to let Madame du Plessis-Bellière leave the city.

'When I think it's Desgrez who's in charge of this!' she thought. 'He could have helped me, but now he won't. He will give me all possible information about my husband's disappearance, and all kinds of advice, but he will also do all he can to obey the King's orders.'

She clenched her fists and gritted her teeth as she ordered the coachman to turn the horses around. This interference with what she wished to do aroused all her fighting instincts. Joffrey de Peyrac, helpless and hunted though he was, had managed to get into Paris. Well, she would manage to get out this very day!

She sent a messenger to Saint-Cloud, and shortly after Florimond arrived with his tutor, who told her that in accordance with her instructions he had begun negotiations for the sale of Florimond's position. Monsieur de Loane wanted it for his nephew and was offering a good price. 'We shall see about that,' Angélique said. She did not want to go away and draw down the wrath of the King until she had taken all precautions for the safety of her children.

'Why should I sell my appointment?' Florimond asked. 'Have you got some better job for me? Am I going back to Versailles? I was getting on very well at Saint-Cloud. Even Monsieur noticed what a good job I was doing.'

Charles-Henri welcomed him with shouts of joy. He worshipped his elder brother, and Florimond returned his affection. Every time he came to Paris, Florimond would take him in hand, give him piggy-back rides, let him play with his sword. Florimond went into raptures again over Charles-Henri's good looks.

'Isn't he the handsomest child in the world, Mama? He should be the Dauphin instead of the nitwit who is.'

'Better not let anyone hear you say that, Florimond,' warned the Abbé de Lesdiguières.

Angélique took her eyes from her two sons – Charles-Henri, so fair and pink and plump, gazing with adoring blue eyes at the dark-complexioned Florimond. Whenever she looked at the curly head of her son by Philippe, she felt strangely helpless and regretful. Why had she ever entered into that marriage? Joffrey de Peyrac had sent an emissary to seek her out, and had learned from him that she had remarried – a shocking situation from which there was no escape. God should not have let such a thing happen!

She took pains to conceal the preparations for her departure. She would send Charles-Henri and Barbe, his nurse, with the other servants to Plessis in Poitou. Even in anger, the King would not revenge himself on the child and the property of his former marshal. But for Florimond she had other, more oblique plans. 'The King will probably be very angry with me,' she said to herself by way of reassurance. 'But how can he object to my taking a little trip to Marseilles? I'll come back. . . .'

In order to divert suspicions and give some proof of her compliance, she summoned her brother Gontran, saying that at last she had found time to have her children's portraits painted. While she was struggling with her account books so as to leave all her affairs in order, she heard Florimond inventing diversions to keep his little brother quiet.

'Little angel with the smile of a cherub, you are a darling. Little glutton, fat as a priest, you are a darling,' he kept reciting in a parody of the litany.

Then she heard the voice of the Abbé de Lesdiguières. 'Florimond, you should not make fun of such things. You have far too irreverent an attitude. It disturbs me.'

Paying no attention to him, Florimond went on chanting: 'Little woolly lamb browsing on sweetmeats, you are a darling. Little will-o'-the-wisp, full of mischief, you are a darling. . . .'

Charles-Henri was laughing uproariously. Gontran was grumbling as usual, and the blond and dark heads of Angélique's children were taking form on the canvas. Florimond de Peyrac, Charles-Henri du Plessis-Bellière – each a reflection of the two men she had loved.

One evening Florimond came to Angélique as she was sitting before the fire. 'Mother,' he said directly, 'what is happening? I don't think you are the King's mistress any more, the way he keeps you doing penance in Paris.'

'Florimond!' exclaimed Angélique in some confusion. 'What business is it of yours?'

Florimond knew his mother's volatile nature, and took care not to fall foul of it. He pulled up a footstool and sat at her feet, lifting his dark shining eyes up to hers in a way he knew well was disarming and irresistible.

'Aren't you the King's mistress?' he repeated with an innocent smile.

Angélique wondered whether she should not end the discussion then and there with a smart slap, but she restrained herself for the time being. Florimond had no ulterior motive. He was asking the same question that everyone in Court was, from the first gentleman down to the last page, namely, what would be the result of the duel between Madame de Montespan and Madame du Plessis-Bellière? But since the latter was his own mother, he was more interested than most, especially since the rumours of her high position in the royal favour had given him considerable prestige among his colleagues. These embryonic courtiers were already training themselves in intrigue and so endeavoured to win his friendship. 'My father says your mother can get the King to do anything she wants him to,' young d'Aumale remarked to him. 'You're in luck! Your career is all set. Just don't forget your old friends. I've always been on your side, now haven't I?'

Florimond carried his head high, pretending he was another Father Joseph, the unobtrusive influential adviser of Richelieu. He promised Bernard de Chateauroux that he could be Admiral of the Fleet, and Philippe d'Aumale that he could be Minister of War. But now, here was his mother dragging him out of Monsieur's household, talking of selling his post as page to the little princesses, and living herself in retirement in Paris, far from the Court of Versailles.

'Have you displeased the King? Why?'

Angélique laid her hand on the boy's smooth forehead, parting the thick dark ringlets that tumbled about his head. She felt the same melancholy that had oppressed her the day Cantor had asked permission to go off to the wars, the same shock all mothers sense when their children suddenly become persons in their own right, thinking their own thoughts.

She replied to Florimond's question softly: 'Yes, I have displeased the King, and he is very cross with me.'

He knitted his brows in imitation of the distraught and anxious expressions he had seen on the faces of courtiers in disgrace. 'What a blow! What's going to become of us? I bet it's that whore Montespan's doing. That bitch!'

'Florimond, what language!'

Florimond shrugged. That was the way they talked in the royal antechambers. Suddenly he seemed resigned, as if he were facing the facts with the philosophical outlook of one who had seen plenty of houses of cards rise to great heights and then collapse in ruin.

'I hear you're going on a trip.'

'Who told you that?'

'I just heard.'

'What a bore! I don't like everyone to know my plans.'

'I won't tell a soul, I promise. But just the same I should like to know what you intend to do about me now that everything's so topsy-turvy. Are you going to take me with you?'

She had thought of taking him, and then had decided against it. The whole undertaking was in the lap of the gods. She did not even know how she was going to get out of Paris, or what information she could get from Father Antoine in Marseilles, or in what direction it might turn her. A child, even so sharp a one as Florimond, might well prove a liability.

'Now let's be reasonable, my boy. What I am going to propose to you may not sound very attractive, but the time has come for you to get some knowledge into that donkey head of yours. I'm going to turn you over to your Jesuit uncle, who has agreed to enter you in one of his Order's colleges in Poitou. The Abbé de Lesdiguières will go with you, and will continue as your counsellor and guide while I'm away.'

She had indeed gone to Father Raymond de Sancé and entreated him to take care of Florimond if need be, and to see to his education.

As she had expected he would, Florimond pouted. For a long moment he brooded, frowning. Angélique put her arm around his shoulders to help him swallow this unpleasant news. She was about to discourse to him on the joys of study and college life, when he raised his head and said matter-of-factly:

'Well, if that's all there is in store for me, I can see the only thing for me to do is go and find Cantor.'

'Good lord, Florimond,' Angélique exclaimed, 'don't talk that way, for heaven's sake! You aren't thinking of dying, are you?'

'Certainly not,' the boy said calmly.

'Then why do you say such a dreadful thing as that you're going to join Cantor?'

'Because I want to see him again. I'm bored. I'd rather go to sea than chant Latin with the Jesuits.'

'But . . . Cantor is dead, Florimond.'

Florimond shook his head. 'No, he's gone to join my father.'

Angélique felt faint. Was she losing her mind?

'Wha-a-t? What are you saying?'

Florimond looked her straight in the eye. 'Yes, my father . . . the other one . . . you know . . . the one they tried to burn in the Place de Grève.'

Angélique was speechless. She had never told the boys about that. They did not play with Hortense's children, and her sister would have cut out her own tongue rather than mention that terrible scandal. She had been sedulous in keeping them from any gossip, anxiously wondering what she would tell them when they found out the reputation and the fate of their father. But they had never asked her a single question about him, and it had not been till this moment that she realised this silence of theirs was unusual. They had never asked her because they already knew!

'Who told you that?'

As if to put his thoughts in order and prepare a reply, Florimond gave a hesitant look and turned to the fire, picking up the tongs and rearranging the logs that had burned through in the middle. How naïve she was, that mother of his! And how sweet! For years Florimond had thought her quite stern. He was afraid of her, and Cantor used to cry because she would always go out just at the time they had hoped she would come and play with them. But for some time now he had been aware that she had her weak moments. He had probed the anguish that lay behind her smile, and because he had endured the venomous remarks surreptitiously passed in his hearing on the subject of the 'future favourite', he had developed a more mature attitude toward her. Some day he would be grown, and then he would protect her.

Florimond turned his radiant smile on her and held out his hands in a winning gesture. 'Mother dear. . . .' he whispered.

She clutched his curly head to her breast. Surely there was no lovelier, no sweeter child in the whole wide world. He had inherited all the instinctive charm of the Comte de Peyrac.

'Do you know how much you look like your father?'

'Yes, I know. Old Pascalou told me.'

'Old Pascalou! So that's how you knew!'

'Yes and no,' said Florimond pompously. 'Old Pascalou was a good friend of ours. He used to tootle on his fife and tinkle his little tambourine for us, and tell us all kinds of stories. He always said I looked like that unfortunate gentleman who had built the Hôtel de Beautreillis. He had known him as a child and he said I looked exactly like him except that his face was scarred from a sword cut. Then we used to ask him to tell us more about that fabulous person who knew how to do everything, even how to make gold out of dust. He would sing so fascinatingly that no one moved a muscle. He duelled with all his enemies. Finally people were so jealous of him that they wickedly burned him alive in the Place de Grève. But Pascalou used to say it was pretty certain he had escaped them, because Pascalou had seen him when he came back here to his house after everyone thought he was dead. Pascalou used to say that now he would die happy knowing that the great man who had been his master was still alive.'

'That's all true, my darling. He is alive, very much alive.'

'But for a long time we did not know that man was our father. We used to ask Pascalou what his name was, but he wouldn't tell us. Finally he told us as a huge secret: the Comte de Peyrac, Prince of Toulouse and Aquitaine. I remember we were alone with him in the servants' hall that day. Of course, Barbe had to appear. She heard what we were talking about, and she turned all colours of the rainbow. She told Pascalou he shouldn't be telling us such terrible things. Did he want the curse of the father to fall on the children after all their mother had done to rescue them from their sad fate? She kept on raving and ranting, and we didn't know what she was talking about, and neither did Pascalou. Finally he said: "Old lady, do you mean these boys are his children?" Barbe's mouth fell open and she looked like a fish out of water. Then she began stammering and stuttering and she was awfully funny. But she was silly to think she could get out of it that easily. We never stopped asking her: "Who was our father, Barbe? Was he the Comte de Peyrac?" One day Cantor and I tied her to a chair in front of the fire, and said that if she didn't tell us the whole truth and all she

29

knew about our real father, we'd burn the soles of her feet, the way highway robbers do. . . .'

Angélique let out a little cry of horror. Was it possible that these infants who could have taken communion without confession . . . ! Florimond began laughing at the memory of it all.

'When she began to roast a little, she told us everything, but she made us swear we would never breathe a word of it. And we kept the secret, but we were happy and proud that our father had got out of the clutches of those wicked men. Then Cantor got the idea he should go and look for him by sea.'

'Why by sea?'

'Because it's so vast,' he said with a sweep of his arm. He seemed to think of the sea as something he had no true notion of but which nonetheless was a gateway to realms where every wish came true. Angélique could understand.

'Cantor made up a song,' Florimond continued. 'I don't remember all the words, but it was very pretty. It was the story of our father. He used to say: "I will sing this song everywhere I go, and plenty of people will recognise him and tell me where he is. . . ." '

Angélique felt her throat tighten and her eyes grow moist. She could picture the two of them plotting the quest of the little troubadour for that legendary man.

'I didn't agree with him,' Florimond said. 'I didn't want to go, because I liked my job at Versailles so much. You don't get very far in a career by going off to sea, do you? But Cantor went. Barbe used to say: "That one's worse than his mother when he gets an idea firmly in his head." Mother, do you think he has met my father?'

Angélique stroked his hair without replying. She could not bring herself to tell him again that Cantor had paid with his life, like the Knights of the Holy Grail, for chasing a phantom. Poor little knight! Poor little troubadour! She could see his face, eyes and lips closed, floating in the transparent emerald depths of the bottomless seas, drifting like an image in a dream.

'. . . by singing,' Florimond murmured, his thoughts wandering on in the same pattern.

She had never known before what lay behind his frank eyes. The world of childhood, with its strange mingling of wisdom and nonsense, had long since passed beyond her ken.

'All children get foolish ideas,' she said to herself. 'The worst of it is, mine put them into effect.'

Florimond remained silent for a while, then raised his head, his mobile face suddenly registering embarrassment and sadness.

'Mama,' he continued, 'did the King condemn my father? I've thought about that a lot, and it's worried me, for the King is a just man.'

It hurt him to think the King he idolised might fail. To reassure him Angélique said: 'It was jealous men who caused your father's ruin. The King pardoned him.'

'Oh, I'm glad of that,' Florimond exclaimed. 'I love the King, but I love my father still more. When will he come back? Since the King pardoned him, can't he regain his rank?'

Angélique sighed. Her heart was heavy.

'It's such a tangled story, so hard to unravel, my poor little boy. Until just a little while ago I too thought your father was dead. Even now there are times I think I must be dreaming. He did not die, but escaped, and came back here to find his gold. It's true, and yet it's impossible. All the gates of Paris were watched. Guards were placed all around the house. How could he have got inside?'

She noticed Florimond looking at her with a superior smile. Suddenly she realised that the child must know. In astonishment she exclaimed: 'You, you know?'

'Yes.' He leaned toward her and whispered: 'By the tunnel from the well.' He leaped up and grasped her hand. 'Come with me.'

As they passed through the long hall he took a vigil light from near the entrance door and pulled his mother down the steps into the orchard. By the dim light of the half-moon they proceeded along the paths among the round-trimmed orange-trees until they reached the outer wall at the end of the garden where old-fashioned herbs grew in profusion. A broken pillar, a weathered scutcheon on a bench, the ancient well with its wrought-iron canopy recalled the splendour of the fifteenth century when this whole neighbourhood was one great palace with innumerable courtyards in which lived the kings and princes of France.

'Pascalou showed us the secret passage,' Florimond said. 'He said my father himself had supervised the reconstruction of the old tunnel when he was building the house. He paid the three workmen a lot of money to keep quiet about it. Pascalou was there. Then he showed us everything because we were his sons. Look.'

'I don't see a thing,' Angélique said as she bent over the dark pit. 'Wait.'

Florimond set the vigil light inside the big wooden bucket bound with copper hoops which hung from the well-chain, and lowered it gently.

The light glistened against the damp walls. When it was half-way down, the boy stopped playing out the chain.

'There! If you lean way over you can see a small wooden door in the wall. That is the entrance. When the bucket stops directly before it, you can open the door and enter the tunnel. It's very deep. It goes under the cellars of the neighbouring houses and under the ramparts of the Bastille until it comes to an exit in the Faubourg Saint-Antoine, where it joins the ancient catacombs and the former bed of the Seine. But when my father had it rebuilt, he extended it to the forest of Vincennes. You come out into a little ruined chapel. My father was very far-sighted, wasn't he?'

'How do you know that this tunnel is still usable?' Angélique whispered.

'Oh, it is. Old Pascalou kept it in good repair. The bolt on the door was always kept oiled. It open with just a touch, and the spring that lets you out into the chapel works well too. Old Pascalou said everything had to be kept in readiness for the day the master would come back. But he hadn't come back then, and sometimes all three of us – Pascalou, Cantor and I – would wait for him in the chapel. We would listen and hope to hear his footsteps – the footsteps of the Great Cripple of Languedoc.'

Angélique looked at him sharply. 'Florimond, you're not asking me to believe that you and Cantor went down the well?'

' 'Course we did,' Florimond replied nonchalantly. 'More than once, if you want to know.' He began to haul up the bucket, puffing with his exertions. 'Barbe used to sit here waiting for us and saying her rosary, as nervous as a hen with a brood of ducklings.'

'That old fool knew about it too?'

'She had to help us pull up the bucket.'

'She should never have let you do such a dangerous thing. And to think she never told me about it!'

'She had to. She was scared we'd toast her feet again.'

'Florimond, you ought to be spanked!'

Florimond did not answer, being busily engaged in recovering the vigil light from the bucket. The well had become dark and mysterious again. Angélique passed her hand over her face, trying to order her thoughts.

'What I don't understand . . .' she said. She thought a moment more. 'But how could he get out of the well alone, without anyone to help him?'

'It's not hard. There are iron rungs set into the wall for just that purpose. Pascalou didn't want us to use them, though, because we were too small, and he was getting too old. So we had to put up with Barbe and all her complaining to help us back up again. When old Pascalou thought he was dying he sent for me. I was at Versailles then. The Abbé and I jumped on horseback and came to him. Mama, it's a sad thing to see an old servant die. I held his hand till the very end.'

'You did right, Florimond.'

'He told me: "You must see to the well for when the old master comes back." I promised him I would. Every time I come back to Paris I go down the well to see if all the machinery is still working.'

'Alone?'

'Yes, I've had enough of Barbe. I'm big enough now to manage all by myself.'

'You go down by means of the iron rungs?'

'Yes. It's easy, I tell you.'

'Doesn't the Abbé try to stop you?'

'He never knows. He's asleep. I don't think he ever suspected anything about it.'

'How well my children are looked after!' Angélique said bitterly. 'Weren't you afraid, Florimond, to be alone like that at night in a tunnel?'

The boy shook his head. If from time to time he had been afraid, he was not going to admit it. 'My father was interested in mines, I've heard. Perhaps that's why I like to be underground.'

He looked up at her, flattered by the admiration she could not repress. In the moonlight she recognised in the scornful twist of his lips and the sparkle of his dark eyes the devilish look of the last of the troubadours who loved to scandalise and shock the timorous complacency of the bourgeoisie.

'If you'd like me to, mother, I will take you through.'

CHAPTER FOUR

The royal galley slowly entered the harbour of Marseilles. Like a blue mirror the roadstead reflected the flames of its crimson silk pennons, their golden tassels flying in the wind. At the peaks of the masts floated the scarlet escutcheons of the Admiral's flags and the crimson naval standards embroidered with golden fleurs-de-lis.

On the dock there was a general air of excitement. The fishmongers and flower-vendors seized their baskets of figs and mimosa, melons and carnations, sea-skate and shellfish, and headed for the spot where the handsome ship would tie up, chattering loudly as they ran. Then came the dandies followed by their little dogs, and the red-capped fishermen who had stopped mending their nets. Two Turkish longshoremen in red and green trousers, their mahogany-coloured chests streaming with sweat, let fall the enormous bales of dried fish they were carrying, and sat down to draw their long pipes from their sashes. The arrival of the galley would allow them a few puffs while the anthill-like activity of the dockside relaxed. The captains supervising the loading of a vessel, the shouting merchants running up and down followed by their clerks and bookkeepers, decided to lay down their scales and catch their breaths for a moment. They flocked to the galley as to a pageant, less to admire its winged grace as it skimmed over the water and its lace-trimmed officers than to see the convicts at the oars. It was a horrible sight which caused the women to cross themselves, even though they never tired of seeing it.

Angélique rose from the gun-carriage where she had sat waiting for many long hours. Flipot followed her, carrying her bag. They mingled with the crowd.

Near the Tour Saint-Jean the galley seemed to hesitate like a huge red bird, the sunlight sparkling on its gilded carving. Finally it glided toward the dock with great sweeps of the twenty-four oars that churned the water into white swirls. It tacked about, turning toward the offing its long slim prow of ebony terminating in a gigantic siren of gilded wood, and displayed to the spectators on the pier its sculptured, gilded poop surmounted with an awning of red and gold brocade – a huge square tent, sometimes called the tabernacle, where the officers gathered.

A little before landing, the oars rose and remained motionless. The whistles of the overseers of the galley-slaves and the reverberations of the gong that was stopping the momentum of the oars sounded along the embankment; then dominating all the other sounds came the abusive language of the captain to the sailors who were furling the sails.

A group of officers in full regalia appeared on the quarterdeck near the gilded wood staircase. One of them leaned forward and, removing his plumed hat, began to signal with it in Angélique's direction. She turned around and to her considerable relief saw a group of young ladies and gallants who had just got out of a carriage. It was them the officer was saluting. One of the young women, dark-haired and sharp-

34

featured and starred with beauty-patches, exclaimed in delight: 'Oh, that darling Vivonne! In spite of being an admiral and more powerful in Marseilles than the King himself, he is still so charming and simple! He saw us and he didn't hesitate a minute to wave at us!'

As she recognised the Comte de Vivonne Angélique lost herself in the crowd as quickly as she could. Madame de Montespan's brother set his red heels on the sticky pavement and headed straight for the dark-haired girl, his arms outstretched.

'How delightful to find you on the docks, my lovely Ariane. And you too, Cassandra. And isn't that dear Calistro over there? What bliss!'

In a sophisticated confusion that left the sightseers open-mouthed in amazement, the Admiral and his friends exchanged salutations. The Comte de Vivonne was at his best in his rôle as viceroy. His sunburned complexion went well with his blue eyes and his long, thick blond hair. His considerable height detracted from a slight corpulence. Like a consummate actor, he was playing his part to the hilt. Gay and lively and quick-witted, there was much in him of his brilliant sister, the King's mistress.

'It's just by chance that I could put into port today,' he said. 'In fact, I must set sail again in two days for Candia. But a storm did so much damage, and the health of the crew was so bad, that I had to put in at Marseilles. Now, seeing that you are here, I invite you all to a couple of days of feasting.'

A sharp report like a pistol shot made the group jump. One of the guards of the galley-slaves was cracking his whip and urging the crowd to scatter.

'Let's move along, my dears,' said Monsieur de Vivonne, laying his hands, which were encased in white-leather, perfumed gloves, on the shoulders of the young ladies. 'The convicts are about to debark. I have permitted some fifty of them to return to their encampment in the cove of Rocher to bury one of their number who was stupid enough to give up the ghost while we were entering the harbour. That's why we were slightly delayed. My second-in-command suggested – and I approved – that his body be thrown overboard as is customary when the galley is at sea. But the Chaplain objected. He said there would not be enough time for him to say the usual prayers and other rituals, and that we could not treat a Christian soul as if it were a dog's, and, in short, that he wished to bury it. I agreed because we were so near the port and also because I have learned by experience that that little Lazarist Father always wins in the end. Nothing – neither persuasion nor force – can change him once he gets a notion into his head. So let's move on. I want to take you to Scevola's for some pistachio sherbet and Turkish coffee.'

They wandered away while the convict-keeper continued to crack his whip at the foot of the gangplank like a lion-tamer urging his beasts from their cage into the sands of an arena.

From within the hull rose fearful sounds of dragging chains and rasping voices. A murmur ran through the crowd as the first of the convicts appeared at the head of the gangplank, their bodies encumbered by long chains which they carried over their shoulders or at the end of their arms so that the weight would not endanger their precarious footing. One behind the other they crossed the plank that linked the galley with the dock. They were chained in fours. Filthy rags knotted around their ankles where the irons fitted were supposed to protect their flesh, but many of these rags were stained with blood. Both men and women crossed themselves as the convicts passed by.

They walked barefoot, scratching at their lice, keeping their eyes lowered. Their clothing, consisting of a shirt and a pair of red wool trousers knotted to a wide, once-white belt, was stained with sea water and exhaled an unbearable stench. Most of them were bearded. A red woollen cap pulled down to their eyebrows covered their matted hair. The caps of some were green, denoting that these were 'lifers'.

The first passed by without looking around. Others provided the show the crowd was waiting for. Their eyes glittering, they accosted the women in foul language and with obscene gestures. One of the lifers picked on a placid citizen whose only wrong in the convict's eyes was that he was not in his place.

'Big joke, hey? You damn bloated wine-cask!'

The convict-keeper raised his whip high and whistled its hempen lash across the pale skin already scarred with sores and scabs. The women gasped in pity.

However, a new group was appearing, each one carrying his cap in his hand. The lips of these convicts were moving, and presently one could hear the mumble of their prayers. The crowd fell solemnly silent. Two convicts descended the gangplank carrying a body wrapped in sail-cloth. Behind them walked the Chaplain, whose black cassock contrasted vividly with the mass of red tatters.

Angélique stared at him intently. She had not been sure she would recognise him. It had been ten years since she had seen him, and that was in circumstances unpleasant to remember.

Already the little band had moved off, their chains clanking on the paving-stones. Angélique grasped Flipot by the cuff.

36

'Go and follow that priest. Father Antoine is his name. As soon as you catch up with him, tell him – now, listen closely – tell him: "Madame de Peyrac is here at Marseilles and would like to meet you at the inn of the Golden Horn." '

'Come in, Father,' said Angélique.

The priest hesitated in the doorway of the room where sat this great lady in her simple but expensive costume. He was obviously embarrassed by his thick shoes and his rusty black cassock, the ragged cuffs of which hung short of his red, brine-chapped wrists.

'Forgive me for receiving you in my rooms,' Angélique said. 'I am here on a secret mission and I do not wish to be recognised.'

The priest indicated that he understood and that it made no difference to him. He accepted her invitation to take a seat on a stool. Now she recognised him – just as she had seen him squatting that evening before the blaze of the Paris executioner, his shoulders hunched, looking like a frozen cricket, his dark eyes blazing when he opened them wide.

She sat down in front of him. 'Do you remember me?' she asked.

A smile flickered over the thin lips of Father Antoine. 'I remember you.'

He peered at her attentively, comparing the woman before him with the haggard, swollen, distraught creature he had last seen wandering one winter twilight around the embers of a pyre which the wind was scattering.

'You were expecting a child then,' he said gently. 'What did it turn out to be?'

'A boy,' she said. 'He was born the same night. And already he is dead. He lived to be only nine years old.' The thought of Cantor made her turn her head away toward the window. 'The Mediterranean took him from me,' she added pensively.

Evening was falling. Shouts, songs, calls rose from the alleys where people of many nationalities – Turks, Spaniards, Greeks, Arabs, Neapolitans, Negroes and English – were moving about noisily as the taverns and brothels began to open for business. Not far away a few chords on a guitar preceded the warm, vibrant voice of a serenader. Yet under all the raucous tumult the ever-present sea boomed like a swarm of bees.

Father Antoine kept staring at her, lost in thought. This woman of such startling beauty bore so little relation to the young creature of

37

despair he remembered. She seemed so sure of herself now, so alert, so commanding. He looked again for some mark upon her of the hardships she had endured. He would not have recognised her and would have had difficulty identifying her if it had not been for the touch of sadness in her face when she mentioned her drowned son.

She turned back to face him. The Chaplain folded his hands on his knees as if preparing for a long session. Suddenly he was afraid to say anything. She would compel him to tell her everything and that would lay a great burden of responsibility upon him.

'Father,' said Angélique, 'I have never known – and now I want to know – what the last words of my husband were at the stake. . . . At the stake,' she repeated. 'At the last moment. What did he say?'

The priest raised his eyebrows. 'Your desire comes rather late in the day, Madame,' he said. 'You must forgive me for not remembering. Years have gone by since then and I, alas, have ministered to many other condemned men. Believe me, I cannot tell you precisely.'

'Well, I can, then. He said nothing. He said nothing because he was already dead. It was a dead man they tied to the stake. And my husband, still alive, was being dragged through a tunnel while the crowd watched the blaze fulfilling the sentence unjustly meted out to him. The King admitted all this to me.'

She watched for a gesture of surprise, perhaps of protest, on the part of the priest. But he remained impassive.

'You knew this, didn't you?' she said with a sigh. 'You have always known it.'

'No, not always. The substitution was so cleverly made that at the time I hadn't the least suspicion. They had put a cowl over his head. It was only later that . . .'

'Later? Where? When? *Who* told you?' She leaned forward, her breast heaving, her eyes ablaze. 'You have seen him, haven't you? You saw him after the fire.'

He stared at her fixedly. Now he fully recognised her. She had not changed at all. 'Yes,' he said, 'I saw him. Listen to me.'

Then he began his astonishing story.

It happened in Paris in the month of February 1661, on the same freezing night that the monk Bécher died, 'tortured by demons', shrieking: 'Forgive me, Peyrac. . . .'

Father Antoine was praying in the chapel, when a lay brother came to tell him a poor man insisted on seeing him – a poor man who nonetheless had slipped a piece of gold into the lay brother's palm. The lay brother had not dared put him out. Father Antoine returned to the parlour. The man was there, leaning on a stout crutch, his swaying, almost deformed shadow projected on the whitewashed wall in the light of the oil-lamp. His garments were adequate. He was wearing a black steel mask. When he raised it, Father Antoine sank to his knees beseeching Heaven to deliver him from horrible visions, for before him stood a ghost, the ghost of the sorcerer he himself had seen burned in the Place de Grève.

The ghost smiled derisively. He tried to speak, but the only sounds that came from his mouth were so hoarse as to be unintelligible. Suddenly the apparition vanished. It was a few moments before Father Antoine realised that the wretched man had simply fainted and was lying at his feet on the flagstones. He calmed himself and leaned over the unconscious visitor, still alive but half-dead, his strength ebbing fast. His body had no more substance than a skeleton, but his purse contained a dazzling fortune in gold coins and jewels.

For many days the visitor hovered between life and death. Father Antoine, after sharing his secret with the Father Superior, took care of him.

'He had come in the last stages of exhaustion. You could hardly imagine how his body, so tortured by the executioner, could have made the effort. One of his legs, the lame one, bore horrible sores on the knee and thigh from the torture of the boot. The sores had remained open almost a month, for he had been walking all that time. Such willpower is a tribute to the human race, Madame!'

The once powerful Comte de Toulouse had said to the humble prison chaplain: 'From henceforth you are my only friend!'

It was the little priest he had thought of when after gathering all his remaining strength for his return to the Hôtel de Beautreillis he had thought himself dying of exhaustion. To have come so far only to die on the brink of success! He had left the hôtel by a secret door in the garden to which he had the key, then had dragged himself through Paris to the house of the Lazarists, where he knew he would find Father Antoine.

Now he had to take flight, for he could not remain in France. Father Antoine was leaving to accompany a gang of convicts bound for Marseilles, and to take up new duties there.

Joffrey de Peyrac conceived the idea of mingling with the convicts for the trip to Marseilles. He had found his Moorish servant, Kouassi-Ba, again. Father Antoine hid the gold and jewels in his own clothes and returned them to him after their arrival. Shortly after the Comte and his Moor escaped in a fishing smack, and disappeared.

'Have you never seen them since?'

'Never.'

'You have no idea what became of the Comte de Peyrac after his escape?'

'None whatever.'

She looked in his eyes again, then almost timidly asked: 'Didn't you come to Paris a few years ago to inquire after me? Who sent you?'

'I see you know about my visit to Desgrez.'

'He told me himself.'

She was hanging on his words and, since he hesitated to reply, she repeated insistently: 'Who sent you?'

The Chaplain sighed. 'To tell the truth, I never knew him. It happened several years ago when I was in Marseilles, where I was chiefly occupied with the convicts' hospital. An Arab merchant came to see me, one of those who come and go in this port. He informed me in great secrecy that a certain party wanted to know what had become of the Comtesse de Peyrac. He asked me to go to the capital. A lawyer named Desgrez could perhaps give me some information, as well as a few other persons whose names he gave me. For my services I received a purse containing a sizable sum which I accepted, thinking of my poor convicts, but all my attempts to find out from the messenger who had sent him failed. He only showed me a gold ring set with a topaz which I recognised as one of the Comte de Peyrac's jewels. I went to Paris to fulfil my mission. There I learned that Madame de Peyrac had become the wife of the King's Marshal, the Marquis du Plessis-Bellière. She was quite rich and stood high at Court, and so did her sons.'

'Weren't you shocked to hear that? I married again while my first husband was still alive! Perhaps your ecclesiastical conscience will rest more easy when I tell you the Marshal was killed in the Franche-Comté and that thereafter I have been considered twice a widow.'

Father Antoine was not offended. He even smiled a little as he said that he had known of many strange situations, but had to admit that Providence certainly had led Angélique down twisting paths. He pitied her deeply.

'So I came back to Marseilles, and when the merchant came back, I told him all I had learned. I have not heard a word from him since. That is everything I know, Madame, truly all.'

'That Arab,' said Angélique, 'where did he come from? Do you remember his name?'

The Chaplain knit his brows in thought. 'I've been trying these last few minutes,' he said at last, 'to remember all I could about him. His name was Mohammed Raki, but he was not one from Arabia. I noticed his clothes. The Arab merchants of the Red Sea tend to dress like the Turks, whereas those from the north coast of Africa wear full woollen cloaks called burnouses. This one came from Algeria or Morocco. But that's all I know, and it's not much to go on. Except that I remember chatting with him about one of his uncles whose name has just occurred to me – Ali Mektub. I was talking to him about an Arab slave I had known in the galleys, whose rich uncle had purchased his freedom. Ali Mektub did a big business in pearls, sponges and all kinds of trinkets. He lived in Crete and so far as I know he still does. Perhaps he could tell you something more about his nephew Mohammed Raki.'

'In Crete?' Angélique was lost in thought.

Angélique and Flipot went down to the waterfront in the hope of finding a vessel that would take them on the long voyage to the islands of the Levant. While they were walking along, Angélique suddenly stopped and rubbed her eyes, thinking she must be dreaming. A few steps ahead of her was a little old black-clad man standing on the edge of the quay in a deep reverie, quite oblivious of passers-by and of the mistral whipping his beard. From his ship cap, his big tortoise-shell spectacles, his old-fashioned clothing, his oiled-silk parasol and the vials in the wicker basket at his feet, she knew beyond a doubt it was Savary the apothecary she had met at Court.

'Maître Savary!' she shouted.

He was so startled he almost fell into the water as he peered at Angélique through his spectacles.

'So it's you, my little diplomat! I never thought I'd find you here.'

'Indeed! As a matter of fact, I'm here purely by chance.'

'Hmm! It's chance that brings all adventurous folk together. Do you know a better spot for embarking on strange undertakings? Sooner or later your ambition would have led you to Marseilles. It's written on your forehead. Don't you smell the intoxicating perfumes of these shores – the odour of wondrous voyages?' He lifted his arms in exultation. 'The spices, ah, the spices! Can't you sniff them, the sirens that lure the bravest sailors . . . ?' He began counting them on his fingers. 'Ginger, cinnamon, saffron, paprika, cloves, coriander, caraway, and the prince of them all – pepper! Pepper!' he exclaimed again ecstatically.

She left him to his dreams, for she saw Flipot returning with a big fellow in a sea-captain's red bonnet.

'So it's you who are offering a fortune for a passage to Crete?' he exclaimed, raising his arms skyward. 'I thought you'd be some old fool who had nothing to lose but her bones. Haven't you got a husband to knock some sense into your head? Or are you anxious to end your days in the harem of the Grand Turk?'

'I said I wanted to go to Crete, not Constantinople.'

'But Crete is in the hands of the Turks. It's full of eunuchs, both black and white, who come there to buy flesh cheap for their masters. You'll be lucky to get there without being stolen on the way.'

'But you're going to Crete, aren't you?'

'Oh, I'm going there all right,' the Captain growled. 'But I didn't say I was going to get there.'

'To hear you talk, anyone would think the Barbary pirates were waiting just outside the harbour here.'

'That's just what they are doing. Only last week a Turkish galley was spotted manoeuvring around the Hyères islands. Our fleet isn't strong enough even to scare them. By God, it's a shameful thing!

'You can be dead sure you'd be discovered before long, and all the slave merchants of the Mediterranean – white, black, brown, Christians, Turks, Berbers or pirates – would fight for the chance to sell you to some old wheezing pasha. How do you think you'd like being batted around in a game like that?' he asked, pointing at a fat Turkish merchant and his suite coming down the quay.

Angélique stared at the procession, common enough in Marseilles but entirely new to her. Their huge turbans of green and orange muslin bobbed above their dark faces like pumpkins. Their shoes with toes turned up in points from which pearls dangled, the parasols negro pages held over their heads, all made it seem more like a scene from a pageant than a sinister mission.

'They don't look so evil,' Angélique said to tease the Captain, 'and they are certainly handsomely dressed.'

'Bah! All that glitters is not gold. They know we're on our home ground here. Merchants always are on their very best behaviour in Marseilles. But once past the Château d'If all they think of is piracy and more piracy. No, Madame, it's no use your looking at me that way. I won't have a thing to do with this undertaking of yours. The Holy Mother would never forgive me if I did.'

'What about me?' Savary asked. 'Will you take me?'

'Are you going to Crete too?'

'To Crete and farther. If you must know, I'm going to Persia, but don't tell anyone.'

'How much are you offering me for the trip?'

'I'm not very rich, as a matter of fact, so I suggest thirty *livres*.'

The Captain frowned. 'Nothing doing! Neither for you nor for Madame here. Thirty *livres* wouldn't get you as far as Nice. With all I'd be risking, it isn't worth it. You, Madame, would draw the Berbers down on me like a carcase draws sharks, if you'll pardon the expression.' Raising his bonnet with a lordly gesture, he went back to his boat moored beside the quay.

'They're all alike, these Marseilles sailors,' said Savary angrily. 'Greedy and mercenary as Armenians.'

'It's no use my talking to other captains,' Angélique said. 'As soon as I do, they all start talking about harems and slavery. You'd think no one ever went to sea that she didn't wind up in the Grand Turk's seraglio.'

'Or the Bey of Tunis's, or the Dey of Algiers' or the Sultan of Morocco's,' Savary added. 'Yes, that's the way things often turn out. But anyone who doesn't want to take chances shouldn't go travelling by sea.'

Angélique sighed. Ever since morning all she had got in answer to her requests for transportation were the same attitude of surprise, the same shrugging of the shoulders, the same refusals. A woman going to Crete all alone! Sheer madness! Why, you'd have to be convoyed by the royal fleet itself!

Savary had encountered similar difficulties, but only because of his lack of money.

'Let's join forces,' Angélique said to him. 'You find me a boat, and I'll pay your passage along with my own.'

She gave him the address of the inn where she was staying, and after he had gone in search of another boat, she sat for a while on a new cannon, one of a considerable number in the port which had doubtless been forgotten by some naval equipper and now seemed designed more to serve as benches for strollers along the waterfront than to fire ammunition at the Barbary galleys.

The women from the Canebière section of the city were knitting there and gossiping while they waited for the fishermen to return, and the merchants were hawking their wares.

Angélique's feet hurt, and her head ached from the strong sunlight. She looked enviously at the women whose broad-brimmed straw hats shaded faces of classical beauty with great ox-eyes and full lips. They

43

had a certain imperial quality about them even when they were calling down curses on the passers-by who would not buy the carnations and posies they held out to them, or heaped words of warm tender affection on those who stopped by their stalls.

'Buy this codfish from me,' one of them importuned Angélique. 'It's the last one I've got. Look, it's as shiny as a new coin.'

'I wouldn't know what to do with it.'

'Why, eat it of course! What else would you do with a codfish?'

'I'm a long way from home, and I have nothing to carry it in.'

'Put it in your stomach. It won't bother you there.'

'Eat it raw . . . ?'

'No, fry it over the brazier of the Capuchin Fathers. Look, here's a sprig of thyme to put in its stomach while it's cooking.'

'I haven't any plate.'

'Get a stone off the beach.'

'And no fork.'

'How complicated you make things! Use your fingers.'

To get rid of the woman Angélique finally bought the fish. Holding it by its tail, Flipot wandered over to a corner of the quay where three Capuchin friars ran a sort of open-air kitchen, ladling fish soup out of a big pot and distributing it to the poor. For a few *sols* they allowed people to cook over two braziers. The smell of the frying fish and the soup made Angélique's mouth water, and she discovered she was hungry.

Now was the time when the citizens, even the stuffiest bourgeois, would come down to the waterfront to sniff that strange and wonderful aroma.

Not far from Angélique an elaborately dressed woman was alighting from a sedan chair, followed by a little boy who was looking enviously at the street urchins turning somersaults on the bales of cotton.

'Can I play with them, mother?' he begged.

'No, don't even think of it, Anasthase,' the woman answered indignantly. 'They're nothing but ragamuffins.'

'They have a lot of fun,' the boy said sulking.

Looking at him fondly, Angélique thought of Florimond and Cantor. She herself had played with urchins.

It had been hard for her to persuade Florimond not to follow her. The only way she had succeeded was to say that she would be gone just a few weeks, perhaps only two, if she was lucky. In the time it would take her to go by public coach to Lyon, then down the Rhône by boat, find the Chaplain and return, Angélique could possibly get back to her house in Paris before her absence was detected by the King's police. 'It would be the best trick I've ever played on you, Monsieur Desgrez,' she said to herself.

As she reviewed her hazardous escape, her heart beat faster. Florimond had not misled her; the tunnel was perfectly usable. The medieval vaulting restored by a hand skilled in mining engineering had withstood the ravages of dampness for a long time. Florimond had guided his mother to the abandoned chapel in the Forest of Vincennes. It was in ruins. Angélique promised herself that she would see to it that everything was in readiness for the return of the master. But why, she wondered, now that he had been gone so long?

It was not without emotion that she had embraced her son as dawn was waking the forest. How brave he was, as proud as she, and how well he could keep a secret! She had told him as much before they parted. She watched the trap-door close slowly over his curly head. Before letting it fall into place Florimond had winked at her. For him it was only a game that thrilled him and gave him a great feeling of importance.

Thereafter Angélique, followed by Flipot carrying her bag, set out on foot to the next village where she hired a carriage to take her to Nogent. There she had taken the public coach.

She had arrived at her goal, Marseilles. Now a second destination loomed – Crete. Her talk with the Chaplain had suggested a new trail for her to follow, difficult and tenuous. . . .

The next link in the chain was an Arab jewel-merchant whose nephew had been the last man to see Joffrey de Peyrac alive. How to find this jewel-merchant in Crete already presented several problems. Would he help find his nephew? But, Angélique said to herself, Crete was a lucky omen. It was the island for which she had purchased the office of Consul of France. However, she did not know how she could make use of her title since she was in the process of committing a grave offence against the King of France. For that reason, and for many others, she knew she ought to get out of Marseilles as quickly as possible and above all avoid meeting people of her own class.

Flipot did not return. Could it be taking him all this time to fry a fish? She looked for him and discovered him in conversation with a man in a long brown coat who appeared to be asking him questions. Flipot seemed embarrassed. Juggling the smoking hot fish he was hopping from one foot to the other, his antics making it clear that the fish was burning him. But the man seemed in no hurry to let him go.

Finally, with a shrug he went away and was soon lost in the crowd. Angélique saw Flipot start off in exactly the opposite direction from where she was sitting.

Then a little later he reappeared, zigzagging to escape her attention. Angélique went after him and caught him in a dark alleyway where he was pretending to hide behind the column of a portico.

'What does all this mean?' she asked. 'Who was that man talking to you just now?'

'I don't know. . . . At first I didn't trust him. . . . Here's your fish, Madame Marquise. There's plenty left. I dropped some when I was running.'

'What did he ask you?'

'Who I was. Where I came from. Who I worked for. I just said: "I don't know." "Come, come," he said, "you don't think I'm going to believe you don't know your master's name. Go on that way, and I know whom I'll have to deal with – the police!" I kept saying: "Yes sir, no sir, I don't know. . . ." Then he turned nasty. "That isn't the Marquise du Plessis-Bellière over there by any chance, is it? What inn is she staying at?" What did you want me to say?'

'What did you say?'

'I thought up a name of an inn on the spur of the moment – the White Horse. It's way the other side of town.'

'Come along. Quick now!'

As they hurried up the steep streets, Angélique tried to solve the puzzle. Were the police following her? Why? Was it possible that her flight had been discovered so quickly by Desgrez and had he sent his stool-pigeons after her? Suddenly she thought she had the answer. Monsieur de Vivonne had noticed her in the crowd the other day when he disembarked. At the time he had not been able to think of her name, but he knew her face was familiar. Now he had remembered and had sent his servants to find her again. Was it out of curiosity? Or friendship? Or out of respect for a courtier of the King?

Whatever the reason, she was not particularly eager to see him, but still his interest did not disturb her. Vivonne was too often away from Versailles on some campaign or other to keep up with the finer points of Court intrigues and did not know the latest about Madame du Plessis-Bellière, the future royal mistress. She was sure of that. Hence, there was no doubt that . . . Unless the man had been sent by the Chaplain, the only person who knew she was in Marseilles. Perhaps he had some information to give her about Ali Mektub or Mohammed Raki. But if he had, he would have sent his emissary to the inn of the

46

Golden Horn, since he knew where she was staying.

When she arrived at the inn she was damp with perspiration, and her heart was beating wildly.

'It's not wise to get yourself into such a state,' the innkeeper told her. 'You Paris ladies think you have to hurry-scurry all the time. Come this way, I've prepared you a fine dish of eggplant and tomatoes with just a touch of pimento and oil, and you can tell me the news.'

The innkeeper had doubtless been inspired to such maternal solicitude by Angélique's well-filled purse. She rather wanted to be in on any plots afoot, for she was well aware of the modesty of her inn, and had perceived at once that Angélique was a fine lady, accustomed to being served by an army of servants, yet who did not wish to attract attention here. Ah, love, love. . . .

'Come this way,' she said to Angélique. 'Here's a quiet corner over by the window. You will be quite alone at this little table, and my other guests won't be able to ogle you so far away. What would you like to drink? A little rosé from Var?'

She set a pewter goblet before Angélique and a glazed earthenware pitcher sweating from the cool liquid within it.

Angélique raised her eyes and caught sight of Flipot standing in the doorway and making emphatic signals to her. As soon as the innkeeper had turned her back, he dashed over to his mistress and whispered: 'He's coming . . . that evil man . . . the wickedest of them all.'

She glanced out of the window to see climbing the street, wrapped in a purple silk greatcoat, a silver-headed stick in his hands which he carried crossed behind his back, none other than Police Lieutenant François Desgrez heading for the inn.

CHAPTER FIVE

Angélique's first reaction was to push back her chair, leap down the two steps that separated her alcove from the principal room of the inn, and dash through it to the staircase that led to the upper floor.

'Follow me,' she said to Flipot.

The innkeeper raised her arms to the ceiling. 'Madame, what's the matter? What about the *ratatouille* I was making you?'

'Come here,' Angélique commanded. 'Come with me quick. I have something to tell you.'

Her expression and her voice were so imperious that the innkeeper dashed after her without asking for any explanation.

Angélique pulled her into her room, holding her by the wrist and digging her nails into her plump flesh without noticing. 'Listen, there's a man coming to the inn any minute now, wearing a lavender coat and carrying a silver-headed cane.'

'Is he the one who had a message brought you here this morning, perhaps?'

'What do you mean?'

The innkeeper delved into her capacious bodice and drew out a letter written on parchment. 'A boy came and left this for you just a little before you came back.'

Angélique snatched the missive from her and unfolded it. It was from Father Antoine, telling her of a visit from Desgrez, the lawyer he had had the honour of meeting in Paris in 1666. He had not deemed it advisable to conceal the fact that Madame du Plessis was in Marseilles, or her address.

Angélique crumpled the letter. 'It's of no interest to me now,' she said to the innkeeper. 'If the man in question asks you about me, you don't know who I am, have never seen me. As soon as he leaves, come and tell me. Here, this is for you.'

She held out three gold pieces, which so delighted the innkeeper that she made no remark, just winked knowingly and sidled out like a conspirator.

Angélique proceeded to pace the floor feverishly, biting her nails in her impatience. 'Get my things together,' she ordered Flipot, who was watching her anxiously. 'Pack my valises. Be ready.'

Desgrez had acted quickly, but she had no intention of letting herself be recaptured or led back to the King in chains like a slave. Now the sea would be her only means of escape.

Night was falling, and as on the previous evening the guitars began to strum and Provençal love-songs sounded from the dark alleys between the houses that rose in tiers from the waterfront.

Angélique would escape from Desgrez and from the King. The sea would carry her away. She went to the window and stood quietly there listening to the sounds of the inn.

Someone tapped at the door.

'You have no light,' whispered the fat innkeeper as she slipped into the room. She struck a flint and lit the lamp. 'He's still there,' she continued. 'Oh, he's a fine looking man and very polite, but he has a strange way of looking at you. Not that it bothered me! "As if I didn't know who's staying in my inn!" I said to him. "I certainly would have noticed a lady like you describe if she were in my house. But I tell you

48

I've never laid eyes on her." At last he believed me, or at least he pretended to. He wanted supper, and he wanted it served in the same little room where I had laid a place for you. He sniffed all around it as if he were looking for something with his long nose.'

'My perfume,' said Angélique to herself.

Desgrez would surely have recognised it, for it was a blend of verbena and rosemary especially prepared for her by a famous perfumer in the Faubourg Saint-Honoré. Desgrez had often sniffed its fresh country scent on her body when she had let him kiss and fondle her. Ah, what's the use of living when something betrays you to a fiend like that!

'And suddenly,' the innkeeper went on, 'his gimlet eye lit on the gold pieces you gave me. I still had them in my hand. "You have generous guests, mother," he said. I got nervous. Is that man your husband, Madame?'

'No!' Angélique said emphatically.

The woman shook her head several times. 'I see,' she said. Then she cupped her ear in her hand. 'Who's coming out there? None of my guests has a walk like that. I know them all.' She opened the door a crack, then slammed it shut. 'He's out there in the hallway, opening the doors of all the rooms.' She put her arms akimbo as she said indignantly: 'I'll show that fresh jailer what kind of stuff I'm made of!' Then she changed her tone. 'No, that might spoil everything. I know these policeman types. You start out being saucy to them and you wind up sobbing and crying into your handkerchief.'

Angélique grabbed her purse. 'I've got to get out of here . . . absolutely have to. I haven't done anything wrong.' She held out a handful of gold.

'Come this way,' whispered the innkeeper. She pulled Angélique out on to the little balcony, and removed one of the iron rails. 'Jump! Go on, jump to the next roof! Don't look down. Over there! You'll find a ladder on your left. When you're on the ground in the courtyard, knock. Tell Mario the Sicilian I sent you and that he's to take you to Santi the Corsican. No, it's not far, just to Juanito's and then to the Levantine quarter. I'll take care of that snooper to give you time.' She added a few words of luck in Provençal, crossed herself, and went back into the room.

The flight of Angélique and Flipot was like a game of hide and seek. Without stopping to catch their breaths they dashed past skylights, dropped into dark gardens, flitted by windows beyond which families were calmly eating supper without so much as raising their eyes from their plates as the fugitives passed, scrambled down stairways, wove in and out of a Roman aqueduct only to dodge past a Greek temple, brushed against hundreds of red and blue shirts hanging on the lines stretched across the alleys, slipped on piles of watermelon rinds and fish heads, were hailed by deafening shouts and songs and solicitations in all the languages of Babel, and finally took refuge, panting, with a dark Spaniard on the edge of the Levantine quarter. Now, he told them, they were far, far away from anything that might resemble the Inn of the Golden Horn. Did the lady wish to go any farther? The Spaniard and Santi the Corsican looked at her inquisitively.

Angélique mopped her face with her handkerchief. The long-dying glow of twilight was vying in the west with the lights of the city. Strange monotonous rhythms seeped through the closed doors and shutters of the cafés. There the street-porters and the Arabs and Turkish merchants lolled on soft cushions smoking their narghiles and sipping an eldritch brew from the shores of the Bosphorus out of little silver cups. A foreign smell mingled with the heavy odours of frying food and garlic.

'I want to go to the Admiralty,' Angélique said. 'To Monsieur de Vivonne's. Can you take me there?'

The two guides shook their ebony locks until their heavy gold earrings jangled. The Admiralty neighbourhood seemed much more dangerous to them than the stinking labyrinth through which they had led Angélique. But because she had been so generous to them, they agreed to give her explicit instructions for finding her own way there.

'Did you understand them?' she asked Flipot.

The boy shook his head. He was scared to death, having no knowledge whatever of the rules this variegated underworld of Marseilles lived by, except that he was sure its inhabitants would be quick with a knife. If his mistress were attacked, how could he protect her?

'Don't be afraid,' said Angélique.

This old city of the Phoenician colonists did not seem hostile to her. Desgrez did not control things here as he did in the heart of Paris.

Night had fallen now, but the transparent sky cast a bluish tinge over the city, outlining the remnants of its ancient past – a broken column, a Roman arch – among which ruins half-naked children were playing as silently as cats.

Vivonne's brightly lit residence loomed around a bend in the street. Sedan chairs and carriages were arriving and leaving, and through the open windows drifted the music of lutes and violins.

Angélique stopped for a minute to smooth out her gown and make herself as presentable as possible. She saw a broad-shouldered man leave a group and come toward her as if she were expected, but since the light was behind him, she could not recognise his face. Once he was near her, he stared at her closely, then took off his hat.

'Madame du Plessis-Bellière, isn't it? Yes, of course it is. Let me introduce myself – Carroulet, Chief of Police here in Marseilles. I'm a good friend of Monsieur de la Reynie. He wrote me about you, as he wanted your stay in our city to be as pleasant as possible.'

Angélique noticed that he had a kindly, fatherly face, with a big wen at the corner of one nostril. His voice was unctuous.

'I have also seen his lieutenant, Monsieur Desgrez, who arrived here yesterday morning. Thinking you might perhaps intend to pay a call on the Duc de Vivonne, who he knows is one of your friends, he instructed me to wait for you at the entrance here so that no embarrassing misunderstanding . . .'

Suddenly Angélique was filled with rage rather than fear. Do Desgrez had put all the police of the city on her trail, even up to Carroulet, well known for concealing a hand of steel under a velvet glove!

'I have no idea what you're talking about, Monsieur,' she said coldly.

'Hmm,' he replied indulgently. 'But, Madame, you were very fully described. . . .'

A coach was drawing up beside them. The Chief of Police moved to flatten himself against the wall. Angélique, however, practically threw herself under the hooves of the horses, and taking advantage of the time it took the coachman to steer around her, mingled with the guests who were crowding the entrance to the hôtel of the Duc de Vivonne. Servants with torches lit up the great staircase that led to the entrance hall. She climbed it confidently and mixed with the other guests.

Flipot was at her heels, carrying her purse. Angélique ducked into the shadow of the stairway like a woman who has just noticed her garters slipping down.

'Escape while you can,' she whispered to the little page. 'Conceal yourself in the servants' quarters – I don't care where – so long as no one notices you. I'll meet you tomorrow morning at the waterfront when the royal fleet sails. Try to find out just where and when that will be. If you aren't there, I'll sail without you. Here's some money.'

She emerged from her place of refuge and with the same confident steps climbed the marble flight that led to the upper floors.

She had hardly reached the first landing when the policeman she had just dodged appeared below. Angélique's curiosity was stronger than her terror, and she leaned over the banister to spy on him, trusting he would not see her in the shadows.

Carroulet did not seem happy. He accosted a servant and began questioning him closely. The man kept shaking his head, then drifted off. Shortly afterward the Duc de Vivonne appeared, laughing at some joke or other. The Police Chief bowed to him obsequiously, for the Admiral of the Fleet was a person of considerable importance. He was high in the King's favour, and everyone knew that his sister was the acknowledged mistress of the King. Since he was quite a touchy young man into the bargain, his manner was not gracious.

'What are you trying to tell me?' Vivonne exclaimed in his bull-like voice. 'Madame du Plessis-Bellière among my guests? Better look for her in the King's bed according to the latest news from Versailles.'

As Carroulet insisted, Vivonne lost patience. 'Your story doesn't hold water. She was here, you say, and now she's not here. Either you must be blind, or you're having hallucinations. You'd better take a physic.'

The Police Chief made up his mind to withdraw, crestfallen. Vivonne shrugged his shoulders. One of his friends came up to him and apparently asked him what had happened, for Angélique heard the young Admiral reply crossly, 'That boor was claiming that I was entertaining here in my house the lovely Angélique, the King's latest flame.'

'Madame du Plessis-Bellière?'

'The same. Heaven help me if I ever have that intriguing whore under my roof! My sister has almost gone out of her mind from all the affronts that woman has made her endure. She has written me desperate letters. If that green-eyed siren got what she wanted, Athénaïs would have to haul down her flag, and the Mortemarts would have a sorry time of it.'

'Do you suppose she is in Marseilles? Her beauty, I hear, is enough to haunt your dreams. I've always been dying to meet her.'

'You'd only die in vain. She's a flirt, cruel to the point of murder. Her admirers know how vain it is to try to get anywhere with her. She doesn't waste time in love talk when she sees anything she wants to get. And what she wants right now is the King. She's a sly one, I tell you. My sister said in her last letter . .

Angélique missed the rest of their conversation, for they moved on into one of the salons.

'You'll pay for that, my dear,' Angélique said to herself, furious at the way Vivonne had slandered her.

She groped her way down the dim corridor until she found a door, the handle of which she slowly turned. The room was empty and illuminated only by the gleams of light coming through the open window. Exhausted, Angélique stretched out on a deep oriental divan covered with rugs and cushions. Her foot struck a kind of copper platter lying on the floor, and it rang with the sound of a gong. She listened anxiously, then found a candle to show her where she was. The suite of rooms – a bedroom, a dressing-room and a bathroom – must be the Duc de Vivonne's. It was obviously the apartment of a seafaring man who, once ashore, did nothing but indulge himself. It did not take her long, as she surveyed the general disorder, to pick out charts and maps and uniforms, and a clothes closet in which were hanging a considerable number of nightgowns and filmy negligees.

Angélique selected a white embroidered *mousseline de soie*. She washed in a basin prepared for the master – and his mistress – filled with water scented with Provençal lavender. She brushed the dust out of her hair. Sighing with comfort, she wrapped the gauzy garment around her, and returned in her bare feet to the dressing-room. She was so tired she was shaking. After listening for a moment to the muffled shouts coming from the salons, she sank again on to the divan. To hell with the future, and all the policemen in the world! She was going to sleep.

'Oh!'

The sharp scream woke Angélique. She raised herself, shielding her eyes from the bright light.

'Oh!'

The dark-haired girl with beauty-patches all over her face was standing at her head, a picture of astonished indignation. Quickly she turned and gave someone a resounding slap.

'Well, you swine, is this the surprise you were keeping for me? Congratulations, it worked! I don't ever intend to forget so exquisite an insult. I shall never see you again in my whole life.'

With a great swishing of her dress and clicking of her fan she swept out of the room and vanished. The Duc de Vivonne, holding his smarting cheek, turned from the doorway and saw Angélique.

His servant was the first to recover his wits. He set the two candlesticks he was carrying on a table, bowed to his master – and accidentally to Angélique – then glided out, closing the door softly behind him.

'Monsieur de Vivonne . . . I am distressed,' murmured Angélique, forcing a contrite smile.

Now that she spoke, he seemed at last to realise he was dealing with a creature of flesh and blood, not a ghost.

'So it's true what that boor said. You were in Marseilles. You were under my roof. How could I have guessed? Why did you not introduce yourself?'

'I did not want to be recognised. Several times I've almost been arrested.'

The young man put his hand to his forehead, and went to his ebony writing-desk, from which he took a decanter of brandy and a glass.

'So Madame du Plessis-Bellière has all the police in the kingdom on her tracks! Have you murdered someone?'

'No. Worse! I refused to go to bed with the King.'

The courtier's eyebrows rose in astonishment. 'Why?'

'Out of loyalty to your dear sister, Madame de Montespan.'

Vivonne regarded her speechless, the decanter still in his hand. Then his face relaxed and he burst out laughing. He poured himself a glass of brandy and sat down beside her.

'I should think that would have cost you your life.'

'Perhaps it will. But not so soon as you think.'

She continued to flash her timid little smile at him. Her eyelids, still heavy with sleep, fluttered over her green eyes, and her lashes cast long shadows on her smooth cheeks.

'I was so tired,' she sighed. 'I had walked for hours over this whole city. I had lost my way. I came here for refuge. Forgive me, I know it was indiscreet of me. I washed in your bathroom and I took this dressing-gown out of your closet.'

She smoothed the sheer white material over her bare body. Beneath it glowed pink the curving line of her thighs and her hips. Vivonne glanced at the negligée, then turned his eyes away. He swallowed his brandy in one gulp.

'A damned embarrassing situation!' he grumbled. 'The King is going to find out you were here and accuse me of being your accomplice.'

'Monsieur de Vivonne,' Angélique said, rising to her feet, 'don't be silly. I thought you were more devoted to your sister's fortunes . . . on which your own depend to a certain degree. Would you really like to see me in the King's arms, and Athénaïs in disgrace?'

'No indeed!' stammered Vivonne, perplexed by a situation that was becoming more and more like a play by Corneille, 'but I should not like to offend His Majesty. *You* may refuse his attentions if you like. But why are you in Marseilles? And at my house?'

She laid her hand gently on his. 'Because I want to go to Crete.'

'Huh?' He jumped as if a bee had stung him.

'You're leaving tomorrow, aren't you?' Angélique persisted. 'Take me with you.'

'Bolder and bolder! I think you must be out of your mind. Do you really mean to go to Crete? Do you even know where it is?'

'What about you? Do you even know that I am Consul in Crete? I have very important business and interests there, and it's a good time for me to tend to them and let the King's passion cool for a while. Don't you think that's a good idea?'

'It's madness . . . Crete!' He rolled up his eyes as if the insanity of her proposal defeated him.

'Yes, I know,' said Angélique. 'The harem of the Grand Turk, the Barbary pirates, et cetera, et cetera. But, you see, with you, I would have nothing to fear. What could happen to me if I were escorted by the Royal French Navy?'

'Dear lady,' said Vivonne solemnly, 'I have always respected you deeply . . .'

'Perhaps too much,' she suggested with a playful smile.

Her interruption so discomfited the young Admiral that he stammered before he could go on with what he intended to say.

'What difference does it make? Hmm! Well, regardless, I have always regarded you as a sensible woman with a good head on her shoulders. Now, to my great disappointment, I am forced to see that you have no more sense than any other young flibbertigibbet who speaks before acting and acts before thinking.'

'Like the pretty brunette who left us a few minutes ago? I should have liked to explain myself to your charming mistress. Now she is so angry she'll spread the news that I'm here.'

'She does not know your name.'

'She will be quite able to describe me, and people I don't want to know I'm here will recognise me. Take me to Crete.'

The Duc de Vivonne felt his throat tighten. Angélique's eyes were making him feel giddy. He went to his writing-table and poured himself another glass of brandy.

'Never,' he said in answer to her last request. 'I'm too sensible for that. By becoming an accomplice in your flight – which is what I will be sooner or later – I will incur the wrath of the King.'

'And the thanks of your sister.'

'I am sure to fall into disgrace.'

'You underestimate Athénaïs's power, my dear. However, you know her better than I do. Now she is the only one in the King's favour, and he is very fond of her. She hasn't forgotten the wiles she used to lure him in the very beginning. Don't think she isn't strong enough and clever enough not to take advantage of my absence and repair what little damage I may have done.'

Vivonne knit his eyebrows, deep in thought. 'Bah!' he said. Then he must have had a vision of the dazzling Mortemart, must have heard the echo of her scornful laugh and her inimitable voice, for he grew calm again. 'Bah!' he said again. 'We can depend on her.' He shook his head several times. 'But you, Madame, what about you?' He watched her out of the corner of his eye.

Each time he looked at her she observed he was growing more and more conscious of her presence there in his house at that hour – a woman who had been one of the jewels of the Court and coveted by the King. He was studying her perfection with a kind of astonishment, as if he were seeing her for the first time. There was no flaw in her beauty. Her complexion was peerless, more golden than many blondes', and her clear green eyes had jet-black pupils. At Versailles he had looked upon her in her Court costume as on an idol, which used to make the Montespan blanch with rage. Now in her present state of undress she was wholly feminine and pulsating. For the first time in his life he thought of the King, murmuring to himself: 'Poor man! If it's true that she refused him. . . .'

Angélique did not break the weighty silence between them. It amused her to keep a Mortemart in suspense; it was a piece of luck very few could boast of. The high spirits and the explosive nature of the family never seemed to subside. Either you hated them or worshipped them – even the oldest, the Abbess of Fontevrault, whose madonna-like beauty swathed in veils and wimples fascinated the King and enthralled his courtiers. Age had not quenched the fires of her spirit as she read the Early Fathers and ruled her convent and directed her nuns along paths of sublime virtue.

Vivonne had the best qualities and the worst defects of his sisters, capricious and easygoing, vibrating between coarseness and suavity, stupidity and genius. In the same way that a kind of friendship – that of the warrior for the lover – had attracted Angélique to Athénaïs, so that she had always looked upon the Duc de Vivonne with half-serious interest. He seemed to be made of finer stuff than the other noblemen who dogged the steps of their master and lived off his subsidies.

She smiled her subtle smile at him again and remembered that in the last analysis she really did like these terribly greedy, foolish, handsome Mortemarts. Slowly she raised one arm to support her head and flashed a teasing look at the young man.

'Well, what about me?' she said.

'You are a strange woman, Madame. Have you forgotten that you sought to turn my sister out? Yet here you are, taking just the opposite position and trying to give her the advantage. What are you after? What do you expect to get out of all this shamming?'

'Nothing except more worries.'

'So?'

'Haven't I the same right as any other woman to try little whims?'

'Certainly! But choose your victims. With the King that can take you far.'

Angélique pouted. 'Is it my fault that I don't like taciturn men with cranky dispositions who have little sense of humour and are so meticulous about intimate matters that they're almost vulgar?'

'Whom are you talking about?'

'The King.'

'Well! So you go so far as to sit in judgement on him. . . .' Vivonne was visibly offended.

'My dear, when it comes to bedroom matters, let me speak as a woman and not a subject.'

'Fortunately, not all women reason the way you do.'

'Let them submit and be bored if they want to. But those things I can't countenance. Titles, favours, honours never balanced that kind of submission and constraint so far as I'm concerned. I gladly leave them all for Athenais.'

'You are . . . unspeakable!'

'What did you expect? Is it my fault if I prefer gay young men full of spirit . . . like you, for instance? I like gallant gentlemen who have some time for women. To hell with those single-minded bores who have no time for anything but business. I like someone willing to step out of the road to success a little to pick a few flowers.'

The Duc de Vivonne turned his eyes away, mumbling: 'Now I see your game. You have a lover waiting for you in Crete, some little ensign with a handsome moustache and no other purpose in life than women.'

'You're quite mistaken. I have never been in Crete and no one is waiting for me there.'

'Then why do you want to go to that pirates' den?'

'I've already told you, I have business there. Besides, it seemed like a good way for me to forget the King.'

'He will not forget you! Do you think you're a woman men forget easily?'

'He will forget me, I tell you. Out of sight, out of mind. Isn't it that way with you, with all other men? He'll discover his Montespan all over again, and be perfectly happy with her for the rest of his life. He's not a complex man, nor a sentimental one.'

The Duc de Vivonne, who had felt his throat tighten strangely, now could not help bursting out with: 'How wicked you women are!'

'Believe me, the King would be grateful to you if he learned you had come to my assistance and thus rid him of a fruitless passion. Now he won't have to act the tyrant and throw me into a dungeon. Time passes, and he will laugh at his anger, and Athénaïs will be able to make good use of the service you could render her by whisking off the person she most wants to get rid of.'

'But what if the King does not forget you?'

'Well, there'll still be time for me to change my mind. Perhaps I shall have thought things over and seen the error of my ways. The devotion of the King will move my heart. I shall fall into his arms and become his favourite and . . . I won't forget you either. Don't you see, you should think of the future. By helping me you can win either way, my little courtier.'

She had spoken those last words with just enough scorn in her voice to sting him. He blushed to the roots of his hair, and protested loftily: 'Do you think I'm a scoundrel, a bootlicker?'

'I never did think so.'

'Well, understand that I'm quite as capable of telling the King what I think as you are.'

'I don't doubt it.'

'But that's not the point,' replied the young Admiral severely. 'You forget a little too easily, Madame, that I am in command of a squadron, and that the mission on which the royal fleet is sailing tomorrow is a military one, which is to say a dangerous one. I am entrusted with the responsibility of policing this madhouse of a Mediterranean in the name of the King of France. My orders are strict: no passengers, much less female ones.'

'Monsieur de Vivonne. . . .'

'No!' he roared. 'Remember, I am master on board my ship, and I know what I have to do. An expedition in the Mediterranean is no pleasure-ride on the Grand Canal. I know how important my mission is, and I am confident the King would say and do just what I am now.'

'Do you think? . . . On the contrary, I am confident the King would not turn up his nose at what I'm offering you.'

She spoke seriously. Vivonne changed colour again. The blood was pounding in his temples. He stared at her like an inquisitor. It seemed to him that life itself lay in wait for him in the soft slow heaving of her breasts peeping through the lace of the negligee.

He was dumb with surprise. Madame du Plessis had a reputation for being haughty and difficult to approach, and she had admitted she was capricious. Courtier that he was, it had never occurred to him that he might be offered what had been refused the King. His lips felt suddenly parched. He swallowed his brandy and set the glass back carefully on the writing-table as if he thought it might drop from his grasp.

'Let's be sure we understand each other,' he said.

'I think we do . . . very well,' murmured Angélique. She pursed her lips into a rosebud and looked straight into his eyes.

He fell on his knees beside the divan, throwing his arms around her slim waist. With a gesture of homage he had not planned he bent his head and touched his lips to her satiny skin just above her swelling breasts, and remained in that mysterious darkness fraught with the heady perfume of Angélique.

She did not stir except to let her lashes veil the shining glory of her eyes.

Then he felt her bending toward him, yielding to his caress. A mad desire seized him to devour that golden flesh, grained like fine porcelain. Greedily he ran his lips over her, seeking her smooth, round shoulders, the hollow of her throat where the warmth made him giddy.

Angélique's arms encircled him, pressing his head against her. Then she gently laid her hand on his cheek and made him look up at her. Her emerald eyes met the hard blue ones of the Mortemart clan, and for once they yielded to her. Vivonne had never before encountered such a creature or experienced a more electric delight.

'Will you take me to Crete?' she asked.

'I think . . . I think I could not do otherwise,' he answered thickly.

Angélique knew every trick of a casual sexual encounter. She had promised to satisfy him, and he was too sophisticated to be content with a passive affection. Sometimes cajoling and laughing, then suddenly as ferocious as a frightened animal, she would give herself to him, then retreat from his new demands until he had to plead with her that he was dying of frustration.

'Is it the wise thing to do?' she said.

'Why should we be concerned with that?'

'I don't know. . . . We scarcely knew each other yesterday.'

'That's not true. I have always worshipped you silently from afar.'

'And I must admit I found you very taking, but this evening it's as if I were seeing you for the first time. You are much more . . . disturbing than I thought. You frighten me a little.'

'Frighten you?'

'I've heard so much about how cruel the Mortemarts are.'

'Nonsense! Forget your fears, my darling.'

'No . . . Monsieur! Oh! Let me catch my breath, for heaven's sake. Listen, I have some principles. There are some things one doesn't do except with a lover of long, long standing.'

'You are adorable! I'll see to it you forget your principles. Don't you think I can?'

'Perhaps. I don't know.'

They kept whispering passionately in the dim light of the candle's flickering flame. Angélique yielded to his gentle yet fearsome attacks, though she trembled within the strong arms bending her, subjecting her to his will. The candle guttered out. They were enveloped by the darkness, which seemed to drag her deeper into his designs. She allowed herself to glide blindly and willingly into the ever new and zestful gulfs of voluptuousness. Forgetting everything, she groaned with abandon as she struggled bravely and blissfully, every pain wringing shocks of pleasure from her senses.

Still clasping her, he fell asleep. But in spite of the delicious languor and the languishing dizziness that engulfed her, she refused to sleep herself. It would not be long till dawn, and she wished to be awake when he opened his eyes, particularly since she put no trust in the promises of men once their desire had been gratified.

She lay with her eyes open, staring into the deep-blue screen of the night beyond the open window through which came the sullen booming of the sea on the pebbled shore. Mechanically her hand caressed the sinewy body of her sleeping lover, reviving for her the old tenderness she had longed for when years ago she had lain beside Philippe.

Daylight turned the sky a clear grey mottled with purple like the breast of a mourning dove, then softly changed it to a pale green-and-white iridescence that shimmered like mother of pearl.

Someone was scratching at the door.

'Admiral,' came the voice of the valet, 'it's time.'

Vivonne was instantly awake like a man accustomed to alerts.

'Is that you, Giuseppe?'

'Yes sir. May I come in to help you dress?'

'No, I'll take care of that. Just tell the Turk to get my coffee ready.'

He smiled knowingly at Angélique as he added to the valet: 'Tell him to bring two cups and some pastry.'

The valet went away.

Angélique smiled knowingly back at Vivonne, and laid her hand on her lover's cheek. 'How handsome you are!' she said.

The fact that she addressed him so familiarly sent a thrill of ecstasy through him. She had refused the King!

'You're beautiful too. I think I must be dreaming.'

In the half-light, her long hair streaming around her, she seemed almost a child.

'Will you take me to Crete?'

He seemed shocked. 'Of course! Do you think I'm such a blackguard as not to keep my promises after you have kept yours so marvellously? But we must hurry, for we have to put in an appearance within the hour. Have you your luggage with you, or should I send for it?'

'My lackey should be waiting for me near the pier with my bag. While I'm waiting, I'm going to rummage in that wardrobe so well furnished with everything to please a woman's heart. Are they your wife's clothes?'

'No,' Vivonne said soberly. 'My wife and I live apart. We do not see each other any more, since that viper tried to poison me last year in order to replace me with her lover.'

'That's right. I remember. I heard about it at Court.' She laughed mirthlessly. 'Poor dear, what a terrible thing to have happen to you! Did she really poison you?'

'I was sick as a dog.'

'That's all over now,' she said gently, patting his cheek. 'So these gowns belong to your mistresses, who according to rumour are as various as they are numerous. But I shouldn't complain. I'm going to find what I need.'

She laughed again. The gambols of love had left a spicy fragrance on her body, and when she passed before him he instinctively held out his arms to grasp her and clutch her to him.

But she escaped laughing. 'No, my lord. We're in a hurry. We shall meet again later.'

'Ouch!' he said with a wry face. 'I don't know whether you've thought how uncomfortable a galley is.'

'Pooh! We'll find plenty of occasions to embrace here and there.

Don't you ever put into port in the Mediterranean? Aren't there islands with clear blue streams and beaches of soft sand?'

He sighed deeply. 'Be still. You're driving me crazy.'

Whistling, he pulled on his silk stockings and his blue satin breeches and came to the doorway of the bathroom. She had poured some water out of the copper pitcher into the marble basin and was splashing herself with it.

'Let me at least look at you,' he begged.

She glanced at him indulgently over her wet shoulder. 'How young you are!'

'Not any younger than you, I think. I'd even go so far as to say I'm three or four years older. If I remember correctly, the first time I saw you was – yes, I'm sure of it – when the King entered Paris. You had all the biting, untamed freshness of your twenty years. I was twenty-four then, and thought I was a grown man full of experience. I'm just beginning to realise that I really know nothing.'

'But I grew old faster,' said Angélique gaily. 'I'm terribly old. I'm a hundred.'

A Turk with a face like a fruitcake under his green turban brought in a copper tray on which tiny cups of a black beverage were steaming. Angélique recognised the brew as the same she had drunk with the Persian ambassador Bakhtiari Bey, and the same that impregnated the Levantine quarter of Marseilles with its aroma. She could hardly touch her lips to it, its bitter odour repelled her so. Vivonne, however, drank several cups, one after another, and then asked her if she was ready to leave.

Angélique felt panic sweep over her again. What if the police were still nosing after her in the sleeping city?

Luckily, however, the Admiral's hôtel gave directly on to the arsenal, and they reached the pier merely by crossing the courtyard.

In the distant roads the galleys were waiting. A gold and white longboat was crossing the harbour toward the pier. Angélique thought she would faint with anxiety as she waited for it to arrive. The Marseilles cobblestones were scorching her feet. At any moment Desgrez might appear to nullify all her plans and destroy her hopes. She kept looking around her at the jetties, the moorings, the slips, the harbour and the city above it wrapped in a brownish mist.

Vivonne was talking with his officers while the servants tossed the luggage into the longboat.

'Who goes there?'

Angélique spun around. Two forms were timidly creeping out from between some cases of goods and moving toward the group. She let out a great sigh of relief as she recognised Flipot and Savary.

'This is my suite,' she said, introducing them. 'My doctor and my lackey.'

'Tell them to get into the boat. You too, Madame.'

They still had to wait while the longboat bobbed and bumped against the pier. Someone had forgotten the charts and had to go back for them.

The port was coming to life. Fishermen dragging their nets were stepping down the ladders into their smacks. Others were leaving their anchored boats to come ashore and warm up their breakfast on the braziers of the Capuchin friars.

A Greek or perhaps Turkish prostitute began to dance, swaying her veils and raising her hands high as she clicked her copper finger-cymbals. It was neither the time nor the place to invite men to sample her wares. Perhaps, though, she was dancing a salute to the rising sun after a sordid night in the oriental quarter. The exotic tinkle of her castanets seemed out of place on the almost deserted waterfront.

The oars of the dinghy swished out of the water, then dipped into it again. Soon they were out in the waves, and Angélique could see the first rays of the sun sparkle on the Tour Saint-Jean.

Angélique cast one last look behind her. Marseilles was retreating into the distance. But she thought she saw the form of a man coming out on to the pier. He was too far away for her to distinguish his features, but she was sure it was Desgrez. Too late!

'I've won, Monsieur Desgrez!' she thought with a thrill of triumph.

PART TWO

Crete

CHAPTER SIX

Angélique was staring pensively at the golden tassels of the tabernacle awning as they tossed over the waves and danced in the spray of the wake. The six galleys were sailing before a fresh wind, their long bowsprits rising and dipping in graceful curves, their gorgeously decorated hulls leaping over the blue billows. The gilded figureheads gaily parted the waves, while on the carved poops the conch-blowing tritons, the rose-crowned cupids and the full-bosomed sirens dazzled her eyes as their gilded contours rose dripping from the water and sank into it again. On the masts the pennants and banners whipped with a joyous sound. The flaps of the afterside of the tent had been drawn back, and the sea air, laden with the scent of myrtle and mimosa wafted from the nearby shores, prickled her nostrils.

The Duc de Vivonne had furnished the tabernacle in oriental style, with rugs, low divans and cushions, and made it a mess-room for the officers. Angélique found it quite comfortable, and preferred to lounge there rather than in her narrow cabin between decks, which she found damp and dismal. Here the sound of the surf against the hull and the heavy canvas of the tent drowned the incessant gongs of the overseers and the raucous oaths of the guards. It was almost like being in a salon.

A few feet away from her a junior officer, Monsieur de Millerand, was scanning the shore through a telescope. He was still almost a beardless youth, but tall and well built. His grandfather, an Admiral, had schooled him in the traditions of the royal navy and, being fresh from school and observant of rules, he did not approve of having a woman aboard. He had never been known to smile, and he stalked about haughtily, studiously avoiding the company of the other young officers who at certain hours would gather around Angélique. They were far less stiff than he, and clearly enjoyed her company, which at least lent some flavour to their expedition.

The coastline revealed a long, sheer rocky palisade of a purplish hue, behind which rose mountains covered with dark-green vegetation composed of low bushes and fragrant herbs. In spite of the beauty of the colours, the place had a wild look. Not a single tiled roof, not a sailing-boat in the blue coves carved out of the pink cliffs, as charming and inviting as jewel-caskets. Only here and there a lonely little town girdled by ramparts.

The Duc de Vivonne appeared, wreathed in smiles, followed by his Negro page carrying a candy box. 'What are you doing, my dear?' he asked as he kissed Angélique's hand and proceeded to sit beside her. 'Would you like some oriental sweets? Noticed anything, Millerand?'

'No, my lord, except that the coast is deserted. The fishermen have left their isolated hamlets to escape the Berbers who come here on slave raids. They must have taken refuge in the towns.'

'We have just passed Antibes, haven't we? With a little luck we can impose on the hospitality of my good friend the Prince of Monaco tonight.'

'Yes, my lord, providing another of our good friends – I mean Rescator – doesn't appear to interfere with our cruise.'

'Have you seen anything?' Vivonne repeated, rising to his feet and taking the spyglass from the officer.

'No indeed. But knowing him as we do, that's what surprises me.'

Vivonne's second-in-command, Monsieur de la Brossardière, followed by two other senior officers, the Comte de Saint-Ronan and the Comte de Lageneste, entered the tent, and on their heels came Savary. The Turkish servant appeared and with the assistance of a young slave began to prepare coffee while the gentlemen seated themselves on the cushions.

'Would you like some coffee, Madame?' Monsieur de la Brossardière asked Angélique.

'I don't know. I suppose I should get used to it.'

'Once you are used to it, you can't do without it.'

'Coffee is good for keeping the humours of the stomach from rising to the head,' said Savary pedantically. 'Mohammedans love it, not so much for its medicinal qualities as because, according to tradition, the Archangel Gabriel invented it to rally the strength of the great Mohammed.'

'Let's drink coffee then!' Vivonne exclaimed gaily, throwing Angélique an ardent look.

These healthy young men kept gazing at her without attempting to conceal their admiration. She looked truly magnificent in a pale lavender gown which showed off the sheen of her skin glowing from the sea air, and her blonde locks. With a gracious smile she acknowledged the tributes these men paid her with their eyes.

'I recall drinking coffee like this with Bakhtiari Bey, the Persian ambassador,' she said.

The young slave was handing around damask napkins fringed with gold. The Turk poured the coffee into cups of fine porcelain, while the little Negro was passing two silver candy dishes, one containing lumps of white sugar, the other cardamom seeds.

'Take some sugar,' La Brossardière recommended.

'Grate a little cardamom into it,' Saint-Ronan suggested.

'Drink very slowly, but don't let it get cold.'

'You should always drink coffee scalding hot.'

Each imbibed his coffee in little sips. Angélique did as they advised and discovered that, even if the coffee was unpleasant in itself, its aroma was delicious.

'This cruise is beginning under delightful auspices,' said La Brossardière smugly. 'It is our good fortune to have on board one of the queens of Versailles, and, what's more, I hear that Rescator is en route to visit his ally Mulai Ismail, the King of Morocco. With him gone, the Mediterranean will be peaceful.'

'Who is this Rescator who seems to haunt your mind so?' asked Angélique.

'One of the lawless bandits we are directed to pursue and capture,' Vivonne said soberly.

'Is he a Turkish pirate?'

'Pirate he certainly is, but whether or not he's a Turk I don't know. Some say he is one of the brothers of the Sultan of Morocco, but others maintain he's French because he speaks our language so fluently. I'm rather inclined to think he is a Spaniard. It's hard to know what to believe about him, because he is always masked. That's not uncommon for these renegade Christians. They often mutilate themselves so as not to be recognised after they have renounced their religion. They also say he's dumb, having had his tongue cut out and his nostrils slit. But who knows? Those who think him a Moor or a Spanish Moor say that he is one of the victims of the Inquisition. On the other hand, those who think he's a Spaniard accuse the Moors of mutilating him. In any case he can't be very good looking, for no one can boast of having seen him unmasked.'

'But that doesn't keep him from being quite successful with the ladies,' La Brossardière said with a laugh. 'I've heard his harem includes some priceless beauties, and that he's bid against the Sultan of Constantinople himself in the slave market. The head of the Sultan's white eunuchs – you know, that handsome Caucasian Shamil Bey – will never get over Rescator outbidding him for a blue-eyed jewel of a Circassian girl.'

'You're making our mouths water,' said Vivonne. 'But should you be telling these stories in front of a lady?'

'I'm not listening,' said Angélique. 'Please go on with your tales of the Mediterranean, sir.'

La Brossardière said he had got the story from a Knight of Malta, the Bailiff Alfredo di Vacuzo, an Italian, whom he had met in Marseilles. The Knight was returning from Crete, where he himself had taken some slaves, and remembered vividly that auction at which Rescator had thrown sack after sack of gold coins at the feet of the Circassian beauty until by the end they reached to her knees.

'He certainly must be rich!' said Vivonne in one of his sudden fits of anger that made him turn red to the edge of his periwig. 'He's obviously not nicknamed Rescator for nothing. I suppose you don't know what that name means, Madame?'

Angélique shook her head.

'In Spanish it means a trader in contraband money, a counterfeiter. There used to be some practically everywhere, little craftsmen who were neither dangerous nor even annoying, but now there is only one – Rescator.'

He began to ponder this solemnly. Millerand, the young lieutenant, who was rather sentimental and timid by nature, plucked up the courage to enter the conversation. 'You said his slit nose did not keep Rescator from being pleasing to women, but these pirates use only the slaves they buy or have taken by force, and so it seems to me you can't judge their powers of seduction merely from the number of their wives. Take for example the renegade of Algiers, Mezzo-Morte, that fat pig, the greatest slave merchant in the Mediterranean. To see him, no one could suppose a single woman would ever yield herself to him out of love, much less out of taste.'

'Lieutenant,' said La Brossardière, 'what you say sounds logical, but you are wrong on two counts. First of all, Mezzo-Morte, even though he is the biggest slave-trader in the Mediterranean, has no women in his harem, because he prefers . . . young boys. They say he keeps more than fifty of them in his palace in Algiers. Secondly, Rescator does have a reputation for being loved by many women. He buys plenty, but keeps only those who choose to live with him.'

'What does he do with the others?'

'Sets them free. That's his hobby. He frees all his slaves, men or women, when he feels like it. I don't know how true all that is, but it's certainly part of the legend.'

'Legend!' grumbled Vivonne in rather bitter disgust. 'That part of his legend is true. He does free his slaves. I've seen him do it myself.'

'Perhaps he does it to compensate for renouncing his faith,' Angélique said.

'It's possible, but more likely he does it just to start trouble. He does it to . . . to embarrass . . . everyone!' roared Vivonne. 'For his own amusement, that's it, for his own amusement. Don't you remember, Gramont, when you were in my squadron at the battle of Cape Passero, those two galleys he captured? Do you know what he did with the four hundred convicts aboard? He took them out of irons and landed them in Venice. You can imagine how pleased the Venetians were with that gift! It created an international incident, and His Majesty remarked to me, not without irony, that when I let my galleys be captured I should at least choose a regular slave-merchant for my victor.'

'Your stories are exciting,' said Angélique. 'The Mediterranean seems to be full of interesting characters.'

'Heaven help you if you ever meet any of them. Whether they're mere adventurers or renegade Christians, slave-traders or simple merchants, anyone who deserts to the Infidels to oppose the Knights of Malta or the King of France ought to be burned at the stake. You have yet to hear of the Marquis d'Escrainville, a Frenchman; or of the Dane, Eric Jansen; or of Mezzo-Morte, who's already been mentioned; or of the Salvador brothers, Spaniards; or of plenty of other minor sea-raiders. The Mediterranean is infested with them. But we've talked enough about such scum. It's getting cooler, and I think it's a good time for you to inspect the galley. I'll go see if everything is shipshape.'

As the Admiral walked away, the other officers took leave of Angélique in turn, and returned to their posts.

It was then that Angélique noticed Flipot. The little lackey must have run up the stairs from the hatches, for he was panting and pale, and he stared at his mistress with popping, haggard eyes.

'What's the matter with you?' she yelled at him.

'There,' he stammered. 'I've seen him.'

She ran over and started shaking him. 'What? What did you see? Who?'

So certain was she that she had seen Desgrez on the quay as she left that she thought he might be going to spring up before her like a jack-in-the-box.

'Say something,' she ordered Flipot.

'I've seen him. . . . I've seen . . . the slave-keeper. Ah, Madame Marquise . . . it scared me to death . . . I can't . . . I can't tell you . . . there . . . down there in the slave pits.'

He retched, and, wrenching away from her, ran to the rail and vomited.

Angélique relaxed. The poor boy just hadn't got his sea-legs yet. The sight of the convicts and the odours of the pit must have upset him. Angélique asked the Turk to pour her a cup of coffee.

'Stay there,' she said to Flipot. 'The fresh air will do you good.'

'Oh, good lord, to have seen that!' he kept repeating. 'It made my blood run cold.'

'It will do,' said the Duc de Vivonne, returning. 'In a few days we'll be ready for the tempests. Madame, come inspect this galley on which you have been so rash as to embark.'

The gilded railing of the tabernacle and its crimson brocade curtains divided a heaven from a hell. As soon as Angélique stepped out on the poop-deck, the wind brought her the nauseating odour of the galley-slaves below, bending to the oars, then rising, in a slow monotonous rhythm that made her dizzy. The Duc de Vivonne held her hand to help her down the steps, then took the lead as he escorted her on the tour of the ship.

A catwalk ran almost the entire length of the galley. On either side were the stinking pits which contained the slaves' and convicts' benches. No bright colours or gilt there, only the rough wood of the benches to which the oarsmen were chained in fours.

The Admiral moved forward slowly strutting to show off his well-turned calves encased in red silk stockings with golden clocks, and taking care how he set his fine shoes with their scarlet heels on the slimy planks. His suit was of blue brocade, with wide red lapels, and a broad white sash fringed with gold encircled his waist. His jabot and cuffs were of precious lace; his hat so bedecked with ostrich plumes that in the wind it looked like a nest full of birds ready to take flight. He kept pausing to inspect everything minutely. Near the cook's galley on the port side, where the oarsmen's food was prepared, he came to a stop. Over a little hearth hung two huge cauldrons steaming with the weak potato and black bean soup which was the oarsmen's daily fare.

Vivonne tasted the soup and found it horrible. He took pains to explain to Angélique that he had personally seen to the improvement of this cook's galley. 'The former apparatus weighed five thousand pounds. It was unsteady, and in a heavy sea the nearest convicts usually got scalded. I had it lightened in weight and lowered as you see now.'

Angélique made a vague gesture of approval. The revolting stench of the oarsmen, to which the soup added its far from appetising odour, was making her queasy. But Vivonne, happy to have her with him and taking pride in his ship, did not spare her anything. She had to admire the beauty and seaworthiness of the two lifeboats, the beautiful lines of the pinnace and the little dinghy, and praise the emplacements of the swivel-guns on the gunwales.

For quarters the marines had only the narrow gunwales near the cannons. There was hardly enough room there, and they had to crouch or sit still all day long so as not to tilt the heavy ship. They had no other amusements at their disposal than to curse at the convicts below them or yell at the guards and jailors. It was hard to maintain discipline.

Vivonne explained that the oarsmen worked in three shifts, each bossed by a guard. Generally two shifts rowed while the other rested. The oarsmen were recruited from the prisons of France and from foreign captives.

'An oarsman has to be very strong, and must have been a murderer or a thief. The convicts they send us from the prisons die like flies, because they haven't enough muscle. That's why there are so many Turks and Moors.'

Angélique was looking at a group with long light-coloured beards, most of whom wore wooden crucifixes around their necks. 'Those hardly seem to be Turks, and that's no crescent hanging on their chests.'

'They are Turks by dint of being captured. Actually they are Russians we bought from the Turks. They're excellent oarsmen.'

'What about those over there with long beards and big noses?'

'They are Georgians from the Caucasus, purchased from the Knights of Malta. These here are the real Turks. They're volunteers. We hire them as head rowers because of their extraordinary strength. They keep discipline when the ship is under way.'

Angélique watched their spines bend beneath their red uniforms, then snap back to reveal their bearded faces, mouths straining open with the effort. Even more repellent than the thick stench of sweat and filth were the ferocious expressions of the convicts feasting their eyes on this woman above them as if she were an apparition.

Her dress was the colour of springtime, and the plumes of her huge hat tossed in the wind. A sudden gust whirled her skirt till its embroidered scallops brushed the face of a convict chained next to the catwalk. With a quick turn of his head he seized the material in his teeth.

Angélique let out a shriek of terror as she tugged at her skirt to free it. The oarsmen burst into savage laughter.

The keeper rushed up, his whip brandished high, and rained blows down on the head of the convict, but the wretch would not let go.

73

Beneath his green cap a tangle of matted hair half hid the evil gleam in his black eyes. It was so bold a look, so ferocious, and so intense that Angélique was unwillingly fascinated by it. Suddenly she shivered, and the blood drained from her face. That greedy, mocking look, like a hungry wolf's, was not unfamiliar to her!

Two other guards leaped into the pit, and beat the man with their fists and cudgels until they knocked out his teeth. Finally they kicked his blood-drenched body under his bench.

'We apologise, my lord. We apologise, Madame,' the guard in charge of the shift kept saying. 'That one's the worst of all, a real ungovernable trouble-maker. We never know what he'll be up to next.'

The Duc de Vivonne was livid with rage. 'Tie him to the bowsprit for an hour. A little dip in the ocean will calm him down.' He put his arm around Angélique's waist. 'Come along, dear. I'm sorry.'

'It's quite all right,' she said, recovering her aplomb. 'He did frighten me, but it's all over now.'

As they moved away, a hoarse shout rang out from the pit: 'Marquise of the Angels!'

'What did he say?' Vivonne asked.

Angélique turned around, deathly white. At the edge of the catwalk two chain-laden hands were groping like talons toward her feet. In the hideously swollen face leering up at her she suddenly saw only two black eyes emerging from the depths of her past.

'Nicholas.' It was the shepherd boy, son of one of her father's serfs, whom she had known in their childhood and again as Calembredaine in the Paris underworld.

Admiral Vivonne helped her back to the shelter of the tent in the stern.

'I should have been more careful with those dogs. A man is not a pleasant thing to behold from the catwalk of a slave pit. Certainly it's nothing for a lady to see, yet most of my lady friends are rather fond of it. I didn't think you were so sensitive.'

'It's nothing,' Angélique said in a weak voice.

She wanted to vomit, just as Flipot had done a while back, when he too had recognised Nicholas Calembredaine, the one-time star performer of the Court of Miracles and notorious robber of the Pont-Neuf, whom everyone had thought dead since a skirmish at the Saint-Germain fair, but who for ten years now had been expiating his crimes on a galley bench in the King's navy.

'My darling, what is wrong with you? You seem so sad.'

The Duc de Vivonne had stolen up on her, taking advantage of finding her alone, and was standing behind her watching the twilight steal across the waves. She was so lost in reverie that he felt alarmed.

She turned and gripped his strong shoulders. 'Kiss me,' she whispered.

She needed the touch of a clean, powerful man to dispel the sights of misery and abject poverty that had been haunting her thoughts for the last few hours. The persistent boom of the gong dinned into her heart like leaden hail, awakening within her the voice of despair, of inescapable destiny.

'Kiss me.'

As he touched her lips, she surrendered to him passionately. She wanted to sink into forgetfulness.

He kissed her again and again, his desire churning his blood till it coursed through his veins like a mountain torrent. His hand glided from her waist to her bosom, and she shivered with excitement when he stroked the perfect globes of her breasts as if he could not get enough of them. She clung to him tightly.

'No . . . listen, my dear,' he said, as he drew away panting. 'Not tonight. It's impossible. We must be on the alert. The sea is full of dangers.'

She did not insist, merely rubbed her forehead over his golden epaulets, which scratched her skin with a slight pain that made her feel better.

'Dangers?' she asked. 'Is a storm brewing?'

'No, but the pirates are on our trail. Until we land at Malta, we have to be on guard.' He grasped her to him tightly again. 'I don't know what you do to me,' he said. 'You inflame me with such desire. You are so changeable, so full of mystery, so full of surprises. Sometimes you are so radiant that we are all like tame sheep under the spell of your eyes and your smiles. But now I see you weak and helpless, as if you were overwhelmed by fear of something that might harm you. I want to protect you from it, something I've never felt before except with little children.'

Gently he pushed her aside and drew apart to lean his elbows on the railing. From time to time the spray of the waves splashed his face, quenching the fire in his lips that Angélique had kindled. He still felt her mouth imparting its heat to his. He was ravening to touch her lips again, feel them open to his, sense the thrill of her teeth meeting his like a barrier to his onslaught, a defence which made the surrender of her lovely face all the more voluptuous, tilted back, eyes closed, responding to his advances.

A woman who could kiss like that! A woman who knew how to laugh and weep from the depths of her heart so sincerely! He didn't care if she was sensitive and capable of being hurt. Still he could not forget that she had made the indomitable Athénaïs bow to her in their treacherous, merciless rivalry.

Thoughts like these were driving him to distraction. He had to know what lay beneath her moods.

'I know why you are so sad,' he said. 'I knew from the moment when you first told me about your son. You're thinking of him, aren't you – the boy you entrusted to my care and who drowned during a battle?'

Angélique buried her face in her hands. 'Yes,' she said in a strangled voice, 'that's it. The sight of this glorious blue sea that robbed me of my child torments me.'

'It was that devil Rescator did it. We were rounding Cape Passero when he swooped down on us like a sea-eagle. No one had seen him coming, for he was using none of his topsails and hence could remain unnoticed for a long time because of the high seas running that day. When at last we saw him, he was already upon us. His twelve cannons fired only one round, and we lost two galleys. Rescator sent his janizaries aboard the *Flamande*, the ship my household was aboard, including little Cantor. . . . Perhaps he panicked at the sight of the chained slaves fighting in the pits, or at the Moors with their scimitars. My squire Jean Gallet heard him shout: "Father! Father!" One of the boarders seized him to drag him off. . . .'

'Then?'

'The galley split in two, and sank amazingly fast. Even the Moors who had boarded it were washed into the sea. The pirates fished them out, and we did the same for our men still afloat. But almost all my household perished – my chaplain, my choir-boys, my four stewards – and the lovely child whose voice was like a nightingale's.'

A moonbeam glided into the tabernacle, turning the tears on Angélique's cheeks into pearls. Passionately he said he loved to see her weep, for she had such power over men's hearts. What was her mystery? He only vaguely remembered a scandal out of the distant past, something to do with a sorcerer burned in the Place de Grève.

'Who was his father? The one your boy called out to as he was drowning?' he asked bluntly.

'A man who vanished long ago.'

'Dead?'

'Probably.'

'Funny how people think of those things as they are about to die.

Even a child knows when he is dying.' He sighed deeply. 'I loved that little page. You don't hate me because of what happened to him, do you?'

Angélique made a gesture of surrender to fate. 'Why should I, Monsieur de Vivonne? It was not your fault. The war itself was to blame – or life, so cruel, so meaningless.'

CHAPTER SEVEN

Before leaving Spezia, where the French squadron had been lavishly entertained by a relative of the Duke of Savoy, Angélique thought she noticed the precautions increasing. Capricious though he was, Admiral Vivonne could be a farsighted and meticulous naval commander when the occasion demanded. And though the second galley of the fleet was already under way, he stayed behind to watch it from the tabernacle of the *Royale*.

'Brossardière, order it to return at once!'

'But, my lord, that will have the worst possible effect on the Italians who have been watching our sailing manoeuvre.'

'As if I cared what those cake-eaters think! What I see, and what you don't seem to notice, is that the *Dauphine* lists to port. She's loaded too high. I bet her hold is empty. She'll capsize in the slightest squall.'

His subordinate pointed out that the provisions had to be stowed on deck. If stowed in the hold, they would get wet, especially the flour.

'I'd rather have wet flour than another foundering ship like the one we lost recently right in the harbour of Marseilles.'

La Brossardière went to execute his chief's orders. Another galley, the *Fleur de Lys*, stood out to sea.

'Brossardière, have the rowers amidships reinforced.'

'Impossible, Admiral. You know they are the Moors we captured on that boat with the contraband silver.'

'More allies of Rescator harassing us, and obstinate to boot. See that they get two lashes apiece, and are put on bread and water.'

'They are already, my lord, and the doctor says we'll have to set some of them ashore, they're so weak.'

'The doctor can mind his own business. I will never set any of Rescator's men ashore, and you know very well why.'

Brossardière approved. As soon as they touched land, whether they were dying or not, these men of Rescator's would vanish as if by magic. They were probably scheming for that, especially as their master paid a special bounty to anyone who restored his men to him. They were seamen by choice, but when captured they showed a greater passive resistance than other captives.

'And now we are going to make for the open sea,' Vivonne announced when the six other galleys had cleared the harbour. 'At last! For the ten days or so since we set out I'd been beginning to think the galleys couldn't do anything but hug the shore. Hoist the mainsail,' he ordered.

The order was relayed from galley to galley.

The sailors tugged at the ropes and pulleys. On the spars the furled sails were loosed to explode like bombs as the wind filled them.

This was the first time Angélique had ever been to sea. The shores of Tuscany disappeared behind them, and wherever she looked she could see only water and then more water.

Not till noon did the lookout call: 'Land ahead!'

'It's the island of Gorgonzola,' the Duc de Vivonne explained to Angélique. 'We'll see if any pirates are hiding there.'

For its approach to the island the French fleet formed a semicircle in order to surround it. The island was rocky and barren, bristling with little promontories. Aside from three fishing smacks from Genoa and two from Tuscany which were setting their nets for tuna there was no sign of pirates. The island was almost uninhabited. A few goats were browsing on the sparse vegetation, and Vivonne wanted to buy them, but the head fisherman said no, they were their only source of milk and cheese.

'Tell them,' Vivonne ordered one of his officers who spoke Italian, 'that we would at least like to have some fresh water.'

'They say they haven't any.'

'Then catch the goats.'

The marines ran skipping over the rocks and killed the animals with their pistols. Vivonne summoned the head fisherman and offered him money for the goats, but he refused to take it. Suspicious of him, the Admiral had the man's pockets turned inside out. Several gold and silver coins spilled on to the deck. Vivonne had the man thrown overboard. He swam back to his boat.

'Let them tell us who gave them that money, and we'll set some cheese and wine ashore for them in payment for the goats. We are not thieves. Translate that.'

The fishermen seemed neither surprised nor hostile. To Angélique they looked as if they had been carved out of charred wood, as mysterious as the black Virgin she had seen in the little sanctuary of Notre-Dame de la Garde at Marseilles.

'I'll warrant these so-called fishermen are only pretending to be after tuna. They're out there just to inform the enemy of our route.'

'They seem harmless.'

'I know them, I know them well,' Vivonne said, making threatening gestures to the impassive fishermen. 'They're spies in the pay of all the bandits of these latitudes. These coins are Rescator's.'

'You see enemies everywhere,' Angélique said.

'That's my business as a pirate-chaser.'

La Brossardière came to call their attention to the sunset, though not because he found the violet sky streaked with gold-edged purple clouds beautiful.

'In a couple of days we're going to get a south wind. It would be wiser to go back to sailing close to shore.'

'Never!' said Vivonne.

The coast belonged to the Duke of Tuscany, who at the same time that he was promising entente with France was also giving shelter at Leghorn to English and Dutch merchants, and especially to Berbers. Leghorn, next to Crete, was the most important slave-market. If they went there, they would either have to make a big demonstration of naval power, or pretend not to notice. His Majesty preferred to stay on good terms with the Tuscans. Consequently they had to be content with merely policing the islands.

'We will head farther south, and Madame du Plessis will be able to see, and report to the King, that a galley can sail on the open sea by night under full sail.'

In fact, the wind died completely as night fell, and the ship progressed under oar-power. The watch was doubled for the sake of caution. But only one shift of oarsmen were rowing by the light of lamps which cast the shadows of the continually moving slave-keepers on the catwalk. The other convicts slept in fours on planks beneath their benches, wallowing in their filth.

At the other end of the galley Angélique tried to close her mind to the thought of their suffering only a few feet away from her. She had never gone back to the catwalk, hence could not let Nicholas know she had recognised him. The slave belonged to a bitter page of her life, the horrors of which had erased even the memories of their childhood when they had first been intimate. She had ripped out that page and destroyed it, and she would not let mere chance revive it. The dragging hours of the trip were torture to her in her impatience to get to Crete.

The deep blue light was almost phosphorescent owing to the reflection of the lanterns in the waves. Each stroke of the oars left a luminous

79

wake after it. In the sterns of the ships burned enormous beacons of gilded wood and Venetian glass, shaped like a man, in which twelve pounds of candles were lit every night.

She heard Lieutenant Millerand report to the Admiral. The marines were complaining about having to spend the night aboard in their cramped quarters.

'What are they grousing about? They aren't in chains, and they had good goat stew tonight. War is war. When I was a cavalry colonel I often slept on my horse and went without food. All they have to do is get used to sleeping sitting up. It's just a matter of habit.'

Angélique began to arrange the cushions on the divan to stretch out upon them. The Negro page came to help her. It was useless to ask Flipot for help, he was so seasick.

The Duc de Vivonne kept coming and going, with the little Negro and his candy boxes following him everywhere. The Mortemart appetite was legendary, and the young man owed his becoming stoutness to his craving for oriental sweetmeats.

As he munched the candied nuts and sucked the soft Turkish paste, he pondered the strategy of his campaign. He had advised his officers to get a little rest and they were sleeping on mattresses, but he had made up his mind not to do likewise. He seemed preoccupied, and in spite of the darkness summoned the master cannoneer to him.

A man with greying hair appeared in the light of the beacon.

'Master cannoneer, are your guns ready for action?'

'I have put your orders into effect, my lord. The pieces have all been overhauled and oiled, and I have had the cases of powder, balls and small shot brought up on deck.'

'Good. Go back to your post. Brossardière, old man. . . .'

Roused from sleep, the officer put his periwig back on, smoothed out his cuffs and almost immediately was standing before his superior.

'Sir?'

'Order Chevalier de Cléans, in command of the flanks, to take a centre position. He is carrying our reserves of powder and shot, and he'll have to be able to furnish us with more at once if we get involved for long. Call me the head of the musketry division also.'

When that man appeared, he said: 'Distribute muskets, bullets and powder. Keep a special eye on the swivel-guns. Don't forget we have only three cannons forward. The swivel-guns and muskets are our only real defensive weapons in case of a surprise attack.'

'All is ready, sir. The last drill should have let everyone know where his post is.'

During these preparations Savary put in an appearance, and announced that the saltpetre in his medicine chest was damp, which indicated there would be a change in the weather during the next twenty-four hours.

'I don't need your damned saltpetre to be aware of that,' Vivonne growled. 'If bad weather is coming, it won't come right away, and the surface of the water will show the change first.'

'Am I to understand that you fear an attack?'

'Master apothecary, understand that an officer of His Majesty's fleet fears nothing. Rather say that I foresee an attack, and go back to your phials.'

'That's what I wished to ask you, my lord, whether I might put my precious drugs in the safety of your council room. A bullet might break one of the phials.'

'Yes, if you think you ought to.'

The Duc de Vivonne sat down beside Angélique.

'I'm nervous,' he said. 'I think something is going to happen. I've always been that way. When I was a child and there was a storm at night, I'd keep fiddling with things. What should I do to calm down?'

He went in search of one of his pages, who returned with a lute and a guitar.

'We're going to sing for a while in honour of the starry night and the love of women.'

The brother of Athénaïs de Montespan possessed a sweet voice, possibly a little high, but well pitched. He could sing Italian songs beautifully. The time began to pass more pleasantly and the big hourglass that marked the minutes had to be turned twice.

Angélique felt a shiver run along her spine.

'Listen,' murmured the Comte de Saint-Ronan, 'the slaves are singing.

The sound of their humming in quartet carried over the water like the moaning of a conch-shell. It went on for a long time, full of the loneliness of the sea. Then a still youthful voice rose in a solo, singing the refrain of the chanty:

> I remember my old mother
> Would tell me to be good,
> Not like my wicked brother
> Chained to a bench of wood.

I robbed not on the highway,
But I did not do as told;
And now I row my life away
Chained in a galley's hold.

The song died away. In the silence that followed, the sound of the surf against the hull seemed louder.

A seaman called: 'Unidentified light five leagues to starboard.'

'Prepare for battle! Extinguish the beacons and leave only riding lights. Four squadrons of the guard on duty!'

Vivonne seized his telescope. After a long moment he asked Brossardière's opinion.

'We are approaching Cape Corsica. I think it's probably a boat out fishing for tuna, trying to catch them at night by driving them into nets. Do you think we should put in at the cape to make sure?'

'No. Corsica belongs to Genoa, and, besides, its coasts are almost always full of Berbers lying in ambush at anchor. The inhabitants are such partisans that they do not permit anyone at all to enter their roadsteads. All navigators, pirates, or corsairs, know enough to avoid that island. Let us follow the strategy we worked out when we left, and proceed to the island of Capraia, which belongs to the Duke of Tuscany and which has often given asylum to Turkish pirates.'

'When will we raise it?'

'By dawn, if the weather holds. Did you hear something?'

They strained their ears. From a distant galley came a prolonged howling, which presently stopped abruptly.

Vivonne swore. 'Now those Moorish dogs are baying the moon.'

La Brossardière, who had sailed in the Levant for many years, and knew Arab customs, said: 'They are howling for joy. That's their cry of victory.'

'Joy? Victory? They must be excited tonight.'

The forward watch sent one of its members. 'My lord, the chief of the watch has just climbed to the lookout. He asks you to turn your telescope in the same direction the light came from and see if those don't look like signals.'

Vivonne raised the spyglass again, and La Brossardière watched through his field-glasses.

'The watch is right, I think,' he said. 'They're signalling from the tops of the Rigliano mountains of Cape Corsica, doubtless to call their fishing fleet in.'

'Yes,' Brossardière replied. 'Doubtless.'

A new howling echoed over the water from the same galley, the *Dauphine*.

Savary reappeared and whispered to Angélique. 'Have you noticed how joyful the Moors on the *Dauphine* have suddenly become? The signal fires on the coast have warned them.'

Vivonne just caught his last words. He seized the old man by the collar of his old-fashioned greatcoat. 'Warned them of what?'

'I can't say, my lord. I don't know the code.'

'What makes you think they were trying to contact the Moors?'

'Because those are Turkish lights, my lord. Didn't you notice the blue and red of the rockets? I know, my lord, because I was once engaged as fireworks master by the grand master of artillery at Constantinople. He hired me to make rockets out of powder mixed with mineral salts to burn with different colours. The secret comes from China, but the whole Mohammedan world uses it. That's why I thought it could not be only Turks and Arabs sending messages to other Turks and Arabs, and since I saw hardly any other lights on the horizon except those of our galleys . . .'

'You go too far, Maître Savary,' said the Comte with humour.

A longboat with two beacons ablaze was approaching. La Brossardière shouted at it to extinguish its lights. A voice shouted back through the darkness: 'My lord, we have trouble aboard the *Dauphine*. The Moors amidships are up in arms because of the fires on the mountain.'

'Are they the Moors we captured on that felucca that was carrying the illegal silver?'

'Yes, my lord.'

'I suspected as much,' said the Admiral between his teeth.

'One of them keeps leaping up on his bench and shouting incantations.'

'What does he say?'

'I do not know, my lord. I don't understand Arabic.'

'I know,' said Savary. 'I heard him. He is shouting, "Our deliverance is at hand!" The others were answering him with shouts of joy as if he were a muezzin.'

'Take that instigator and execute him!'

'By hanging, my lord?'

'No, we haven't time, and the sight of him dangling from the yards might excite the other fanatics. Shoot him at the base of the skull with a pistol, and throw his body overboard.'

The longboat departed. A few minutes later two shots cracked out.

Angélique wrapped her cloak about her. The breeze had freshened suddenly, and she was cold.

The Admiral swept the coast once again, but everything had been swallowed up in darkness.

'Hoist the sails and put the other three shifts of slaves to work. With a little luck we'll be at Capraia by morning. We can revictual there with goats, of which there are a great many, and get some fresh water and some oranges.'

Angélique thought she could stay awake, but she must have dropped off for a nap, because suddenly she realised it was daylight. The shimmering light of dawn revealed an island ahead of them. In the counter-light from the pale gold, pink and light blue sky, it was only a mass of dark muddy blue reflected in the almost glassy surface of the water.

Angélique perceived that she was not alone under the awning of the tabernacle. She straightened her gown, fixed her hair, and stepped outside to sniff the morning air. The staff had moved forward. She was hesitating about crossing the catwalk when Lieutenant Millerand noticed her and graciously escorted her.

The Duc de Vivonne was in an excellent mood. He handed her his field-glasses.

'See how attractive that island is, Madame. Notice there is no surf at the base of those volcanic rocks. That means we will approach in complete calm. Nothing untoward to come alongside.'

Angélique had some trouble adjusting the glasses to her eyes, but finally she shrieked with pleasure at discovering a cove hidden among the flowering lilacs and the seagulls swooping above them.

'What's that – that round shining light over to the left?' she asked.

She had hardly spoken when the light shot up into the sky, then fell as it died out.

The officers looked at one another. Savary said calmly: 'Another signal rocket. You are expected.'

'Clear the decks for action!' Vivonne shouted through his megaphone. 'Gunners in position! We will force a passage. What the devil, we're a whole fleet!'

In spite of the wind they could hear the howling on board the *Dauphine* quite near and ahead of the Admiral's galley.

'Make that rabble shut up!'

But a piercing voice soared above the other noises, chanting with ear-piercing shrillness:

La illaha ilallah
Muhammadu, rasul ullah

Finally it subsided.

The Duc de Vivonne continued to give orders. 'Give the signal for regrouping according to the importance and manoeuvrability of the vessels. Keep the reserves of artillery in the centre. I will be in the centre, too, to keep an eye on things. The *Dauphine* and the *Fortune* take the lead. The *Luronne* take the left flank. The three others to the rear in a semicircle.'

'Flag on the cliff,' signalled the lookout.

Vivonne raised his telescope. 'There are two flags. One white, but raised by hand, a declaration of war in the Christian manner. The other is red with a white border and its emblem. That's funny, I seem to make out the silver chisel of Morocco. That's . . . that's impossible . . . !'

'I understand what you mean, my lord. The Berbers are not accustomed to raise their standards, and the Moors never use a white flag beside their emblems. Only Christians interpret a white flag as a declaration of war.'

'I don't understand it,' said Vivonne thoughtfully. 'I wonder what kind of enemy we're dealing with.'

In spite of the rolling sea, the galleys approached in line under reduced sail, and began to group into battle formation, pointing to the cliff that marked the mouth of the creek.

At that moment two Turkish feluccas appeared. The Admiral handed the telescope to his officer, who looked through it and then handed it to Angélique. But she was already watching through the old, very long one covered with verdigris that Savary had fished out of his luggage.

'I don't see anything in those boats except Negroes and some wicked looking muskets,' she said with disappointment.

'It's an insolent provocation!'

Vivonne came to a decision. 'Instruct the *Luronne*, our lightest ship, to give chase and run them down. Those fools don't even have any artillery.'

The *Luronne* obeyed the signals and set out in pursuit of the two feluccas. A little later the cannon fired and its boom echoed along the coast. Angélique gave the telescope to Savary to cover her ears with her hands.

The feluccas were not hit, but headed for the open sea.

The *Fleur de Lys* and the *Concorde* who had them in line of fire got

85

excited over this easy prey and took the initiative of falling out of line to advance on the target. The cannon boomed again several times.

'A hit!'

The triangular sail of one of the feluccas was trailing in the waves. In a few seconds the hull sank. The black heads of some who escaped appeared on the crests of the waves. The other felucca tried to manoeuvre to pick them up, but a well-aimed volley from the *Fleur de Lys* and the *Concorde* encircled it. She had to take to flight again.

'Bravo!' said the Admiral. 'Have the three galleys turn back toward the roads.'

The ships performed the manoeuvre with some difficulty owing to the by now quite rough sea. There followed a certain confusion in the disposition of the battle order.

It was then that the lookout shouted: 'War xebec to starboard, making for us!'

A boat under full sail had just come into sight at the mouth of the cove, and was crossing the strait between the cliffs at considerable speed.

'Come about to face the enemy!' thundered Vivonne. 'Fire the three cannons when I give the order. 'Fire!'

The big cannon in the middle recoiled on its tracks from the shock of discharging its load. Angélique was deafened by the shot, and the smell of powder tickled her nostrils. Through the smoke she heard the following orders, crisply given, precisely obeyed.

'Starboard swivel guns in position. The xebec is outsailing us. All muskets fire. Ready to come about into range. Fire!'

The salvos increased, topping the still vibrant echoes of the cannon. But the xebec had not been hit and was still too far away to be reached by the musket balls.

Savary was watching through his telescope with all the delight of an entomologist examining a fly under his microscope.

'It's a handsome ship, built of Siamese teak, a priceless wood. After the bark is stripped off, it's five years before the tree is ready to be cut down, and then seven years of weathering before it's ready to be sawed up. The white flag on the mainmast and the pennant of the King of Morocco on the poop and a special emblem – red with a silver crown in the middle.'

'That's the emblem of Monsieur Rescator,' Vivonne said bitterly. 'I might have guessed!'

Angélique's heart leaped. So she was about to meet the terrible Rescator, who had caused the death of her son, and whom the brave officers of His Majesty's navy seemed justifiably to dread. She ignored

Vivonne's and Brossardière's exchange of opinions as she kept her eyes focused on the manoeuvres of the enemy.

'That devil Rescator has a new ship. Sleek lines, low in the water, hardly up to the range of our guns – that's why we missed him just now when we had him across our bows. Twenty-two cannons in all. Damnation!'

Through the portholes in the hull of the xebec gleamed the round muzzles of the cannons, and wisps of smoke drifted from them, indicating that the cannoneers were at their posts ready to light the fuses at the first command. Signal flags ran up the halyards: 'Surrender or we will sink you.'

'Does that insolent bastard think he can scare the fleet of the King of France that easily! He's too far off to sink us. The *Concorde* is moving up and soon will have him in range. Hoist the white flag of war on the forward mast, and the fleur-de-lis in the stern!'

Presently the enemy changed course, describing an arc so as to avoid the cannons in the prows of the French ships which were pointed toward the shore to the east. The ship moved with amazing swiftness, all its sails set. Several cannon shots boomed out. The *Fleur de Lys* and the *Concorde*, which had fallen for the trick of the xebec manoeuvres, returned and were trying to land a direct hit on their assailant.

'Missed!' said Vivonne in disgust. He fished some sugared pistachio nuts out of his candy box. 'Now we have to be careful. He knows it takes time for us to reload. He's going to double back on us and try to sink us. Get ready to come about to face him. If we can take that position, he'll have to sail against the wind to get at our sides.'

The galley swung around. The enemy seemed to be adjusting to this new manoeuvre. For several moments there was a heavy silence on the ship, broken only by the rhythmical clanging of the slave-drivers' gongs that beat like a heart in pain.

Then in the distance they saw the pirate ship get under way again, returning toward them just as the French Admiral had predicted. It flew like a sea-eagle well to the rear of the whole flotilla, then suddenly stopped and tacked about.

'That damned pirate is a clever strategist,' La Brossardière growled. 'Pity he's our enemy!'

'This doesn't strike me as quite the right moment to admire his skill, Monsieur de la Brossardière,' Vivonne remarked drily. 'Cannoneers, have you reloaded?'

'Yes, my lord.'

'Then fire at once when I give the order.'

But the twelve cannons on the pirate's port side fired first. The sea seemed to turn into an immense geyser which hid the enemy in its spray. All kinds of debris soared into the air, and a deafening explosion echoed from side to side. Then an enormous wave crashed down on the *Royale*'s slave-pits and several oars on the port side snapped like matchsticks.

Soaked to the skin, Angélique clung to the gunwale of the galley as it slowly righted itself. The Duc de Vivonne, who had been knocked to the deck, was already on his feet again.

'Not bad,' he said. 'He missed us. Give me my telescope, Brossardière! I think now that . . .'

He broke off, his mouth dropping open, bewilderment and disbelief on his face. Where the supply galley had been there was now only a kind of whirlpool spinning like spokes a mass of broken spars and oars. The ship and its hundred slaves, and, more important than anything else, its four hundred tons of ammunition, had sunk.

'There go our reserves of ammunition!' Vivonne gasped. 'That bandit! We let ourselves fall for his trick. He wasn't aiming at us but at the supply ship. When the other galleys went after him, they left it exposed. But we'll sink him. . . . We'll sink him yet. The game isn't over by a long shot.'

The young Admiral tore off his dripping hat and his sopping periwig and threw them violently on the deck. 'Have the *Dauphine* take the lead. She hasn't fired yet, and her ammunition is intact.'

In the distance the enemy lay in wait, manoeuvring to tack about for a broadside charge. The *Dauphine* got into position rapidly. Angélique noticed that it was on this ship that the captured colleague of Rescator were at the oars, the ones who had kept up that singsong chant in Arabic the night before, and whose leader had been executed. She thought it hardly prudent to use these prisoners in such a difficult battle manoeuvre.

The thought had no sooner occurred to her than she saw the long oars amidship get out of rhythm and foul the others. The *Dauphine*, which had just come about, shuddered like a wounded bird, then suddenly heeled over and capsized. There was a tremendous sound of cracking timbers, but the shrill cries of the Moors dominated the din.

'Every galley's pinnace and longboat to the rescue!'

All this took time. Angélique put her hands over her eyes to blot out the sight of the sinking galley. Most of the seamen and all of the slaves were doomed to suffocate in the hull, or to drown. The marines who had been hurled into the sea were struggling to swim, but their heavy equipment was weighing them down. They were screaming for help.

When she thought she dared look again, she saw ten white sails flapping in the wind almost on top of her. The xebec was now hardly five hundred feet away. She could see the highly varnished wood of the hull glisten in the sunlight, and clearly distinguish the dark figures of the musket-armed Berbers, wrapped in huge white cloaks girt with brightly coloured sashes, crowding the gunwales from stem to stern.

In the prow, surrounded by a guard of janizaries in green turbans and carrying short swords, stood two men watching the *Royale* attentively through their telescopes. At first, in spite of their European dress, Angélique thought they too were Moors, for their faces were dark, but presently she saw their hands were white and gathered that they were wearing masks.

'Look at the taller,' said Vivonne softly, 'the one in black with a white cloak. That's he, Rescator. The other is second-in-command, a man named, or nicknamed, Jason. A dirty adventurer but a good sailor. I suspect he's French.'

Angélique reached a trembling hand for Savary's telescope. In its circular lens the two men now appeared more clearly, as different from each other as Don Quixote and Sancho Panza, but by no means laughable. Jason was a strapping fellow in military dress with a huge sabre clapping his boots. In contrast, Rescator was tall and thin, and wore a black costume of a rather old-fashioned Spanish cut. The cuffs of his tight boots were trimmed with gold tassels, and he wore a red kerchief about his head in pirate style, topped with a big black hat trimmed with red feathers. The one indication of his Islamic persuasion was his full cloak of white wool embroidered in gold, floating in the breeze.

With a shiver Angélique realised how closely he resembled pictures of the Devil himself, and his whole being seemed to emanate a fascinating cruelty. So this was the man who had stood coldly by while on a sinking galley a little child raised his arms to heaven, calling for his father!

'Why don't we sink him?' she exclaimed in desperation. 'What are we waiting for?'

She had forgotten the spectacle of horror going on around her – the capsized *Dauphine*, whose sailors were clinging with an heroic effort to her sides. Nothing could save her now that she was shipping water faster than the pumps could bail, and she began slowly to sink beneath the surface.

A longboat was being lowered from the xebec. The second it touched the water, Rescator's lieutenant leaped into it.

'They are asking for a parley,' Vivonne said in some surprise.

Shortly thereafter the pirate came on board and, after introducing himself to the officers, bowed deeply in the oriental fashion.

'Greetings, Admiral,' he said in perfect French.

'I have no truck with renegades,' replied Vivonne.

A subtle smile spread over the masked features of the lieutenant. He crossed himself. 'I am as much a Christian as you, sir, and so is my master Rescator.'

'Christians do not lead the forces of the infidels.'

'Our forces are composed of Arabs, Turks and whites, just like yours, sir,' said the lieutenant casting a glance at the slave-pit. 'The only difference is that ours are not in chains.'

'Enough of this. What do you want?'

'Let us set free and recover our Moors whom you have as prisoners aboard the Dauphine, and we will withdraw without continuing this engagement.'

Vivonne glanced at the sinking galley. 'Your Moors are going to perish with that ship.'

'That's not necessary. We are offering to right it.'

'That's impossible!'

'We can do it. Our xebec is swifter than . . . than these tenders you call galleys,' he said scornfully. 'But you had better make up your mind quickly. In a few minutes it will be too late to act.'

Vivonne recognised his dilemma. He knew he could do nothing in time to save *Dauphine* himself. To accept the offer meant rescuing the splendid ship and several hundred men, but it also meant surrendering to an enemy of inferior strength. Since, however, he was responsible for the royal fleet, he had no choice.

'I accept,' he said between his teeth.

'Thank you, Admiral. I salute you.'

'Traitor!'

'My name is Jason,' said the man with considerable irony.

He stepped to the ladder. The Duc de Vivonne spat on the deck where he had been standing.

'A Frenchman! For you are a Frenchman. Your speech leaves me no doubt as to that. Wretch! How could you betray your own countrymen?'

The pirate turned, his eyes flashing behind his mask. 'It was my countrymen who betrayed me first,' he said. He pointed toward the slave-pit. 'I have rowed on the King's benches – for years and years – all the fine years of my youth. Yet I had never done anything wrong.

'Naturally.'

The longboat was rowing away. The Duc de Vivonne, his hands clenched, could not contain himself. To be given orders by an escaped convict, to be insulted by a former galley-slave! And all the time, Rescator watching and grinning. What a laugh for him!

'My lord, are you going to trust the word of an infidel?' asked one of the lieutenants, trembling with indignation.

'I am certainly not going to ask your advice, you little fool! Sometimes the word of a pirate is better than that of a prince. What do you think about all this, Brossardière?'

'It's a bargain I never hoped for, my lord, and very much in the style of this sinister joker. I wouldn't have said so much if we had been dealing with Admiral Mezzo-Morte, or some of the Berber captains who are, generally speaking, all rogues.'

'Run up the parade pennon and announce a truce.'

The xebec moved to reveal its starboard side, also equipped with twelve cannons.

'It's going too fast. It's going to miss its mark. This is a trick,' said Lieutenant de Saint-Ronan excitedly.

Suddenly the enemy ship came into the wind, reducing its speed, and moved up to the *Dauphine* on a different tack that brought it just astern of the foundering vessel, around which the pinnaces and longboats were finally beginning to pick up some of the floundering seamen. The xebec's decks were alive with activity. The Moors fixed a rope to the base of the central mast, and ran it to a windlass.

On board the *Royale* the officers were holding their breath. The sailors and marines looked as if they had been turned to stone.

Rescator seemed to have abandoned his scornful immobility. Now he could be observed talking animatedly with his lieutenant, picturing the coming manoeuvres in his gestures. Then, at a signal, a janizary came to take his cloak and hat. Another handed him the end of a rope, the remaining coil of which he slung over his shoulder. Clambering up the forward gunwale of the xebec, he crawled several feet along the bowsprit with astonishing agility.

The lieutenant was yelling through his megaphone to the captain of the *Dauphine*.

'He's telling Tournève to play out the anchor from the prow to keep the boat from pivoting when the xebec begins to pull. He's advising him to transfer all possible weight to starboard, then get back on the port side as soon as the galley begins to right itself so as not to be thrown off on the other side.'

'Do you think that black devil plans to throw that rope like a lasso to

91

hook the starboard side of the *Dauphine*?'

'That's what it looks like to me.'

'Impossible! That rope must weigh a tremendous amount. He'd have to be a Hercules to . . .'

'Look!'

Suddenly they saw him silhouetted against the sky. The rope whistled through the air, and the knot at its end wrapped around a protuberance on the starboard side of the *Dauphine* about midship.

Cheers broke out on board the xebec. The Moors were waving their muskets in the air as a sign of joyful approval.

La Brossardière let out a profound sigh. 'An acrobat on the Pont-Neuf could not have done better!'

'Look, look, my dear,' laughed Vivonne bitterly. 'Here's a good one for your little history of the Mediterranean. The legend of Monsieur Rescator won't languish for want of new anecdotes.'

Now the xebec was tacking so as to withdraw gradually to the rear. Its sailors ran to the bridge and set up six huge oars to help catch the wind. The rope tautened. All the men left on the unlucky galley scrambled to starboard to lean on the gunwale where the rope was hitched. The submerged side rose abruptly from the water with a loud sucking sound. At a shout from Tournève the crew dashed to port to counterbalance it.

Once on its keel again, the *Dauphine* rocked violently from side to side until gradually it came to rest. A final order vibrated across the waves like a cry of deliverance: 'To the pumps! All hands bail!'

Cheers rang from the other galleys. A little later the longboat of the corsair ship was launched again and headed toward the *Dauphine*.

'They've got a portable forge with them and blacksmith's tools. They're going to knock the irons off the prisoners.'

This operation took a long time. Finally the freed Arab slaves began to appear on deck along with ten or so of the strongest Turks.

The Duc de Vivonne turned scarlet. 'Traitors! Pirates! Infidel dogs!' he shouted through his megaphone. 'You don't keep your promises. You said nothing about freeing any but your Moors. You have no right to take the Turks too.'

'Blood money for the Moor you executed,' replied Jason.

'Compose yourself, sir,' La Brossardière said to his superior, 'or we shall have to bleed you. I'm going to summon the doctor.'

'He has other things to do than bleed me,' replied the young Admiral in a mournful voice. 'See how many dead and wounded we have.'

Under full sail the pirate xebec was disappearing into the distance.

CHAPTER EIGHT

The Duc de Vivonne got into the longboat and raised his head to Angélique on the deck of the galley. 'I'll see you soon, dearest. In a few days I'll be meeting you in Malta. Pray that our arms will be victorious.'

Angélique forced herself to smile back down at him. She unfastened her sky-blue silk sash fringed with gold and tossed it to him. 'A token of victory for your sword!'

'Thank you,' shouted Vivonne as the longboat rowed away. He kissed the sash and proceeded to tie it around the hilt of his sword. Then once again he waved goodbye to her.

Angélique wondered why she did not feel more forlorn at this parting. Vivonne had decided to pursue Rescator and track him down in the waters around Malta, where the galleys of the Knights of St John of Jerusalem might lend the French assistance. The Admiral's galley, the *Royale*, was too heavy and not manoeuvrable enough for a pursuit of this variety. It devolved upon the *Luronne*, and Angélique was left in the care of La Brossardière and some soldiers. The *Royale* was to proceed more slowly and by gradual stages to Valetta, together with the *Dauphine*, which required repairs.

The war galleys formed into line, then disappeared into the darkness of a storm that was rapidly approaching from the south-east. Angélique retired to the tabernacle while the rain beat down on the decks and the *Royale* rocked and pitched violently.

'First the pirates, now the sea,' said La Brossardière.

'Is this a storm?'

'Not yet, but it won't be long in coming.'

The rain stopped, but the sky remained slate-coloured and the sea rough. The air was stifling in spite of the damp wind which occasionally swept them.

The conversation of Savary and Lieutenant Millerand, who had unfrozen a little now that Vivonne, of whom he was insanely jealous, had departed, did little to keep Angélique from dying of boredom.

'What is there for me to do aboard this galley?' she asked Savary.

She smiled sadly to herself as she thought of Versailles and of Molière and his farces.

As night fell Monsieur de la Brossardière advised her to go to her cabin, but she could not bring herself to do so, and said she preferred to stay where she was until the situation got out of hand. The violent pitching of the ship eventually rocked her to sleep in spite of the wind which had risen and the buffeting of the waves against the hull.

She awoke as from a nightmare. The night was black as soot. As she half raised herself up from the divan, she was aware that something unusual was going on. The ship was still pitching violently, but the wind seemed to have died.

Suddenly she realised what had awakened her – the silence. The gongs no longer sounded. It was as if the entire galley had been deserted and was tossing about in the waves like a shingle. Terror swept over her.

'Monsieur de la Brossardière!' she called.

No answer.

She struggled to her feet with difficulty and took a few halting steps, then bumped into something soft and almost fell.

Angélique leaned down. Her hand touched the braid of a uniform. She grasped the shoulder of the prone man and shook him vigorously.

'Monsieur de la Brossardière, wake up!'

He made no response. Feverishly Angélique groped for his face. Its icy touch made her recoil in terror.

She rose to search for her bag which she always kept within reach near her couch, extracted her little travelling lamp and struck a flint to light it. A mischievous gust of wind blew out the flame three times before she could set the red-tinted glass chimney over the flame and explore the darkness around her.

Monsieur de la Brossardière was stretched out on the deck, his eyes already glassy and a fearful wound oozing blood over his forehead.

Angélique stepped over him to the entrance of the tabernacle. There she bumped into another body lying across it, a soldier also quite dead. Quietly she lifted the curtain and looked out. In the darkness she could pick out some lights in the slave-pit and distinguish shadows moving about on the catwalk, but they were not those of the slave-keepers with their long whips. Red-clad shapes were moving to and fro and she could catch their hoarse voices.

Angélique let the curtain fall and withdrew to the depths of the tabernacle, oblivious of the spray which from time to time splashed her when an extra large wave dashed against the poop. She was in a panic of terror, for at last she knew why the gongs were silent. The sound of a naked foot sliding over the planks brought her to her feet, painfully alert.

Nicholas stood in the entrance, clad in the red tatters of a galley slave. He looked at her from under his matted hair and filthy beard with the same smile that had first terrified her when he lay in wait for her outside the windows of the tavern. When he spoke, his incoherent, raving words seemed to prolong the nightmare.

'Marquise of the Angels . . . my beauty . . . my dream . . . you see me at last! For you I have broken my chains . . . one blow for the keeper . . . one blow for the guard. Ha! Ha! a blow here, a blow there . . . I've been waiting a long time to deal them . . . but it was you that unleashed them . . . to see you there . . . alive! . . . as I've seen your face in the skies these ten years in the galleys . . . and you belong to that other fellow, eh? . . . you were kissing him, caressing him . . . I know you! . . . you've been leading your life while I've been leading mine. . . . It's you who have won . . . but not for always. The wheel has turned . . . it has brought you back to me. . . .'

He stretched toward her his wrists scarred by the irons he had endured these long months. Nicholas Calembredaine had tried twice to escape during his years as a slave. Now, the third time, he had succeeded. He and his fellows had killed the entire crew, the marines, the officers. They were masters of the galley.

'Why do you say nothing? . . . Are you afraid? . . . When I held you in my arms, you had no fears then!'

A bolt of lightning illumined the sky outside, and the rumble of thunder echoed through the night.

'Don't you recognise me?' continued the convict. 'It's not possible . . . I know you recognised me the other day down there.'

She smelled the sweat and salt crust on his rags and cried out in revulsion: 'Don't touch me! Don't touch me!'

'Ah, so you do recognise me. Tell me who I am.'

'Calembredaine, the robber.'

'No, I am Nicholas, your master from the Tower of Nesle. . . .'

A sudden wave dashed over them, and Angélique had to cling to the railing so as not to be washed overboard as it swept back into the sea. Beyond, a sinister snapping sound answered the demonic din of the thunder. A young galley-slave appeared in the entrance.

'Chief, the main mast is broken. What should we do?'

Nicholas shook his dripping garments. 'Spawn of a pig!' he rattled in his throat. 'If you didn't know what to do, why did you demand that I cut the throats of all the sailors? You said you knew how to sail.'

'But there are no more sails.'

'A fine mess! Well, we'll row. Put the others to work, the ones still chained to the benches. You beat the gong yourself. I'll see those black rebels work!'

He went out, and soon the monotonous clanging of the gongs began again, rising above the whistling tempest. The galley, which for an endless moment had seemed to reel and tip to the side where the broken mast was lying, righted itself after Nicholas had taken a hatchet to the stump still holding it and a wave had dragged it into the sea. The pumps were manned, and the oars struggled to make headway.

Now that she could clarify her nightmare, Angélique recovered her courage. Often in her life she had thought she would die of fear, but once the tension had passed, her rage and her combative spirit won out. Her wet gown stuck to her legs and hindered her from moving. She dragged herself back to her bag, opened it, and got new clothes. Taking advantage of the occasional steadiness of the ship, she succeeded after several attempts in stripping off her dress and her soaking undergarments.

She had foreseen that her quest might well involve a great deal of walking, and so had provided herself with masculine attire made of grey cloth, which she now drew on as well as she could. With her legs encased in knee breeches, and her body protected by a jacket that buttoned up to a white linen collar, she felt more prepared for dealing with shipwreck – and the convicts. She pulled on high boots, pinned her hair tightly around her head, and pulled a grey felt hat down over it. She had the presence of mind to reopen her bag and take out of it all the gold she had left, which she stowed in her belt with her letters of credit. It was an exhausting process doing all this and trying to keep her balance while waves swept the deck and the body of the unfortunate La Brossardière kept sliding around about her feet in the wash.

'Angélique,' shouted Nicolas as he re-entered. He saw only a young man before him, and for a moment did not know what to make of it. 'Ah, it's you after all,' he said with relief. 'I thought you might have been washed overboard when I didn't see your gown.'

'Washed overboard?'

'You will be soon if this show keeps up.'

The canvas walls of the tabernacle split in two, and the wind carried them away.

'That's too bad,' he growled. 'I think we're heading toward shore.'

An old convict with a white beard and only one eye had come with him.

'You can see it from here,' he said, leaning out over the stern into the wild night. 'There . . . over there, see the dancing lights. . . . There's a harbour there, I tell you. We'd best take shelter.'

'Are you crazy? Fall into the hands of the keepers again?'

'It's a little fishing cove. We can scare them enough to keep them quiet, and we'll only stay there till the storm passes. If we don't put in there, we'll crack up on the rocks like so many crates.'

'I do not agree.'

'What do you suggest then, Chief?'

'Try to stay at sea until the storm dies.'

'You're foolish to do that, Chief. This old wooden shoe won't ride it out.'

'We'll put it to a vote. Come on,' he said, seizing Angélique by the arm. 'You're going to take shelter in the cabins. You'll be swept overboard here, and I don't want the sharks to get you. You belong to me.'

In the darkness she could only guess at the confusion in the dismasted galley. The slave-pit was half full of water. Under the lashes of their former companions the foreign convicts – Russians, Moors, Turks – were rowing fiercely, crying out from time to time in despair and fright.

Where were Savary and Flipot?

Nicholas was at her side again. 'They want to make the port we saw over there,' he shouted to her. 'I do not. With a few other of the brethren we can put to sea and sail away. Come, Marquise.'

She tried to escape from him, foreseeing that there was greater safety on the mutinous galley than in the shelter of a port. But he seized her and lifted her in his arms to carry her to the waiting longboat.

The boat was dancing on the crests of the waves like a walnut-shell when day broke. Soon the sky was clear, but the sea remained violent and green, as it drove toward the shore these fragile human beings who had dared to defy its wrath.

'Every man for himself!' shouted Nicholas as the red cliffs rose nearer and nearer to them.

The convicts leaped into the water.

'Do you know how to swim?' Nicholas asked Angélique.

'No.'

'Come on just the same.'

He leaped into the water with her, struggling to keep her head above the waves.

She swallowed a great gulp of salt water and choked. A wave snatched her from Nicholas and carried her toward the shore as if she were on horseback. She dashed up against a rock and clung to it with all her strength. The wave drained away from her, almost succeeding in sucking her back with it. Angélique climbed a little higher on to the rock. The wave swept over her again, enveloping her in its cold shroud, then left her only to return. Yet each time she managed to scramble up a little higher. Finally she felt the sand of a beach under her. Just a little bit more! Then she found a dune covered with dry grass, crawled into it and fainted.

When she opened her eyes and saw the hard blue sky above her, and recalled what had happened during that terrible night, she remembered that not once had she thought of entrusting her soul to God. Her forgetfulness frightened her as much as if an unconfessed sin were weighing on her conscience. Now, in mortification, she did not dare correct her omission by thanking Providence for granting her another morning of life.

She stood up with difficulty, feeling a little sick from all the salt water she had swallowed, and took stock of her state. Did Providence deserve to be thanked? A few feet away from her she had just noticed the convicts around a fire they had built on the beach.

The sun was high in the heavens and its warmth had dried her clothes and her hair, but her hair was full of sand and her sunburned cheeks smarted. Her hands were badly scratched and torn. Little by little her senses returned, first sight, then hearing. She could catch the rough voices of the ten or so convicts. Two of them were busy cooking something over the fire, but the others, standing around it, seemed from their tone of voice to be arguing.

'No, that won't do, Chief,' shouted a big blond gangling fellow. 'We've done everything you ordered us. We respected your rights, now you respect ours.'

Nicholas's back was toward Angélique, so she did not hear his reply.

'You're the one said she belonged to you before.'

'You can't make us believe that. She's a woman of quality. What would she be doing with a louse like you?'

'Don't try to fool us, Chief. That's not the way things happen.'

'Even if it was true what he says, it makes no difference. Paris law is one thing; galley rules are something else.'

A bony old fellow, toothless and bald as an egg, spoke up, wagging his finger. 'You know the law of the Mediterranean: "The cormorant gets the body, the pirate gets the loot, and the women belong to everyone."'

'Yes, to everyone,' the others took up the cry as they moved menacingly toward their leader.

Angélique looked up at the summit of the cliff. She would have to try to get farther inland where perhaps she could hide in the underbrush or in the little groves of cork trees that crowned the shore. Doubtless the place was not uninhabited, and she could get some protection from the fisherfolk.

Cautiously she began to creep away on her hands and knees. If the convicts started to fight, she would gain time. But the quarrel seemed to be settled. She heard a voice say: 'All right, that goes. You're the chief, so you have a right to the first bite. But leave some for the rest of us. . . .'

A great burst of laughter followed these words. Angélique saw Nicholas striding in her direction. She tried to flee, but in a moment he had caught up with her and seized her by the wrist. His eyes gleamed wildly, his lips drawn back over his teeth black from chewing tobacco. He was so obsessed with his frenzy he did not notice she had recoiled from him, and proceeded to drag her at a run over the rough goat path at the base of the cliff. The laughs and obscene jokes of the convicts who had remained on the beach followed them.

'Take your time, Chief, but don't forget about us. . . . We got the same urge you have. . . .'

'As if I'd let them have her!' grumbled Nicholas. 'She is mine. Mine!'

He darted over the pebbles and the dry undergrowth, dragging her behind him, while the wind tore her hair loose from the knot she had wound it in and whipped it across her face like a blinding silk scarf.

'Stop!' she shrieked.

The convict kept on running.

'Stop! I can't go any farther.'

Finally he heeded her and came to a halt, gazing about him as if he had just awakened.

They had followed the rim of the cliff, and now the sea was at their feet, its dark blue contrasting with the azure of the sky where seagulls were tracing white curlicues. The tangy air well-nigh choked them.

The escaped convict suddenly seemed to discover he was bound no more. 'All that!' he murmured gazing at the limitless expanses around him. 'All that for me. . . .'

He released Angélique's hand to swing wide his arms and inhale to the very bottom of his lungs, swelling his chest and rolling his shoulders which toil at the oars had rendered even more powerful than formerly. His muscles bulged and knotted beneath his tight-fitting red shirt.

Angélique leaped to one side and began to run.

'Come back!' he bellowed, setting out after her.

When he caught up with her she faced him with hands spread like the claws of an angry cat. 'Don't come near me! Don't touch me!' Her eyes darted such sparks that he froze in his tracks.

'What's come over you?' he grumbled. 'Don't you want me to kiss you? It's been such a long, long time. Don't you want my love?'

'No!'

The man frowned deeply, as if her words were penetrating his brain so slowly that he found it hard to grasp their meaning. He made another attempt to catch her, but she evaded him. He groaned at her deception.

'What's come over you? You can't treat me like this, Angélique! I haven't had a woman for ten years, not even touched one, hardly seen one. Then you came, you were there. . . . *You!* I destroyed everything just to be near you, to take you away from that fellow. Haven't I a right to touch you?'

'No.'

The convict's black eyes rolled in his head as if he had suddenly been smitten with madness. He leaped upon her, and succeeded in holding her, but she scratched him so furiously that he let go of her again to stare uncomprehendingly at the deep bloody furrows beginning to swell along his arms.

'What's come over you?' he repeated. 'Don't you remember me, my darling – how you would snuggle up to me to sleep in the Tower of Nesle when I used to take you in my arms and make love to you as much as I liked . . . and you liked? That was no dream, it was real. Are you trying to tell me that never happened, that I ever craved anyone but you . . . that you wanted me on your wedding night? But that's all true! I've always loved you. Don't you remember Nicholas, your old friend Nicholas, who used to pick strawberries for you?'

'No! No!' she shrieked, fleeing from him in desperation. 'Nicholas died long ago. You are Calembredaine the robber, and I hate you!'

'But I love you!' he yelled.

They started running again as he chased her through the thorny underbrush. Angélique stumbled over a root and fell. Nicholas was almost upon her, but she got to her feet again. He grasped her tightly around her waist, even though she kept pounding her fists into his face.

'But I love you,' he kept repeating. 'I have always yearned for you. I shall never get over you. For years and years at those oars I would burst with desire for you. And now, I can't even reach you. . . .'

He tried to strip off her clothing, but her masculine attire did not make the job an easy one. She continued to defend herself with super-human strength, but he did succeed in tearing the collar of her coat and exposing her breast.

'Let me take you,' he pleaded. 'Try to understand. I'm ravenous, dying of longing for you.'

They struggled madly and fiercely among the tufts of juniper and myrtle while the wind buffeted them.

Suddenly she realised that the convict was being hauled up as if torn by the roots from the earth, and thrown on the ground a few feet away. A man had just appeared out of the underbrush. His torn blue uniform exposed a chest and shoulders striped with contusions, his face swollen and streaked with dried blood. Still Angélique could recognise him as the young Lieutenant Millerand.

Nicholas recognised him too as he got to his feet. 'Oh, mister officer,' he said with a grin, 'so the fishes didn't find you very tasty when we helped you overboard? Pity I didn't come to your help so you couldn't have come here to interrupt. . . .'

'Scoundrel!' growled the young man. 'You'll pay for this.'

Nicholas rushed at him, but a violent blow from the Lieutenant toppled him. The convict roared with rage and sprang back to the attack. For what seemed an endless time they rained deadly blows upon each other. They were almost of the same height and of equal strength, and several times the King's officer crashed to the ground so hard that Angélique feared he could never rise again with Nicholas hammering on him from above. Then with a quick movement, the Lieutenant rolled on to his back and kicked his adversary in the stomach. A second later he was on his feet once more. Another blow to the stomach made Nicholas blanch under his filthy beard, totter, and bend double.

'Scum!' the convict growled. 'All the time you were eating ortolans, I was sipping the delicate bean soup of the galleys. . . .'

Relentlessly Millerand struck him in the face, causing Nicholas to back farther and farther toward the edge of the cliff as the blows hailed down on him, until he was staggering on the brink of the precipice.

'No!' shrieked Angélique.

But as she screamed, Nicholas lost his footing and tumbled backward into the blue depths. The echo of her voice ended only with the crack of his body on the purple rocks below.

Lieutenant Millerand wiped his forehead. 'Justice has triumphed,' he said.

'He's dead,' exclaimed Angélique. 'This time, he is really dead. Oh, Nicholas! Oh, this time you'll never come back.'

'Yes, he's dead. The sea is already carrying him away.'

Stunned by the battle he had just won, he could not understand her sobs, or why she should be on her knees at the edge of the cliff, weeping and wringing her hands.

'Don't look, Madame, It's no use. He's good and dead. You have nothing more to fear. Come along, and keep quiet, or you'll attract the other convicts.'

He helped her up, and together they stole away from the scene of the tragedy.

CHAPTER NINE

For a long time they walked over the desolate island until they at length caught sight of the dark keep of a castle on a promontory.

'God be praised!' murmured the Lieutenant. 'We can ask hospitality of the lord of this place.'

The young officer was close to exhaustion after his night afloat in the icy water, fighting fatigue and cramps and despair. Finally at dawn he had been cast unconscious upon the shore, and when he came to he had found some shellfish to nourish him. Then he had dragged himself into the inner part of the island to look for help, had heard a woman screaming for help and had run to the spot where Angélique was struggling with Nicholas.

His anger at seeing the leader of the mutiny that had cost his comrades their lives restored enough of his strength to avenge them. But he had received many painful blows in the encounter and now was almost at the end of his tether.

Half-dead from thirst, Angélique was hardly more alive.

The sight of the castle revived them and they quickened their steps. Presently the wild, uninhabited landscape began to take on some aspect of life. On a distant beach they could make out human forms, and as they rounded a bend in the path they came upon a herd of goats calmly browsing on the short grass.

Millerand looked at them, and scowled. He dragged Angélique behind a rock and motioned to her to lie down.

'What's going on?'

'I don't know. But those goats look suspicious to me.'

'What's the matter with them?'

'I wouldn't be surprised if they were set to wander along the shore with lanterns around their necks.'

'What do you mean?'

He laid a finger on his lips as he crawled toward the edge of the cliff. After a moment of observation, he beckoned her to join him.

'I was not wrong,' he whispered. 'Look!'

Beneath them a wide stream was flowing into the ocean just below the sombre bulk of the castle. Among the rocks floated the wreckage of a shipwrecked vessel – masts, oars, sails, pieces of gilded railing, casks and planks, which the waves were heaving to and fro, and here and there a dead body. Other bodies had been washed up on the rocks, their tell-tale red garments reflected in the tide pools. On the beach, where the seabirds were piping and screaming, men and women armed with boat-hooks were hauling ashore everything left afloat. Others were pushing the stranded corpses back into the water. Still others were setting out in little boats toward the carcase of the ship impaled on the sharp rocks at the mouth of the stream.

'They're shipwreckers,' Millerand murmured. 'Scavengers of the sea. They tie lighted lanterns on the necks of their goats at night, so that ships off their course will think them harbour lights and steer toward them only to crash on the rocks.'

'So the galley-slaves thought they could find shelter here?'

'They got what they deserved. But what is Monsieur de Vivonne going to say when he learns of the loss of his flagship? Poor old *Royale*!'

'What are we going to do?'

The noiseless appearance of ten sunburned men behind them kept the Lieutenant from replying.

The shipwreckers bound their hands behind their backs and took them to Signor Paolo di Visconti, who ruled this region from his donjon of volcanic rock.

He was a Genoese with the build of an athlete, so heavily muscled that he seemed ready to split his satin tunic. His dazzling smile and fierce expression clearly revealed him to be a bandit. For such he was, and nothing else, lording it over Corsican vassals as barbarous as he.

He seemed very pleased to see the two prisoners. The booty of an old galley and a few wretched slaves had seemed pretty thin to him.

'An officaire of His Majesty ze King of France!' he exclaimed. 'I zink you have a family who is fond of you, signor, a family perhaps wiz plenty money? *Dio mio, che bello ragazzo!*' he sighed as he stroked Angélique's chin with a heavily ringed and dirty hand.

Lieutenant Millerand stiffened. 'Madame du Plessis-Bellière,' he said by way of introducing her.

'A woman! *Madonna! Ma guarda che carina! Che bella ragazza!* I like ze young people but a woman like this – that is verree rare!'

From him Lieutenant Millerand learned that the storm had carried them to the coast of Corsica, a wild and abandoned land actually under the sway of Genoa.

Out of respect for their rank the Italian invited them to dinner. His hospitality was a curious blend of luxury and rustic simplicity. The lace tablecloths were of wondrous workmanship, but there were no forks, and the few pewter spoons were used for serving. They ate by dipping their fingers into a silver dish that bore the hallmark of a famous Venetian goldsmith.

The Signor di Visconti offered roast sucking-pig garnished with fennel and chestnuts. Then the servants brought in a huge pewter pot full of a broth yellow with saffron and containing bits of pastry and toasted cheese.

In spite of her apprehensions Angélique ate as much as she could. The Genoese kept eyeing her as he filled her silver-gilt embossed goblet with a dark aromatic wine that quickly brought the blood to her cheeks. She kept darting panicky looks at Millerand, who understood their meaning and came to her rescue.

'Madame du Plessis is extremely tired. Couldn't she take a little rest in some quiet spot?'

'Tired? The signora is perhaps your sweetheart, signor?'

The young man blushed to the roots of his hair. 'No.'

'Ah! I feel bettaire. I can breathe again,' said the Genoese, spreading his hand over his chest. 'I would not have liked to embarrass you. But everyzing is all right now.' He turned to Angélique. 'You are tired, Signora? I understand. I am ze brute. I weel take you to your . . how do you say in French – apartment?'

At the very top of the tower was a well-ventilated room containing a bed with embroidered sheets and brocaded coverlets. The room was full of Venetian mirrors, French clocks and Turkish armour. Angélique thought of how much it resembled the thieves' storeroom in the Tower of Nesle.

The Corsican maidservant insisted that she take a bath and put on a rather pretty dress she took out of a wardrobe where hung many others, all doubtless pillaged from the trunks of too daring travellers.

Angélique was glad to soak in the tub of warm water and to stretch out her cramped legs which had suffered badly from the sun and salt water, but she insisted on dressing herself again in her own clothes, stained and torn though they were. She made sure her sash, still stuffed with gold pieces, was in place. The masculine clothes and the money would provide her a certain protection.

It seemed to her that the bed was heaving like a storm-tossed ship, tapping her ebbing strength. The faces of Nicholas, the convicts, Signor Paolo kept circling round her, staring and leering. Finally she slipped into a tortured sleep.

A knocking at the thick, iron-barred window shutter that served as a door aroused her. A muffled voice was calling: 'Mistress! Mistress! It's me. Madame Marquise, open up!'

She rubbed her forehead. An icy wind was whistling through the room.

'It's me. Flipot!'

She got up and groped for the door, outside which she found her lackey with an oil lamp.

'How are you, Madame Marquise?' he asked, grinning from ear to ear.

'But . . . but how . . .' Gradually it began to make sense to her. 'But, Flipot, where did you come from?'

'From the fleet, just like you, Madame Marquise.'

Angélique put her hands on his shoulders and kissed him. 'My boy, I am so glad to see you! I thought you had been either killed by the convicts or drowned in the shipwreck.'

'No. Calembredaine recognised me while we were still on the galley. "He's one of us," he said. I asked him to spare the old apothecary too, as he couldn't possibly do them any harm. They shut us up in a store-room, but Monsieur Savary picked the lock. It was dark and right in the midst of the storm. The slaves were howling in the pits, and those who weren't chained were crawling about everywhere. When we found out you were not still on board, Monsieur Savary and I managed to get the longboat launched. He's some sailor, that old boy! Still he couldn't keep us from being caught by Signor Paolo's fishermen. But we were all in one piece, and they gave us something to eat. When we found out that you, too, had been rescued, we were happy as could be.'

'Yes, my boy, it is something to be alive, but look at the mess we're in. We're in the hands of notorious robbers.'

'That's why I came after you. A ship is about to put to sea. Yes, a merchant Signor Paolo detained, who is trying to slip away quietly. He's willing to wait an hour for us, but we've got to hurry.'

It did not take Angélique any time at all to make up her mind. Everything she possessed she was carrying on her person. She glanced around the room, and foreseeing that one of the daggers hanging on the wall might come in handy, she slipped it up her sleeve.

'How do we get out of the castle?' she whispered.

'We can only try. But the people here have been drinking to celebrate the wreck of the galley. They found several undamaged wine casks on it. They're drunk as pigs.'

'What about Signor Paolo?'

'Not a sign of him. Probably he's passed out in some corner, too.'

Angélique asked about Lieutenant Millerand, but Flipot told her he had been shut up in a solitary dungeon and would have to be left to his fate.

They crept down flight after flight of stairs at a snail's pace, the draughts almost extinguishing their lamp and even causing the bracketed wall-torches to flicker. In the last of all the Genoese was reeling about, his smile as he saw them boding no good.

'Ah Signora *che cosa c'é*? Have you come to keep me company? I am delighted!'

Angélique, still with a few more steps to descend, took in the situation at a glance. Above Signor Paolo di Visconti a lath-work frame supporting four thick tallow candles hung from the ceiling by a string that passed through a pulley fastened to the wall of the stairway. It didn't take Angélique two seconds to pull out her dagger and cut the cord.

She never knew whether the crude chandelier landed on the Genoese's head or not, for all the lights went out. But they heard him bellowing and gathered that if he wasn't dead he at least was in an awkward position.

Taking advantage of the confusion and the darkness, Angélique and Flipot succeeded in reaching the gate, and crossed the courtyard without any trouble. The building was so ruined, they thought they might still be inside its crumbling walls until Flipot spotted the path leading to the meeting place. Wind-driven clouds masked the full moon.

'This way,' said Flipot.

They could hear the sea pounding on the shingle of a beach as they slithered through the underbrush until they came to a little cove where some forms were hovering around a boat.

'So it's you who want to go and get yourself eaten by the fish off Corsica and Sardinia?' asked a voice with a Marseilles accent.

'Yes, it's I,' replied Angélique. 'Wait, here's something for your trouble.'

'We'll talk about that later. Get into the boat.'

A few feet away Savary, looking like a genie in the darkness, was hurling imprecations into the windy night: 'Your greed will bring you misfortune, you insatiable Moloch, you giant octopus, you foul leech on the wealth of others. I offered you everything I had and you spurned it.'

'I'll pay for him,' Angélique said.

'There'll be too many on board,' the Captain growled.

Then he went to take the tiller and pretended not to see the old man climb aboard with his bag, his umbrella and his phials.

The moon, since ancient times the friend of fugitives and smugglers, had long been hidden in the clouds. The boat had time to get beyond the rocks, where the Genoese sentinels were on watch, without being seen. When the silvery light beamed forth again, the beacon on top of the donjon was already fading into the distance.

The Provençal Captain heaved a sigh of relief. 'There!' he said. 'Now we have time for a song. Take the helm, Mutcho.'

He pulled a guitar out of a chest and tuned it carefully. Soon his bass voice was soaring across the Mediterranean.

'Well, if it isn't the lady from Marseilles who wanted to see the Grand Turk's harem? Well, you've certainly got your own way!'

In the light of day Angélique had no trouble identifying the captain of the *Joliette*, the same skipper who, back in Marseilles, had so sternly warned her about the perils of her voyage. His name was Melchior Pannassave, a man in his forties, with a cheerful, deeply tanned face topped with a red and white striped Neapolitan-style bonnet. Several turns of a wide sash bound his black trousers about his waist. For a long time he chewed on his pipe, grinning to himself, before turning to one of his men.

'When a woman's got her mind set on something,' he remarked, 'God Himself can't keep her from getting it.'

The old toothless sailor named Scaiano, who appeared as taciturn as his captain was talkative, showed his assent with a long jet of tobacco juice.

The crew also included a Greek boy named Mutcho.

'Well, here we are on board, Madame,' the Captain said. 'There's not too much room, what with my cargo. I never expected to have a lady passenger either.'

'Why don't you just treat me like a boy? You wouldn't be the first to take me for a gentleman.'

'Perhaps that's the best thing to do after all. But while there's just us here, we don't have to play games, do we?'

'If you did, you'd get used to the idea, so that if we get stopped by the infidels . . .'

'My poor little girl, with all due respect, you're just dreaming. The minute they saw your pretty little face, whether you're a boy or a girl, you'd go right into their pot. Just ask Mezzo-Morte, the Admiral of the Algerian fleet. Ha! Ha! Ha!' He winked knowingly at the silent sailor.

Angélique shrugged her shoulders. 'It's really absurd to keep pretending we're doomed to a fatal encounter with the Berbers or the Grand Turk.'

'It's no illusion, Madame – excuse me – Monsieur – I myself have been captured by them ten times. Five times I was exchanged almost at once, but the other times cost me thirteen years of captivity in all. They made me slave in the vineyards on the shores of the Bosphorus, and in the bakeries of some pasha or other with a villa near Constantinople. Can you see me as a baker! What a fate for a fisherman! Especially having to roll out their old pancakes as thin as handkerchiefs and stick them into the oven. I managed it, of course, but what bothered me most was being surrounded by eunuchs with swords in their hand, always watching to see I didn't get even a glimpse of the little girls behind the harem shutters.'

The weather had cleared up. Big white, bright-edged clouds streamed across the sky, driven by a dry whistling wind that flecked the waves with foam.

'What luck to have the storm die as soon as we got away from shore,' continued Pannassave, puffing on his pipe. 'From here to Sicily we'll have nothing but clear sailing.'

'Except for the Berbers,' hissed Savary, 'waiting in the wings.'

'What I don't understand,' said Angélique, 'is how you have the courage to keep going back to sea after all the mishaps you've had of one kind or another. What makes you do it, I wonder.'

'Ha! You're beginning to catch on. It's a good sign. Why do I sail? Why, it's my business, Madame. I coast from one port to another with a little stock in trade. At the moment, those little bundles you see there, wrapped in tinfoil, contain sage and borage. I'm going to trade them in the Lavant for Siamese tea. Herb for herb, you might say.'

'But tea doesn't belong to either the myrtle or the fennel family,' said Savary pedantically. 'It's the leaf of a shrub that looks like oleander. Infusions of it purify the brain, brighten the eyes and are a specific for wind on the stomach.'

'I like it all right,' said Pannassave mischievously, 'but I like Turkish coffee better. I sell my tea to the Knights of Malta, and they trade it with the tribes of Barbary – the Algerians, Tunisians and Moroccans. They're all great tea drinkers apparently. I'll also bring back a little cargo of coral, and a few fine Indian Ocean pearls hidden in my belt. So, there you are!'

The Provençal Captain stretched himself out on a bench in the sun. Angélique, in the prow, was struggling with her hair. She decided to face the wind, and let it float behind her in great whirls of burnished gold, as she raised her face to the scorching kisses of the sun.

Melchior Pannassave kept watching her through half-shut eyes. 'Ha! Why do I sail?' he repeated, smiling. 'Because there's nothing finer in the world for a son of Marseilles than to wander in a nutshell like this between the blue sea beneath and the blue heavens above. And when there's a pretty girl with her hair streaming in the wind, to boot, well . . . well, anyone would say. . . .'

'Lateen sail to starboard,' called the old sailor.

'Shut up, you fool, you're disturbing my day-dreams.'

'It's an Arab ship with sails and oars.'

'Run up the Order of Malta flag.'

The cabin boy went astern to unfurl a red flag with a white cross in the middle. The eyes of everyone on board the little sailboat watched, not without anxiety, to see how the Arab ship would respond.

'They're going away,' said Pannassave, lying down again. 'There's no better antidote for anything flying the poisonous crescent than the flag of those good monks of the Order of Saint John of Jerusalem. Obviously they aren't in Jerusalem any longer, or in Cyprus, or even Rhodes; but they're still in Malta. For centuries the Moslems have had no worse enemy. That's why I didn't hesitate to spend all of a hundred *livres* to fly their flag. I also have a French one, one with the emblem of the Duke of Tuscany, another which with a little bit of luck might scare off the Spaniards, and one that's a passport with the Moroccans. That last is a real treasure, and there aren't many who have one. I keep it for last. You see, Madame, Berbers or no, we are prepared.'

There was no cabin or quarters for the crew on the little boat. Mutcho, the cabin boy, hung up two hammocks, and unrolled a canvas waterproofed with linseed oil to protect Angélique from the spray at night. The wind veered and died, but almost at once sprang up again from a different quarter. The sailors applied themselves to reefing the sails before it grew completely dark.

'Aren't we going to light any lanterns?' Angélique asked.

'So we can be seen?'

'By whom?'

'Who knows?' said the Captain, sweeping the vast horizon with his arm.

Angélique listened to the deep murmuring of the sea. A little later the moon rose, tracing a silver path over the water right up to their sides.

'It's time for a song,' said Melchior Pannassave, taking up his guitar.

Angélique listened as the twanging notes of a Neapolitan ballad spread over the silent water. An idea began to form in her mind. Everyone seemed to sing here on the Mediterranean. The convicts forgot their woes; the sailors forgot the dangers lying in wait for them. Rich, full voices had always been a trait of these southern people since time out of mind.

'The one they used to call Golden Voice,' she thought, 'hadn't he sung so that his fame spread over land and sea?'

Inspired with sudden hope, she took advantage of a moment when Pannassave was catching his breath to ask whether he had ever heard in the Mediterranean of a singer with a particularly lovely and appealing voice. The Captain thought a moment and then named for her all who had acquired a reputation for their voices from the Bosphorus to the coasts of Spain, not omitting Corsica and the shores of Italy. But none answered to the description of the troubadour of Languedoc.

She dropped off to sleep still wondering.

The sun was already high when she awakened. The sea was calm. The boat was moving slowly, the skipper dozing at the helm. The old sailor was lying down, chewing tobacco. Angélique could see Flipot all curled up, trying to forget his troubles in sleep, and the little cabin boy equally sound asleep, his open red shirt exposing his sunburned chest. But there was no trace of Savary.

Angélique leaped up and shook the Captain awake. 'What have you done with Maître Savary? Did you put him ashore in the night?'

'If you go on getting so excited, little girl, I may have to put you ashore too.'

'Oh, how could you do such a shameful thing! Just because he hadn't any money! I told you I would pay his way.'

'There, there, softly, softly. You're a real dragon, aren't you? How do you think a boat could get into port at night and then get out without a lot of hullaballoo and visits from the authorities? You must have been sleeping soundly indeed not to have noticed all that.'

'But where is he then?' Angélique shouted. 'Did he fall overboard?'

'Well now, isn't that amazing!' said the Captain glancing around him.

As far as the eye could see, the water was blue and sparkling.

'Here I am,' said a cavernous voice, which might have been that of some sea god.

A coal miner's face appeared from under a hatch, and the old scholar proceeded to haul himself up out of the hole. He wiped his grimy face with one hand, while he kept scrutinising a black object held in the other.

The Captain roared with laughter. 'Don't wear yourself out, Grandpa, you can't crack that pine-nut. It's tougher than a nutgall.'

'Funny substance,' said the scholar. 'Rather like lead ore.'

A wave threw him off balance, and the object he was holding fell with a dull, heavy sound.

Melchior Pannassave flew into a rage. 'Why can't you watch what you're doing! If that had fallen overboard I'd have to pay a thousand *livres* fine.'

'Lead ore has become quite expensive in your book,' said the apothecary thoughtfully.

The Captain apologised for his hasty words, and calmed down. 'I just said that in a manner of speaking. There's nothing wrong in carrying lead ore, but I'd rather you pretended you'd never seen anything. What were you doing in my hold anyway?'

'I didn't want my phials to get broken and I was looking for a safe place to stow them. By the way, have you a little fresh water I could clean myself up in?'

'I don't have any to spare for that. There isn't any water or soap that could possibly help you out anyway. You need lemon juice or strong vinegar, and I haven't any of that either. You'll have to wait till we land.'

'Funny substance!' the scholar repeated as he went away to sit in a corner, resigned to looking like a coal miner.

Angélique made herself comfortable on a folded sail in the bottom of the boat out of the wind, and munched grudgingly on the salt pork and crackers and sweet pepper Pannassave served his passengers. As she brooded on the 'pine-nut', old memories revived in her mind. Learned as he was, Savary still was not aware that the 'pine-nut' was not crude lead but badly tarnished silver which had been exposed to sulphur fumes to blacken it. It was the same kind of camouflage the Comte de Peyrac used to smuggle silver from his mines in Spain and England, and she had heard that many smugglers in the Mediterranean did the same.

When noon came and Melchior Pannassave retired to his favourite bench for his brief siesta, Angélique sat down beside him.

'Monsieur Pannassave,' she whispered.

'Yes, lovely lady.'

'May I ask you a modest question? Are you carrying silver for Rescator?'

The Captain was in the process of unfolding a big kerchief with which to shield his face from the blazing sun. He sat up abruptly, his expression no longer merry.

'I didn't quite hear what you said,' he replied drily. 'It's risky to gossip in public, you know. Rescator is a Christian pirate in league with the Turks and the Berbers, which is to say he is a desperate man. I have never seen him, and I don't want to see him. And what I'm carrying in my hold is *lead*.'

'In my country the miners call it *matte*. You call it 'pine-nut'. But it's the same thing – crude silver in disguise. My father used to carry it to the coast on mules and ship it out in the form of thin black wafers without the King's stamp. I know I'm not mistaken. Listen, Monsieur Pannassave, and I'll tell you everything.'

She told him how she was searching for a man she loved who used to be involved in mining.

'So you think he might still be involved in it?'

'Yes.'

Had he ever heard in the course of his trading of a very learned man, lame, with a scarred face?

Melchior Pannassave shook his head. Then he asked: 'What is his name?'

'I don't know. He must have had to change it.'

'No name, eh? Well, I reckon they're right to say love is blind and chooses its victims at random.' He plunged into deep thought, his face relaxed but his eyes wary.

'Listen, little girl,' he resumed at length, 'I don't want to discuss your tastes or ask you why you still persist in this love when the world is so full of fine, good-looking young fellows who aren't ashamed of the name God and their parents gave them at baptism. No, it's not up to me to preach you a sermon. You aren't a child any longer. You must know what you're doing and what you want. But I don't have to deceive you either. Carrying "pine-nut" has always been done in the Mediterranean and always will be done. Your lover didn't start it. Want me to tell you something? My father used to ship "pine-nut". He was a "rescator" too, they said – oh, just a minor one, not so big and powerful as the real one.

'He's a regular shark. He came from South America, where, they say, the King of Spain sent him to steal the Incas' gold and silver. Afterward he struck out for himself. As soon as he appeared in the

Mediterranean, he gobbled up all the smaller fish. Everyone had to work for him or be sunk. He acquired a monopoly, you might say.

'But no one blames him for that. Business is better now in the Mediterranean. Barter is easier, and things aren't so hectic. Formerly you had to go to a lot of trouble to find a little silver on the market. It used to circulate in driblets, and everyone had to tighten his belt. When a merchant wanted to make a big deal in silk or other oriental goods, he often had no recourse but to borrow the money at exorbitant interest rates from the bankers. The Turks naturally didn't want to have to whistle for their money, and operations of that kind got completely out of proportion. Now there's plenty of silver. Where does it come from? Why does anyone need to know? The point is, it's there.

'Naturally, not everybody likes it this way – people who hoard their money and never lend it except at five times its worth – little countries, petty princes. The King of Spain, for instance, thinks all the wealth of the New World belongs to him, and there are other greedy souls like the Duke of Tuscany and the Doge of Venice and the Knights of Malta. They have just had to put up with the course of events.'

'In other words, Rescator is your benefactor.'

The Captain's face darkened. 'He is not my benefactor. I don't want to have anything to do with that damn pirate.'

'Still, if you're carrying silver and he has a monopoly . . .'

'Listen, little girl, let me give you a piece of advice. Hereabouts you don't have to know all the facts. No one investigates things too closely. You don't need to know where the chain you're a link in begins or even where it ends. I usually take on a cargo at Cadiz or somewhere – generally in Spain – and I'm supposed to carry it to the colonies in the Levant, not always to the same place. I unload my goods, and I get paid in coin or by a letter of credit I can present anywhere in the Mediterranean – at Messina, Genoa, even Algiers if I take it into my head to go there. After that, it's over and done with. Melchior, go back to the Canebière!'

With these words the Captain spread out his kerchief to indicate that he had said everything he was going to say.

Angélique shook her head. *It doesn't matter where the chain you're a link in begins or ends.* She could not submit to the rules of this region where there were so many conflicting interests, and you had to forget your benefactors and generally keep a short memory. She would not let go of the tiny clue she had until she followed it to its end.

Still from time to time this thin thread seemed to slip from between

her fingers and melt into the blue of the sky. The lazy motion of the
sea, the warmth of the sun, made reality disappear into fantasy. It was
easy for her to understand how the myths of the ancients could have
sprung into being on these shores.

*Do you suppose I'm believing a myth myself . . . some legend of a
vanished hero no longer in the land of the living . . . trying to discover the road he took here where no one asks for details and all the
mirages blend together into one great unattainable dream. . . .*

She roused herself from her reverie to say: 'Thank you, Monsieur
Pannassave. You have told me some very interesting things.'

The Captain dismissed her thanks with a gallant gesture, and
stretched himself out on his bench. 'Nonsense,' he said modestly, 'I've
just been around a little.'

As evening drew on, they caught sight of a snow-capped mountain
sparkling in the setting sun.

'Vesuvius,' Savary said.

The cabin boy, who had been curled up on a coil of rope by the mast,
called out that there was a boat in sight. They watched it come nearer –
a brigantine of imposing size.

'What flag?'

'French,' shouted Mutcho gleefully.

'Run up the Order of Malta flag,' Pannassave ordered.

'Why don't we fly the fleur de lis, seeing they're our countrymen?'
Angélique asked.

'Because I am suspicious of my countrymen when I see them on a
Spanish warship.'

The galleon seemed to be trying to cut across the little *Joliette*'s path.
Oriflammes were flying from all its halyards.

Melchior Pannassave stifled an oath. 'What did I tell you! They want
to come aboard. That's not regular – they're in Neapolitan waters and
France is not at war with the Order of Malta. This is some fancy trick
or other. Just you wait and see!'

The galleon was taking in sail. Then to her surprise Angélique saw
the French flag lowered and an unfamiliar flag run up in its place.

'The flag of the Grand Duke of Tuscany,' said Savary. 'That means
the ship has Frenchmen on board but has purchased the right to do
business at Messina, Palermo and Naples.'

'They don't have us yet, children,' whispered the Captain. 'Get ready
for the fun if they insist.'

They could see a man in a long red coat and a plumed hat standing
on the poop and watching them through a spyglass. When he put the

telescope down, Angélique noticed he was wearing a mask.

'That's a bad sign,' Pannassave grumbled. 'When they wear masks for a parley they're not good Christians.'

A man with a face like a hangman's, apparently the lieutenant, was handing the man on the poop a megaphone.

'What's your cargo?' he shouted in Italian.

'Lead from Spain bound for Malta,' Pannasave answered in the same tongue.

'Is that all?' he shouted arrogantly in French.

'Some herbs too,' replied Pannassave in French also.

A burst of olympian laughter came from the men leaning on the galleon's rail. Pannassave winked.

'Those herbs are a good idea. They'll turn their stomachs!'

Then, after conferring with his lieutenant, the man with the hat took up the megaphone again. 'Lower your sails and get ready for inspection. We are going to examine your bills of lading.'

Pannassave turned ruddy. 'What does he think he's doing, handing down the law to innocent people? I'll get ready for him!'

A longboat was being lowered over the side of the brigantine. Sailors armed with muskets were taking their places in it under the command of the ugly lieutenant, one of whose eyes was covered with a black patch which did not enhance his appearance.

'Mutcho, take in the sail. Scaiano, get ready to take the tiller when I tell you to. Grandpa, you're cleverer than you look. You stroll over next to me so they can see you. Turn your back on them. That's right. Here's the key to the powder chest. Take out some bullets too. I'm going to come about so we'll be out of sight. The cannon is already loaded, but we'll keep it in reserve. Don't take its cover off yet, I don't think they've seen it.'

The sail bellied and the *Joliette* began to drift with the wind. The longboat rowing toward them disappeared behind a wave only to reappear closer to them.

Melchior Pannassave shouted through his megaphone again: 'I refuse you the right to board me.'

Scornful laughter was the answer.

'This'll do for distance,' muttered the Captain. 'Take the tiller, Grandpa.'

He snatched off the canvas hood camouflaging the cannon, and picked up a fuse which he held in his teeth, lit it with a tinder box and slipped it into the cannon's breech.

'Hang on, children, and God help us!'

The cannon roared, and the blast that shook the boat threw them all on the deck.

'Missed, God damn it!' swore Pannassave.

He groped around in the thick smoke trying to load the cannon again. The shot had managed only to spray the boarders, and after the smoke cleared they could be seen safe and sound. They hurled oaths at the boat and began to load their muskets.

The *Joliette* was still drifting, an easy prey to the superior enemy.

'The tiller, Scaiano, the tiller! You, Grandpa, try to scull with it.'

A hail of musket-balls splashed into the water all around them. The Captain let out a howl and clutched at his right arm.

'Oh, you're wounded!' screamed Angélique, rushing to him.

'The bastards! I'll make them pay for that. Grandpa, do you know how to fire a cannon?'

'I was artilleryman for Soliman Pasha.'

'Good! Close the breech and get a fuse ready. Take the helm, Mutcho.'

The longboat was not more than fifty fathoms away, and with its prow toward them was a difficult target. The rough sea and an unsteady wind were making the sailing boat and its antagonist bob up and down.

'Surrender, you fools!' shouted the man with the black patch.

Melchior Pannassave, still clutching his wounded arm, turned toward his companions. They all shook their heads.

Then he shouted: 'A Provençal captain never surrenders!' Raising a finger to Savary, he muttered: 'Fire!'

A second explosion rocked the boat. When the smoke cleared, oars and planks were floating all around, with men clinging to them.

'Bravo!' murmured the Captain. 'Now, set all sails! We'll try to escape.'

But a dull shock shook the *Joliette*. It seemed to Angélique that the gunwale she was clinging to melted like butter. Cold water was streaming over her feet. Then there was a salty taste in her mouth.

CHAPTER TEN

The captain of the corsair ship removed his mask to reveal a still youthful face whose tan contrasted pleasantly with his grey eyes and blond hair. But a network of tiny wrinkles gave him a sardonic expression, and heavy pouches under his eyes indicated the excesses of his life. He was greying at the temples.

'In all my career,' he remarked, a supercilious look on his face, 'I have never seen so shabby a crew. Save for that fellow from Marseilles who's well enough put together except that he's got a bullet in his shoulder, only two emaciated boys and a couple of stunted old men, one of them, for some reason or other, disguised as a Negro.'

He grabbed Savary's beard and pulled him closer. 'What did you think you were going to gain by changing colour? Negro or not, I would not bid twenty sequins for your old carcase!'

The lieutenant with the black eyepatch, a thick-set, swarthy fellow, pointed a trembling finger at the old man.

'That's the one . . . that's the one who . . . sank . . . our boat . . . with the cannon ball.'

His clothes were wringing wet and his teeth were chattering. He had been fished out of the water with three others, but five of the crew of the *Hermes* had died as a result of the encounter with the harmless looking little sailing-boat.

'Indeed? So that's the one?' repeated the pirate, his snake-like eyes piercing the shrivelled old man whose appearance was so piteous it gave the lie to the lieutenant.

He shrugged his shoulders and turned from the hardly glamorous group of Savary, Flipot, the cabin boy and old Scaiano, all dripping salt water from their garments over the deck, to the husky Marseilles captain stretched out on the deck, his face contorted with pain.

'Those Provençal fools, how proud they are! You think they're just shamming and yet they aren't scared to attack a whole fleet. Idiot! What have you got out of all your audacity? If your boat weren't such a good one, I'd have sunk it right to the bottom of the sea. But now let's see to this young man who seems to be the only piece of good merchandise of the whole damned lot.'

He strolled over to Angélique, who was standing apart from the rest. She too was shivering in her sopping garments, for the sun was low on the horizon and the wind had turned cool. Her dripping locks hung down on her shoulders.

The Captain examined her with the same cold scrutiny with which he had inspected the other victims of the shipwreck.

She felt ill at ease as his eyes wandered over her, aware that her suit was clinging to her, revealing her shape. The pale brows of the pirate came nearer and nearer, his eyes narrowed to slits, an evil smile on his lips.

'Well, young man,' he said, 'how do you like travelling?'

He drew out his sword and pressed its point against Angélique's chest at the neck of her shirt which she was trying instinctively to fasten

together. She felt the sharp steel prick her skin, but she did not wince.
'Brave, eh?'

He leaned a little on the sword. Angélique's nerves almost cracked under the strain. Suddenly the blade slipped into the opening of her shirt and slashed the cloth away, revealing her white bosom.

'Well, a woman!'

The sailors burst into howls of laughter as Angélique quickly pulled the torn shirt across her exposed breasts. Her eyes were flaming.

The corsair continued to smile. 'A woman! This is certainly a day for jokes aboard the *Hermes*. An old man disguised as a Negro, a woman disguised as a man, a Provençal disguised as a hero, and even old Coriano here disguised as a sea god.'

The laughter broke out afresh at the sight of the ugly lieutenant with the eyepatch, who answered to the name of Coriano.

Angélique waited until the noise died down. 'And a swine disguised as a French nobleman!' she said.

He acknowledged the insult without ceasing to smile. 'Well, well! More surprises! A woman with a gift for repartee! That's a rare item in the seaports of the Levant. Maybe the day won't turn out so badly for us after all, gentlemen. Where do you come from, my beauty? From Provence like your friends?'

When she made no reply, he approached her and laid his hand on her waist. Paying no attention to her retreat, he stripped her of her dagger and her sash. He weighed the latter in his hand with a knowing smile, then opened it and let the gold pieces slip from one hand to the other. The men came closer, their eyes shining. A glance from him, however, and they withdrew again.

He rummaged some more in her sash and fished out the letters of credit she had wrapped in a sheath of waterproof canvas. When he unfolded it he looked puzzled. 'Madame du Plessis-Bellière . . .' he said. Then, making up his mind: 'Allow me to introduce myself. The Marquis d'Escrainville!'

The way he bowed indicated a certain upbringing and that his title of nobility must be authentic. She began to hope that out of regard for their equal positions in society he would show her some regard.

'I am the widow of a Marshal of France,' she said, 'and I am going to Crete to look after my late husband's interests there.'

His lips curved into a sinister smile, but his eyes remained cold. 'They call me the Terror of the Mediterranean,' he said.

Then after reflection he had her taken to a cabin which he apparently reserved for distinguished passengers, especially if they were females.

There in a messy old copper-bound chest Angélique found European and Turkish feminine attire, some veils, imitation jewels and slippers. She hesitated to take her clothes off, for she felt no sense of security on this boat. It seemed as if leering eyes were peering at her through the gaps in the boards of the cabin. Still her garments were clinging to her like an icy shroud, and she could not stop her teeth from chattering. At length she made a supreme effort and stripped off her clothes to put on with disgust a white dress that almost fitted her, but which was very unstylish and hardly suitable for the occasion. It made her look like a scarecrow, she thought. A Spanish shawl about her shoulders improved her appearance. She curled up on the couch and remained there a long time in a state of considerable depression. Her hair was sticky and reeked of sea water just as the damp wood of the cabin did, and the rank odour made her feel sick.

Here she was quite alone in the middle of the sea, as lost and abandoned as a shipwrecked mariner clinging to a raft. With her own hands she had broken all the bonds between her and her once brilliant career, and there was no one to help her across this chasm to the next stage. Where would the broken ends be joined? Even if this nobleman-pirate chose to take her to Crete, what would she do there? She had no money now. She had only one hope to rely on, an Arab merchant named Ali Mektub. Then she recalled the Frenchman who was managing her position as consul and who could possibly help her. She could go to him. She tried to remember his name: Rocher? . . . Pocher? . . . Pacha? . . . No, it wasn't any of those. . . .

Presently she heard a key rattle in the lock of the cabin door. Coriano appeared with a lantern, followed by a Negro boy carrying a tray. He hung the lantern up by the skylight, and ordered the tray to be set on the floor, his one eye roving greedily over the prisoner. Then, pointing to the tray with his stubby, heavily bejewelled finger, he commanded her to eat.

Once he was gone, Angélique could not resist the appetising aroma coming from the tray, on which were fried shrimps, a soup of shellfish and oranges, and a bottle of good wine. Angélique wolfed it down. She was at the end of her strength, worn out with fatigue and worry. When she heard the heavy footsteps of the Marquis d'Escrainville outside, she thought she would scream.

The pirate turned the key in the door and entered. He was so tall he had to stoop in the low-ceilinged cabin. In the ruddy light of the lantern he might have been handsome, with his greying temples and his clear eyes, if only that cruel grin had not distorted his mouth.

'Well,' he said as he looked at the empty tray, 'Madame has apparently enjoyed her repast.'

She scorned to answer him and kept her head turned. He put his hand on her naked shoulder. She broke away and fled to the narrow corner at the rear of the room, casting her eyes about for a weapon, but finding none. He kept watching her like a cruel cat.

'No,' he said, 'you shan't escape me. Not tonight, anyway. Tonight we add up the score, and you are going to pay it.'

'I don't owe you a thing,' Angélique protested.

He laughed. 'Well, if not you, then your sisters. Bah! You have done enough to other men to deserve a hundred punishments. Tell me, how many men have you seen crawling at your feet? How many?'

The insane gleam in his eyes filled her with panic. She searched for a way of escape.

'So you're beginning to be afraid, eh? I like to see that. You're not so proud now. Soon you'll be on your knees to me. I know how to take that.'

He unbuckled his baldric and threw it together with his belt on a hassock. Then he did the same with his sword-belt and began to take off his clothes with a cynical disregard for modesty.

She picked up a little stool and threw it at him, but he dodged it and came toward her, grinning evilly, until he had seized her in his arms. As he leaned his face over hers, she bit him on the cheek.

'Damn!' he shouted.

Mad with rage, he grasped her wrist and tried to throw her to the floor. In the tiny cabin they struggled silently and savagely, while the wooden walls shook under the shock of their entwined bodies.

Angélique felt her strength ebb quickly. She fell. Panting, d'Escrainville pinned her to the floor with all his weight, watching her last gasps of anger subside. She felt all the power drain from her limbs, leaving her only the strength to turn her head from side to side to avoid the grinning mask pressing upon her.

'Quiet down, my beauty! Quiet down! There, now you're behaving better. Let me look at you more closely.'

He ripped open her bodice and with a groan of pleasure pressed his greedy lips upon her breast. She kept twisting in revulsion, struggling to escape him, but he only tightened his hold upon her and began spreading her legs apart to take possession of her. Just as he was about to succeed, she gave a tremendous heave with all the strength left in her body. He swore and hit her violently, causing her to howl with pain. For interminable minutes she had to endure his blind fury devastating her, and allow him to glut his passion upon her with all the delicacy of a rutting boar in its lair.

When finally he stood up, she was burning with shame.

He lifted her to her feet and then, after gazing at her livid face, he let her fall again heavily at his feet.

'That's the way I like to see women,' he said. 'There's nothing left for you to do but weep.'

He put on his red clothing again and buckled his sword-belt.

Angélique was supporting herself on one arm, and smoothing down her rumpled dress with the other. Her yellow hair hung like a veil over her face covering her drooping neck.

D'Escrainville gave her a final kick. 'Weep! Go on and weep!'

But the tears did not come till after he had left. Then a burning flood streamed down her cheeks. Painfully she hoisted herself up on the couch. The severity of the perils she had endured these last few days, her everlasting struggles with lust-crazed men, were beginning to take their toll of her courage and her powers of resistance. Violent sobs shook her until, toward the middle of the night, she heard a scratching at the door which rallied her out of her despair.

'Who is there?'

'I Savary.' The old man's face, still blackened by the 'pine-nut', appeared in the crack as she opened the door. 'Let me come in.'

'Yes, indeed,' Angélique said, pulling her dress around her. What luck that brute of a pirate had forgotten to lock the door behind him!

'Hmm!' said Savary, taking in the tell-tale disorder in the cabin. He sat on the edge of the couch, his eyes discreetly lowered.

'Alas, Madame, I must admit that since I've been on this boat, I have not been very proud to be a member of the male sex. I ask your forgiveness for it.'

'It's not your fault, Maître Savary,' said Angélique, as she dried her tear-stained cheeks and smoothed her hair. 'It is my fault. I was not very far-sighted. Now the wine's been poured, we must drink it. After all, I'm not dead yet, and neither are you, and that's all that matters. How is poor Pannassave?'

'Badly off. He's delirious with fever.'

'What about you? Aren't you risking dire punishment for paying me a visit here?'

'The whip, the bastinado, and being strung up by my thumbs to a yard-arm – such are the diversions of our distinguished Marquis.'

Angélique shuddered. 'He's a horrible creature, Savary. I think there's nothing he's not capable of doing.'

'He's an opium smoker,' said the old apothecary. 'I could see that the moment I laid eyes on him. The drug drives all who use it to acts of sheer madness. We're in a tight spot.'

He rubbed his thin white hands against each other. This frail old man, Angélique thought, in tatters, his white hair straggling over his cadaverous greenish-blue face, was all that was left her by way of comfort and support.

In a low voice Savary started to tell her not to lose courage. In a few days they could escape.

'Escape! Do you really think that's possible? How?'

'Shh! It's by no means an easy matter, but what will help us is that Pannassave is one of Rescator's men, one of the many skippers, fishermen and traders who help him in his commerce. Pannassave explained it all to me, and you suspected it before, too. In that gang the humblest carrier of 'pine-nut', be he Moslem or Christian, can be assured of never rotting in a slaver's hull. Rescator has means everywhere of freeing men. That's why so many work for him.'

Savary leaned over, his voice dwindling to a murmur. 'Even here on this boat, there are accomplices of Rescator. One of those mysterious passports Pannassave carries in his oilskin envelope will identify him and get him help from his guards.'

'Do you truly believe the watchmen of this frightful d'Escrainville are his accomplices? They're risking death. . . .'

'. . . Or fortune! In that gang anyone who helps a prisoner escape is in line to receive a fabulous sum, it seems. Such is the decree of that shadowy figure named Rescator whom we had the dubious honour of encountering. No one knows whether Rescator is a Berber, a Turk or a Spaniard, a renegade Christian or a Moslem by birth, but one thing is certain, which is that he has not parted company with the pirate traders of the Mediterranean, who, black or white, are all slave-traders. And you, Madame, who have so befriended me, and have such a respect for scientific pursuits, do not deserve to disappear into the labyrinth of some harem just to become a plaything for one of these lascivious Moslems. I am going to put everything to work to spare you that fate.'

'Do you mean that this is the fate the Marquis d'Escrainville has in store for me?'

'I would be very much surprised if he hadn't.'

'It's not possible! He may be a dirty freebooter, but he is still a Frenchman like us and he comes of an ancient family of the nobility. He wouldn't even think of such a hideous thing!'

'He is a man who has always lived in the Levant, Madame, regardless of his French antecedents. They're like cast-off clothes to him. His soul – if, indeed, he has one – is oriental. It is hard to escape from that too,' Savary said with a little laugh. 'In the Orient it's as customary to humiliate a woman as it is to drink coffee. D'Escrainville is going to try either to sell you or keep you for himself.'

'I must admit neither of those prospects exactly pleases me.'

'Then why beat your head against a stone wall? We're going from here to Messina, the nearest slave-market. I only hope Pannassave will be well before we get there, so we can pursue our plans.'

As the boat sailed onward, Angélique kept telling herself she was getting closer and closer to her destination. She had dreamed of such a sea voyage since the day her brother Josselin had exclaimed to her: 'I'm going off to sea. . . .'

The boat was carrying her to her love, but her love kept moving always farther toward the horizon. 'Will Joffrey de Peyrac remember me?' she wondered. 'Will he want me again? I have renounced his name, and he may have renounced my memory.'

One morning she awoke with a shattering headache. Her head felt like lead. Her mouth was dry, and her clothes seemed to burn her flesh.

'Where are we?' she asked the little Negro slave who brought her tray.

'Off the coast of Sicily. Last night you could have seen the glow of the volcano.'

'Sicily . . .' she repeated mechanically.

Ashes from Mount Etna were drifting in through the porthole. 'I shall die under these ashes,' Angélique said to herself. 'I'm stifling hot, and they're scorching me, but I know no one will come to my aid.'

At that moment the door opened and the light of a lantern penetrated the smoky gloom of the cabin. The face of d'Escrainville, with its skin like crackled china, bent over her.

'Well, my fine fury, have you decided to be more docile?'

She was lying on her stomach, her head on one arm, like a marble statue, her hair spread out over her gleaming shoulders, but her lack of movement was not due to sleep.

He knit his brows and set the lantern on a little stand. As he bent to raise her, her body went limp in his arms, and her head fell heavily against him.

Her skin was fiery to his touch, and he jumped back in surprise. Then he raised her face to examine it. Her head lolled as if the weight of her hair were pulling it. She was mumbling some words incoherently, among them two which made him smile: 'My love, my love.'

He laid her back on the bed and spread the coverlet over her. Stepping to the door he spoke to someone outside. 'This woman is sick. Take care of her.'

The ship was riding at anchor, Angélique sensed from the gentle sway that lulled her in her bed. The sun was pouring through the porthole. She concluded its broiling heat had awaked her, and she shifted her position to get out of its rays. Outside there were loud noises and the sound of confusion. Bare feet padded past her door. Shouts and whistles rose above the din and the shuffle of scurrying feet.

'Where am I?'

She passed her hands over her face to try to wipe away the mists that seemed to shroud her brain. How thin, almost transparent, her fingers looked! Her hair, however, felt clean and soft, as if it had been carefully brushed and even perfumed. She looked around for her clothes until she spied them neatly folded on the chest. She got up and started to dress, but was surprised to find how big her clothes were for her. When she could not locate her own shoes, she put on a pair of Turkish slippers. Then she searched high and low for her sash.

'Oh, that's right. The pirate took it.'

Bit by bit her memory returned. When she stood up, though, her legs were wobbly. Nevertheless, by leaning on the woodwork, she managed to get out of the cabin.

The deck of the boat was deserted just outside, but forward there was a noisy crowd. The cool air made her stagger, and she almost fell. Then she let out a weak cry of delight. Before her lay an island, and on the crest of a hill a little ancient temple raised its white outlines into the sky of gold. It seemed like a ship of fancy preparing to sail off to the Elysian fields. Around it rose white columns, lifting their heads like lilies from the grass, indicating that once there had been other temples, other altars, now vanished, leaving only ruins.

Just beside Angélique a door banged open and a man burst out. He passed her without seeing her, but she recognised his slightly faded red greatcoat with its frayed embroidery, and above all his swarthy face seamed with tiny wrinkles which gave him at first glance an expression of insane rage. *The Marquis d'Escrainville*. She had last seen him bending over her while she struggled against a terrible sense of suffocation.

His grin recalled their fearful struggle. She recoiled and tried her best to make herself invisible.

All the crew of the ship had gathered in the prow, so that she could see the crowd of slaves made up of all sorts of people in the bottom of the hold – women and children, men old and young, of every race and colour and clad in all sorts of costumes from the brilliantly embroidered jackets of peasants from the shores of the Adriatic to the white burnouses of the Arabs and the dark veils of the Greek women.

D'Escrainville stared at them as if he were having hallucinations, then addressed Coriano who was plodding toward him slowly and philosophically.

'That's what comes of not being strict!' he shouted. 'I let that old crow of an apothecary flatter me. Now, look what he's done. *Escaped!* The second slave who's got out of my clutches within a month. It's never happened to me before – to me, the Terror of the Mediterranean! I didn't get that nickname for nothing. And yet I let myself be taken in by a miserable louse like him who wouldn't have fetched me fifty piastres at Leghorn. He wheedled me into coming to these damned islands by saying I would find a fortune out of some miracle product that could be had for the taking. And to think I believed him, donkey that I am! I should have remembered I picked him up with that damned Provençal who escaped in his sailing-boat, after I went to the trouble of recaulking it to sell at a good price. No one ever fooled me like that before. And now, this apothecary!'

'It's certain someone helped him, either some watchman or some one of the slaves.'

'That's what I'm going to find out, Coriano. Is everyone here?'

'Yes, sir.'

'Then let's have a good laugh. Ha! Ha! No one makes sport of the Marquis d'Escrainville for long! If I ever catch that damned apothecary again, I'll crack him in two like the louse he is. And I won't forget it was that old demon who sank our longboat either. Everyone come here!'

Since everyone was already there, no one stirred. They stood in apprehensive silence, staring at the Captain.

'Someone is going to pay for this. The longboat is gone. I know from experience no one will confess, so lots will be drawn to determine who's guilty. The oldest and the youngest of the Christian slaves will draw. No one under ten years of age, though. I'm no monster.'

Angélique stared with popping eyes at the hysterical figure in the red coat. The silence of death reigned on the ship; then the wails of the women rose from the hold as mothers tried to protect the children clinging to them.

'Hurry up!' yelled d'Escrainville. 'Justice is swift on a ship, so . . .'

At that moment a violent explosion seemed to come from the bowels of the ship, drowning the words of the maniac. There was a moment of dumb stupefaction, then the cry broke out: 'A fire!'

White smoke began to issue through the latticed ventilators in the stern of the *Hermes*.

The slaves began to panic, but the whips of their guards soon restored them to order.

D'Escrainville and his lieutenant dashed to the stern.

'Where is the first mate?' he shouted.

A squad of marines pushed forward hesitantly, white with terror.

'Four men raise the hatch and four more go down to see what's happened! It's coming from the provisions storeroom next to the galley.'

No one budged an inch. The spectators seemed turned to stone by the unusual occurrence.

'It's devil's fire, sir,' stammered one of the marines. 'Look at that smoke. That isn't good Christian smoke. . . .'

As a matter of fact, the clouds belching from the hatchway were creeping heavily along the deck, first like a thick white paste, then suddenly scattering like a mist rising from a damp hollow. D'Escrainville approached as if he wanted to take some into his hand and raise it to his nostrils.

'It has a strange odour.' He got control of himself and snatched the pistol out of Coriano's belt. 'I'll shoot you in the arse,' he roared, 'if you don't get down there at once as I ordered.'

Suddenly the hatch seemed to rise of its own accord amid the vapours. The bystanders howled with fear, and d'Escrainville himself stepped back a foot or two.

'A ghost!'

In a particularly thick cloud appeared a form wrapped in a damp white sheet, from which a stifled voice emerged: 'I beg you, sir, don't be alarmed. It's nothing at all. . . .'

'What does . . . what does this mean?' stammered the pirate. 'You accursed alchemist, isn't it enough for you to make us run our legs off this morning without setting fire to the ship too?'

The figure seemed to be shedding its cocoon. A moment later Savary's bearded head appeared. He sneezed and coughed; then picking up his winding-sheet made some gestures of reassurance to the crowd and plunged down again into the hatchway, which closed over the head of the apparition.

Angélique and all the rest believed they had been witnessing some sort of witchcraft. But soon Savary climbed up the ladder, calm and in excellent spirits, even though he was covered with soot and his tattered garments were impregnated with a disgustingly sweetish odour. He explained with dignity that there had been no fire. The explosion and the vapours had merely been the result of 'an experiment which might mean great things for science in general and maritime navigation in particular'.

The pirate leader eyed him from head to foot furiously. 'So, you did not escape!'

'I? Escape? But why? I'm very happy on your ship, sir.'

'But what about the longboat? Who put it overboard?'

The ruddy face of a young marine with a turned-up nose rose over the gunwale. He climbed up the rope ladder that hung over the side of the ship and stopped in surprise to see the assemblage.

'The longboat, Captain? Why, I took it to go after wine on the island this morning.'

D'Escrainville relaxed, and Coriano permitted himself to laugh.

'Ha, Captain, ever since that damn Provençal escaped you've been seeing escapes everywhere. I told Pierrik myself to go fill the casks this morning.'

'Fool!' He shrugged his shoulders in annoyance and turned away.

It was then that he first saw Angélique. His tense features relaxed, as if he were making an effort to be gentle and seem friendly. 'Ah, here is our beautiful Marquise. Are you all right at last? How do you feel?'

She remained leaning against the wall, looking at him with mingled horror and disbelief. Finally she murmured: 'I am sorry, sir, but I haven't yet come to understand what happened to me. Have I really been sick?'

'For more than a month.'

'A month! Oh, good Lord, where am I now?'

The Marquis gestured toward the island. 'Off Ceos, dear lady, in the middle of the Cyclades.'

CHAPTER ELEVEN

Angélique remembered she had fallen asleep when they were off the coast of Sicily. Now, here she was, a month later, at the end of the world so far as she was concerned, wandering among barren Greek islands that even their gods had forsaken, at the mercy of a piratical slave-trader.

She took refuge again in her cramped cabin, and tried in vain to recall what had happened. Finally realising it was all a blank to her, she sent for Savary.

'Yes,' he said. 'I took care of you, helped by a Greek slave girl named Hellice. While you were out of your head she bathed you and brushed and anointed your hair, which looks lovely now. Soon you will be as beautiful as ever again.'

'Give me a looking-glass,' said Angélique in some trepidation.

She regarded herself with a grimace. Her cheeks were pale and hollow, her eyes haggard. Perhaps, she thought, now the pirates won't sell me after all.

'Where is Flipot?' she asked the old scholar.

'D'Escrainville sold him at Messina to an Italian nobleman who wanted a tutor to teach his son French. D'Escrainville got a good price for your little lackey.'

'Flipot a French teacher!' In spite of her disappointment she had to laugh. She made up her mind to ask the slave trader if he remembered the Italian's name so that she might repurchase Flipot. Then she recalled with alarm that if d'Escrainville's plan succeeded, she would never be able to do so. No one ever escaped from a harem.

'Do you suppose Pannassave will help us?' she asked plaintively.

'Alas, poor Pannassave could not wait for you to recover. He had to put his own plans into action or be sold into slavery before he could even try them. And I had to use all my powers of persuasion on our captor to keep me on board.'

'So you remained all on account of me,' Angélique said, touched by his loyalty.

'How could I leave you?' the old man said modestly. 'You were desperately sick and you still have not completely recovered. But you will.'

'Haven't you been sick too? Your skin is all covered with blue spots.'

'It's still the effect of the "pine-nut" – Pannassave's lead. It's hard to get it off. I have tried lemon juice and spirits of wine, but I think I'll have to shed my skin to get rid of it completely,' Savary said humorously. 'But it's of minor importance. The really important thing is to get ourselves out of the hands of these wicked pirates.' He let his eyes rove around the room cautiously. 'Shh! I have a plan.'

'Do you think the Marquis d'Escrainville is really going to Crete?'

'Indeed I do. He intends to introduce you to the batistan.'

'Who is that?'

'It's not a person. It's the inn where high-priced slaves are put up for sale. The others are offered in the bazaars and the public square. The batistan of Crete is the largest in the whole Mediterranean.'

Angélique felt the gooseflesh prickle along her arms.

'Don't get excited,' continued Savary, 'for I have a new plan. But to effect it I'll have to persuade our greedy buccaneer to take us all over the Greek islands so that he can make his fortune from the use of their rare products in perfume.'

'Why?' asked Angélique.

'Because we need accomplices.'

'Do you think you'll find them in the Greek islands?'

'Who knows?' said Savary mysteriously. 'Madame, I may appear quite indiscreet, but since we're in this sorry mess together, I'm sure you won't object to your old friend asking you some questions. Why, for instance, did you ever set out all alone on this perilous voyage?'

Angélique sighed. After hesitating a moment, she resolved to confide in the old scholar. She told him how, after believing for years that her husband, the Comte de Toulouse, had been executed, she had acquired convincing evidence that he had escaped his doom. And how, after following up one clue after another, she had had to set out for Crete, where there was a slim chance of finding some traces of him.

Savary waggled his beard, but said nothing.

'Do you think I'm out of my mind?' asked Angélique.

'Yes. But it's forgivable. I'm an old fool myself. I leave everything to encounter unforeseen dangers. In my search for knowledge I follow my dreams just as you do, because in the bottom of our hearts there burns an undying flame – in your case, your love which guides you like a star in the desert. Are we really such fools? I doubt it. Beyond reason there is an instinct in us both, which guides us even though it terrifies us. It's like a divining rod that tells us where hidden waters are.

'Have you ever heard of Greek Fire?' he said, changing the subject. 'In the days of ancient Byzantium, a learned sect possessed its secret. Where did they come from? Well, my researches indicate that they were Zoroastrian fire-worshippers from around Persepolis on the border between Persia and India. It was that secret that made Byzantium invincible for as long as the Byzantine scientists possessed the secret of this unquenchable fire. Alas, it vanished when the Crusaders invaded Byzantium about 1203. Now, I am positive the secret lies in mineral moumie, which burns eternally, and when properly treated exhales a volatile gas which is extremely inflammable and almost explosive.

That is what I was experimenting with this morning, using only an infinitesimal amount. You see, Madame, I have rediscovered the secret of Greek Fire!'

In his excitement his voice had risen, and Angélique had to remind him they were still only wretched slaves in the hands of a pitiless master.

'Don't be afraid of anything,' Savary assured her. 'If I tell you about my discoveries, it's not that I am indulging my hobby, but rather because they will help us regain our freedom. I have my plans and I promise you they will succeed if only we can get to the island of Thera to the south of us in this same archipelago of the Cyclades.'

'Why Thera?'

'I will tell you when the time comes.'

As evening approached, the ship was filled with new sounds. Women's screams rose in the air, mingled with men's voices and oaths. There was a noise of bodies falling, and of bare feet scurrying along the labyrinthine passageways of the boat; then loud weeping and tortured howls, half drowned by the deep voices of the pirates and their obscene laughter.

Angélique looked out of her porthole. The pirates were bringing in a new load of slaves, which they were examining for their market value. If the women were beautiful they were set to one side, reserved for the gratification of their future masters' pleasure. But a sizable number were herded together to be sold as mere labourers. The men prodded the bellies of each one to see if she were pregnant, for a woman big with child brought a higher price, since the purchaser would be getting two slaves for one.

Angélique put her hands over her ears, shrieking that she had had enough of this barbarism and wanted to get out. When Coriano appeared with two Negro boys bringing her a tray laden with food, she hurled abuse at him and refused to swallow a morsel.

'But you must eat,' exclaimed the one-eyed lieutenant. 'You're nothing but skin and bones.'

'Then make them stop tormenting those women.' She kicked at the tray and upset all the covered dishes on it. 'Stop those screams!'

Coriano vanished as fast as his short legs could carry him. Then she heard d'Escrainville bawling: 'So you think she has character, do you? Well, I hope you got what you want! If my crew can't get in a little fornication on their own ship . . .'

Then he strode into the cabin in a foul mood. 'It seems you refuse to eat?'

'Did you think your orgies would whet my appetite?'

She was so thin and her clothes hung so baggily that she looked like a headstrong adolescent, and the pirate could not help smiling.

'All right! I have given orders, so you be agreeable too. Madame du Plessis-Bellière, will you do me the honour of dining with me on the poop?'

Cushions had been placed around the low table. Round basins of silver were passed them, filled with thick sour cream in which were meatballs wrapped in scented vine leaves. The table was heaped with dishes containing different sauces – onion, pimento, paprika, saffron – like green and yellow and red spots on the tablecloth.

'Taste this dolma,' Coriano said, heaping her plate with it. 'If you don't like it, we can bring you some fish.'

The pirate chief looked at his lieutenant mischievously. 'You make a good nurse. No doubt about it, that's what you were born to be.'

Coriano resented his teasing. 'Someone has to take the trouble to repair the damage,' he roared. 'It's lucky for us she isn't dead already. If she were to die now, I'd never hear the end of it.'

The Marquis was angry now. 'What do you want me to do now?' he shouted. 'I let her take the air. I invited her to dinner as politely as I know how. We all go on tiptoe so as not to disturb her when she's asleep. My men have to act like choirboys and go to bed at eight. . . .'

Angélique burst out laughing.

The two buccaneers looked at her in open-mouthed amazement.

'She's laughing!'

Coriano's hairy face lit up. 'Madonna! If she could only laugh like that on the auction block, she'd fetch twenty thousand piastres more.'

'You idiot!' said d'Escrainville. 'How many have you ever seen laugh on the auction block? Besides, this isn't her style. We can count ourselves lucky if she just keeps her mouth shut. Why are you laughing, my dear?'

'I can't cry all the time,' Angélique said.

She yielded to the enchantment of the calm blue evening. The little island before them seemed to drift away into the light mist like a boat in a dream, its temple touched with silvery rays from the rising moon.

The Marquis d'Escrainville followed her eyes. 'Once there were six temples to Apollo here, and every day they worshipped his beauty in dance and song.'

'And now you have replaced all that with a reign of terror.'

'Don't be so sentimental. These degenerate Greeks have to serve some purpose.'

'Is that why you tear infants from their mothers' arms?'

'They would only die of hunger on these barren islands.'

'And what about those poor old men, so weak they could hardly climb aboard?'

'They're different. I'm doing them a service by capturing them.'

'Really,' she said sarcastically.

'Yes indeed. Perhaps you don't know that on Ceos there's a custom that when a man reaches the age of sixty, the other inhabitants either poison him or exile him. They don't like old men hereabouts.' He watched her, smiling sardonically. 'You have many things to learn about the Mediterranean, lovely lady.'

A slave brought him a Turkish water-pipe. He leaned back and began to puff at it.

'See how starry the sky is. Tomorrow at dawn we'll set out for Kyouros. There under the oleanders the god Mars lies sleeping, not yet ground into chalk by the natives. Every time I go there, I visit him. Do you like statues?'

'Yes. At Versailles the King's gardens were full of them.'

The temple emerged from the mists which remained below it, looking as if it were suspended in the deep blue sky.

In a whisper Angélique said: 'The gods are dead.'

'But not the goddesses.' The Marquis was gazing at her through half-shut eyes. 'That costume suits you quite well, everything considered. It leaves enough concealed to set one guessing.'

Angélique pretended not to have heard him. She began to eat, since she could not resist the demands of her stomach any longer, and the aroma of the food was enticing.

'Are we far from Crete?' she asked.

'Not very. We'd be there now if that devil of an apothecary hadn't wheedled me into wasting my time hopping from island to island. But, what's the difference? One of the joys of the East is letting time slip by without any sense of hurry.' He blew out a long column of smoke. 'Are you in a hurry to get to Crete?'

'I'm in a hurry to learn what fate is in store for me. Would you really sell me into slavery?'

'Why did you think I was keeping you here?'

'Listen,' she said inspired with a sudden ray of hope. 'If it's money you want, I can pay you a ransom. In France I am very rich.'

He shook his head. 'No, I don't want to get mixed up in any trans-actions with the French. They're too tricky. To get the money, I'd have to put in at Marseilles. That would be dangerous . . . and it would take too long. I can't wait that long. I have to buy a new ship. Have you enough money for that?'

'Perhaps.'

Then she remembered the sorry state in which she had left her affairs when she set out. She had had to mortgage her own ship and its future cargo to pay the expenses she had incurred at Court. Furthermore, her position in France, now that the King was angry with her, was rather precarious. She bit her lips in despair.

'You see,' he said, 'you are entirely in my hands. I am your master and I can do with you whatever I wish.'

Every evening thereafter the Marquis d'Escrainville invited her to share his dinner on the poop. He was as courteous as he knew how to be, for doubtless Coriano had lectured him, but sometimes his basic nature got the upper hand and he spoke familiarly to her and told her dirty stories. Then at other times he remembered his former train-ing and entertained her with conversation. She discovered he was quite erudite, that he knew oriental languages and could read classical Greek. All in all, he was a strange combination of traits.

He allowed her to go ashore on the island, where Savary was gather-ing the balms and extracts he swore were of such great value. The ground was covered with sweet basil plants, the scent of which made her dreamy, and as the sun warmed her, she felt at last how good it was to be alive.

Once she felt someone staring at her, and looked up to see d'Escrain-ville scrutinising her as she leaned against the fluting of a white column, pressing her lips to a sprig of the fragrant herb. From his eyes she drew the premonition that he would end by killing her; she was too feminine for him, too alluring. He realised she was something he could never possess. Possibly that was why he smoked his opium. Only in the dreams it brought him could he ever attain her. She drew back in alarm.

'Come here,' he said with an imperious gesture.

She moved towards him, keeping her eyes on the treacherous pebbles of the path which hurt her feet through the thin Turkish slippers she was wearing. She noticed how well turned and tanned his calves were below the silver buckles that fastened his trousers at the knee.

D'Escrainville took her by the arm. 'Don't look at me as if I were about to eat you. Do you think I'm a monster?'

'No, I know what you are.'

'Which is . . . ?'

'The Terror of the Mediterranean.'

He relaxed the pressure of his hand on her arm, apparently pleased with her reply. They walked on till they came to the peak of the island, below which the *Hermes*, riding at anchor in a pool of azure blue, seemed only a toy ship on the rippling sea.

'Close your eyes,' d'Escrainville said.

Angélique shuddered. What cruel trick was he going to play on her now? He grinned to see her troubled face.

'Close your eyes, you stubborn mule.'

To make sure she could not see, he put his hand over her eyes and led her farther along the path, holding her close to him. His hand left her waist, and she felt it caress her cheek.

'Look!' he said.

'Oh!'

They had come to a kind of terrace from which rose the ruins of a temple. Flowers sprouted from between the marble flagstones, and the spot was surrounded with wild strawberries and yellow and pink laurel. Two long rows of undamaged statues depicted a dance of frozen motion, glistening white against the incandescent azure of the sky.

'What is it?' murmured Angélique.

'The goddesses.'

He led her down the aisle between the figures, smiling their silent joy, their graceful arms reaching out with the melancholy entreaties of forgotten divinities worshipped only with the incense of the plants and hymned only by the far-off murmur of the sea.

She was so lost in wonder she did not notice how his arm had tightened about her.

At the end of the aisle stood an altar on which a naked child – a triumphant tiny god – was bending his bow.

'Eros!'

'How lovely he is!' sighed Angélique. 'He is the god of love, isn't he?'

'Have you never felt his dart?'

She did not wish to answer him, but moved away to investigate a shaded niche where reclined a voluptuous Aphrodite.

'You could be as beautiful as she if only you were more loving,' he said after a long moment of silence.

She could not read his eyes this time, as he glanced from the statue of the goddess to her and back again, but she could sense he was in torment. What would he do now?

'Do you think you have impressed me with your lofty airs, and that is why I do not treat you as you deserve at night?' he said. 'You are vain enough to think so, I'm sure, but don't fool yourself, for that is not the reason. There is no slave in the world who can so impress the Terror of the Mediterranean. Yet I've had enough of your screams of hatred and your unsheathed claws. Once is enough; it lends a little zest to the adventure. But after a while it gets tedious. Couldn't you bring yourself to be a little more agreeable?'

She looked at him coldly, but he did not see her, for he had begun to pace up and down, his boots ringing on the marble paving-stones, the noise overcoming the incessant zee-ing of the locusts.

'You can be so beautiful when you are loving,' he repeated; 'when, as happened one night, your face was upturned to mine and your eyes were closed, and through half-opened lips you murmured: "My love!" '

Then, in answer to her bewildered expression, he continued: 'You don't remember? You were sick, delirious perhaps. But I shall never forget. How ravishing you could be in the arms of a man who loved you!'

He paused in his pacing and raised his eyes to the little god Eros, all snow and gold. 'I should like to be that man,' he said piteously. 'I should like you to love me. . . .'

It was almost a prayer, but Angélique could not wait for him to finish it. 'Love you?' she cried. 'You?'

The whole situation suddenly seemed so absurd to her that she burst into laughter. Didn't he realise what a loathsome creature he was to her? A heartless, soulless torturer? Did he think she could ever love him? Her laughter shattered the silence of the deserted spot, returning as a piercing, mocking echo which the wind was slow to dissipate. 'Love you? You?'

The Marquis d'Escrainville turned white as the marble forms around them. Advancing on Angélique, he struck her twice with the back of his hand. The salt taste of blood was on her tongue. He struck her again, and she fell at his feet, blood trickling from the corner of her mouth.

'That laugh!' he shouted. He opened his mouth as if trying to catch his breath. 'Whore! How dare you! You are worse than all the rest! I will sell you! I will sell you to a vicious pasha, to a bazaar merchant, to a Moor, to any brute who will destroy you. But you shall never show others your look of love. I forbid it! Now, get out. Go away. I have no notion of letting Coriano and my men get ahead of me. Go away before I kill you!'

Two days later the ship dropped anchor off Thera. The Marquis d'Escrainville came out of his cabin, where for the last two days he had lain in an opium trance.

Angélique went ashore for exercise. Her walk led her to the youths' gymnasium decorated with motionless dancers. The ground was littered with arms and fingers broken from the statues, Angélique tried to lift one, a graceful arm of some long dead youth, but it was too heavy for her. It seemed to embody all the weight of the centuries it had seen pass. She lay in the grass beneath the statue of a discus thrower. The blows she had received still pained her, and she was overwhelmed with grief. She thought of trying to escape into the interior of the island, but the barrenness of the landscape discouraged her.

Presently she heard the sound of sheep bells, and down the path came Savary, accompanied by his inevitable goats from whose wool he extracted the resins which brushed off on it, and which he gave to d'Escrainville as the essence of perfumes. He had with him this time a Greek to whom he was talking intimately.

'Let me introduce Vassos Mikoles, Madame,' he said, his face beaming. 'What do you think of this handsome boy?'

Angélique tactfully concealed her surprise. She had often admired the beauty of the Greek men who still retained all the grace and strength of the same youths dancing here in marble, but the present specimen did not resemble them at all. In fact, she found him particularly unattractive and stunted. His dark face was fringed with a straggly brown beard, and his thin, hollow-chested body made him look rather like his companion. Angélique's eyes went from one to the other.

'Ah, yes,' said Savary delighted, 'you have guessed it. He is my son.'

'Your son, Maître Savary? Do you have children?'

'A few here and there throughout the Levant,' the old man said with a sweeping gesture. 'What did you think? I was younger and nimbler than I am today when I first set foot on Thera some thirty years ago. I was only a little Frenchman like all the rest – poor but chivalrous.'

He went on to explain that as he was passing by some fifteen years later he had observed with satisfaction that the memento he had left of his first visit was becoming a first-class apprentice fisherman. During this voyage he had left with the Mikoles family, who regarded him as a traveller worthy of the veneration due Odysseus himself, a whole flask of mineral maumie which he had brought back from Persia at the risk of his life.

'Just think what that means, Madame. A whole flask! Now we are saved!'

Angélique could not quite see how, nor how this offspring of the Paris apothecary could be of much help to them against the whole crew of freebooters. But Savary was confident. He had found his accomplices. Vassos and his uncles would join them in Crete with the flask of maumie.

CHAPTER TWELVE

For several hours the *Hermes* had been at anchor in the harbour of Candia, the principal city of the island of Crete. The light was fading, but the violent colouring evoked the Orient, and the land breeze was tainted with odours of hot oil and oranges. The red sun stained the stones of the quay with crimson, and a pinkish dust dyed the whole city and the Venetian fortifications still fresh with the blood of the recent fighting. Crete, formerly a Christian island, had recently come under the sway of Moslems. Its new masters betrayed their presence by the white candle-like minarets rising among the towers of the Venetian churches and the domes of the Greek ones.

As soon as they arrived, d'Escrainville had headed for shore in the longboat.

Angélique stood on deck looking at the town and waiting to see how her crazy wanderings were going to end.

Of ancient Crete, home of the Minotaur and its fabulous labyrinth, only Candia remained, a rapacious and explosive city and a modern labyrinth in which were inextricably mingled all the races of the earth, for it was situated at an equal distance from the shores of Asia, of Africa and of Europe, and united all three continents in a Gordian knot.

The Turks, however, were not much in evidence. It was enough for a corsair frigate to fly the green and white flag of the Duke of Tuscany for the red Turkish flag with its white crescent to signal from the top of the fortress permission to enter the harbour.

Twenty galleys and warships and several hundred sailing-boats were riding at anchor in the roadstead or along the quay.

Angélique noticed a saucy bark with ten newly-polished cannons. 'Isn't that a French ship?' she asked, suddenly hopeful.

Savary, who was sitting near her, his umbrella between his knees, looked up anxiously. 'It's a Maltese galley. See the red flag with the white cross. The Maltese fleet is the finest in the Mediterranean, for the Knights of Christ are very rich. At any rate, what could you, a captive, expect from the French at Candia?'

He explained that whether Candia was Greek, French, Venetian or

Turkish, it would remain just as it had been throughout long ages – a haven for Christian pirates, just as Alexandria was for Turkish ones, and Algiers for the Berbers.

Exempt from paying duty to the Turkish governor, the sea-rovers flew the flags of Tuscany, Naples, Malta, Sicily and Portugal, and often these banners protected the worst specimens of Christianity, who kept returning to Candia to trade there.

Angélique contemplated the goods piled up on the quay and on the barges: bales of cloth, fish, barrels of oil and piles of watermelons, but the meagre quantity and variety of these goods bore scant relation to the vast number of boats.

'They are mostly warships,' she remarked. 'What are they doing here?'

'Well, what are we doing here?' said Savary with a twinkle. 'Look at most of these ships. Their holds are shut, whereas ordinarily a merchant ship with a legitimate cargo would keep them open in port. Look at the bayonets of the watchmen on their decks. What are they guarding? The most precious merchandise of all.'

Angélique could not keep from shuddering. 'Slaves? Are all those slaves-traders?'

Savary did not reply. A wretched longboat was weaving its way out to the *Hermes*. A European in a hat trimmed with drooping feathers and clad in sorry raiment stood in the stern waving a flag no larger than a pocket handkerchief, bearing gold lilies on a silver field.

'A Frenchman!' Angélique exclaimed. In spite of the sarcastic advice of the scholar, she persisted in looking for countrymen who might help her.

The man in the longboat heard her, and after a little reflection tipped his hat to her. 'Is d'Escrainville on board?' he shouted.

No one bothered to reply, and so he clambered up the ladder which hung over the side. The few sailors on guard showed no surprise at or objection to this untimely visit, and continued cracking sunflower seeds between their teeth and playing cards.

'I asked if your leader is here,' repeated the new arrival coming up behind one of them.

'Maybe you can find him in the town,' said the other without stirring.

'Didn't he leave a package for me?'

'I'm not the storekeeper,' said the other, spitting out some seed hulls and returning to his game.

The man rubbed his stubbly chin in vexation. Hellice, the Greek slave girl, came out of a cabin. She smiled at him, then went to whisper to Angélique: 'That's Rochat, the French Consul. Don't you want to talk to him? Perhaps he can help you. I'll bring you some French wine.'

'Oh, now I remember,' said Angélique. 'Rochat is the name of my deputy here in Candia. Perhaps he can do something for us.'

But Rochat had already noticed that the young man he saw in the stern was indeed a woman in man's clothing, and was coming toward her.

'I see my old friend d'Escrainville still holds his luck. Allow me to introduce myself, lovely traveller: Rochat, Vice-Consul of the King of France at Candia.'

'And I,' she said, 'am the Marquise du Plessis-Bellière, Consul of the King of France at Candia.'

Rochat's face was a picture of astonishment and incredulity, apprehension and distrust.

'Didn't you hear that I had bought the title?' Angélique asked calmly.

'Indeed I did, but permit me a little shock of surprise, Madame. Supposing you really are the Marquise du Plessis-Bellière, what could have induced you to wander here? I should like some proof of what you say.'

'You will have to take my word for it, Monsieur. Your "friend", the Marquis d'Escrainville, stole my papers including my title patent when he captured us on the sea.'

'I understand,' said the shabby diplomat, cocking an increasingly insolent eye at her and Savary. 'You are, as it were, guests of my friend d'Escrainville against your will?'

'Yes. And Maître Savary here is my steward and counsellor.'

Savary immediately assumed the role she had just bestowed on him. 'Let's not waste valuable time,' he said. 'Monsieur, we propose a little deal that will soon net you a hundred *livres*.'

Rochat grumbled that he didn't see very well how captives . . . He seemed to be having an argument with himself. He straightened his jabot of frayed lace.

Hellice returned with a tray bearing a decanter and several glasses, and set it before them. Then, like a proper servant, she withdrew. Her deferential attitude toward Angélique seemed to convince Rochat that he was not dealing with an ordinary slave but with a lady of high rank. After a little conversation during which they exchanged names of people they knew in common, the deputy was completely persuaded. But this plunged him into a frightful quandary.

'I am sorry, Madame. Falling into d'Escrainville's hands is the worst thing that could have happened to you. He despises women, and it is hard to get him to relent once he has decided to avenge himself on one. Of myself I can do nothing. The slave-traders have the freedom of the city here and, as the saying goes, "the booty belongs to the pirate". I have no power either as a financier or an administrator, so don't count on me to interfere with the plans of the Marquis d'Escrainville or risk losing the little influence I have as deputy consul.'

Then, still trying to adjust his disorderly clothing and staring at his worn shoes, he undertook to justify his conduct. He was the youngest son of the Comte de Rochat and, having no inheritance, was sent at the age of eight to a diplomatic centre in the Levant as a language student. That was one way of disposing of poor younger sons, namely, to allow them to learn the language and customs of a country in order to become an ambassador's interpreter later. He had been brought up in the French quarter of Constantinople, had completed the curriculum of a Moslem school there, and had played with the sons of the pashas. That was where he had met d'Escrainville, also a language student. They had graduated together and the young d'Escrainville had begun a rather brilliant career as a colonial administrator which lasted until the day he fell in love with the beautiful wife of the French Ambassador to Constantinople. She had a lover who was in debt. To pay these obligations without bringing them to the Ambassador's attention, she got young d'Escrainville to forge some notes. Out of his fascination for her, he did so.

Naturally it was he who had to pay when the fraud came to light. The beauty denied everything and even found a few more accusations to hurl at him.

The story became common knowledge. D'Escrainville lost his head over it. He sold his post and bought a little boat in which to go buccaneering on his own. In fact, he chose a better way out than his friend Rochat, who had struggled to advance his diplomatic career but was lost through not being close to the intrigues by which the courtiers at Versailles sold these posts over and over again. All he knew was that he had a right to two and a half per cent of the value of all French merchandise passing through Candia. But for four years now neither the Marseilles Chamber of Commerce nor Colbert, the Minister of Finance, had remembered to pay him, but had apparently continued to pour his dues into the pockets of the former beneficiary of the position.

'Aren't you constructing the situation in your own favour?' asked Angélique. 'Accusing the King and his Minister is a serious thing. Why didn't you go to Versailles with your case?'

'I don't have the means. How would I know I'd even get there alive or without getting into trouble with the Turks? If you think I'm exaggerating, let me tell you that an official of much higher rank than mine – our ambassador to Turkey, Marquis de la Haye – is in prison in Constantinople for debt simply because the Minister has not paid him for years. You see, I have to get out of this mess. I have a wife and children, for heaven's sake!'

With a sigh he concluded: 'Just the same I can try to give you some help providing I don't get into trouble with your owner, the Marquis d'Escrainville. What can I do for you?'

'Two things,' said Savary. 'First, find in this city, which you must know very well, an Arab merchant named Ali Mektub who has a nephew named Mohammed Raki. Then ask him, if he wants to please the Prophet, to be on the Candia waterfront when the French pirate's ship unloads to auction off its slaves.'

'I can probably do that,' said Rochat with relief. 'I think I know where that merchant lives.'

But the second half of the plan he said would be more difficult, namely to turn over immediately to Savary the few sequins he had in his pocket. Finally, he consented, but not without a twinge of pain.

'Since you assure me that these forty sequins of mine will earn me a hundred *livres* . . . But what about the proceeds from the sale of my sponges at Marseilles? D'Escrainville promised to bring me a cask of Banyuls wine, too. Where is it?'

Angélique and Savary hadn't the faintest idea.

'So much the worse! I haven't time to wait for the master of the house. When you see him, tell him his old friend Rochat was here demanding payment for his sponges and the cask of Banyuls he was promised. No. On second thoughts, don't say anything. It will be better if he doesn't know we've been talking. One never knows!'

'In the Orient the right hand never lets the left know what it's doing,' said Savary sententiously.

'Right! He should never even suspect I've loaned you captives money. What a nuisance! I wonder whether my generosity won't lose me my head in the long run. My situation is getting more complicated all the time. Well!'

He departed without even emptying his wineglass, so troubled was he at the lack of caution that had led him into what he was now involved in.

When the slaves were being unloaded that evening, an Arab in a hooded cloak was waiting near the pier. Angélique had just set foot on the quay under the watchful eye of Coriano. Savary had arranged for them to be loosely bound. Suddenly he thrust a purse of sequins into Coriano's hand.

'Where did you get that money, you old toad?' growled the buccaneer.

'It wouldn't make you any richer to know . . . or to tell your captain,' whispered the apothecary. 'Let me have five minutes alone with that Arab over there, and I'll give you still more.'

'So you can plot an escape with him?'

'Even so, what difference would it make? Do you think the price you'd get for my old carcase would equal even the thirty sequins I gave you?'

Coriano jingled the copper coins in his hand, hesitating for a moment between justice and practicality, then turned his head and gave all his attention to the division of the lots of merchandise: the old men and the sick into one corner; the well-built men into another; the young and beautiful women to one side, and so on.

Savary trotted over to the Arab. Shortly afterward he returned and sidled up to Angélique.

'That's Ali Mektub all right. He has a nephew named Mohammed Raki, too, who lives in Algiers. Nevertheless his uncle says he remembers that his nephew went to Marseilles for a white man for whom he had worked a long time in the Sudan, where that man, who was very learned, was mining gold.'

'What did that man look like? Could he describe him?'

'Don't get excited. I couldn't ask him a thousand details the moment I arrived. But I'm going to see him at greater length this evening or tomorrow.'

'How will you manage that?'

'That's my business. Just trust me.'

Coriano separated them. Angélique was taken under a strong guard to the French quarter of the city. Evening was falling, and from the open-fronted taverns along the street came the music of tambourines and flutes.

The house they entered was like a little fortress. D'Escrainville was there, surrounded by a semi-European scheme of decoration in which fine furniture and gold-framed portraits were side by side with oriental divans and the ubiquitous water-pipe. The stench of opium permeated everything.

He invited Angélique to take coffee with him, something he hadn't done since that memorable evening on the island among the marble goddesses.

'Well, my beauty, here we are in port. In a few days all the admirers of lovely girls who are willing to part with a goodly sum to acquire a rare object, will be able to inspect your figure in detail. We'll give them plenty of time, you may be sure.'

'You're a crude sort,' said Angélique. 'But I don't think you're going to have the audacity to put me up for sale . . . and naked too.'

The pirate laughed loudly again. 'The more I display you, the better chance I have of getting the twelve thousand piastres I want for you.'

Angélique leaped up, her eyes flashing. 'That shall never be,' she shouted. 'Never will I accept such shame. I am not a slave. I am a great lady of France. Never, never will I endure it. Try to treat me that way, and I'll make you regret it a hundred times more than you can possibly imagine.'

'Insolent whore!' he roared, seizing his whip.

The one-eyed lieutenant interceded. 'Let her alone, Captain. You are going to damage her. It's not worth the trouble to get her all bruised. A little sojourn in the dungeon will take some of the starch out of her.'

The Marquis d'Escrainville was incapable of listening to reason, but his lieutenant jostled him aside cautiously and he went to stretch out on the divan, letting his whip fall to the floor.

Coriano grasped Angélique's arm, but she pulled it away, saying she was quite able to walk by herself. She had never taken much of a liking to this fellow with his hairy, tattooed arms, who truly looked the part – a low pirate with his black eye-patch and his head tied in a red bandana from under which his long, greasy hair straggled down his unshaven cheeks. He shrugged his shoulders and led her through the winding passageways of the old house, half-fortress, half-inn. After forcing her down a flight of stone stairs, he stopped before a door heavily barred with medieval iron, pulled out a bunch of keys and turned the squeaking locks.

'Get in there!'

Angélique hesitated on the sill of the dark cavern he pointed out to her. He pushed her in and locked the door.

Now she was alone in a gloomy dungeon lit only by a small barred window near the ceiling. There wasn't even any straw for her to lie on; the only furnishings were three thick chains with irons for wrists and ankles fastened into the wall. At least the brute had not locked her into these.

'And they were afraid of damaging me,' she said to herself.

Her shoulders smarted where the whip had wrapped itself around them. She let herself fall to the ground. The silence was as profound as in a tomb. At least she could collect her wits here, if not in comfort, then at least without distraction. She discovered that her serenity came from the recent news that Savary had whispered to her concerning the Arab merchant Ali Mektub.

Angélique kept repeating every one of his words over and over to herself so as not to lose hope. She could not be mistaken. She had been right to try, in spite of the worst vicissitudes, to get to Crete. The frail thread had not been broken and hope still gleamed at the end of her road. Now she did not have to delude herself. For a long time nothing so definite had shown up in her quest. When and where would she be able to meet the nephew of Ali Mektub? She did not know even in what way she could regain her freedom or whether the dreaded destiny of the harem awaited her.

Nevertheless, she must have dropped off to sleep and slept soundly, for when she awoke she found beside her a copper tray on which were some Turkish coffee exhaling an appetising aroma, some candied pistachio nuts and some honey cakes.

She was finishing her refreshments when voices echoed down the subterranean corridor. Footsteps were drawing near. The key squeaked in the lock, and the one-eyed pirate thrust in two other women, one of whom was veiled, and both of whom were screaming violent oaths at him in Turkish. Their jailer abused them roundly in the same language, and, after locking them in, went away grumbling.

The two women retreated into a corner of the dungeon and stared in terror at Angélique until they discovered she, too, was a woman. Then they began to laugh hysterically.

By this time Angélique had got used to the dimness, and could see that the veiled woman was wearing Turkish trousers, a black silk blouse and a bolero of velvet. Her thick black hair, rendered even darker by being dyed with green henna, was topped with a red velvet cap from which hung a gauze veil that concealed her face. Seeing that she was in the presence of only another woman, she took this off and revealed long bluish lashes curling over doe-like eyes. She would have been a great beauty if her nose had not been so prominent. Around her neck was a gold chain from which hung a crucifix, which she proceeded to kiss, and then crossed herself.

When she saw how Angélique reacted to this gesture, she went to sit down beside her and began to talk – to Angélique's great surprise – in French, not fluently but correctly. She was an Armenian from Tiflis, in the Caucasus Mountains, and hence of the Orthodox faith, but she had learned French from a Jesuit father who taught her and her brothers. She introduced her fair companion, a Russian, who had been captured by the Turks near Kiev.

Angélique asked how she happened to fall into d'Escrainville's power, but she could hardly explain because she had just recently arrived from Beirut in Syria, having started in Erzerum and come via Constantinople. Both of them considered themselves very lucky to be in Crete, for they knew that this time they would not be treated like cattle and exposed for sale naked in the public square, but rather be offered as valuable properties in an enclosure reserved for such precious merchandise.

Angélique kept looking at her uneasily as she talked. The woman, whose name was Tchemitchian, must have been months en route, exposed naked in all the bazaars of the Levant. Yet no one had robbed her of the heavy gold bracelets on her wrists and ankles, nor her long, heavy girdle made of gold sequins. In fact, there were several *livres* of gold on her person, enough, it would seem, for her to redeem her freedom.

The Armenian burst out laughing. It was not so much a question of money as it was of finding a protector with power and authority. She was sure she would find such a one more easily here in a country that had so recently belonged to the Christians and which was still the loading port for European corsairs, just as it was the unloading place for the ships that came there to trade with Westerners. She had seen Orthodox priests in the streets, and that sight had given her hope.

The Russian was much more reserved. She seemed indifferent to her fate, but proceeded to pre-empt most of the space in the cell by stretching out to sleep.

'She won't be much competition,' said the Armenian with a knowing wink. 'She is pretty, but you can easily see she lacks something to be really attractive. On the other hand, I certainly hope your presence here won't hinder me from finding a good master.'

'Haven't you ever thought of escaping?' asked Angélique.

'Escape? I? Where would I go? It's a long way back to the Caucasus where I come from, and the road runs entirely through Turkish territory. Haven't they conquered Crete already? Furthermore there's no one left at home. The Turks are there. They slaughtered my father and my older brothers, and my younger ones were castrated right before my eyes to be sold as white eunuchs to the Pasha of Kars. No indeed, the best thing for me is to find as powerful a master as possible.'

Then she began to question Angélique, asking with a touch of deference whether she had come from the slave markets of Malta.

'Why? Do you think there's some honour attached to being raped by the monks of the Order of Malta?' Angélique asked with considerable irony.

'They are the most powerful Christian lords in the Levant,' said her companion, rolling her eyes. 'Even the Turks are afraid of them and show them respect, for the Knights' commerce extends to every part of the Mediterranean and they are fabulously rich. Didn't you know the batistan here in Candia belongs to them? I heard one of their galleys was at the quay here, and that the Order's slave-master would be at the auction when we are sold. But I forget you are French and you must have slave markets in France. They say France is a powerful nation. Is it as big as Malta?'

Angélique corrected her. No, France had no slave-markets, and it was ten times bigger than Malta.

The Armenian laughed in her face. Why should a Frenchwoman be inventing tales more fantastic than even the Arab fantasies? Everyone knew there was no Christian nation larger than Malta.

Angélique gave up trying to convince her. She said the prospect of being sold in the batistan of the noble Knights of Malta was no consolation for the loss of her freedom, and she hoped soon to find some means of escape.

The Armenian shrugged. She did not think anyone could escape from the clutches of a slave-market as important as the 'French peerat'. She had been in the hands of the Turks for nearly a year and she had never, never heard of a successful attempt at escape on the part of any woman. The most 'successful' were those found stabbed or eaten by the dogs and cats.

'Cats?' exclaimed Angélique.

'Some Moslem tribes train cats to guard their captives. A cat is much more ferocious and swift than a dog.'

'I thought it was the eunuchs guarded the women.'

She learned that the eunuchs guarded only those who were lucky enough to be elevated to the status of the harem. Mere captives were relegated to the surveillance of cats and dogs, to which the rebellious were sometimes thrown to be eaten alive. These obscene animals began by clawing out the eyes and gnawing off the breasts.

Angélique shuddered. She was not afraid of death, but, if it came in that fashion, it was a different matter altogether.

The remains of the food that had been left for Angélique did not go far when divided into three parts, especially as the Russian ate most of it. The prisoners began to suffer from thirst. In spite of their appeals –

particularly sonorous on the part of the Armenian – no one came to their help. But as the night grew cooler, their thirst was somewhat appeased, only to redouble at daybreak. Still no one came near them. Gusts of hot wind blew through the narrow grating at the top of their dungeon. Soon they were not only thirsty but hungry as well. Still no one came. The light outside changed to pink, then to purple, then dwindled away. It was night again, worse than the one before. Angélique's back pained her frightfully where the pirate's whip had broken the skin and the blood had glued her garments to her flesh. But in the morning they were awakened by a delicious odour quite near by.

'It smells like real Caucasus shashlik,' said the Armenian, her nostrils quivering.

Then they heard the welcome clatter of metal dishes in the corridor.

'Put it here,' said the voice of d'Escrainville.

At the same moment the lock turned, letting a ray of light into the dungeon.

'A little fasting, and some companions to give you plenty of information about your lot, should have knocked some wisdom into you, my beauty. Have you decided to act more like a dutiful slave? Bow your head and say: "Yes, master, I will do everything you want" . . .'

The pirate was under the influence of wine and his drugs. He was badly shaved. When Angélique did not answer him, he swore and informed her that his patience was at an end.

'I can't do any bargaining at the auction before I have humbled that girl. Otherwise she'll spoil everything. Repeat after me with your head bowed: "Yes, master . . ." '

Angélique clenched her teeth. The slaver spat with rage. Once more he raised his whip, but again the one-eyed lieutenant stopped him. Calmed a little, the pirate chief made an effort to control himself.

'The only reason I don't flay you alive is that it would lower your price.' He turned to the sailors who were carrying the dishes. 'Take the other prisoners into the next dungeon to eat and drink, but not this stubborn mule.'

To Angélique's great astonishment the Armenian and her gluttonous Russian companion refused to accept what she could not share. It was the unspoken law that prisoners stuck together.

Their torturer condemned all women to the devil, swearing that such a breed should not be allowed to exist, and with a great to-do had all the dishes carried back.

The day dragged on, and night again brought hunger to the three captives. Angélique could not sleep. Yet she would have to endure still another day of misery before the auction sale in which the three would doubtless be the chief attraction. Savary had promised to extricate her from her desperate situation, but the chances of a poor old man, penniless and himself a captive, with only ignorant Greeks to help him, were considerably slimmer when some of the most notorious pirates were competing to dispose of the goods necessary to their survival as slave-traders.

Toward the middle of the night she thought she saw two eyes gleaming in the darkness. 'A cat!' she screamed.

But it was only a double-wick lamp.

The night seemed endless. She would have liked to sleep, but she decided she had better not, for Savary might still come. Toward dawn she heard the sea roar as in a storm. She curled up under the window, and eventually dozed.

'Madame du Plessis, will you write a letter?'

Angélique woke with a start. She could barely make out the old apothecary trying to slip a sheet of paper through the bars of the window together with an inkhorn and a pen.

'How can I? I have no writing desk.'

'No matter. Lean against the wall, or spread it on the floor.'

Angélique rested the paper against the rough stone. 'Who is this letter to?' she asked, her spirits reviving.

'Your husband.'

'My husband?'

'Yes. I have seen Ali Mektub again. He has decided to go to Algiers to find his nephew and question him. It's barely possible that his nephew can lead him straight to your husband's hiding place. If so, it would be a good thing for him to have a letter in your handwriting to authorise his mission.'

Angélique's hand trembled on the wrinkled paper. Write to her husband! He was no longer a phantom but a living being. The thought that his hands might touch this letter fresh from her hands, that his eyes might read it, seemed insane to her. But, she thought, she did believe in the resurrection of the body, didn't she?

'What should I say, Maître Savary? I don't know what . . . What should I put in the letter?'

'It doesn't matter, just so long as he can recognise your writing.'

148

Angélique wrote, grooving the paper deeply in her tense excitement: Remember me who was once your wife. I have always loved you. – Angélique.'

'Should I tell him what a tight spot I'm in? Let him know where I am?'

'Ali Mektoub will tell him.'

'Do you really think he can find him?'

'He will do all he can, at any rate.'

'How did you get him to agree to go for poor penniless slaves like us?'

'Moslems don't always look for material rewards,' Savary answered. 'They are more likely to indulge some idiosyncrasy of their own, and when the spirit moves them to do so, there's no stopping them. Ali Mektub regarded you and your husband's story as a sign from Allah. God has mysterious plans for the two of you, and regards you with special favour. Your quest is a holy one, and he thinks Allah might punish him if he did not go. He will make this pilgrimage as devoutly as if he were going to Mecca, and at his own expense. He loaned me the hundred *livres* I promised Rochat. I know he will do it.'

'Perhaps it is a sign that Heaven is taking pity on me. But the voyage will be a long one. What will happen to me in the meantime? You know they say they're going to sell me in a couple of days.'

'I know,' said Savary anxiously, 'but don't give up hope. Perhaps I will have time to effect your escape. If you could just gain a few days before being put up at auction, it would help my chances.'

'I've thought of that. My fellow prisoners here told me that sometimes captives mutilate or disfigure themselves to keep from being sold. I haven't the courage for that, but I thought if I cut off my hair right down to the scalp, I would frustrate my jailors. They're putting all their hopes and expectations on the fact that I'm blonde, because the Orientals like fair women. Without my hair I wouldn't fetch so high a price. They wouldn't dare sell me that way when all they would have to do is wait till my hair grew out again. That would gain us some time.'

'It's not a bad idea. But I'm afraid of that wretch d'Escrainville's temper.'

'Don't worry about me. I'm beginning to get used to it. All I need is a pair of scissors.'

'I'll try to slip some in to you. I don't know if I can get back here myself, for I am being watched closely, but I'll find someone to do it. Keep up your courage. In sha Allah!'

Her third day of captivity dawned. Angélique expected her captor's cruelty to increase. Her head felt light and her legs weak, and she thought she might be catching a fever. When she heard footsteps in the outer passageway, she began to shiver dolefully.

Coriano appeared, ordered her out of the dungeon, and without saying a word led her to the salon where the Marquis d'Escrainville was pacing in his usual concentrated fury.

When he saw Angélique he looked at her evilly, then pulled a pair of scissors out of the tail-pocket of his coat.

'This is what we found on a Greek boy who was trying to slip them through the ventilator into your cell. They were intended for you, weren't they? What were you planning to do with them?'

Angélique looked away scornfully and did not answer. Her plan had failed.

'She must have had some plan in the back of her mind,' said Coriano. 'You know how many things they can dream up to get away. Remember that Sicilian girl who drank acid? And that other one who threw herself off the battlements? Both total losses.'

'Don't bring up those things!' said the pirate.

He started pacing the floor again. Then he seized Angélique by the hair and tipped her head back to look in her face.

'You have made up your mind that you will not be sold, haven't you? You would do anything to get away, isn't that right? Are you going to scream? Howl? Struggle? Is it going to take ten men to strip you?' He let her go and resumed his pacing. 'I can see that from here. A fine scandal that will be! The Knights of Malta, who own the batistan, don't like that. And neither do the fanciers of docile women.'

'We could drug her,' said Coriano.

'You know perfectly well that won't do. It makes them look too listless. I need those twelve thousand piastres!' He stopped in front of Angélique. 'If you are docile I can surely get them. But if you're not, you'll cheat us. I'm telling you, Coriano, I'd pay anyone to take that hussy off my hands.'

The lieutenant gave a groan of exasperation. 'We have got to tame her, that's all.'

'How? We've tried everything.'

'No!' His one eye lit up. 'She hasn't been taken on a little tour of the battlement dungeons yet. That'll let her know what's in store for her if she swindles us out of a good sale.'

A hideous leer spread over his toothless mouth. D'Escrainville replied in kind.

'Good idea, Coriano! We can still try that.' He approached his captive. 'Would you like to know the kind of death I'm planning for you if you spoil our sale? Would you like to know the end I'm reserving for you if you don't fetch us our twelve thousand piastres? If you arrange things so our buyers don't like you?' Holding her by the hair again, he thrust his face into hers, suffocating her with his opium-tainted breath. 'For die you shall! Don't hope for any pity from me. Unless I get twelve thousand piastres out of you, you shall die. Now, do you want to know *how* you shall die?'

The door of a new dungeon shut upon her. Like the other one it was damp and dark, but otherwise seemed no different. She remained a long time on her feet, then sat on a wooden bar in one corner. She had no mind to show the Marquis d'Escrainville the fright consuming her, but that did not prevent her from experiencing a deathly fear. Just as he was shutting the door, she was on the point of throwing herself at his feet, begging him for mercy, promising anything he wanted, but one last flash of pride had kept her from it.

'I'm afraid,' she said aloud. 'Dear God, how afraid I am.'

The place was like a tomb. She covered her face with her hands and waited. Then she thought she heard a soft thud as if something had fallen rather near her. Then silence again.

But she was not alone in the dungeon. Some undetected presence she sensed staring at her. Slowly she spread her fingers, and screamed with horror. In the middle of the dungeon stood a huge cat, its eyes gleaming in the gloom. Angélique froze.

Then another cat appeared between the bars of the ventilator and leaped down into the cell. A third followed it, and a fourth and a fifth, until she was completely surrounded by the slinking, creeping beasts. All she could see in the darkness was their glowing eyes. One of them squatted on its haunches, preparing to spring upon her, aiming, she was sure, at her eyes. She tried to kick it away, and the beast responded with a frenzied miaowing that the others took up in fiendish chorus.

Angélique had leaped to her feet, trying to reach the door. Then she felt a weight on her shoulders and sharp claws digging into her flesh while others tore at her clothing.

Her arms over her eyes, she began to howl like a madwoman: 'No, not that! Not that! Help! *Help!*'

The door flew open, and Coriano entered, whipping and kicking the cats aside, and cursing at them. Even he found it hard to disperse them,

for they were starving. He dragged Angélique outside, so beside herself with terror that she writhed howling on the stone flooring.

D'Escrainville watched her as she grovelled, finally beaten. Now, at
last, her weakness had overcome her will, and she was no different from
any other woman.

The skull-like grin spread over the pirate's mouth. This was his finest
triumph, and his bitterest. Suddenly he wanted to cry with pain. He
ground his teeth to stop himself.

'Now do you understand? Now will you be docile?'

Sobbing, she repeated: 'No . . . not that . . . not the cats! Not the
cats!'

He raised her head. 'Will you be docile? Will you go tamely to the
batistan?'

'Yes. Yes.'

'Will you let us exhibit you naked?'

'Yes. . . . Yes. . . . Anything. . . . But not the cats!'

The two buccaneers looked at her.

'I think we've won, Captain,' said Coriano. He bent over Angélique,
still writhing and sobbing on the floor, and showed where her shoulder
had been torn by the claws of the murderous cats. 'I went in as soon as
she began to call for help, but even so they had time to give her a
fine clawing. The head man of the batistan and Erivan, the auctioneer,
are going to hold that against us.'

The Marquis d'Escrainville wiped the sweat from his forehead. 'That's
the least of our disappointments. We're lucky they didn't claw her
eyes out.'

'You're right. Madonna, she's the stubbornest I've met yet. As long
as I live and no matter what seas I drift in, I will always remember the
French girl with the green eyes.'

After that horrible scene Angélique resigned herself to her punishment as best she could, making no effort to collect her thoughts or
rebel against her fate. Her two fellow-prisoners exchanged knowing
looks when they saw her, once so proud, lying dejected for hours at
a time, staring at nothing. The pirate chief knew how to subdue rebels.
He was a man of wide experience. He could even make a woman feel
proud in bending to his will.

The next day one of the Moorish guards from the *Hermes* came in
with two fat Negroes. At first Angélique took them for men, for they
wore masculine clothes, including a huge turban and a scimitar at

their belt, but when she examined them more closely she concluded they were middle-aged women, for withered breasts hung under their brocaded velvet boleros, and their prune-like faces were beardless. The older planted herself before Angélique and said in a falsetto voice: 'Hammam!'

Angélique turned to the Armenian. 'Hammam? Doesn't that mean "bath" in Persian?'

'Yes indeed,' said the old woman in Turkish. Then she pointed her orange-lacquered fingernail at the Russian. 'Bania.' Then she pointed to herself. 'Hammamchi!'

'That means he's the supervisor of the baths,' said the Armenian.

She explained that they were two eunuchs who had come to take them to the Turkish Bath, where they would have their superfluous hairs removed and be properly attired. She roused herself from her torpor and chatted rapidly with the two hideous characters. Both she and the Russian woman seemed delighted with the prospect.

'They say we can choose the most expensive clothes in the whole bazaar, and jewels too. But first you have to be veiled. The eunuch pretends it's indecent for you to be dressed in man's clothes. He's ashamed of you.'

They brought the three captives back into the house, where refreshments of lemon and orange juice had been set out for them. Angélique shuddered when the eunuch with the long orange fingernails brushed her hair aside to examine her back. The Marquis d'Escrainville entered while all this was going on. The eunuch said something to him emphatically in Turkish.

The Armenian whispered: 'He's asking if d'Escrainville has lost his mind to have punished you so just before the auction. He doesn't guarantee that he can obliterate those scratches before night.'

D'Escrainville replied loudly in the same language. The eunuch pursed his lips like a disappointed old woman, and shut up.

The corsair's eyes were bloodshot, his mouth tense. His wandering glance did not rest on Angélique. After a moment he stomped out of the room.

Slaves brought in street clothes for all the women, and Angélique had to put on a full black chuddar which covered her face except for her eyes, which were veiled by a strip of white gauze. Outside were some ragged urchins holding several saddled donkeys. The Armenian commented that this means of transportation was designed to show off their great value. Then she and the Russian began to talk in Turkish to the eunuchs, which left Angélique quite out of the picture.

The old eunuch seemed to be a rather agreeable, and certainly a talkative party. He began by buying some pieces of quivering red and green jellied paste which he offered the three women, saying it was flavoured with raspberries and mint, but they should not eat too much before their bath. Angélique found it insipid and disgusting, and handed it to the urchin but the Negro took it away and struck the boy with the bull's pizzle.

After so many days of incarceration the air felt good to her. The storm had passed, and the sea, which she could glimpse from time to time at the end of a narrow street, was a deep lavender, flecked with white. The sky was blue and cloudless, and the heat less stifling.

The little procession advanced quite slowly through the crowds which were already swarming into the streets, though the hour was early. At the harbour all the races of the Mediterranean basin hugged the windowless walls of the Greek houses along the alleys or took refuge under the projecting balconies of the little Venetian palazzos that almost touched each other above. The Greeks from the mountains and the peasants from the neighbouring countryside were easily identified by their short white skirts and bare knees. There were Arab merchants in brown hooded cloaks. The few Turks to be seen were distinguished by huge globe-like, gem-encrusted turbans, and by puffed-out trousers held by sashes that encircled their waist with many turns. Olive-complexioned Maltese walked alongside Sardinians and Italians, each in his native costume. These were minor merchants who coasted along the shores. The very fact that they had escaped the pirates allowed them to trade on an equal basis as free men, just as Melchior Pannassave could have done if fortune had been kinder to him. There were many European costumes too – big plumed hats and high cuffed boots or heeled shoes – but more or less shabby, indicating colonial officials forgotten on this distant island. Occasionally a banker from Italy appeared, dressed in velvet and wearing great ostrich feathers in his hat, and fine leather boots. Every hundred feet or so they encountered a black-gowned bearded Orthodox priest, wearing on his chest a huge crucifix of carved wood or silver or gold.

The Armenian asked each one she passed for a blessing which the priest would give her absentmindedly by tracing a cross in the air.

In the tailors' section the head eunuch bought many bolts of cloth of every colour, and jewels. At length he suggested they return via the harbour. They passed piles of dates, melons, watermelons, oranges, lemons and figs stacked on the huge black paving-stones. Then a forest of masts and spars came in view.

On the bridge of a galleon flying the flag of Tunis stood a sort of ogre with long hair and beard, dressed in a gold-embroidered vest and high red-leather boots, who was bellowing like the god of the sea. The eunuchs stopped the donkeys in order to enjoy the sight and exchange observations with the captives. The Armenian graciously translated for Angélique's benefit.

Hence Angélique learned that the man was the renegade Dane, Eric Jansen, who had spent twenty years among the Berbers. In order to save his overloaded ship from wreck during the storm of the previous night he had had to jettison a part of his cargo – almost a hundred slaves bound for Albania. Now the old Viking was storming as he watched the sale of another contingent of slaves 'damaged' in the hold of the storm-tossed vessel. Bruised men, and women and children half dead with fright, were being liquidated at bargain prices here on the Candia waterfront, and he was keeping only the more interesting items of his last raid. This disappointment had put him into a terrible mood, and he kept roaring at his slave-keepers not to spare the whip.

The pathetic band had been hoisted on the piles of spars and the casks on the quay so as to be better seen by the public. White burnoused Arabs from his Berber crew were hoarsely chanting the merits of each piece of merchandise. Prospective buyers were permitted to grope, pinch, and even unveil the women who stood exposed on the edge of the waterfront naked and shivering. Some tried to cover themselves with their hair, but the guards kept striking them to prevent such attempts at modesty. They even forced their mouths open to display how many teeth they had.

Angélique shuddered with shame at the sight. 'It's not possible,' she said to herself, 'that I . . . No, not that!' She looked about her for any source of help whatever, and caught sight of an old orange-seller staring at her through the folds of his full cloak. He made a signal to her, then disappeared into the crowd.

A black trader was dragging a stupefied, wild-eyed woman away from her three shrieking children. 'That,' said the Armenian, 'reminds me of the way they tore my brothers away from my mother.' She listened to what they were saying, and continued: 'That woman was bought for an Egyptian harem deep in the desert. Her purchaser couldn't be bothered with children; they'd die on the trip.'

Angélique said nothing. A kind of indifference had crept over her. 'They are going to sell the children for just a few piastres,' the Armenian resumed. 'Or else leave them here to roam with the dogs and cats. Cursed be the day they were born!' She nodded slowly. 'We're lucky. At least we won't die of hunger.' Then she blithely asked permission to go and admire the Maltese galleys the red flags of which, with their white crosses, were whipping in the breeze.

The sale was about to end. Soldiers of the Order of Malta were using their halberds to keep order in the lines of captives being led away by their new owners. Booted and helmeted, these soldiers were distinguished from ordinary mercenaries by their black chasubles with big, white eight-pointed crosses on their chests.

The Armenian was ecstatic about these members of the greatest fleet in Christendom. The eunuch had to speak sharply to her to get her to come away. He had by no means intended to deprive the captives, who would depart the next day for distant harems, of one last sight of this street scene so dear to the heart of every Oriental that even a condemned man was allowed to see it, but now he had to hurry, for the time of the sale was drawing near.

'Hammam! Hammam!' he kept repeating as he urged them along.

Just outside the Turkish Bath Angélique saw the orange-seller again. When he deliberately stumbled against her donkey, she recognised him as Savary.

'Tonight,' he whispered, 'when you come out of the batistan, be ready. A blue rocket will be the signal. My son Vassos will guide you, but if he shouldn't be able to meet you, do everything you can to get to the Crusaders' Tower by the harbour.'

'That's impossible. How will I ever be able to escape these guards of mine?'

'I think at that moment your guards, whatever they are, may have something else to attend to than keeping an eye on you,' Savary grinned and a diabolical light came into his bespectacled eyes. 'Be ready!'

CHAPTER THIRTEEN

The sun was already low on the horizon as slaves bore the three women in tightly-closed palanquins to the batistan of Candia.

Situated on a rise of ground, this building looked from the approach like quite a large establishment. It was square, and its entrances were wrought-iron grills. The crowd outside it was so thick that the captives, still under the guard of the eunuchs, had to force their way in through the mob swarming around a sort of blackboard of unpolished marble, on which a swarthy man with a prominent nose was writing in Italian and Turkish.

Angélique knew enough Italian to understand the information:

Orthodox Greeks	50 écus, gold
Orthodox Russians	100 écus
Moors and Turks	75 écus
Miscellaneous French	30 écus

Rate of Exchange

1 French	=	3 Moors at Marseilles
1 English	=	6 Moors at Tanta
1 Spanish	=	7 Moors at Agadir
1 Dutch	=	10 Moors at Leghorn or Genoa

The eunuchs shoved Angélique forward, and they all entered a sizable patio with blue tile paths between rose trees, oleanders and orange-trees. A beautiful Venetian fountain bubbled in the middle. Here the racket of the city scarcely penetrated; the thick walls shut out all distracting sounds so that the rituals of high finance might take place in solemn silence. The patio was ringed with carved columns covered with ancient Byzantine paintings like manuscript illumination, which supported a balcony off which were the rooms where the auctions took place. The older eunuch left his flock here to learn the room to which they had been assigned.

Angélique could scarcely breathe under her layers of veils. Everything seemed to be happening in a dream, as if she were caught up in some machine that had suddenly released her at the threshold of these halls where human beings of all sorts and descriptions were to be inspected by covetous eyes. She pushed a veil aside to catch her breath, but the younger eunuch signalled to her emphatically to cover her face again. She pretended not to understand him, and continued to look dolefully at the procession of purchasers – Turks, Arabs and Europeans – crossing the patio and disappearing into the rooms above.

Suddenly she caught sight of Rochat, the deputy consul, coming through the entrance. He had his usual week's growth of beard, and was carrying a portfolio of papers under his arm. Angélique ran to him.

'Monsieur Rochat,' she whispered, 'listen to me. I haven't much time. Your scoundrel friend d'Escrainville is going to put me up for sale. Try to help me and I shall always be grateful to you. I have a fortune in France. Just remember, I didn't fool you about the hundred *livres*

I promised you. I know you cannot intercede for me yourself, but couldn't you get some of the Christian buyers – the Knights of Malta, for instance, who have so much influence here – to take pity on this terrible situation I'm in? I can't bear the thought of being sold to a Moslem and put in a harem. Tell the Knights I am ready and willing to pay any ransom whatever if they'll only win the auction and get me out of the clutches of these infidels. Won't they take pity on a poor Christian woman?'

The French official pretended to be annoyed at first, and almost left her, but he calmed down the more she talked.

'Why, that's a fine idea,' he said, scratching the back of his neck, 'and it's quite possible it would work. The Commissioner of Slaves of the Order of Malta, Don José de Almada, a Castilian, is here tonight, and so is another high-ranking member of the Order, Bailiff Charles de la Marche, from Auvergne, one of your countrymen. I'll undertake to interest them in your case. I don't see why they shouldn't help.'

'Wouldn't it look funny for a member of a religious order to buy a woman?'

Rochat rolled his eyes up. 'My poor child, it's plain you don't know much about this place. For years the Order has been buying and selling women just like any other slaves, and no one has ever objected. We are in the Orient now, and furthermore let's not forget that the good Knights took a vow of celibacy only, not chastity. But probably the ransom would interest them more than a slave for a plaything. The Order needs money to keep up its fleet. I am going to investigate your titles, your rank and your fortune. The Knights are always glad to get on the good side of the King of France, and I've heard that you were quite a figure at Court, close to His Majesty Louis XIV. All this may persuade them to lend you aid.'

'Oh, thank you, Monsieur Rochat. You're my saviour!'

She forgot how ineffectual and unattractive and unshaven he was. He was going to do something for her. She squeezed his hand fervently.

Touched and embarrassed, he said: 'I'm glad I can be of some use to you. Your plight worried me, but there was nothing I could do, was there? Now, just keep your hopes up.'

The young eunuch descended upon them like a screeching hawk and dragged Angélique away by her arm. Rochat departed quickly.

In a rage at the touch of the eunuch's black hands on her arm, Angélique whirled around and smacked his flabby cheeks. The eunuch drew his sword, but seemed unable to make up his mind whether he should use it on such a valuable piece of merchandise. He was young and had come from a provincial harem, where he was used to guarding only very docile females, and no one had ever told him what to do with a rebellious and independent one. He looked as if he might burst into tears.

When the older eunuch heard of the incident, he raised his arms to heaven. The only thing he wanted was to get rid of his responsibilities, and quickly too. Luckily for him the Marquis d'Escrainville appeared just then. The two eunuchs told him all the trouble they had been having.

The pirate looked at the veiled young woman, seeming hardly to recognise in her the young man he had known on the voyage. Angélique's diaphanous silks and veils did a great deal to improve her value by revealing her figure. D'Escrainville ground his teeth. His hand clenched her arm so tightly that she almost fainted from the pain.

'Don't you remember, you whore, what I promised to do to you if you didn't behave yourself? Tonight, either you do what the eunuchs tell you, or it will be the cats again. The cats, understand!'

His expression was so horrible Angélique thought he must truly be a demon from hell. Then as one of the purchasers came up, he calmed down.

The newcomer was a paunchy Venetian banker, elaborately dressed in plumes, lace and gold braid.

'Monsieur d'Escrainville,' he said in a heavy accent, 'I am glad to see you again. How are you?'

'Not very well,' the pirate replied, wiping the sweat from his forehead. 'I have a migraine headache that's driving me crazy. It won't go away till I sell that girl over there.'

'Pretty?'

'Judge for yourself.'

Like a horse-trader he pulled the veil from Angélique's face. The Venetian whistled.

'Whe-e-ew! What luck you do have, Monsieur d'Escrainville. She'll bring you real money.'

'I expect so. I shan't let her go for less than twelve thousand piastres.'

The heavy-jowled face of the banker took on an enigmatic expression as he tried to estimate whether the lovely captive would be within or beyond his means. 'Twelve thousand piastres? Well, she's certainly worth it, but aren't you being a little greedy?'

'There are plenty of collectors here who wouldn't hesitate a minute to pay that. As a matter of fact I'm waiting now for the Circassian Prince Riom Mirza, a friend of the Grand Sultan, who has instructed him to procure this rare pearl, and also for Shamil Bey, Pasha Soliman Aga's head eunuch, who never thinks of price when it comes to pleasing his master.'

The Venetian sighed. 'It's hard for us to compete with the monumental fortunes of those Orientals. But I shall be at the auction. If I'm not mistaken, we're going to have a fine show. Good luck, my friend!'

The auction room looked like a large salon. Fine tapestries covered the walls, with low divans beneath them, facing one another. At the far end of the room was a platform with steps leading up to it. Venetian glass chandeliers reflected in their thousands of prisms the lamps the Maltese lackeys had just finished lighting.

The room was already half full, and the occupants were arguing incessantly. Turkish servants, wearing long moustaches and pointed hats tipped with gold or silver, were busy setting cups of coffee and plates of dainties on low copper and silver tables. Others were supplying the smokers with the inevitable water-pipes, the low burbling of which formed an undertone to the higher-pitched discussions.

Oriental costumes predominated, but there were ten or so white corsairs in gold-braided trousers and embroidered cloaks. Some, like the Marquis d'Escrainville, had taken the trouble to put on their wrinkled tunics, and hats still trimmed with plumes but bearing the marks of pistol shots and sword fights. Their long Dutch pipes looked incongruous among so many narghiles.

Eric Jansen, the renegade Dane, entered with three Tunisian bodyguards, and sat down ostentatiously next to an old merchant from the Sudan, a Negro in a barbaric African robe, the agent of Egyptian merchants who supplied the harems of Arabia and Ethiopia and the African interior.

The eunuchs guided the three women down the length of the room, pushed them up the steps to the platform and then hustled them to the rear of it, where a curtain half hid them and where there were cushions for them to sit upon. The same Armenian who had been writing the rates of exchange at the entrance approached them.

This was Erivan, the auctioneer and master of ceremonies. With considerable deference he greeted Angélique in French, then asked the Armenian and the Russian in Turkish whether they would like some coffee and sherbet to help them while away the time. Then he entered into a lively argument with the Marquis d'Escrainville.

'Why do you want to put up her hair? Can't you see, it's like a cloak of gold.'

'Leave me to my own devices,' said Erivan, squinting. 'Everyone likes a surprise.'

Two servant girls appeared in answer to a clap of his hands. At Erivan's direction they braided Angélique's hair and wound it into a knot which they fastened with pearl-headed hairpins at the back of her neck. Then they draped her veils around her again.

Angélique let them do it without interfering, for her eyes were searching anxiously for the arrival of a Knight of Malta whose aid Rochat had promised to obtain for her. Through a rip in the curtain she tried in vain to find a black cloak with a white cross among the caftans and tunics. Cold sweat broke out on her forehead at the thought that Rochat might not have been able to convince those conservative businessmen he was telling the truth.

The auction began. The first item was a Moor, a master of navigation. An appreciative silence spread over the room at the sight of this statuesque figure whose bronzed body was craftily oiled the better to show off his knotty muscles and herculean proportions.

Then a slight disturbance broke the stillness as two Knights of Malta made their entrance, their black cloaks flaunting the white cross of their Order. As they moved through the room they bowed to the notables of Constantinople, and proceeded up to the platform, where they engaged Erivan in conversation. He pointed out the captives to them.

Angélique got to her feet, full of hope.

The two Knights bowed to her, their hands on the hilts of their swords. One was a Spaniard, the other French, and both belonged to the noblest families of Europe, for to join this greatest of the Orders of Christianity a man had to have at least four quarterings on his coat-of-arms. Their costume might appear sombre, but it was by no means inelegant. Their cuffs and their ruffs were of Venetian lace, their silk stockings were fastened with silver garters, their shoes sported silver buckles.

'Are you the high-born French lady Monsieur Rochat just undertook to tell us about?' asked the older of the two, who wore a white periwig as stylish as any at Versailles. He proceeded to introduce himself. 'I am the Bailiff de la Marche, of Auvergne, and this is Don José de Almada, of Castile, Slave Commissioner for the Order of Malta. This title I quote at such length because it may be of interest to you. It appears that you were captured by the Marquis d'Escrainville, that stinking vulture, while you were voyaging to Crete on a mission entrusted to you by the King of France.'

Angélique silently blessed poor Rochat for having put things that way. He had shown her what line to follow. She emphasised her personal contact with the King himself, named her most important connections from Colbert to Madame de Montespan, mentioned the Duc de Montespan, mentioned the Duc de Vivonne, who had put the royal galley and the entire Mediterranean squadron at her disposal, then related how the enterprise had been intercepted by Rescator.

'Ah! Rescator!' said the Knights, lifting their eyes like martyrs.

She continued with the story of how she had tried to pursue her mission as best she could on a little sailing-boat which had soon fallen prey to another pirate, the Marquis d'Escrainville.

'This is the result of the frightful chaos there has been in the Mediterranean ever since the infidels destroyed good Christian government,' said the Bailiff de la Marche.

Both of them had kept nodding as she told her tale, obviously convinced of her sincerity. The personages she named and the details she gave about her position at Court could not have left them in doubt.

'It's a most distressing story,' said the Spaniard lugubriously. 'We owe it to the King of France and to you, Madame, to extricate you from these woes. But, alas, we are no longer masters of Crete, though, inasmuch as we own the batistan, the Turks owe us some consideration. We are going to bid at the auction. I, as Slave Commissioner of the Order, have funds at my disposal for good investments.'

'D'Escrainville is very demanding,' remarked the Bailiff de la Marche. 'He wants at least twelve thousand piastres.'

'I can promise you double that as my ransom,' Angélique said. 'I'll sell my estates if I have to, and my offices too, and pledge to repay everything you have to lay out. The Church will not regret having saved me from such a dreadful fate. Just think, if I get shut away in some Turkish harem, no one, not even the King of France, can do anything for me.'

'Alas, that is true. But keep your hopes high. We are going to do our best.'

Don José seemed worried. 'The bidding will go high. Prince Riom Mirza, the friend of the Grand Sultan, is in town. The Sultan charged him to procure a white slave of extraordinary beauty. He has already combed the slave-markets of Palermo and even Algiers without finding what he wanted. He hurried here the minute he heard about the Frenchwoman the Marquis d'Escrainville had captured. No doubt, the sky will be the limit for him if he finds Madame du Plessis the one he's been seeking for his imperial friend.'

'I've heard that Shamil Bey and the rich Arab jeweller Naker Ali are here too.'

The two Knights withdrew to discuss in whispers, but quite volubly, what they would do. Then they returned.

'We can go up to eighteen thousand piastres,' said Don José. 'That will give us a wide margin, and certainly ought to discourage our chief competitors. You may depend on us, Madame.'

Somewhat consoled, she thanked them in a faint voice, and watched them depart. But in the bottom of her heart she wondered whether they would have been so generous if they knew she was in disfavour with the King. She still had to meet the present emergency. Master for master, she vastly preferred to be a slave of the Cross rather than of the Crescent.

While the two knights were talking with Angélique, the bidding had begun. The Moor had been bought by an Italian corsair, Fabrizio Oligiero, for his crew. Now a huge blond slave with magnificent muscles was on the block. As a matter of form Don José de Almada bid against the Dane from Tunis. When the slave saw that the Tunisian renegade had won him, he fell on his knees and begged not to be condemned to the galleys for the rest of his life. Never again would he see the grey, windswept steppes of his native Russia. The Maltese lackeys employed by the Knights to keep order in the batistan had to lay violent hands on him to put him into the keeping of his new master. Then a group of white children were put up for sale.

The Armenian captive dug her nails into Angélique's arm. 'Look, over there against that pillar, that's my brother Arminak.'

'I thought it was a girl, he's so painted.'

'I told you he's a eunuch now. You know why they paint these boys. I never expected to see him here, but so much the better. It proves he's worth a good sum. If anyone really rich buys him, he's shrewd enough to get most of his master's fortune into his own hands after a while, if the man's stupid enough to make him his vizier and confidant.'

The old Sudanese pointed a scarlet fingernail at the boy and made a bid in a guttural voice. The Turkish Governor of Candia bid against him. A religious in a black soutane, the Chaplain of the Order of Malta, had sat down beside the two Knights, and was whispering to Don José. The Spaniard caught the attention of the Turkish Governor, who yielded to him with a courtly gesture. The boys began to sing. The Chaplain listened to each one separately and picked out five, among them the Armenian's brother.

'A thousand piastres for the lot,' he said.

A white-skinned personage, doubtless a Circassian, got to his feet and shouted: 'Fifteen hundred piastres!'

The Armenian whispered to Angélique: 'What luck! That's Shamil Bey, head eunuch of Soliman Aga. If my brother gets into that seraglio, his fortune's made.'

'Two thousand,' bid the Chaplain of the Order of Malta.

He finally won the bidding. The Armenian began to weep. 'Alas, my poor Arminak, shrewd as he is, will never get the better of those monks. They don't think of pleasure, only of piling up money to maintain their fleet. I'm positive the priest bought him just on account of his falsetto voice. He'll have to sing in a Catholic church now. What a disgrace! Perhaps he'll be sent to Rome for the Choir of the Pope.' She spat as she pronounced the hated name of the head of the rival church.

The auction was progressing rapidly. There remained only two puny boys whom no one wanted, and who were knocked down to the old Sudanese for next to nothing. The rest of the audience teased him that he was losing his taste and business judgment.

At that moment there was a commotion in the room as the personal envoy of the Sultan of all Believers made his entrance. Prince Riom Mirza was wearing an astrakhan cap and a black silk uniform across the breast of which dozens of little powderhorns were embroidered in gold edged with red. His dagger and his sword were studded with rubies. His bodyguard followed him. After bowing to the Turkish Governor, he proceeded to have a spirited discussion with Shamil Bey.

'They're arguing,' whispered the Armenian. 'The Prince says the eunuch has no right to bid for the beautiful slave, for she is promised to the Sultan of Sultans. I hope he means me.' She swelled out her bosom and swayed her hips.

In spite of herself, Angélique almost broke into sobs. These men were arguing, she was sure, about her disposition. She felt so faint and dizzy that she could hardly pay attention to the remainder of the proceedings – the sale of d'Escrainville's young black eunuchs, then of the Russian captive, and finally of the Armenian. Consequently she never found out whether her friend got her wish to be selected for a princely harem or fell into the hands of the old Sudanese, or, worse, was bought by some pirate who would sell her again as soon as he was tired of her.

Erivan, smiling unctuously as always, was bowing before her now. 'Please follow me, lovely lady.'

The Marquis d'Escrainville was at his heels. He caught Angélique by the shoulder. 'Remember,' he hissed, 'the cats . . .'

Only the thought of the horrible death that awaited her, and her hope of escaping by the intervention of the two Knights, gave Angélique the courage to face the hundreds of lecherous eyes unwaveringly focused on her the moment she made her appearance.

A nervous silence descended on the room. For three whole days Candia had talked about nothing but the coming sale of the beautiful Frenchwoman. The spectators were all leaning forward avidly, inspecting every detail of this veiled piece of costly merchandise.

Erivan motioned to a young eunuch servant who approached Angélique and loosened the veil that covered her face. It fell to the floor. Angélique's eyes flashed at the sight of these tense male faces riveted upon her, and the thought that presently she would be stripped naked before them so revolted her that she froze and turned deathly white. A ghastly shiver ran through her entire body. Her shudder and the proud, well-nigh imperious look in her sea-green eyes seemed to electrify the previously somewhat soporific crowd. Heads began to sway in voluptuous appreciation of her beauty.

Erivan began the bidding. 'Five thousand piastres.'

In the far corner of the room to which he had withdrawn to watch the auction, the Marquis d'Escrainville trembled. It was double the amount agreed on for the opening bid. That damn louse of an Erivan! He had immediately perceived in the audience an atmosphere of intense acquisitiveness that would make the bidding soar way beyond reason. The men were like dedicated gamblers, intent upon nothing but staking their all to win.

'Five thousand piastres!'

'Seven thousand,' shouted the Circassian Prince.

The chief of the white eunuchs muttered a bid. Then in a frenzied desire to win the bidding then and there, the Prince yelled: 'Ten thousand.'

A hush fell over the room. Angélique stole a look at the Knights of Malta, neither of whom had opened his mouth yet. Don José was leaning forward, a smile lurking in the corners of his stern lips.

'Prince,' he said, 'the last high priest of the Grand Sultan used to preach strict economy. I pay my respects to the Sultan's fortune, but isn't ten thousand piastres a large enough sum to buy the entire crew of a galley?'

'The Sultan of Sultans can sacrifice one of his numberless galleys if such should be his august fancy,' the Prince replied drily, looking triumphantly at Shamil Bey, whose fat feminine features wore an expression of deep disappointment. The head eunuch of Soliman Aga would have been unutterably proud to bring home this treasure of a slave to his illustrious master, but he was not unmindful of the extent of his resources and he well knew how far he dared go.

The silence continued. Suddenly Angélique felt the hands of the young eunuch on her shoulders, removing the veiling that covered her bosom. Now she was naked to the hips. A fine sweat broke out on her body, catching the golden light of the candles and lending her skin the iridescence of pearl.

Now the eunuch had removed the pins that fastened her hair, and it tumbled about her shoulders like a shower of golden rain. With the instinctive gesture of any woman feeling her hair come down, she lifted her hands to rescue her silken ringlets, and revealed the firm, perfect globes of her breasts. She was the picture of a woman discovered at her toilet.

A murmur of ravishment rippled through the hall. One Italian pirate swore audibly.

Shamil Bey decided his master would excuse his extravagance, and shouted: 'Eleven thousand piastres!'

The old Sudanese got to his feet and intoned a long melodious chant which Erivan translated: 'Eleven thousand five hundred piastres for a poor old man staking his entire wealth to gain this jewel whose favours would be sought by the sheikhs of Araby, the rulers of Ethiopia, the kings of the Sudan and even the lords of the far distant African plains.'

There was another lengthy pause. Angélique thought with terror that this black old man would discourage the two most powerful bidders by the sheer audacity of his methods of trade.

The Knight of Malta lowered his swarthy eyelids. 'Twelve thousand piastres,' he said.

'Thirteen thousand,' shouted Prince Riom Mirza.

Once more the Spaniard spoke to him sarcastically. 'Do you really believe the Sultan of Sultans will thank you for squandering his fortune? Everyone knows the sorry state of his finances.'

'I am not speaking for the Sultan,' replied the Prince, 'but for myself. I want that woman.' His black eyes never strayed from Angélique.

'In either case, aren't you risking the loss of your head?' the Knight of Malta said.

With a tone of impatience, the Prince said: 'Thirteen thousand piastres!'

Don José sighed. 'Fifteen thousand.'

The gathering began to mutter anew. Shamil Bey was moving his lips in dreadful uncertainty as to whether he should unbalance his budget for years to come and yield to vanity in procuring this rare pearl for Soliman Aga's seraglio.

'Sixteen thousand,' shouted Riom Mirza, apparently suffering himself, for he took off his astrakhan bonnet and mopped his brow.

'Who will say more?' shouted the auctioneer, repeating his taunt in several different languages.

Nothing broke the silence that followed. The European pirates had not opened their mouths, having seen from the first bid that the auction would go far beyond their reach. Damn d'Escrainville! From that woman alone he would get enough to pay his debts and buy still another ship for his armada.

'Who will say more?' Erivan repeated, nodding toward Don José.

'Sixteen thousand five hundred,' said the Knight tonelessly.

The Prince was being stubborn. 'Seventeen thousand.'

The two last bids had been made with the crackling rapidity of rifle shots. Angélique's brain was whirling with the sound of so many voices in Italian, Greek, French and languages she could not identify. She could not tell now what was going on, but she knew she was deathly afraid. She saw Don José's face contort, and the Bailiff's darken. Tremblingly she tried to gather her hair about her. When would this torture ever end?

A tall Arab in a white robe rose in the rear of the room, and strode toward the platform with the lithe grace of a panther. Angélique heard Erivan address him as Naker Ali. Below his red and white striped turban his midnight eyes gleamed in a swarthy, hawk-nosed face edged with a black beard.

Stooping, but not taking his eyes off Angélique, he withdrew from a large pouch he wore on his chest some objects that he spread on his outstretched palm – the most valuable of all the precious stones he had brought back from his last voyage to the Indies: two sapphires, a ruby as big as a walnut, an emerald, a blue beryl, opals, turquoises. From his other hand dangled a jeweller's scale, into one pan of which he placed the stones one by one. Erivan leaned over his shoulder, rapidly calculating on his fingers the worth of the stones. Finally he announced in triumph: 'Twenty thousand piastres!'

Angélique looked in panic at Don José. The limit he had set for his bidding was now passed. The Bailiff de la Marche begged him in a loud whisper: 'Make one more try, brother.'

Prince Riom Mirza was grinding his teeth. He had given up. They couldn't let that superb figure of a woman go to a common Red Sea trader, no matter how rich he might be. She was far too good for a vulgar shopkeeper's harem in some back street of Candia or Alexandria, reeking of rancid oil and fried grasshoppers.

He took Don José aside, and told him he would kill him with his own two hands if he didn't bid higher. The Knight of Malta put on his martyr's expression and like a saint on a Spanish altarpiece waited till the buzzing in the hall subsided. Then he made one last bid: 'Twenty-one thousand piastres!'

The eyes of the Turkish Governor of Candia were full of mischief as he took the stem of his narghile from between his lips and quietly said: 'Twenty-one thousand five hundred.'

Don José gave him a look like a poisoned dagger. He knew for a fact that the Turk did not have that much credit and was only trying to outdo the sovereign state of Malta, the leading Christian nation. He was tempted to stop the auction and let the tricky old Pasha try to scrape up his twenty-one thousand five hundred piastres. But Angélique's piteous expression moved him, much as he hated acting out of sentiment.

Erivan also knew the last bid was nothing but a joke on the part of the Turkish Governor. He stopped the bidding long enough to persuade the Governor not to repeat the game, then turned toward Don José.

'Who will bid more?'

'Twenty-two thousand,' said Don José de Almada.

The silence that followed lasted a long time. But Erivan had not played his last trump. Experience had taught him men's passions are far stronger than their business astuteness. Don José de Almada, who was acting out of principle, would not bring to the auction the same single-minded intensity as a man inflamed with covetousness.

Naker Ali, on his knees at the base of the platform, was raising his eyes toward Angélique as if he were having a vision. His thin lips were trembling, and he kept putting his hand to the pouch on his chest, then taking it away.

The eunuch removed the clasp that held the last of Angélique's veils about her hips. It floated to the floor at her feet.

She could see the men shaken by violent spasms as they leaned forward toward the glistening form revealed to them, lovely as a Greek statue in a grove of oleanders on a forsaken isle. But a living statue, trembling, shivering, promising delights that completely drove a man out of his senses. Each of the bidders dreamed of the intoxication of possessing her, anticipating her surrender to his desire.

A wave of torrid heat swept over Angélique, only to be followed by a sepulchral chill. So as not to face these lewd eyes longer, she put her arms before her face, binding her hands behind her head. Her shame and despair rendered her deaf and blind to everything transpiring around her. Hence she did not see Naker Ali extract a huge diamond from his pouch and lay it, shimmering in light, on his palm.

'Twenty-three thousand piastres,' exclaimed Erivan.

Don José looked away.

'Who'll bid more?' Erivan wheedled. 'Who will bid more?'

Prince Riom Mirza roared with anguish and scraped his nails the length of his cheeks as a token of his despair. A slight smile lit the face of the Arab.

Then Shamil Bey, the head eunuch, rose to his feet. The last bids had given him time to review his finances, work out how he could re-align the dissipated fortunes of his master and cover the deficit. Coldly and impassively he let fall the words: 'Twenty-five thousand piastres.'

The light died on the face of Naker Ali. He gathered his precious jewels into his pouch again, and stole to the shadowy rear of the auction room.

Turning to Shamil Bey, Erivan raised his hammer, but his hand stayed in the air as if he were paralysed. The silence was strangely pregnant, lasting interminably, so complete and so unusual that Angélique grew aware of it and raised her head from her arms. What she saw gave her such a violent shock that she thought she had lost her mind. She shrieked like a madwoman.

At the foot of the platform, where he had come on silent feet, stood a massive form, black from head to foot. A black cloak enveloped his form; his hands were encased in black gloves; a black velvet mask covered his face to the edge of a jet-black beard. He was a shape straight from a nightmare. Beyond the figure she could discern Captain Jason.

Slowly Erivan lowered the arm that held the auctioneer's hammer aloft. He bowed to the ground and murmured unctuously: 'This woman is for sale. Are you interested in her, my lord Rescator?'

'What is the last bid?' The voice that emanated from behind the black mask was deep and hoarse.

'Twenty-five thousand piastres.'

'Thirty-five thousand.'

Erivan's mouth fell open. Captain Jason turned to the assemblage and repeated in a stentorian voice: 'Thirty-five thousand piastres on behalf of my master, Lord Rescator. Who will bid more?'

Shamil Bey collapsed on his cushion without a word.

Angélique heard the hammer fall with a slight tap. The dark figure she was staring at with haggard eyes seemed to increase in size as he drew near and wrapped her in the heavy black velvet cloak he had slipped from his shoulders to hers. It fell almost to her feet. Impulsively she hugged it around her. Never, never in her life would she forget this shame to which she had been exposed.

Unfamiliar hands continued to hold her tight, possessive hands whose strength kept her erect, for her legs were giving way under her, and she knew she would sink to the floor if it were not for this support.

The deep hoarse voice was saying: 'A good night's work, Erivan. A Frenchwoman, and what a one! Who owns her?'

The Marquis d'Escrainville staggered forward like a drunken man, his pupils flashing from a face as white as chalk. He pointed a trembling finger at Angélique.

'A whore!' he said dismally. 'The most shameless in the world. Take care, you cursed sorcerer, she doesn't eat your heart out!'

Coriano rushed forward from the corridor from which he had been watching the sale with his one eye. Exposing his toothless gums in an obsequious smile, he said: 'Don't listen to him, sir. His joy has made him lose his head. She is a charming woman, utterly delightful. Gentle and docile.'

'Liar!' said Rescator. He plunged his hand into the cloth-of-gold pouch he wore at his belt, and pulled out a bag of écus which he flung at Coriano, whose one eye was saucer-wide.

'But, sir, I will get my share of the booty,' he stammered.

'Take this on account.'

'Why?'

'Because I want everyone to be happy tonight.'

'Bravo! Bravissimo!' brayed Coriano, throwing his cap into the air. 'Long live Lord Rescator!'

Rescator raised his hand. 'Let the fun begin!'

Captain Jason issued the invitation to the whole assemblage. The greatest silver trader in the Mediterranean would offer them dancing girls, wines, coffee, music, roast mutton. Whole oxen would be sent to the crews of all the pirate ships moored in the harbour, and thirty casks of wine would be broached in every square of the town. Lackeys would pass among the streets offering baskets of cakes, and scatter comfits from the housetops. Candia would be gay that night in honour of the Frenchwoman. Such were Lord Rescator's wishes.

Everyone – corsairs and princes – relaxed on their cushions in anticipation of the feasting. Only the two Knights of Malta headed for the door. Rescator called to them himself: 'Sirs, won't you be our guests?'

Don José threw him a withering look and withdrew in dignity with the Bailiff de la Marche.

CHAPTER FOURTEEN

Gradually it dawned on Angélique that she had been sold – sold to a pirate who had paid for her the price of a ship and its crew! But in reality all she had done was pass from the hands of one master into those of another, a fate which henceforth would govern her existence as a beautiful, coveted woman. A piercing shriek escaped her into which she poured all her distress, all the horror she had endured, all her revulsion at being so trapped and helpless.

'No. . . . Not sold! *Not sold!*'

She rushed against Rescator's janizaries who were closing around her in an infernal fashion and struggled with them for a moment. But they held her tight, and flung her roughly at the feet of their master. She kept whimpering: 'Not sold! No!'

'Is it the custom for French ladies to appear so scantily clad? Wait at least until you are dressed, Madame.' Rescator's sarcastic voice droned on. 'I have plenty of gowns for you. See if you like them, and choose any one you want.'

Angélique's eyes travelled uncomprehendingly over the black form looming above her until they reached the impenetrable mask beneath which lingered the traces of a scornful smile. He began to laugh.

'Get up,' he said, extending his hand to her.

When she had obeyed, he brushed apart the locks that had fallen over her face and kissed her cheek as if she were an innocent child.

'Sold? No indeed. Tonight you are my guest, that's all. Now, choose what you will wear.'

He indicated three Negro boys in red turbans who brought for her inspection, as in a fairy tale, a dress of pink silk, one of white brocade, a third of blue-green satin trimmed with mother-of-pearl.

'You're hesitating? What woman doesn't. But since the party is waiting for us, I will presume to advise you. That is my choice,' he said, pointing to the blue-green dress. 'To tell the truth, I chose it for you because I heard the Frenchwoman had sea-green eyes. You will look like a siren in it. It rather symbolises the rescue of the lovely Marquise from the waves.'

When she still said nothing, he continued: 'I see what bothers you. You don't understand how, here in faraway Crete, anyone could get gowns like this in the latest Versailles style. Well, don't let it worry your pretty head. I have lots of tricks in my bag. Haven't you heard I'm a sorcerer?'

The ironic twist of his mouth, half-hidden by his short Saracen beard, fascinated her. For a moment a smile flickered on her gloomy face. His slow manner of speaking affected her with something akin to fright. Whenever he spoke to her, he made shivers run up and down her spine. She was utterly stupefied.

She did not react until the two little slaves helping her dress got tangled up in the laces and hooks and buttons of the European-style dress. Their awkwardness got on her nerves, and she fastened the pins and tied the laces herself. Her movements did not escape the notice of Rescator. He tried to suppress his laughter, and ended in a coughing fit.

'Nothing can overcome the force of habit, not even all you've been through,' he said when he caught his breath again. 'Even with one foot in the grave you just couldn't be improperly dressed, could you? Ah, you Frenchwomen! Now, take a look at these jewels.'

He had bent over a casket a page brought him and extracted a magnificent necklace of three strands of lapis lazuli, which he put around her neck himself. When he lifted her hair to fasten the clasp, she felt his fingers pause on the scars the horrible cat had made on her back. But her new master said nothing, just helped her put on the earrings.

Behind the wall of janizaries guarding them, the din was increasing. The musicians had just arrived and with them the dancing girls. Trays piled with fruits and sweetmeats appeared.

'Are you hungry?' asked Rescator. 'Would you like some halva? It's a dessert made of nuts. Are you familiar with Persian nougat?'

She said nothing.

'I know what you want. For the moment not all the sweets and delights in the world can tempt you. You want to cry.'

Angélique's lips quivered, and her throat tightened.

'No,' he said, 'not here. When you are alone with me you may weep as much as you like, but not here, in front of these infidels. You are not a slave. You are the descendant of a Crusader, for heaven's sake! Look at me.'

His flaming eyes pierced hers so keenly she had to draw back.

'That's better. Now take a look at yourself in the mirror. You are a queen tonight – the Queen of the Mediterranean. Give me your hand.'

In her regal gown, her hand on Rescator's, Angélique descended the steps of the infamous auction block. Everyone bowed as they passed.

Rescator seated himself beside the Grand Sultan's representative and made Angélique sit at his right. The dancing girls were waving their long gossamer veils to the rhythmical music of tambourines and guitars.

'Let's have some of that good Candia coffee,' suggested Rescator, handing her a tiny porcelain cup from the tray on the low table before them. 'Nothing is better for cheering up a sorrowful heart. Just sniff its delicate fragrance, Madame.'

She took the cup he offered her and sipped at it. She had learned to like this coffee on board the *Hermes* and welcomed its biting flavour.

The pirate kept watching her through the slits in his mask. It was not an ordinary mask, stopping at the bridge of the nose and barely concealing the cheeks, but reached like a helmet as far as his lips. Its nose was fully modelled, and there were two holes where the nostrils would be. Angélique could not help thinking that the mask concealed a loathsome face. How as a woman could she endure this black velvet face bending over her, knowing it covered frightful mutilations? She shuddered.

'Yes?' said the pirate, as if he had noticed her reaction. 'Tell me what you're thinking.'

'I thought you had had your tongue cut out.'

Rescator threw back his head and roared with laughter. 'Well,' he said, 'at last I know what your voice sounds like, only to learn that you don't think me disgraced enough. Ah, my enemies will never fail to add one more to the score. If I were one-armed and hunchbacked, they'd like it all the better. And dead, too, if possible! As far as I am concerned, it's quite enough to be as covered with scars as an old oak that's withstood the winds and the lightning for a hundred years. But, thank God, I still have enough tongue left to talk to women. I admit it would be a hardship for me not to be able at least to make use of the resources of language to allure those delectable creatures, the jewels of the whole creation.'

He was leaning toward her, talking as if they were alone. She could feel on her neck the warmth of his glances.

'Say something more, Madame. You have a ravishing voice. I know that's not true in my case. My voice cracked one day when I was calling to someone far away. That ruined it.'

'Whom were you calling?' she asked in spite of herself.

He pointed to the ceiling where the smoke of the incense had gathered into clouds. 'Allah. Allah in His Paradise. It's quite far away. My voice broke, but only after it reached Him. Allah heard me and granted what I besought of Him – my life.'

She thought he was making fun of her, and felt a little mortified. But the coffee was restoring her spirits. She even condescended to nibble daintily at a cake.

'At my house,' he remarked, 'I could offer you dishes from all over the world. I've brought home from every country I've visited a man skilled in the arts of his native land. I can give my guests anything they want to make them feel at home.'

'Are there . . . cats in your house?'

The pirate seemed astonished. Then he got her meaning and gave d'Escrainville a murderous look.

'No, in my house there are no cats – nothing that could frighten you or displease you. There are roses . . . lamps . . . windows opening on the sea. Come, let's get out of this chilly atmosphere which doesn't suit you at all. My good friend d'Escrainville must have had a lot of trouble subduing you into licking the boots of a master.'

Angélique leaped up and threw him a stormy look. He laughed again, coughed, and finally was able to speak: 'There! That's just what I was waiting for. You have become the proud Marquise again, the great lady of France, arrogant and fascinating.'

'If only I could become her again!' she muttered. 'I don't think the Mediterranean gives up its prey easily.'

'It's true, the Mediterranean strips people of all their sham disguises. It shatters illusions, but repays with pure gold those who have had the strength to confront it and challenge its delusions.'

How had he guessed she was dreaming less of France than of the impossibility of returning to the bright lights of Versailles as the victorious woman who had ruled over everyone there a few months ago? It all seemed very far away to her, unreal, as if the magic of the Orient had caused it to fade.

Suddenly it was she who sought the enigmatic eyes of the pirate to find an answer there. She kept asking herself what was the power of this man who in such a few words had taken possession of her soul. For days she had been existing as a broken, hunted, humiliated creature. Now Rescator had raised her from the depths of that whirlpool. Like a plant drinking in cool water, she revived and abandoned her humble attitude. She stood straight, and her eyes retrieved their sparkle of thoughtful serenity.

'Proud creature,' he said softly, 'that's the way I like you.'

She looked at him as if she were praying to a god for her life, yet she had no notion that in her eyes was the same hungry look reserved for those who have everything within their power to bestow.

As Rescator returned her gaze, she felt his strength calming her stormy breast. Vanished were the turbaned heads, and sooty faces of the buccaneers under their silk kerchiefs; fading was the cacophony of voices and music. She was alone in an enchanted circle, beside a man devoting his entire attention to her. She inhaled the oriental perfume with which his clothes were steeped, a fragrance that recalled to her the scent of the islands. It mingled with the leathery odour of his mask, the tobacco in his long pipe, the steaming coffee with which their cups were incessantly being filled. A sudden languor, a towering fatigue, overcame her. She sighed deeply and closed her eyes.

'You are tired,' he said. 'You shall sleep in my palace outside the city. You shall recline on the terrace under the stars, but my Arab doctor shall give you a relaxing draught of herbs, and then you will slumber on for as long as you wish. The swish of the sea and the harp-songs of my page will lull you. Does the prospect please you? What do you think of it?'

'I think,' she murmured, 'that you will not be a hard master.'

A spark of merriment danced in the corsair's eyes. 'Perhaps I may become one some day. Your beauty is not long to be withstood. But it shall not be without your consent, I promise. Tonight I shall ask only one thing, priceless to me – a smile from you. I want to be sure you are no longer sad and frightened. Smile at me.'

Angélique's lips parted. Her eyes filled with light.

Suddenly an unearthly bellowing rose above the other noises, and like a red apparition the Marquis d'Escrainville staggered out of the now dense smoke in the room. He was waving his naked sword in the air, and no one dared come near him.

'Now you have her,' he railed. 'It is to you she is showing her face of love, you cursed sorcerer. Not to me. I am only the Terror, not the Sorcerer of the Mediterranean. You hear, you people there, the Terror, not the Sorcerer. But that shall not endure. I am going to kill you.'

He plunged the sword before him. With a kick Rescator sent the tray flying between his legs and the heavy silver samovar after it.

Then while d'Escrainville was off balance, Rescator leaped up, drawing his own sword. The two weapons clashed. D'Escrainville fought with the fury of the demented. They slashed their way through the cushions and the trays right up to the auction block. The Marquis, his back to the wall, had to leap up on it. The dancing girls fled with sharp screams.

It was a fight to the death, red shape against black. Each knew his weapon well. The Maltese lackeys dared not interfere to restore order in the hall they policed. Rescator had tipped each of them twenty sequins apiece and a plug of American tobacco. Consequently there was a solemn silence as everyone present awaited the outcome of the duel.

Finally Rescator wounded the wrist of his mad opponent, forcing him to drop his sword. D'Escrainville was foaming at the mouth. Erivan bravely got his arms around his waist and dragged him away to deliver him to Coriano.

'Pity,' was all Rescator said as he sheathed his weapon.

Had it not been for the intervention of Erivan, the body of the Marquis d'Escrainville would certainly have been offered as a sacrifice for all the victims he had sold at that very spot.

Rescator raised his hands. 'The party is over,' he shouted.

He bowed to right and to left, paying compliments in Turkish, Italian and Spanish. The guests drifted out of the room in a flurry of conventionally polite leave-takings.

Rescator returned to Angélique. Once more he bowed so low as to brush the floor with the black plume of his hat.

'Will you follow me, Madame?'

At that moment she would have followed him to the ends of the earth. She could not even recognise the garden, which a short time ago she had traversed in agony of soul.

The pirate put his elegant cloak about her shoulders. 'The night is cool. But how fragrant!'

In the square before the building a whole ox was being roasted over a huge brazier. The satisfied faces of the crew and the local population gleamed in the light of the coals. From the alleys of Candia rose the songs of the freebooters in praise of the wine. As soon as Rescator came into sight he was cheered lustily.

A long-tailed blue rocket shot up from behind a roof top and blossomed out into shooting rays.

'Look, fireworks!'

Rescator was the first to detect the imminence of something untoward. He parted from Angélique and ran toward the ramparts that towered above the city. The sky was one big rosy glow.

A moving light coming from deep in the town played on the stupefied black faces of the janizaries. They, too, dashed to the ramparts. Bells began to toll. A cry echoed throughout the streets in many different tongues: 'Fire!'

Angélique was shoved aside by the rushing crowd. She had to crawl over the cobblestones until she came to the refuge of a doorway. Suddenly a hand closed over hers.

'Come on! Come on!'

She was looking into the cunning face of Vassos Mikoles. She remembered Savary's words: 'When you come out of the batistan, a blue rocket will be the signal . . .'

She had besought him to rescue her from her purchaser and restore her freedom, and he had kept his promise. But now she was as if turned to stone. Her heart was like ice, and she was totally unable to move a muscle. The little Greek kept insisting: 'Come on! Come on!'

Finally she forced herself to follow him. They ran through the narrow streets to the harbour, caught up in the surging tide of the populace. Commotion there had made its masterpiece. Even the cats, their hair on end, were yowling and leaping from the railings of the balconies like demons with outspread claws. From every mouth came the cry: 'The ships!'

When Angélique and Vassos Mikoles arrived at the waterfront near the Crusaders' Tower, she understood what it meant. The Marquis d'Escrainville's brigantine was flaming like a torch. Already only its burning ribs were left. Brands were falling like rain on the other ships at anchor. The renegade Dane's galley was blazing. Other fires were breaking out, fanned by the breeze, and in the Dantesque light Angélique glimpsed Rescator's xebec. Fire had broken out on its prow, and the crew left aboard were already defeated in their attempts to extinguish it and were retreating before the clouds of suffocating smoke.

'Savary!'

'I have been waiting for you,' Savary said reproachfully. 'You're not looking in the right direction, Madame. Look over there!'

In the shadows of the Crusaders' gate, which its watchman had deserted to run to the fire, he pointed out a bark hoisting its sails to leave. It was almost completely lost in the darkness and only sudden flashes of red light from the fire revealed the tense faces of the fugitive slaves huddled on its decks, and of the sailors trying to get under way. It was the boat of Vassos Mikoles and his uncles.

'Come quickly!'

'But this fire, Savary . . .'

'It's Greek Fire,' the little old scholar shouted, jumping up and down in excitement. 'I have lit at last the inextinguishable fire. Let them just try to put it out. It's the ancient secret of Byzantium. *And I am the one who has rediscovered it!*'

He was dancing with joy like a gnome escaped from hell. Vassos Mikoles hustled him aboard.

Angélique stepped aboard the bark as it moved away from shore. The fishermen were trying to stay in the shadowy region of the promontory, but the gleams of the fire, spreading remorselessly, picked them up no matter where they went. Standing on the poop, Savary was feasting his eyes on the flaming harbour where the populace was swarming like ants in a crushed anthill.

'I stuffed tow into the vulnerable spots in the galleys' hulls,' he explained to her. 'All during the voyage among the islands I went down into the holds every day and got everything ready. Then tonight I sprinkled essence of maumie inside and out. It made them a thousand times more inflammable. The fire spread like a hurricane. . . .'

Beside him, Angélique was so thrilled she could not utter a sound. Savary fell silent. He raised his ancient telescope to his eyes.

'What is he doing? He's crazy, that man!'

They picked out the shape of Rescator on the blazing poop of the *Sea Eagle.* His Moorish sailors had cut the hawsers and the xebec was drifting away from the heart of the fire but was aflame itself. The flames on its decks rose higher and denser. The bowsprit fell off. Then there was a deafening explosion.

'The powder magazine,' muttered Angélique.

'No.'

Still jubilantly dancing, Savary stepped on her feet with his heavy shoes. Vassos Mikoles tried in vain to persuade his father to calm down.

'That white cloud on the level of the water,' shouted Savary. 'What is it? *What is it?*'

A heavy yellow mass was issuing from the bowels of the vessel and drifting over the surface of the water. Presently it had enveloped the ship almost up to the peak of the masts. It blotted out the glow of the fire, and the xebec disappeared in this cocoon of smoke.

The port, still lit by the flames, was dwindling in the distance, as the Greeks rowed at top speed. Soon they hoisted the lateen sail, and the bark of the fugitives fairly leaped over the waves.

Savary set down his telescope. 'What happened? It looked as if that man put out the fire on his ship by magic.'

As he brooded over the mystery, his son took advantage of the old man's abstraction to disappear discreetly into the interior of the boat. For other reasons, Angélique shared the same impression of unreality.

Candia was now hardly visible except for a red glow still reflected in the water. She suddenly noticed Rescator's cloak still about her shoulder. An unaccountable sadness overwhelmed her and, putting her face in her hands, she groaned deeply.

The woman beside her touched her arm. 'What's the matter with you? Aren't you glad to be free?' She spoke in Greek, but Angélique got her meaning.

'I don't know,' she said with a sob. 'I don't know. Oh, I don't know.'

Then came the storm.

CHAPTER FIFTEEN

The storm which had lasted for two long and terrible days subsided only on the morning of the third, but still the boat pitched and rocked, its mast gone and its tiller shivered into splinters. By some miracle all the passengers had been preserved, but as the first clear dawn appeared, they searched the surface of the water for a boat to hail in their distress. The sea was deserted. Not till evening did a Maltese ship appear on the horizon and answer their signals for help.

It was one of the war galleys of the Knights of Malta. The tempest-tossed Greeks were hoisted aboard it, wrapped in blankets, given something to eat, and warmed up with good Asti wine. A little later Angélique was introduced to the captain, a German Knight of about fifty, Baron Wolf von Nessenood, a big blond, slightly grey at the temples, three pale wrinkles seaming his deeply tanned forehead. His reputation as a sailor and a man of war was considerable.

His lieutenant, a French Knight of about thirty, was named de Roguier – an innocent-looking youngster, on whom Angélique seemed to make quite an impression. She informed them of her titles and honours, and recited the saga of her trials and tribulations.

When they docked at Valetta, she was offered the hospitality of a Knight named de Rochebrune, who received her as a distinguished guest. He was a delightful old gentleman who still maintained in Malta all the customs and procedures to which his life at Court had accustomed him. The establishment he modestly called an inn was actually one of eight splendid palaces he maintained as a kind of warehouse, each one representing one of the eight points of the emblem of the Order of Malta, and each consecrated to the national character of the other regions where the Order maintained hospices: Provence, Auvergne, France, Italy, Aragon, Castile, Germany and England, though the last had been suppressed during the Reformation.

She was treated so luxuriously and deferentially that she was in no hurry to leave, for at least in Malta she was under the protection of Christianity's last bastion in the Mediterranean. The city of Valetta was handsome, built of marble pitted by the salt air. It rose like a shaft of gold against the purplish blue of the sky and the sea – a monumental pile of bell towers, domes, palaces perched on the rocky cliffs, battlements studded with cannons reaching from the crest of the island down to the harbour, which itself was a natural defence. Causeways reached like the arms of a giant octopus from the actual port to many little islands, each one heavily fortified.

At this 'inn' of the Comte de Rochebrune, her countryman and an old acquaintance from her days at Versailles, she learned that the Duc de Vivonne had been searching for her everywhere. The French squadron had put in at Valetta for two weeks, during which stay they had had plenty of time for lengthy post-mortems on the depredations of the pirates.

The news that the *Royale* had been wrecked on the shores of Sardinia almost gave Vivonne a breakdown. In so far as he was the King's Admiral, the loss was blow enough to him; but in so far as he was in love with Angélique – as he truly believed himself to be – he was inconsolable at the thought of the horrible fate she must have encountered. First the son, then the mother . . . he had brought nothing but disaster. No one could rally him until he got a message from Lieutenant Millerand, still a prisoner of Baron Paolo Visconti, asking for the trifling sum of a thousand piastres to ransom him from the Genoese brigand. The message confirmed the loss of the *Royale* to the scavengers, and also gave some information about the Marquise du Plessis, who, he said, was safe and sound, had given her captor the slip and had doubtless by now reached Crete on a Provençal sailing-boat.

Immediately the Duc de Vivonne recovered from his depression and once his galleys had been re-fitted in the harbour of Valetta, he set out on his own for Crete, hoping to find the lovely Marquise, who, only a few days after his departure, herself set foot on Malta in the black cloak of Rescator, now salt-stained and faded.

Angélique had to smile at this weird game of hide and seek. Vivonne, the galley-slaves, the apparition of Nicholas like one risen from the dead, his demise – all that seemed now so far away. Could she really have been through all that? Life was moving so fast for her. And now even more terrible and much more recent experiences had left their mark on her.

A week after her arrival in Malta, while strolling through the city, she happened on Don José de Almada. He and his companion, the Bailiff de la Marche, had also just landed on the island.

Twice shipwrecked and thrice a fugitive, Angélique was now too accustomed to untoward vicissitudes even to blush at meeting a man who had seen her naked on the auction block of a slave-mart. And the Slave Commissioner was too sophisticated to indulge in any ill-timed embarrassment. They greeted each other with equal delight, and immediately were recounting their mutual adventures like two old friends. In fact, the austere Spaniard relaxed his formal manner in the quite sincere joy he manifested at seeing her still alive and out of the pirates' clutches.

'I hope, Madame,' he said, 'you aren't too angry with us for abandoning you to the crazy greed and egoism of the bidders at the batistan in Candia. There has never been an auction like that one, and there never will be another. It was absolutely insane. I went just as far as I possibly could.'

Angélique said she appreciated his efforts on her behalf, and that just as soon as she had got free she had remembered his intervention with gratitude.

'God keep you from falling into Rescator's hands again!' sighed the Bailiff de la Marche. 'You are responsible for the most crushing blow of his entire career. Fire or not, to have lost on the same night he acquired her, a slave for whom he had paid the staggering sum of thirty-five thousand piastres . . . That was quite a trick you played on him, Madame. Just be careful!'

They told her what had happened that fearful night in Candia. The fire had spread to the old wooden houses in the Turkish quarter, which flared up like torches. In the harbour itself many ships had been burned to the water's edge, or had been seriously damaged. The Marquis d'Escrainville had had an epileptic fit as he saw the *Hermes* disappear before his very eyes in a geyser of steam and spray. On the other hand, Rescator had succeeded in saving his xebec by putting out the fire on it by some mysterious means.

Thereafter Savary spent all his time at the Hospice of Auvergne or the Hospice of Castile to extract from the two Knights the most infinitesimal details possible of the whole affair. How did Rescator get the fire under control? What means did he use? How long did it take him? Don José had no idea. The Bailiff, however, had heard of some Arab fluid which turned into vapour on contact with heat. Everyone knew the Arabs were highly skilled in some strange science called chemistry. After saving his own ship, Rescator had helped put out the fires on other boats, but the losses were only slightly diminished by his efforts, as the fire had spread with incredible speed.

'I'm not surprised,' cackled Savary, his eyes lighting up behind his spectacles. 'Greek Fire . . .'

He talked so much that he aroused the suspicions of the two Knights. 'Could you have been one of the slaves who engineered that terrible catastrophe? We lost one of our galleys . . .'

Savary prudently excused himself and left. He went to Angélique with his problems. Where should he go from here? Should he return to Paris and write a paper for the Academy of Sciences on his sensational experiments with maumie? Or should he go in search of Rescator and learn the secret of his fire-extinguisher? Or should he continue his voyages, so perilous and so dependent on the twists of fate, to get a new supply of maumie from its source in Persia? He was like a soul in torment now that he no longer had his precious phial of maumie to take care of and carry with him.

And then, what about Madame du Plessis-Bellière herself? Where was she heading? She did not know. But a voice kept whispering to her inner ear: 'Return to the fold. Ask the King's forgiveness and entreat his mercy. Then . . .' But she balked at that solution, and in spite of herself gazed out on the sea with a new hope.

The sun was sinking, and from the towers of the city's hundreds of churches bells were pealing the Angelus. Angélique shut the window. In that sonorous salute to the Blessed Virgin, she couldn't hear herself think.

Rescator's cloak was lying on her bed. Regardless of how stained it was, she had not wanted to lose it, for she thought of it as a kind of trophy. She stretched out on the bed and buried her face in the folds of the velvet mantle. The sea wind and the spray had not washed out its heady perfume. One whiff of it brought back to her that imperious black figure looming above her. She heard again his deep, hoarse voice, and she began to experience once more that strange hour in Candia amid the dreamlike clouds of incense and tobacco smoke, the aroma of coffee, the tinkling of the guitars. And from out of the slits in a black velvet mask two burning eyes were watching her every move.

She groaned, and clutched the frayed garment to her, rolling her head from side to side, haunted by a feeling of loss she could not name or describe.

The dinning of the bells was gradually diminishing. Only one or two were sounding now, like a bass obbligato to the melody of the chimes. Angélique became conscious of a knocking at the door which apparently had been going on for some time, drowned by the booming of the church bells.

'Come in,' she called, getting to her feet.

A page in a black chasuble appeared in the doorway. 'Madame, excuse me for interrupting your rest, but there's an Arab downstairs asking for you. He says his name is Mohammed Raki, here on behalf of your husband.'

The moment his words fully penetrated her consciousness Angélique began to move like an automaton. Without a word she crossed the room, glided like a ghost down the long marble staircase, crossed the entrance hall. Under the Venetian pillars stood a man with the light complexion of the Berber race, dressed like a medieval French peasant and wearing a sparse beard. He bowed low as she watched him, her hands clasped and her eyes eager.

'Your name is Mohammed Raki?'

'At your service, Madame.'

'Do you understand French?'

'I learned it from a French nobleman whose servant I was for a long time.'

'Comte Joffrey de Peyrac?'

A smile stole over the Arab's lips. He said he had never met a man with a strange name like that.

'Well, then . . .'

Mohammed Raki held up his hand to silence her. The man he had served was named Jafar el Khaldun.

'That's his name in Arabic,' he said. 'I always knew he was of high lineage, but I did not learn his title, for he never told a soul. When he sent me to Marseilles four years ago to meet a Lazarist Father and commission him to search for a certain Madame de Peyrac, I was careful to forget that name to oblige the man who was far more of a friend to me than an employer.'

Angélique heaved a great sigh. Her knees were shaking. She motioned to the Arab to follow her into the salon, where she sank on to one of its many divans. The man squatted before her humbly.

'Tell me about him,' Angélique gasped.

Mohammed Raki closed his eyes and began to speak in a slow monotone as if he were reciting a lesson.

'He was a large man and thin, rather like a Spaniard in appearance. His face was so scarred as to be terrifying. On his left cheek the scars went like this.' He traced a V on his cheek. 'Another scar ran from his temple across his eye. Allah must have preserved him from being blinded and reserved a glorious destiny for him. His hair was black and as thick as the mane of a Nubian lion. His black eyes could pierce right through you like a bird of prey's. He was strong and agile. He was a magnificent swordsman and could tame even the wildest horses, but greater still was his knowledge and the acuteness of his mind, with which he greatly impressed the professors at Fez, the greatest university of Islam.'

Angélique felt the warm blood return to her veins. 'Did my husband forsake his Christian faith?' she asked fearfully, though in the same breath she wondered what possible difference it could make to her.

Mohammed Raki shook his head. 'It is not often,' he said, 'that a Christian can take up residence in Morocco without subscribing to our beliefs. But Jafar el Khaldun came to Morocco, not as a slave but as the friend of our deeply venerated hermit-saint Abd el Mekhrat, with whom he had corresponded for years about their researches in alchemy, to which each was equally consecrated. Abd el Mekhrat took him under his wing and forbade anyone to touch a hair of his head. Together they went into the Sudan to search for gold, and that was when I joined the Frenchman's employ. The two were working for a son of the King of Tafilalet.' The man stopped, scowling as if he were trying to recall some important detail. 'A loyal Negro accompanied him everywhere, who answered to the name of Kouassi-Ba.'

Angélique covered her face with her hands. Even more than the extremely accurate description of her husband, the Arab's mention of the name of the faithful Kouassi-Ba removed the last veil between them and revealed the blinding truth to her. Now the road she had followed with so much despair and sorrow shone clearly before her. She had reached its gate. The return of her husband to life was accomplished, and what had hitherto been only a fleeting vision now stood before her in a human form she would soon be able to press to her heart.

'Where is he?' she entreated. 'When will he come to me? Why didn't you bring him with you?'

The Arab smiled indulgently at her impatience. It had been two years since he left the employ of Jafar el Khaldun, when he himself had taken a wife and started a small business of his own. But he often had news of his former employer, who travelled a great deal, and who had settled at Bône, a city on the coast of Africa, where he was continuing to devote himself to scientific inquiries.

'Then all I have to do is go to Bône,' said Angélique.

'That's all, Madame. Unless something has called your husband away on a short trip, you will have little trouble in finding him, for anyone at all can tell you where he lives. He is famous throughout all Barbary.'

She almost sank to her knees to thank God, but the sound of a stick made her raise her eyes. There stood Savary, tapping the mosaics with the tip of his huge umbrella.

On seeing him Mohammed Raki rose and bowed, saying how pleased he was to meet the distinguished gentleman his uncle had told him about.

'My husband is alive!' said Angélique in a voice fraught with emotion. 'He has just assured me. My husband is at Bône, and I am going to join him there.'

The old apothecary examined the man sagaciously over the top of his spectacles. 'Well, well,' he said. 'I did not know Ali Mektub's nephew was a Berber.'

Mohammed Raki seemed both astonished and delighted at his perceptiveness. As a matter of fact, he told them, his mother, Ali Mektub's sister, was an Arab, but his father, whom he resembled, was a Berber from the mountains of Dabilia.

'How does it happen your uncle did not come with you?' asked Savary.

'We were on our way to Candia when a ship we hailed told us a Frenchwoman had escaped and was now in Malta. My uncle went to Candia, for he was in haste to see to his business, but I transferred to the other ship to retrace my steps here.' He looked at Savary half-triumphantly, half-ironically. 'News travels fast in the Mediterranean, sir.'

Then from the folds of his robe he drew a leather pouch and took out of it the letter Angélique had written from prison. 'Isn't this the note you gave my uncle?'

Savary adjusted his spectacles to read it. 'It certainly is. Why didn't this reach its destination?'

Mohammed Raki's face took on a pained expression. In a whining chant he complained of Savary's apparent lack of faith in him. Didn't the honourable gentleman know that Bône was a Spanish settlement in the hands of the Christians, and that two poor Moors, sons of the Prophet, couldn't enter this city of the most fanatical Catholics in the world without risking their lives?

'You got to Malta though,' Savary remarked.

The Arab patiently explained that in the first place Malta was not Spanish, and that, next, he had seized the chance of slipping in in the guise of a servant of Prince Ahmet Sidi, who was going to Malta to negotiate the ransom of Prince Lai Loum, the brother of the King of Aden, recently captured by the Knights.

Savary accepted the explanation. 'Isn't it my duty,' he said to Angélique, 'to be suspicious?' Then he pointed to the Berber. 'What proof do you have that you are Mohammed Raki, former servant of the man we are looking for?'

The man's face darkened again, and he closed his eyes in indignation. Then he relaxed. 'My master loved me,' he said. 'He gave me a token.'

From the same leather pouch he extracted a precious stone set in silver. Angélique recognised it at once – the topaz!

It was not a jewel of great price, but Joffrey de Peyrac attached high value to it because it had been in his family for so many generations. He liked to call it his good-luck stone. She had seen him wear it at the end of a silver chain over his velvet doublet. Later he had shown it to Father Antoine in Marseilles as a token of identity.

She took the jewel from the hands of the Moor and, closing her eyes, touched her lips to it ecstatically.

Savary watched her in silence. 'What are you planning to do?' he said.

'Try to get to Bône, whatever the cost.'

It was no easy thing to convince the Knights of Malta to take the young Marquise on board one of their galleys and land her at Bône. The Comte de Rochebrune, the Bailiff de la Marche, de Roguier and even Don José de Almada all tried to dissuade her from such a mad undertaking. A Christian woman, they said, could not possibly land in Barbary without risking untold dangers. A woman there was no more than a slave assigned to the most menial duties, or at best an odalisque imprisoned in a harem. Only Jewesses could move freely, and yet they were forbidden to go outside the ghetto.

'But I am going to go to Bône,' she insisted. 'It's a Catholic settlement.'

'Worse still,' they said. In settlements like these on the coast of Africa, the Spaniards had burrowed in like ticks to irritate the Berber lions.

What would she, a great lady of France, do among these petty merchants protected by an Andalusian garrison as ferocious as the Moors themselves? What could she possibly find in this lonely spot, one of the most godforsaken on the whole earth? Did she want to get into worse trouble than that she had just so luckily escaped?

Finally Angélique went to the Grand Master of the Order himself, Prince Nicholas Cotoner, a Frenchman of English origin and of high lineage. She spoke to him freely about her tragic love, and how after ten years she had finally learned for a fact that her husband still lived.

The Grand Master listened to her attentively. After she had finished, he remained silent a long time, then sighed. Many things in her story seemed unlikely to him, especially the fact that a noble Christian lord like her husband could have settled in such a wretched spot as Bône.

'You say he used to travel unscathed through these regions?'

'That's what I've been told.'

'Then he must be a renegade. He probably lives like a Moslem with a harem of fifty wives. Finding him will only bring your soul – not to mention your life – into peril.'

'I don't know whether he is poor or a renegade,' she said, her heart breaking. 'I know only this, that he is my husband before God and I am going to find him again.'

The Grand Master's face softened. 'Happy the man to inspire such devotion!' Then he hesitated again. 'Ah, my child, your youth and your beauty distress me. What might not befall you here in the Mediterranean, once a Christian lake, but now delivered into the hands of Islam? What grief it has caused us Knights of Jerusalem to see our forces everywhere retreating! Now we have to recapture not only the holy places, but Constantinople, the ancient Byzantium, where Christianity first found root under the domes of Santa Sophia, now a mosque.' He fell silent, deep in his mystical visions.

Angélique interrupted his reverie. 'I know why you don't want to let me go. It is because you have not got the money for my ransom yet.'

The old prelate's face lit up with amusement. 'I admit I would have liked that excuse for preventing you from committing a folly, but as a matter of fact I have just learned from our bankers in Leghorn that the sum agreed upon has been forwarded by your manager to our Prior in Paris.' His eyes were gleaming. 'Well, Madame, I confess that a human being who has won her freedom can use it to destroy herself if that seems the thing for her to do. Within a week Baron von Nessenood's galley should take to sea again for a crusade against the Barbary Coast. I give you permission to go on it.'

Yet even when Angélique's face beamed with joy, he refused to soften. Frowning and pointing his Cardinal's ring at her, he intoned: 'Remember my warnings. The Berbers are unbelievably cruel. The Turkish pashas themselves are afraid of them, for these pirates accuse them of being only lukewarm in matters of religion. If your husband is friendly with them, it is only because he has become one of them. Better for your salvation that you stay on the side of the Cross, Madame.' Then, seeing that she did not flinch, he added in a gentler voice, 'Kneel, my child, and let me give you my blessing.'

The galley was under way, leaving the amber-coloured ramparts of Malta astern. Baron von Nessenood paced the deck like a self-confident admiral. In the cabin below, two French coral merchants were talking with a pompous Dutch banker and a young Spanish student going to meet his father, an officer in the garrison at Bône. With Angélique and Savary these were the only civilians on board. Naturally, sooner or later, the talk came round to their chances of escaping the Barbary pirates during the voyage.

The galley was more spacious than the royal French one. There was a pleasant retreat under the awning of the tabernacle, where the passengers could take their ease on rustic benches.

Angélique was sick with impatience and, though she could not tell why, with apprehension. This was not at all like her dream. If she had not seen the topaz she would have doubted the messenger who brought it to her. There was something tricky in his eyes. She had been unsuccessful in getting any more details out of him; he had merely spread his hands with a strange smile, as if to say: 'I have told you all I know.'

Desgrez's dire predictions returned to her mind. How would Joffrey de Peyrac receive her after all these years? Years that had branded their flesh and their hearts. Each had known other conflicts, other guests . . . other loves, too. It would be hard for them to meet again.

Now there was a strand or two of grey in her golden hair, but she was still in the first flush of youth, even more lovely than at the time of her first marriage, when her features had not been long enough formed to be truly interesting and her figure had not achieved its full flowering, or her walk the queenly grace that made her so impressive now. All this change had taken place far from the eyes of Joffrey de Peyrac and his influence. The brutal hand of fate had moulded her apart from him.

And what of him? Outraged, harassed with numberless misfortunes, stripped of his wealth, uprooted from his world, had he preserved the nature she had loved so dearly?

'I am afraid. . . .' she murmured to herself.

She was afraid that the transcendent moment when she laid eyes upon him again might be spoiled by some sordid note. Desgrez had warned her of that possibility. But she had never been able to persuade herself that Joffrey de Peyrac could ever decay.

The doubts that beset her almost crippled her. Like a child she kept saying over and over again to herself that she wanted to see 'him' again, her love, her lover of the Palace of Gay Learning, not another, a stranger in a foreign land such as he might have become. She yearned to hear his ravishing voice again. Still, Mohammed Raki had said nothing about that voice. Could one still sing in Barbary? Under that remorseless sun? Among dark-skinned people as ready to chop off one's head as to mow down a field of weeds? Oh, what could have happened to him. . . . ?

She tried desperately to recreate her memories of the past, to visualise once more the presence of the Comte de Toulouse under the arches of the Palace of Gay Learning. But the vision fled from her. Then she wanted to sleep, for slumber would dispel the mists that hid her from her love. Drowsiness was stealing over her, and she could hear a voice murmuring low in her ear: 'You are tired. . . . You shall sleep at my house . . . there are roses . . . lamps . . . windows opening on the sea . . .'

She awoke with a shriek. Savary was bending over her, shaking her.

'Madame du Plessis, you must wake up. You are going to disturb the whole galley.'

Angélique raised herself on her couch and leaned against the woodwork. Night had fallen. The perpetual grunts of the galley-slaves no longer throbbed through the ship, for the galley was under sail alone, and the 120-foot oars had been shipped. In the unnatural silence the only sound was the tread of Baron von Nessenood as he paced the deck. The beacon in the stern had been dimmed so as not to attract the attention of such pirates as were undoubtedly lurking in this channel between Malta and Sicily to starboard and the Barbary Coast of Tunis to port.

Angélique sighed. 'A sorcerer was pursuing me in my dream.'

'If only it remains a dream!' said Savary.

'What do you mean? What are you thinking?'

'I think a pirate as bold as Rescator won't let you elude him without trying to get back what belongs to him.'

'I don't belong to him,' said Angélique in revulsion.

'He paid as much as the cost of a ship for you.'

'From now on my husband will protect me,' she said, though in a slightly dubious tone.

Savary remained silent.

'Maître Savary,' whispered Angélique, 'do you think this could be a trap? I know you were suspicious of Mohammed Raki, yet he had indisputable credentials, didn't he?'

'He did.'

'He surely must have seen his uncle Ali Mektub, since he had my letter. And he has seen my husband. He gave me details I alone could know and which I hardly remembered, but they came back to me at once. Unless . . . Oh, Savary, do you think I may be the victim of some magic spell, the dupe of images projected on some distant screen making me believe that what I want most in the world is only a mirage, the better to lead me into a trap? Oh, Savary, I'm so afraid. . . .'

'Such things can happen,' said the apothecary, 'but I don't think that is the case now. It is something else. A trap, perhaps, but not a magic one. Mohammed Raki was not telling us the whole truth. Wait till we come to the end. Then we shall see.' He had been dissolving a pellet in a pewter cup. 'Take this draught. You will rest better.'

'Is it some more of your maumie?'

'You know very well I have no more maumie,' Savary said mournfully. 'I used it all up in the fire at Candia.'

'Savary, why do you insist on accompanying me on this voyage you do not approve of?'

'How could I leave you?' he answered as if he were reflecting on a difficult scientific problem. 'It's true, I don't approve of it, but I will go to Algiers.'

'To Bône?'

'It's the same thing.'

'Christians are less in danger there than in Algiers.'

'Who can say?' said Savary, shaking his head like a seer in the presence of visions.

Suddenly the night sky was rent by a weird gleaming streak that changed colours several times and ended in a burst of variegated lights.

'A rocket!'

The ship sprang from torpor into confusion. Seamen and marines ran hither and yon calling out to one another. Angélique clung to Savary. The sight recalled to her the opening of the battle between the royal galley and Rescator's xebec.

'Savary, do you think we may encounter that pirate again?'

'Madame, you talk as if I were a military strategist with the supernatural power of being on a Maltese galley and a xebec at the same time. A Turkish rocket doesn't mean Rescator alone. It can mean an Algerian lookout just as well, or a Tunisian or Moroccan.'

'But it looked as if it came from this very ship.'

'Then there is a traitor on board!'

Without waking the other passengers they went on deck. The galley seemed to be pursuing a zigzag course, doubtless in an attempt to throw the enemy off its tracks. Angélique heard the voice of de Roguier as he returned from the prow with the German Knight.

'Brother, the time has come for us to don our armour.'

'No, not yet, brother.'

'Have you searched for the traitor who set off that rocket from our decks?' she asked them.

'Yes, but without success. He'll have to be punished later. Look over there!'

Far beyond the prow she could discern a string of lights. She won-dered whether it was the coast of the mainland or merely an island. The lights seemed to shift and sway, approaching first in a straight line, then in an arc.

'An ambush! Alarm!' thundered the Baron von Nessenood.

Everyone ran to his post and began to erect the six-foot-high palisade used in attacking a ship higher than theirs.

Angélique counted thirty lights moving over the water. 'The Berbers!' she said softly.

De Roguier heard her as he passed. 'Yes, but do not be alarmed. It's only a fleet of little vessels which certainly won't dare attack us unless they have reinforcements. It may be a decoy, though. Were they lying in wait for us? The rocket seems to indicate they were. At any rate, we are not going to waste our ammunition on a skirmish when we can easily escape them. You just heard the captain say not to get into our armour. We won't do that till the moment of joining battle so that our men won't lose spirit in waiting. Baron von Nessenood is a lion in battle, but he has to have at least three galleys confronting him before he thinks it worth while to risk his men and his ship.'

In spite of the Knight's assurances that these boats were no enemy force, she could not help observing that they were gaining rapidly on the heavily loaded galley, which had set all its sails, got all three banks of oars to work, tacked about and was heading for the still wide gap in the hostile circle.

Soon the lights of the fleet faded into the distance. A little later the dark mass of a mountainous island reared quite close ahead of them.

The two Knights consulted their charts by the light of a lantern.

'It's the island of Cam,' said the German Knight. 'The passage into the cove is very narrow, but we'll get there with the grace of God. That will give us a chance to replenish our water supply and at the same time give us a refuge from the galleys of Tunis which won't be long in joining the fleet we just encountered. There are only a few fisherfolk on the island, and they won't hinder our landing. There isn't even a fort or a rifle.'

Noticing that Angélique was standing a few feet away, von Nessenood added crossly: 'Don't think, Madame, that the Knights of Malta are cowards, but I am going to get you to Bône safely, not only because I want to with all my heart but also because our Grand Master entrusted you to my care. We will deal with our antagonists on the return trip.'

She thanked them emotionally.

As the sky lightened, she could see a little beach in the cove fringed with palm and olive trees. She remained on deck, saying to herself that she dared not sleep till they reached Bône, even though she knew this made little sense.

Cautiously the galley waited at the mouth of the cove till full daylight. Baron von Nessenood kept sweeping the surroundings with his telescope as the morning mists lifted. Suddenly he turned to Henri de Roguier, and the two retired at once into the tabernacle. When they reappeared they wore red coats of mail.

'What's going on?' exclaimed Angélique.

The clear eyes of the German were like molten steel. He drew his sword, and the old war cry of the Order leaped to his lips: 'The Saracens! to arms!'

At the same moment a hail of bullets and arrows fell on the deck from the cliffs, splitting the bowsprit.

It was full daylight now, and they could see six batteries glinting in the underbrush, all pointed toward the galley. Over the roar of the cannons the Knight was shouting orders to come about and try to get out of the cove into the open sea. While the manoeuvre was being effected with considerable difficulty, marines were carrying cases of ammunition on to the deck and setting them in place. Others, armed with muskets, were answering the fire as best they could, but they could not find the range. The deck was already covered with wounded and dead. Screams rose from the slave pit, where an entire bank had been decimated by bullets.

Then a mortar on the galley aimed at one of the batteries fired. A Negro tottered and fell from the summit of the cliff into the water. A cannoneer succeeded in demolishing with shrapnel the two operators of another battery on the shore.

'More than four!' shouted de Roguier. 'Let's disarm them. When they run out of ammunition we can overpower them.'

But the summits of the cliffs were already bristling with white turbans, and the cove echoed with their terrifying cries of 'Surrender, you dogs!' Besides, the entrance to the cove was now blocked by the little boats that had chased the galley into this ambush.

At the first shot, Savary had dragged Angélique into the cabin, but she stayed at its door to watch this unequal combat. The Moslems outnumbered the Maltese five or six to one, and the artillery on the galley had been designed for combat at sea level, not to fire at a much higher target. The pirates multiplied, and in excitement at the prospect of easy victory plunged into the water to swim to the galley. Several skiffs had been launched from the shore and, as they approached the ship, disgorged a swarm of swimmers carrying lighted torches.

The best marksmen aimed at them and picked off quite a few. The water turned red with their blood. But the more killed, the more took their places and soon, in spite of the musket fire and the cannon charges, the sides of the galley were covered with this howling human tide, brandishing torches, daggers and sabres as well as firearms.

The Maltese galley resembled a huge wounded seagull beset by an army of ants. The Moors swarmed over it, yelling: 'Va Allah! Allah!'

'Long live the true faith,' answered the Baron von Nessenood, running his sword through the first half-naked Arab to set foot on the deck. But he was followed by others and still others. The two Knights and their fighting brothers had to retreat, though they kept on slashing about them right up to the base of the main mast. Bodies piled up everywhere. No one seemed to think of pillage, only of slaughtering as many as possible of their prey.

Angélique watched in horror as one of the coral merchants gripped two young Moors and wrestled with them, biting and gouging like mad dogs, for none of the three had any weapon.

The only systematic defence was taking place at the base of the mainmast, where the two Knights were fighting like lions. Before them was a semi-circular heap of slain, which had to be crossed by the reinforcements of the Moors. Then a shot from a Moslem sniper, who had taken time to draw careful aim from the prow, struck von Nessenood and felled him. Roguier glanced at his captain, but this momentary distraction cost him the hand that held his sword.

The coral merchant, having vanquished his two assailants, slid down the ladder to the cabin and pushed Angélique inside it. Savary, the other coral merchant, the banker and the young Spanish student had also taken refuge there.

'It's all over,' he said. 'The Knights have fallen. We're going to be captured. Now's the time to throw our papers overboard and get into other clothes, so our captors can't tell our status. You especially,' he said to the young Spaniard, 'pray to the Blessed Virgin they won't find out you're the son of an officer in the Bône garrison. Otherwise they'll hold you hostage, and the first Moor killed under the Spanish ramparts will mean they'll send your father your head.'

All the men, regardless of Angélique's presence, stripped off their clothes, rolled them into a bundle along with their papers, and threw them out of the porthole into the sea. Then they put on shapeless rags they found in a sea chest.

'There isn't a single dress in there,' said one of the merchants in terror. 'Madame, these robbers are going to see right away you're a lady of rank. God knows what fortune they'll want for your ransom.'

'I don't need a thing,' said Savary. 'They always begin by throwing me overboard as worthless.'

At the top of the ladder appeared an enormous Negro, his coal-black face accentuating the ivory white of his eyes as he rolled them over the occupants of the cabin and raised his scimitar on high.

A silence broken only by the groans of the wounded had succeeded the din of battle. The captives were shoved up on deck.

Four low galleys were entering the cove. On the poop of the first stood the admiral of this little fleet. He proceeded to board the Maltese ship, followed by his officers, including a clerk whose business it was to assess the value of the prize, and who pulled a long face at seeing how damaged the galley had been. He made some bitter remarks on this subject, then gave orders for a systematic census of the captives and their possessions.

The galley-slaves of Algerian origin were set free. The others were transferred to the Algerian galleys. The whole Maltese crew was laden with chains. Angélique saw Henri de Roguier pass by, covered with blood, his hands manacled; then the Baron von Nessenood carried by three giants, but also chained, in spite of the terrible wounds from which blood was streaming.

The captives were taken before the admiral, whose name was Ali Hadji. He paid no attention to their disguises, but examined their hands to see how they suited their appearance. The merchants had to confess their identity. Savary, however, threw them into fits of laughter. They set him to one side, reserved, as they said, for the hungriest dogs of Algiers.

The attention of the plunderers was immediately drawn to Angélique. The dark eyes of the Algerian officers examined her with a curiosity not unmixed with deference and even admiration. They exchanged several brief words with Ali Hadji, who then motioned her to him.

Capture by the Berbers was so common for anyone who risked a voyage that Angélique had almost expected it. She had already laid her plans and made up her mind what to do. She would not dissemble, but would stake her all on her fortune and her situation as a woman searching for her husband. The Algerians were not random pirates, attacking and pillaging for the mere joy of doing so. Their 'industry' was run along strict lines. The booty was to be shared down to the last shred of the sails, and it was all carefully catalogued for conversion into money. So far as women were concerned, especially European women, prizes rare and highly valued, avarice generally triumphed over lust. Angélique had already experienced this with the Marquis d'Escrainville. She confronted the hungry eyes of the dark-skinned men serenely.

She gave them the name she had not used for many long years. She was the wife of Joffrey de Peyrac, who was waiting for her in Bône and who certainly would pay her ransom. He had sent her as a messenger one of their own religion, Mohammed Raki, who might be among the prisoners now and could be a witness for her.

The interpreter translated, and Ali Hadji expressed his satisfaction with a smile. He asked the captured Moslem to be brought before him. Angélique had been afraid that Mohammed Raki might have been wounded or killed during the battle, but now she saw him and pointed him out, with the result that an order was given for him to be embarked separately.

The fleet left the cove and headed for the open sea. The little boats were so loaded that no one could move an inch without upsetting the balance of the entire ship and hindering its speed. Only the crew of Negroes and Moors ran up and down the catwalk between the banks of galley-slaves, lashing the Christian ones with their whips.

Ali Hadji took several occasions to look at Angélique. She guessed he was talking about her to his scribe, but she could not understand what they were saying. Savary managed to slide over near her.

'I don't know whether Mohammed Raki will support what I've told them. And what is my husband going to think of all this? Do you think he really will pay my ransom? Will he come to my aid? I was going to him, but now I realise I don't know his whole story. If he has lived this long among the Berbers, he might be better able to deal with our captors than anyone else, though. Was I right to present myself as I did?'

'You were not wrong. The situation is complicated enough without your making it more so. At least you won't risk the final outrages if you come before the courts of Islam. The Koran forbids any of its believers to take as a wife a woman who has a husband still living. They punish the sin of adultery very severely. On the other hand, I heard Ali Hadji say when they brought you before him: "It is she. Yes, it is she. Our mission is accomplished." '

'What does that mean, Savary?'

The old man made a gesture of ignorance.

PART THREE

The Grand Eunuch

CHAPTER SIXTEEN

Aboard the galleys sailing toward shore the only sound was the gentle swish of the prows as they cut through the ripples. Angélique lifted her drooping head and perceived that Baron von Nessenood's eyes were on the land.

'Algiers,' he said.

And in a moment the rumble of the city, as of a thousand grumbling voices, drifted out to them. They could see it now, lying between two great breakwaters, so glistening white as to appear devoid of life.

As the ship entered the harbour, the gold pennon of Ali Hadji at the peak of the mast was but one of hundreds of banners fluttering in the light breeze, among which the most predominant were a red banner with a white device and a green standard bearing the crescent. The foremost galley fired its cannon, and the shot was answered by a volley from the waterfront, followed by shrill cries of joy.

The two Knights of Malta, still in their red coats of mail, were in the van of the prisoners being disembarked on the quay. Then came the sailors and the marines; lastly the passengers. But Angélique was conducted separately under a guard of armed janizaries.

The others, chained in twos and prodded by the victorious Berber crew, were hustled along the quay to the Jenina, where dwelt the Pasha, to whom they had to be shown first in order that he might make his selections from among them.

The populace – white ghosts with faces of dirty yellow – thronged about them on every side, uttering shrill exclamations, and casting hostile eyes upon them. Mingled with them were the pale faces of Christian slaves, bearded and ragged, shouting to the new captives in every tongue of Christendom in the hope that among them might be one or two of their countrymen who could give them news of their families.

'I am Jean Paraguez, from Collioure in the Pyrenees. . . . Do you know? . . . I am Robert Toutain, from Cette. . . .'

The Turkish janizaries lashed out at them with bulls' pizzles, letting the blows fall where they might.

As soon as they came to the slave market, Angélique was taken upstairs to a secluded little room white as chalk, where she crouched in a corner listening to the tumult outside.

Presently the curtain was raised and an old Moslem woman, brown and wrinkled as a withered pear, stepped inside. 'My name is Fatima,' she said, smiling warmly, 'but the prisoners call me Mirelia the Provençal.'

She was carrying two honey-cakes and some water flavoured with vinegar and sugar, as well as a square of lace to protect the face from sunburn. The last precaution came too late, however; Angélique's face was already scarlet from the blazing sun, which even then was spreading its awning of golden silk over the glistening white city of Algiers. She wanted a bath. Her dress was stained by the salt seaspray and spotted with tar from the planks of the deck.

'I'll take you to the bath after the other slaves are sold,' said the old woman. 'It will be a while, because that can't take place before the noonday prayer.'

She spoke in sabir, a conglomeration of Spanish, Italian, French, Turkish and Arabic that all slaves understood. But gradually her native French returned to her, and she told Angélique of her birthplace near Aix-en-Provence. When she was sixteen years old she had been a maid to a great lady of Marseilles, and while voyaging with her to meet her husband in Naples, she had been carried off in a raid by the Berbers. Since she was only a minor servant she had been sold for a few sequins to a poor Moslem, but the great lady had been reserved for a princely harem.

Fatima-Mirelia, now old and widowed, earned a few piastres by seeing to the needs of new captives. Merchants anxious to display their human merchandise to its best advantage, sought her services fairly often. She would bathe and brush and comfort the unlucky women so frequently in a sad state of health and spirits after their desperate voyages, and terrified by their new vicissitudes.

'How pleased I am,' she exclaimed, 'to have been appointed to take care of you. You are the Frenchwoman Rescator bought for thirty-five thousand piastres, and who then escaped from him. Mezzo-Morte had sworn to capture you before his rival could.'

Angélique looked at her in horror. 'That's impossible,' she stammered. 'Mezzo-Morte can't possibly know where I am.'

'Oh, he knows everything. He has spies everywhere. Osman Faraji, the Sultan of Morocco's Grand Eunuch, who came here to find some white women, and he have set out to find you.'

'Why?'

'Because you have the reputation of being the most beautiful white slave in the whole Mediterranean.'

'Oh, how I wish I were ugly!' exclaimed Angélique wringing her hands. 'Misshapen, frightful, hideous . . .'

'Like me,' said the Provençal woman. 'When I was captured I was only eighteen and had fine big breasts. But I was a little lame. The man who bought me and became my husband was a fine craftsman, a potter, who was poor all his life long and never could afford a concubine. I had to work like a beast of burden, but I liked it better that way. Christians like us don't like being traded back and forth, and used by many different parties.'

Angélique pressed her hands to her aching head. 'I don't understand. How could they have set this snare to catch me?'

'I heard Mezzo-Morte sent you his favourite adviser, Amar Abbas, when you were in Malta, to urge you to take ship for a destination where you would be seized.'

Angélique shook her head, afraid to grasp her meaning. 'No . . . I met no one there . . . only an old servant of my husband's named Mohammed Raki.'

'That was Amar Abbas.'

'No! It couldn't be!'

'Wasn't the man a Berber with a short, colourless beard?'

Angélique couldn't force out a single syllable.

'Wait,' said the old woman. 'I've just had an idea. A few minutes ago I saw Amar Abbas talking to Sadi Hasan, the manager here. I'll go and see if he's still around, and if he is, I'll point him out to you.'

A little later she returned, carrying a long veil. 'Wrap this around you right up to your eyes,' she said.

She guided Angélique down the corridor that ran the length of the floor to a balcony from which they could look down upon the square courtyard of the building.

The sale of the slaves had begun. The new ones were naked – the white hairy bodies of the Europeans contrasting with the dark, smooth skins of the eastern captives. To the right, on sumptuous piles of cushions, sat the military officials and old corsairs who had grown wealthy on their depredations and now were enjoying the harems their fortunes had brought them, which they had planted with carefully tended gardens of olive trees, orange trees and oleanders, and kept continually enriching with new purchases. They were surrounded with Negro boys ceaselessly cooling the air about them with long-handled fans.

One of the Pasha's favourites, his chargé d'affaires, took his place amongst them.

'Look,' said Mirelia, 'at that man next to him, talking to him.'

Angélique leaned over the railing and recognised Mohammed Raki. 'That's the one,' she said.

'Well, that's Amar Abbas, Mezzo-Morte's adviser.'

'No!' cried Angélique in despair. 'It can't be. He showed me the letter and the topaz!'

Overwhelmed, she spent the rest of the day trying to understand what could have happened to her. Savary had been right, after all, to be suspicious of the Berber envoy. But where was Savary now? It had not occurred to her to look for him in the wretched herd of slaves being put up for sale. Now that she thought about it, she realised she had not seen the two Knights either.

Little by little the hubbub subsided. The purchasers went home with their new slaves. Darkness descended on dazzling Algiers. In the profound silence of the Islamic night only one sound emerged, deep and rumbling, reaching as far away as the slave market itself.

Fatima-Mirelia lay on the straw matting beside the divan on which Angélique was trying to get some sleep. She raised her wrinkled face and said: 'It's the tavern of the bagnio.'

To put Angélique to sleep, she told her long stories about that singular place where wine and spirits flowed in fountains. There the slaves would meet to exchange what they had stolen for a morsel of food, and there came to be cured all those who were sick or injured. And it was there, when the oil lamps began to smoke and fade as dawn approached, that the best stories in the world were to be heard. Danes and Swedes would tell of their adventures whale-hunting off Greenland, where the nights were six months long; Dutchmen described the riches of the East Indies and the marvels of China and Japan; Spaniards spoke dreamily of the delights of Mexico and the treasures of Peru; the French would recite the wonders of Newfoundland and Canada and Virginia. For all the slaves there had been seafarers.

The next morning they took her to the waterfront to Ali Hadji, who was surrounded by a crowd of young boys dressed in yellow silk drawers, with daggers at their waists and yellow turbans on their heads. Most of them were Moors or Negroes, but a few were merely deeply tanned and one or two had the blue eyes of Nordics. They seemed to regard Angélique with scorn mingled with arrogance and hatred. She felt as if she were encircled by lion whelps or fierce tiger cubs, and the Arab corsair in contrast appeared almost kindly.

A longboat was bobbing at the foot of the ladder that reached from the water to the deck of the galley. Six blond slaves, probably Russians, were at the oars, and a long-moustachioed Turk stood in the prow, his heavily muscled arms folded across his chest. One of the boys vaulted into the stern and took the tiller.

Angélique stepped into the boat under the insolent stares of the boys, who perched like vultures on the gunwales. She wondered where the boat was carrying her, for it swung around the breakwater and out to sea toward a hilly promontory from which were coming bursts of musket fire, and answering pistol shots.

'Where are we going?' she asked.

No one replied. One of the boys spat in her direction, but missed her, only to grin impertinently as the Turk threatened him with punishment. These boys seemed to fear nobody.

Several bullets splashed into the water around them. Angélique nervously took stock of the passengers. Ali Hadji did not budge, but he saw the inquisitive expression on Angélique's face and his mouth spread in a suave smile as he implied with a gesture that she was in reality a guest at a great spectacle.

Two groups appeared around the point of the promontory – a two-masted felucca manned by bearded Christians armed with swords and rifles, and a swarm of young swimmers in yellow turbans who had dived from some distant ships and swum to the felucca in an attempt to do battle with it. They kept diving under the boat only to resurface on the other side at a less well defended spot, then scampered like monkeys up the sides, cut the ropes and fought barehanded with the slaves, dodging their swordthrusts until they were grappling with them hand to hand.

On the poop a man in a short robe and a yellow turban was attentively following this sham battle which he seemed to be directing. From time to time he would pick up his megaphone and bellow a flood of oaths through it in the dialect of the slaves to rebuke such boys as were too awkward or were sluggish about renewing their onslaughts because of injuries or fatigue.

The lion whelps in the longboat were in ecstasies at the sight, and so eager to take part in the game that they leaped into the water like a bunch of frogs and swam rapidly toward the ship. Even the oarsmen slowed their beat, but a couple of lashes brought them back to order. The longboat leaped forward and soon was up to the poop of the felucca.

'I am Mezzo-Morte himself,' said the man on the poop, speaking in French that had a tinge of an Italian accent.

He was a thick-set man, and the diamonds that sparkled in his turban and on his fingers did nothing to conceal his origins as one of the lower class – a poor Calabrian fisherboy still, for all his Arabian Nights costume. This was the Lord High Admiral of Algiers, commander of the most redoubtable pirate fleet in the Mediterranean. He could give orders to the Pasha, and the whole city stood in awe of him.

Angélique made a semblance of a curtsy to him, which seemed to please him immensely. He gazed at her with an air of deep satisfaction, then turned to Ali Hadji and talked with him at length. Angélique could guess from his gestures and from the few words of Arabic she had learned that he was congratulating Ali Hadji for having performed his assignment so successfully. Yet she perceived with anguish that the looks he threw in her direction were more full of menace than the usual stare of a slave merchant evaluating a new captive.

'Admiral,' she said, using the title that even Christendom bestowed upon him, 'will you be so kind as to tell me what fate is in store for me? Please do not forget that I have not tried to deceive you with an assumed name or to conceal from you that I have an enormous fortune back in France, or that I have undertaken this voyage to find my husband, who lives at Bône and can guarantee my ransom.'

Mezzo-Morte nodded his head affirmatively. More and more wrinkles appeared in the corners of his eyes, and she was astonished to see him gasp as if he were strangling with silent laughter.

'That's fine, Madame,' he said when he had caught his breath. 'It's a great consolation to me to know we won't have to go any farther than Bône to negotiate your ransom. But are you sure of what you are saying?'

Angélique insisted she was speaking the truth and that she had nothing to gain by lying. If he doubted her word, he had only to question Mohammed Raki, who had come with her on the same ship from Malta. He had been sent to her as an envoy from her husband in Bône.

'I know, I know,' muttered Mezzo-Morte, the ironic glint in his eyes taking on an almost cruel intensity.

'You know? Oh, good lord!' exclaimed Angélique, light suddenly dawning on her. 'You know my husband? You do know him, don't you?'

The renegade Christian moved his head as if to say, 'Maybe I do and maybe I don't.' Then he guffawed again. His two pages, in liveries of pistachio green and shocking pink, laughed in imitation of their master. He barked an order to them, and they scurried away, only to return almost immediately with a box of Turkish paste. Mezzo-Morte stuffed his mouth with it, then turned to watch the war game still going on below them on the main deck. His love of sweets was a craving he shared with his chief antagonist, the Duc de Vivonne, High Admiral of the French fleet.

'Admiral,' said Angélique hopefully, 'I beg you, tell me the truth. Do you know my husband?'

Mezzo-Morte pierced her with his black eyes. 'No,' he said savagely. 'And, what's more, don't use that tone of voice to me. You are a captive, and don't forget it. We found on your Maltese galley the very worst enemy of Islam, your captain, Baron von Nessenood, who has sunk one thousand and fifty of my barks, thirty-one galleys, eleven cargo boats, eleven thousand men, and has freed fifteen thousand captives. It was a lucky day for me! We have killed two birds with one stone, as they say in France, I think.'

Angélique protested vigorously that she was in Malta only because she had been picked up by one of the Order's galleys when she was on the point of being shipwrecked on her way from Crete.

'So you were coming from Crete? What were you doing there?'

'Practically the same thing I'm doing here,' she said with some bitterness. 'I had been captured by a Christian pirate and sold as a slave. But I succeeded in escaping.' She looked at him defiantly.

'So you are the French slave Rescator bought for that exorbitant price and who got away from him the very same night?'

'Yes, that is indeed who I am.'

Mezzo-Morte went into gales of laughter, slapping his thighs and stamping his feet. His two pages mimicked him. Then, when he had quietened down, he asked her how she had managed to escape the Sorcerer of the Mediterranean.

'I set fire to the harbour,' said Angélique.

'Was that the same fire everyone has been talking about?'

His eyes sparkled with amusement. He asked again if it was true that Rescator had outbid the Sultan of Constantinople and the Order of Malta, who had pushed her price up to twenty-five thousand piastres.

'But why didn't you linger long enough to taste all the delights of that damned sorcerer? Didn't he promise to load you with luxuries?'

'I don't care about such things,' Angélique said. 'I did not venture on the Mediterranean just to become an odalisque for some Christian pirate – or Moslem, for that matter – but to find my husband from whom I have been separated for ten years and whom I thought dead.'

Mezzo-Morte writhed with laughter again, and Angélique became panic-stricken. Was the man insane? The Admiral had gone into hysterics now, and even though his howls of laughter subsided from time to time, they burst out again whenever some new detail of her story struck him as hilarious.

'It's the same one,' he choked out. 'Do you hear, Ali Hadji, it's the same one!'

The Arab laughed too, but more conservatively.

Patiently Angélique undertook to repeat what she had already told them, hoping it would restore them to sanity. She had money, and she could have it sent from France to ransom her. Mezzo-Morte would be well indemnified for the cost of his expedition to the Isle of Cani.

The Italian stopped his laughter. 'So you believe that was an ambush?' he said incisively.

She nodded. Mezzo-Morte raised a finger and said that in his whole long career as a sailor and a raider she was the only woman he had ever met who could see a thing for what it was even in spite of her anxiety at being a captive.

'It's the very same one, Ali Hadji! The same Frenchwoman who drove d'Escrainville out of his mind and whom Rescator bought for the highest price ever paid for a slave, only to lose her because she set fire to the harbour. Hahahahaha . . .'

He watched Angélique like a hawk. Mezzo-Morte was a crude type, but he had a kind of sensitivity to others, and this quickly gave him a certain power over them. The pitiful appearance of his captive – her face burned by the sun, her dress sadly rumpled, her hair in disorder – did not escape him. His dark eyes began to shine like jet, and a fierce, skull-like grin revealed his glistening teeth.

'Now I can understand,' he said softly. 'Yes, she is indeed the same one, Ali Hadji – the same woman described in the letter, whom "he" bought in Candia. What a stroke of luck! Now I have that Rescator! Now he'll have to crawl to me. I've found the chink in his armour, the same one all fools have – a woman! So he thinks he can lord it over us, interfere in our slave trade, act like the master of us all with that money of his! If it weren't for him I would now be the High Admiral of the Sultan, but I know what a disservice he has done me at that Court. Let him go on sneaking from Morocco to Constantinople, let the gold stick to his hands, let him keep all his allies, but I shall be the one to humble him at last! He'll have to quit the Mediterranean, do you hear, Ali Hadji! He'll have to quit and never return!'

He raised his arms in exhilaration. 'Now I shall be the master. I shall have vanquished Rescator, my deadliest foe!'

'You have many enemies, it seems to me,' said Angélique with a trace of sarcasm.

Her tone put an end to the pirate's delight. 'Yes,' he replied icily, 'I have many such, and soon you shall see how I deal with them. I'm beginning to understand how you almost drove poor d'Escrainville crazy, not that he was ever too strong in the head. Sit down.'

Angélique sank, rather than sat, upon the velvet couch he indicated. Her head was swimming. The Admiral of Algiers sat cross-legged across from her and passed her his box of Turkish paste. Angélique felt so fragile and listless that she reached for some eagerly, but no sooner had she stretched out her hand than she drew it back with a sharp cry of pain. Four long streaks welted it. The scarlet fingernails of one of the Admiral's pets had scratched her cruelly.

The gesture seemed to restore Mezzo-Morte's good humour. 'Oh-oh,' he said with a laugh, 'you've made my lambkins jealous. They don't like to see me so near a woman, offering her dainties they think are reserved for them alone. Well, it is a bit unusual for me. No women, that's the one thing that makes for great leaders – and great eunuchs. Women mean sloppiness, weakness, half-baked ideas, poor planning. They're the source of all the stupid things men do. Without them a man can be a colossus. But the eunuchs' way of protecting themselves from temptations seems a little extreme to me. I have merely adjusted my tastes.'

He laughed again and stroked the curly head of his savage little favourite, a Negro boy with a liberally painted face. The other pet was white, with black eyes, doubtless a Spaniard. These children, kidnapped along the shores of the Mediterranean, were destined to forsake their religion either willingly or by force. By showering them first with affection and then with threats, their master inevitably got them to renounce their faith, become circumcised, and pronounce the sacred confession: 'There is no God but Allah, and Mohammed is His Prophet.' The new converts then could go on to become the toys of kings and pashas.

'They're fanatics, these children,' Mezzo-Morte said, 'and devoted to me body and soul. One word from me, and they would pounce on you like wolves and tear you into pieces. Just see how they're looking at you now. When they board a Christian vessel they practically lap up the blood of the Christians. You see, they're forbidden wine. . . .'

Angélique was too despondent to show her revulsion. Mezzo-Morte kept surveying her resentfully, for she had but recently offended him deeply, and he was not a man to forgive such an insult easily.

'You are proud,' he said, 'and pride in women I hate as bitterly as I hate Christians. They have no right to pride.'

Suddenly he began to laugh savagely again, as if he could not stop.

'What are you laughing at?' asked Angélique.

'Because you are so proud, so arrogant. And because I know what is

207

going to happen to you! That is why I am laughing. Now do you see?'

'I must admit I do not.'

'It doesn't matter. You will soon.'

That night Angélique slept on board one of Mezzo-Morte's galleys moored in the harbour. Fatima-Mirelia appeared to wait on her.

Angélique gave her one of her own bracelets and asked her to stay with her throughout the night, for she was haunted by the spiteful jealousy of the yellow-turbaned boys guarding the boat. The old woman lay on a mat across the doorway, and Angélique soon was sleeping the sleep of the dead, so exhausted was she.

The next day a little procession wound its way from the harbour toward one of the gates of the city. On one side the street was bordered by ramparts, and on the other by hovels separated by narrow alleys through which they could see the rays of the sinking sun. Angélique, who walked behind Mezzo-Morte and his habitual guard, kept stumbling over the sharp pebbles. They stopped at the Bab Azun gate, where the officers of the guard bowed low before Mezzo-Morte, who frequently made inspections of their garrison. Such, however, was not the purpose of his present visit. He seemed to be waiting for someone.

Shortly after their arrival, out of a nearby street came a Negro horseman followed by a black bodyguard armed with lances. He alighted and bowed to Mezzo-Morte, who returned his greeting with an even lower bow.

The Italian seemed to have considerable respect for the dark-skinned prince, who was much taller than he. They exchanged several *Salam Aleikums* and other protestations of friendship in Arabic, then turned toward the captive. With hands open and outstretched, the Negro bowed to her again, as Mezzo-Morte's eyes flashed with an ironic pleasure.

'I forgot,' he exclaimed, 'the polite customs of the Court of the King of France. I have not yet introduced to you, Madame, my friend His Excellency Osman Faraji, Grand Eunuch of His Majesty the Sultan of Morocco Mulai Ismail.'

Angélique looked at the huge Negro more in surprise than in terror. Now that she thought about it, she might have known he was a eunuch, for she had noticed the delicacy of his features and his high voice. Yet he was far less fat than most eunuchs, whose jowls and double chins made them look like withered old women, as did the six Negroes in his bodyguard.

So this was Osman Faraji, the Grand Eunuch of the Sultan of

Morocco! She had heard of him, but she could not remember where or from whom, and now she was too tired to ask questions.

'We are waiting for one other person,' Mezzo-Morte told her.

He was jubilant, as if he had staged a kind of farce in which every actor had his proper entrance and exit.

'Ah, here he is.'

The newcomer was Mohammed Raki, whom Angélique had not seen since the fight on the Isle of Cam. The Arab did not give her even a glance, but prostrated himself before the Admiral of Algiers.

'Now we can move on,' said Mezzo-Morte.

They left the city and headed west, the full red glow of the sun smiting their faces. The hills before them were tawny and purple in the sunset. The path led them to a sharp-pointed cliff that seemed in the flaring light to be a precipice of the underworld. It had an unhealthy atmosphere about it, accentuated by the incessant screaming of the gulls and crows and vultures that wheeled about it, mingling their ominous shadows with the lengthening gloom of the evening.

'There!'

Mezzo-Morte was pointing out a little heap of rubble on the slope ahead of them, but Angélique could not grasp what he meant.

'There!' he repeated.

Finally she could make out above a heap of iron shards a white human hand.

'There lie the Knights who were in command of your galley. The natives brought them here to stone them to death at the hour of evening prayer.'

Angélique crossed herself.

'Stop doing that,' shouted the renegade pirate. 'You will bring bad luck on the city.'

He led the way again, and soon they came to the high wall of the citadel. Iron spikes curved like fish hooks studded the wall from top to bottom to catch the victims thrown from the summit and hold them until the birds of prey had devoured them alive. Even now these obscene creatures were tearing at the corpses of two victims.

Angélique was about to turn her eyes away, but Mezzo-Morte commanded her to look carefully.

'Why?' she asked. 'Is this the fate you are reserving for me?'

'No,' he said laughing, 'that would be a pity. I am no connoisseur, but a woman like you ought to serve some better purpose than decorating a wall of Algiers merely to glut the appetite of the vultures and cormorants. But look closely. Don't you recognise one of them?'

For a dreadful moment Angélique thought it might be Savary. In spite of her loathing she glanced up at the wall and somewhat to her relief saw that the bodies were Moors.

'I beg your pardon,' she said ironically, 'but I don't have your fondness for looking at corpses. These do not remind me of anyone.'

'Then I shall tell you their names. On the left is Ali Mektub, the Arab jeweller of Candia to whom you gave a letter for your husband. . . . Ah, I observe "my" corpses are beginning to arouse your interest. Would you like to know the other's name?'

She looked at him intensely. He was playing with her like a cat with a mouse, practically smacking his lips.

'Well, it is Mohammed Raki, his nephew.'

Angélique gave a gasp and turned to the man who had come to her at the hospice in Malta and who seemed very much alive to her at this very moment.

'I can read your mind,' said Mezzo-Morte. 'It's all perfectly simple. This man here is a spy I sent you. A false Mohammed Raki. The real one is up there.'

'Why?' was all Angélique could think of to say.

'How inquisitive women are, always asking for explanations! Well, I'll be a good fellow and tell you. We won't waste time on how that letter fell into my hands. I read it, to learn that a great French lady was looking for her husband who had disappeared years ago, and that she was ready to do anything and go anywhere to find him. An idea took root in my mind. I questioned Ali Mektub: was the woman beautiful? Rich? Yes. I made up my mind. I would capture her. All I needed was to set a trap with her husband as the bait. I questioned the nephew Mohammed Raki. He had known the man and had worked for him a long time in Tetuan where he had been bought by an old alchemist whose assistant he became, and later his heir. He was a man easy to identify; a scarred face, tall, thin, dark, with a lame leg. And as an extra piece of luck he had given Mohammed Raki a jewel which his wife could not fail to recognise. My spy listened closely, and took the jewel. Then the only thing left to do was find the woman who might have been sold at Candia meanwhile. But I soon got news of her. She was in Malta after having escaped from Rescator, who had paid thirty-five thousand piastres for her.'

'I thought it was I who told you that.'

'No, I knew it already, but it amused me so much I wanted to hear it again. Well, everything thereafter was extremely easy. I sent my spy to you in Malta under the name of Mohammed Raki, and we set the ambush on the Isle of Cam, which went off splendidly thanks to the accomplices my spy had smuggled aboard your ship. As soon as a carrier pigeon brought me the news of the successful ambush, I had Ali Mektub and his nephew put to death.'

'Why?' asked Angélique feebly.

'Dead men tell no tales,' said Mezzo-Morte with a cynical smirk.

Angélique shivered. She hated and scorned him so much that he no longer even terrified her.

'You are a scoundrel,' she said, 'but, even more, you are a liar. Your story doesn't hold water. Are you trying to make me believe that to capture a woman you had never seen and whose ransom you could not calculate beforehand you commissioned a fleet of six galleys, and thirty feluccas and longboats, and lost at least two crews in the engagement at Cani? Without counting the ammunition, you spent more than a hundred thousand piastres for a single captive! I can easily believe you are so greedy, but not that you are so stupid!'

Mezzo-Morte had listened to her attentively with half-closed eyes. 'How did you know all these figures?'

'I can count.'

'You would make a good shipowner.'

'I am a shipowner. I own a vessel that trades with the West Indies. Oh, I beseech you, listen to me. I am very rich and I can – yes, I can – not without trouble – but I can pay you an exorbitant ransom. What more do you want out of capturing me? It has probably been a mistake on your part and you are probably regretting it already.'

'No,' said Mezzo-Morte shaking his head gently. 'It was no mistake, and I am not sorry for it. On the contrary, I congratulate myself.'

'I tell you I do not believe you,' shouted Angélique in anger. 'Even if you did succeed in accomplishing the death of the two Knights of Malta, your worst enemies, that doesn't justify all your schemes where I am concerned. You were not even sure I would embark on a Maltese galley. And why didn't you think of getting in touch with my husband to achieve your ambush? You were relying only on my stupidity in believing your spy and his weak proofs. I might have suspected them and demanded evidence in my husband's handwriting.'

'I did think of that, but it was impossible.'

'Why?'

'Because he is dead,' said Mezzo-Morte. 'Yes, your husband – or your supposed husband – died of the plague three years ago. It claimed more than ten thousand victims in Tetuan. Mohammed Raki's master, the learned old Christian named Peyrac, ended his life there.'

'I do not believe you,' she said. 'I do not believe you. *I do not believe you!*'

She was shouting right into his face in order to erect a barrier between her hopes and the despair that these words of his had just aroused in her. 'If I weep now, everything is lost,' she thought.

The Admiral's youthful bodyguard, who had never seen anyone behave in such a way to their master before, were growing excited and kept their hands on the hilts of their daggers.

'You have not told me everything. . . .'

'Possibly not. But I am not going to tell you any more.'

'Let me go! I will pay ransom.'

'No! Not for all the gold in the world, do you hear, not for all the gold in the world would I do that. I can look beyond mere wealth – to Power. And you are my means of achieving it. That's why the cost of capturing you meant nothing to me. You don't need to understand.'

Angélique raised her eyes to the wall, the detail of which was disappearing in the darkness. The Mohammed Raki impaled there on a hook was the only man she knew who had known Joffrey de Peyrac in his second existence, and now he would never speak again!

'If I were to go to Tetuan,' she thought, 'perhaps I could find others who knew him. But to do that I need my freedom.'

'This is what will be your lot,' said Mezzo-Morte. 'Now that I can see your beauty is as great as was reported to me, I am going to include you among the presents I am sending by His Excellency Osman Faraji to my very dear friend the Sultan Mulai Ismail. Now I am turning you over to His Excellency. You will learn from him how to be less proud. That is what eunuchs are good for. Unfortunately there is no institution like them in Europe.'

Angélique scarcely heard him. She understood only as she saw him depart followed by his escort, and felt the hand of the Grand Eunuch on her shoulder.

'Please follow me, noble lady.'

She uttered no word, made no gesture, merely followed him calmly and obediently. The Negroes made their way back toward the Bab el Wed gate.

The night was deathly still. The moonlight cast the lacy shadow of the wrought-iron grill of the window on the floor of her chamber. The air was perfumed with the scent of mint and tea. Angélique roused herself from her state of prostration and sat up. The silence was suddenly pierced by a distant scream, as of an animal caught in a trap.

The trap had been sprung upon her. As on many other occasions when her impulsiveness had led her into hopeless situations, she was furious with herself. The thought of what Madame de Montespan would say, were she to know the fate that had overtaken her rival, seared Angélique's mind like a branding iron. 'Madame du Plessis-Bellière. . . . Have you heard? Ha-ha-ha! Captured by the Berbers! Ha-ha-ha! They say the High Admiral of Algiers has offered her as a present to the Sultan of Morocco. Ha-ha-ha! Isn't that funny! The poor dear. . . .'

The mocking laughter of the beautiful Athénaïs rang in her ears. Angélique got up and looked for something she could smash against the wall. There was nothing in the room – a barren cell stripped like a monk's of everything comfortable, even a divan of cushions, and containing just the pallet of straw on which they had thrown her. There was not even a window, only that single opening barred by the wrought-iron grill. Angélique rushed to it and began to shake it.

To her surprise it yielded at her first touch. At first hesitantly, then more speedily she slipped through the opening into the corridor that opened in front of her.

The dark form of a eunuch rose out of the shadows and followed her. At the top of a staircase she met another with a pike who barred her passage.

With a tremendous burst of strength Angélique pushed him aside, but he grasped her by the wrist. She struck his flabby cheeks, seized him around the neck and hurled him to the floor. The two eunuchs began to screech like monkeys as Angélique ran down the stairs, only to find at their base three other Negroes against whom she struggled in vain. Their falsetto voices rose to a new high pitch as she fought them like a tigress. But soon they had overpowered her. One of the shapeless mounds of fat was whirling his whip, a long lash studded with knots, as he shouted in shrill outrage that she should be given a severe lesson in behaviour.

Osman Faraji, who had appeared after being summoned to quell the commotion, motioned him to put up the whip. But the eunuch kept insisting that the hour had come for this rebellious slave to be given an exemplary punishment. Osman Faraji ignored him. He let his calm eyes fall on Angélique and softly said in French:

'Would you like some tea? Or some lemonade? Would you care to have some skewers of broiled mutton brought you? Or some minced squab with cinnamon? Or some almond paste cookies? You must be both hungry and thirsty.'

'I want my freedom,' said Angélique. 'I want to see the sky. I want to get out of that prison.'

'If that is all,' the Grand Eunuch said softly, 'then please just follow me.'

The guards were quite as happy to see her go as she was to leave them. She had become a thing of terror to them.

She went back up the narrow staircase, then another, and another, until finally she found herself on a terraced roof top with the whole starry vault of the sky spread out above her. A silvery light tinted the cool mist rising from the sea into a bluish vapour that enveloped everything, even the dome of the nearby mosque. Its minaret seemed almost transparent in the rays of the moon, and it made her slightly dizzy as it seemed to sway in the shifting light.

Osman Faraji was watching Angélique closely. As if he had had a sudden inspiration, he said: 'Would you like some Turkish coffee?'

Angélique's nostrils quivered. At once she knew that this was what she had missed most since she had been in Algiers.

Without waiting for her assent, Osman Faraji clapped his hands and gave a brief command. In a few moments a carpet was unrolled and cushions strewn around on it. A low table was fetched, and presently the aromatic vapour of the coffee mingled with the scent of the jasmine in the warm darkness.

Osman Faraji dismissed the slaves. Sitting cross-legged opposite Angélique, he undertook to serve her himself, offering her the customary ground pepper and apricot liqueur as well. But she preferred to drink it with only a little sugar. Her eyes closed as she was seized with a strong nostalgia.

'The odour of the coffee recalls Candia to me . . . and the auction room where its aroma mingled with the tobacco smoke . . . I should like to be back in Candia to relive that moment when a hand raised my head . . . and I was wafted on the wings of bliss . . . and the coffee smelled so sweet. I was happy then in Candia. . . .'

She took a few swallows and then began to weep, her throat becoming tight with the sobs she was trying to repress. This was the last thing she really wanted – to collapse before the Grand Eunuch, not to mention her absurd confession. In Candia she had been no more than a miserable, ill-treated slave, up for sale at auction. But in Candia she had still had hopes of achieving her goal. And she had had with her there her old friend the hard-working, ludicrous Savary, to encourage her, comfort her, direct her, pass her letters to sign through the bars of her underground dungeon, make secret signals to her from under his disguise of beggar's rags. Where was he now, poor Savary? Perhaps they had put out his eyes and made him turn a grindstone like a donkey. Or perhaps they had thrown him into the sea, or to the dogs. They were quite capable of either.

'I do not understand,' said Osman Faraji, 'why you should be weeping. You'll only wear yourself out that way.'

'Ah, really,' said Angélique between sobs, 'cannot you understand how a woman might want to weep when she is far from her own people and in prison! I am not the only one either. Just listen to that other one howl.'

'But with you it is not the same thing.' He lifted his hand and fanned out his long jewelled fingers with their scarlet nails. 'The woman who drove d'Escrainville, the Terror of the Mediterranean, crazy . . . who made Don José de Almada, the most cautious trader I know, bid up to twenty-five thousand piastres . . . who escaped the invincible Rescator . . . who dared scream insults right into Mezzo-Morte's face . . that's quite a record. Such a woman as that, Madame, does not cry or have an emotional crisis.'

Angélique sniffled a little, found her handkerchief, and swallowed the rest of her coffee which had grown cool by now. The tribute Osman Faraji had paid her was rather impressive after all, and her spirits rose.

'Would you like some pistachio nuts? They come from Constantinople. Are they good?'

Angélique nibbled at one and said she had tasted better.

'Where?' said Osman Faraji with concern. 'Do you remember the name and address of the man you bought them from?'

He added that it was his responsibility to see that the tastes of Mulai Ismail's hundred wives were gratified. The harems of Mulai Ismail were the best furnished with luxuries in all Barbary, thanks to his pains. When she got to Meknès she could see for herself.

Angélique stood up, her hands tensed into claws. 'I will never go to Meknès. I want my freedom.'

'What would you do with it?'

His question was so softly uttered that it quite deflated Angélique. She might have cried out that she wanted to get back to her own people and see her native land again, but suddenly she did not know what she wanted any more, and her whole existence seemed a mockery to her. She had no more attachments apart from her two young sons, and even them she had forsaken in the pursuit of her wild projects.

'Here or there,' the Grand Eunuch was saying, 'wherever Allah wills us to be, let us taste the joys of life. Women have a great knack for being adaptable. You are afraid because our skins are black or brown and our language is unknown to you, but what is there in our ways that could possibly frighten you? You are fearful, Madame, because you do not know what Islam is. You are just like all other Christians in thinking us savages. You will see our great cities of the northern coast of Morocco and Fez, whose names means "gold", and Meknès, the Sultan's citadel, which looks as if it were built of solid ivory. Our cities are handsomer and richer than yours.'

'That's impossible. You don't know what you're saying. You can't compare Paris to this collection of white building blocks.'

She motioned toward Algiers, lying asleep far below them, and stopped. It was an unconceivable kind of world, removed from time, existing, as it were, only in a dream. A city built by the magic of the moonlight out of translucent porcelain and set beside a sea of amethyst. A true dream, revealing beneath the garish tinsel of the pirates' lordship the slow, meditative soul of Islam.

'You were never made to be afraid,' said Osman Faraji. 'Be docile and no one will harm you. I will give you time to get used to our Islamic ways.'

'I doubt I shall ever get accustomed to the small value you put on human life.'

'Does human life deserve such concern? True, Christians have an astonishing fear of death and torture, and that makes me think your religion does little to prepare you to look upon the face of God.'

'Mezzo-Morte said something almost like that to me.'

'He is only a renegade, a professional Turk,' said the Grand Eunuch without concealing his scorn, 'but I like to believe it was something more than his lust for money and ambition that attracted him to you. Perhaps it was that freedom of belief which gives one a zest for life and a zest for dying, not the fear of either one such as you Christians have.'

'It's too bad you never could become a priest, Osman Bey. You preach a good sermon. Do you think you shall succeed in converting me?'

'You will have no choice. You shall become a Moslem by dint of becoming one of the wives of our great lord Mulai Ismail.'

Angélique bit her lip to keep from answering impertinently, but she thought to herself: 'Don't count on that too heavily!'

This Moroccan bogeyman they were keeping for her was still fortunately far away. Between here and then she would have to find some means of escaping. And find them she would! Osman Faraji had been quite right in asking her to take coffee with him.

And immediately thereafter she found Maître Savary – a sure sign that Heaven was watching over her.

The establishment in which the Moroccans were staying in Algiers was larger than the batistan of Candia, but like it in that it combined the facilities of an hotel and a warehouse. Both were of the same design: a large rectangular frame enclosing a colonnaded patio in which was a garden of oleanders, lemon and orange trees, and three fountains. There was but one entrance, continually guarded by armed soldiers. No window opened on the street, all the outer walls being of solid masonry. The roofs were flat, providing a kind of parade ground for the sentinels always on duty there. Several areas on the ground floor were set aside for stables, and it was there that Angélique wandered one day to inspect the camels and other strange beasts of burden.

A heap of straw was suddenly pitched aside to reveal the stooped figure of the old apothecary, his garments even more tattered than before.

'Savary! Oh, my dear Savary!' she murmured trying to check her joy, 'what are you doing here?'

'When I learned you were in the hands of the Grand Eunuch I could not rest till I had got as close to you as I could. I encountered a piece of luck in being purchased by a Turkish street porter who has the franchise of taking care of these stables, and is so important a personage he has to have a slave to do his sweeping and cleaning for him. So here I am.'

'What is going to become of us, Savary? They're going to take me to Morocco for the harem of Mulai Ismail.'

'Don't be concerned. Morocco is a very interesting country, and I have wanted to go back there for a long time now. I have many old friends there.'

'Another son?' asked Angélique with a faint smile.

'No. Two! I have to confess that I have no descendants here in Algiers, and that makes our chances of escaping rather difficult. Are you being well treated?'

'Osman Faraji has been very attentive to me. I am free enough. I can come and go in this establishment, and even leave the women's quarters. It really isn't a harem yet, Savary. But the sea is so nearby, wouldn't this be a good time for us to try to escape?'

Savary only sighed and took up his broom and began sweeping again. Eventually he asked her what had become of Mohammed Raki. Angélique told him, and added that now all her hopes had been shattered. She wanted only one thing – to escape and get back to France.

'Everyone wants to escape,' Savary agreed, 'only to regret it later. That's the magic of Islam. You'll see for yourself.'

That evening Osman Faraji politely asked her whether the old Christian slave cleaning the stables was her father or perhaps her uncle or some other relative. Angélique blushed at discovering that she had been so closely watched, even when she thought herself most unobserved. She replied that the old man was her travelling companion and that she was very fond of him and that he was a great scholar, but the Moslems had set him to cleaning the stables as a way of humiliating him because he was a Christian. It must be their way of showing their superiority, to put a master in the position of a servant.

'You are mistaken,' he said, 'just like all other Christians. The Koran says: "On the Day of Judgment the ink of the scholar will outweigh the gunpowder of the soldier." Is this venerable old man a doctor?'

When she answered in the affirmative, the Grand Eunuch's face lit up. The Icelandic slave was sick and so was the pygmy elephant he was taking to the Sultan – two of his most precious gifts. It was a pity that they should be in such poor condition even before leaving Algiers.

Savary was lucky enough to be able to reduce the fever of these two creatures, thanks to a remedy of his own devising. Angélique was astonished at the way he had managed to keep throughout all his vicissitudes so many powders and pills and secret herbs in the depths of his pockets. The Grand Eunuch gave him a decent garment to wear and attached him to his household.

'You see,' said Savary. 'They always begin by wanting to throw me into the sea or to the dogs, and then pretty soon they can't do without me.'

Angélique no longer felt so alone in the world.

CHAPTER SEVENTEEN

The Grand Eunuch's company and his conversation continued to interest Angélique. He seemed to take particular interest in his French captive, and she could not help being flattered, try as she would not to yield to it. She kept wondering to what extent this coldly intellectual Negro might become her friend and ally. For the time being she was completely dependent upon him.

He proved a most agreeable teacher, patient and skilful, and Angélique soon found she was enjoying his tutoring sessions. They served as a sort of distraction for her, and she realised that a knowledge of Arabic could not be anything but useful to her and might help her gain accomplices and even escape some day.

But how? And when? And where to? Of that she knew nothing. All she could cling to was the belief that if she remained in possession of her faculties and her life, she would eventually succeed in escaping. But to what new destiny or for what purpose were questions too deep for her to plumb. And while she waited she still had to endure her lot as a privileged captive.

Among the many things she had to get used to was the fact that her own ideas of time did not exist in the Orient. Consequently, when the Grand Eunuch had told her over and over again that they 'were going to leave at once' for Morocco, Angélique believed him to the letter. Every day she expected to see herself mounted on a camel in a caravan. But day after day went by, and Osman Faraji kept cursing the laziness and thievery of the Algerians without making any visible signs of leaving the city, where, he said, 'there were more thieves than Jews or Christians'. Every time their departure seemed imminent, some mysterious motives – if, indeed, there were any at all – cancelled the order for leaving, and Osman Ferradji resigned himself to wait for some new sign or omen.

One of the things that delayed them was the health of the pigmy elephant which Osman Faraji knew would greatly delight Mulai Ismail, who had a great predilection for rare animals. Every day Savary, in his new rôle as veterinarian, was consulted. And there was endless bargaining over the purchase of other gifts for the Sultan.

Angélique listened to all this dickering, which seemed to her little more than women's gossip. Sometimes she was astonished that she could have taken this Negro seriously at first. She thought now that he was as tricky as any pedlar, and as talkative and capricious as any woman. He gave her the impression that he was continually shuffling about, as if he were groping his way.

'Make no mistake,' Savary said to her when she told him her suspicions, 'this Osman Faraji is the one who made Mulai Ismail Sultan of Morocco. Right now he is trying to make him the head of all Islam, and perhaps of Europe too. Treat him with respect, Madame, and pray

Heaven he will help us get out of the Sultan's clutches.'

Angélique shrugged. Savary was talking like that crazy d'Escrainville. Perhaps he was beginning to get a little soft in his head, as well he might after all his experiences. For the ingenious old apothecary, usually brewing some secret conspiracy, to be surrendering himself to God's mercy, was strange indeed. But perhaps he considered their present situation extraordinarily serious.

Savary was free to roam about the city as a 'mukanga', or witch-doctor. As he prowled the shops and bazaars in search of the herbs and drugs he needed for his medicines, he gathered quite a harvest of news from recently captured slaves. In Algiers one could get from the constant assemblage of people from every quarter of Europe more information than the kings of France, England and Spain could derive. But these innumerable slaves never mentioned a lame man with a scarred face named Joffrey de Peyrac.

She had been able to establish with certainty that he had come into the Mediterranean, but for years now every trace of him seemed to have vanished. Would she have to accept Mezzo-Morte's version of the story that the Comte was dead of the plague? When she thought of that eventuality, she drew a little comfort from it, for uncertainty is the worst torture of all. *I have followed my hopes too much.* . . .

At times she thought she was understanding Savary better. For years he had lived for nothing but the hot pursuit of his 'mineral maumie'. His great bravura act, the burning of Candia, had been only an experiment for him. Like her he was being dragged on and on by some blind destiny. Was life, after all, nothing but a groping after something that never could be found? No. She did not wish to grow soft in the gilded cage that enclosed her now. She wanted to escape. That itself was an end for her to keep in view. Then she would find new traces of her husband, and, if necessary, become convinced he was dead. In the meantime she would not permit herself to become the victim of mere events. But first she would learn Arabic thoroughly, since that was the surest key to her deliverance.

She applied herself with a new diligence to the parchments with which Osman Faraji had furnished her, striving to master the strange signs that represented the sounds of the oriental tongue. Every time she felt the Grand Eunuch's eyes upon her, however, her hand grew shaky. She would forget he was in the room with her. Yet it seemed to her that he had always been with her, priestlike and mystical, his long legs always crossed under the folds of his white wool robe.

'Will-power is a magical and dangerous weapon,' he remarked.

Angélique looked at him with sudden anger. Every time he spoke like that he seemed to be reading her mind.

'Do you mean it's better to let life and events overwhelm you, like a wounded dog at the mercy of the waves?'

'Our destiny is not in our hands. What is written is written.'

'You mean no one can change his fate?'

'Yes, one can,' he said soberly. 'Every human being possesses a boundless potentiality for counteracting fate. That is why I said will-power is a magical and dangerous weapon. It is the force of nature. It is dangerous in that one often pays too dearly for the results one achieves. That is why Christians who use their wills for every advantage and every wicked purpose are always at war with their destiny and bring down upon their heads the woes of which they so continually complain.'

Angélique shook her head. 'I cannot understand you, Osman Bey. We belong to two different worlds.'

'Wisdom cannot be acquired in a day, especially when one has been reared in foolishness and lack of logic. But because you are beautiful and good I want to protect you from the woes that will come upon you if you persist in forcing fate as you know it, while heeding not the ends and means Allah has designed for you.'

Angélique wanted to look away from him and answer proudly that it was impossible to compare an education derived from the Koran to the rich inheritance of the Greek and Roman classics. But she felt too baffled, as if she were being followed and kept apart from herself by a clear, calm spirit which had the power of darting beams of radiant light into the still dark corners of her destiny.

'Osman Bey, are you a seer?'

The smile which flickered over the lips of the Grand Eunuch was not ungracious. 'No, I am only a human being stripped of those passions and desires which so often rob one of vision. I want more than anything else to remind you, Firousi[1], that Allah always answers prayers when they are constant and just.'

Finally the long train of the caravan got under way, slithering like a huge worm across the wild country under the deep blue vault of the sky toward the Aurès range of the Atlas Mountains. It consisted of two hundred camels, as many horses, and three hundred donkeys, not to mention the dwarf elephant and a giraffe. A large contingent of armed horsemen, most of them Negroes, led it; another formed a rearguard,

1. The Arabic word for 'turquoise'

and here and there along the flanks were little knots of defenders. It was, as its leader the Grand Eunuch Osman Faraji remarked, 'the most important and impressive caravan to be seen in the last fifty years'.

The camel- and horse-borne vanguard was constantly riding ahead of the column every time they came in sight of a hill or a pass to spy out any perilous ambush that might be lurking there. Sentinels climbed every cliff to watch for raiders and signalled with their guns when it was safe to continue. Other signals were given with mirrors which flashed the sunlight back to the main body of the caravan.

Angélique rode in a palanquin perched between the humps of a camel. This was a signal honour, for many of the women, even the ones designed for the harem, either walked or rode donkeys.

They progressed across mountains that sometimes were utterly barren and at other times covered with cedars and acacias. The porters were principally Arabs, whereas all the Negroes, even ten-year-old children, rode horses and were armed.

Osman Faraji was the undisputed leader of this motley gathering. He advanced slowly on his snow-white horse in a cloud of golden dust, returning every so often to inspect the column, keep in communication with his lieutenants, restrain the exuberance of the young soldiers, and bring frequent refreshments to the most interesting of his female captives. It was he who parleyed with the bandit chieftains whenever they were lured into a skirmish that looked as if it might turn into something serious. These robbers were so numerous that to massacre them all would have required too great a waste of ammunition; it was frequently better to pay them a toll of money or wheat. They were mostly Berbers or Kabyles, tribes of mountaineers or farmers, whose wretched existence forced them into attacking caravans to survive. Their bows and arrows, however, were no match for the muskets of the sovereign of Morocco.

Osman Faraji was in a hurry to gain the frontiers of his chosen kingdom. The importance of the caravan and the wealth of its possessions were drawing bandits to it as honey draws flies. Savary gave Angélique an itemised list of the gifts the Admiral of Algiers was sending to his most powerful lord Mulai Ismail: a throne of gold, sparkling with precious gems, which Mezzo-Morte had plundered from a Venetian galley, which had seized it from a pirate ship coming from Beirut, where it had been stolen from the Shah of Persia on his tour of inspection of his Ishmaelite tribes; its gold alone was worth eighty thousand piastres. There were also two copies of the Koran encrusted with jewels; a richly embroidered drapery from the door of the Kaaba; three scimitars studded with gems; a toilet set consisting of seventy-nine articles of gold; a thousand yards of mousseline for turbans; two bolts of silk from Persia; and five hundred bolts of Venetian silk. Then there were a hundred young boys, twenty black eunuchs from Somaliland, Libya and the Sudan; ten black Ethiopians and ten white; sixty Arab horses; the pygmy elephant in a harness of gold and pearls, and the giraffe in trappings of scarlet, and lastly twenty women from among the loveliest of every race.

Angélique estimated the value of all this treasure at not less than two million *livres*. It revealed to her the prestige of the Italian renegade she had treated so insultingly. Yes, Mezzo-Morte must indeed be a powerful man! Yet she had stood up to him. She would stand up to Mulai Ismail too, regardless of how awe-inspiring he might prove! With that resolution Angélique emerged from the torpor in which she had been steeped by the long days of nauseating swaying on her camel.

In the evening tents were pitched, and the smoke of the bivouac fires smudged the cool clearness of the orange- and lemon-coloured sky. To entertain the women destined for the harem Osman Faraji sent them several acrobats, a snake-charmer, a dervish and a dancer. There was also a blind minstrel who played on a tiny guitar and sang endless ballads devoted to the glory of Mulai Ismail.

One night, as the blind man chanted, the tall figure of Osman Faraji appeared near Angélique.

'Do you understand enough Arabic,' he asked amiably, 'to follow the song?'

'Enough to have nightmares about it. Your Mulai Ismail seems to me nothing but a bloodthirsty savage.'

Osman Faraji did not reply at once, but sipped at the cup of steaming coffee a slave had just brought him.

'What empire,' he said at length, 'was not built on murder, war and blood? Mulai Ismail has just barely finished his struggle against his brother. He is a descendant of Mohammed on his father's side. His mother was a Negress from the Sudan.'

'Osman Faraji, are you seriously thinking of offering me to your sovereign as one of his innumerable concubines?'

'Hardly. Merely as his Number Three Wife with the title of Favourite.'

Angélique had resolved to try a trick no woman in the world does willingly. She had decided to add five – no seven – finally ten – full years to her actual age. Consequently she admitted to the Eunuch that she had passed forty. How could he dream of giving so demanding a sovereign a woman in her declining years to gratify his pleasures, when he himself had told her that concubines who had passed their prime were relegated to some distant quarter so that the harem might be constantly rejuvenated?

Osman Faraji listened to her with a smile on his lips. 'You are old?' he said.

'Very old,' Angélique said firmly, much as she hated to.

'That won't bother my master. He is quite up to appreciating the wit, the wisdom and the experience of an older woman, especially one whose body hides in its youthful seductiveness any trace of the maturity of the mind.' He looked her straight in the eye with a touch of mockery. 'A young woman's body, a mature woman's looks, the strength and the languor and all the knowledge of the art of love – and perhaps a little perverseness – of a woman in the full flower of her beauty – all that you have. Such stimulating contrasts will not escape the notice of my master. He himself will discern them the first time he lays eyes on you, for in spite of his own youth and his extremely voluptuous nature, he is very quick about people. He can subdue the passions of his Negro blood sufficiently to enjoy the variety of delights he will see you promise him. He can bide his time to satisfy his appetite, for he is physically and mentally superior to temptation as well as to fatigue. Without overlooking the attractions of his concubines – or, rather, by knowing how to overlook them from time to time – he is quite capable of attaching himself to one woman alone if he can truly see in her the reflection of his own mental vigour. Do you know the age of his Number One Wife, his Favourite, whom he continually consults? She is at least forty years old – truly so. She is terribly fat and a head taller than he, and black as the ace of spades. When you see her you will wonder what power she can possibly hold over him.

'His Number Two Wife, in contrast, can't be more than twenty. She is English, captured by pirates while she was travelling with her mother to Tangier, where her father was an officer of the garrison there. She is pink and white and extremely graceful. She delights the soul of Mulai Ismail, but . . .'

'But?'

'But Leïla Aisheh, the Number One Wife, has him under her thumb, though she does nothing without asking him first and always obeys him. I have tried in vain to free him from her influence. Little Daisy, whom we call Valina now that she has become a Moslem, is by no means vapid, but Leïla Aisheh, the Sultana, lets nothing get by her.'

'Aren't you a loyal servant of your Sultana Leïla Aisheh too?' asked Angélique.

The Grand Eunuch bowed deeply several times, touching his shoulder and his forehead with his hand to indicate that he was completely devoted to the Sultana of all Sultanas.

'What about the Number Three Wife?'

Osman Faraji rolled his eyes up, as he usually did at such a question. 'The Number Three Wife will have the firm, ambitious mind of Leïla Aisheh, and the white and gold body of the English girl. My master can savour every delight in her to such a degree that soon there will be no other woman in his eyes.'

'And she will follow unquestioningly all the advice of the Grand Eunuch, won't she?'

'If so, she will prosper, and so will my master, and so will the Kingdom of Morocco.'

'So that is why you were so kind to me in Algiers?'

'Doubtless.'

'Why didn't you have me whipped, as everyone thought you would?'

'You would never have forgiven me. No word, no promise, no favour would ever have erased your resentment if I had. Isn't that so, little Firousi?'

Angélique nodded. Whenever she chatted this way with Osman Faraji, no matter how touchy the subjects they discussed, she always felt calm, for he had the art of putting everything into its proper perspective. Yet because she felt herself slipping into a kind of temptation to submit to her captivity and adapt herself to it because it was in some ways so comfortable, she said fierily:

'Don't count on me, Osman Faraji! My destiny is not to become an odalisque of a half-breed Sultan.'

The Grand Eunuch never moved a muscle. 'What do you know about it? Is the life you are leaving behind so much to be regretted?'

Where would you like to live, then? For what world were you created, sister Angélique? her brother Raymond had said to her, looking straight into her soul with his Jesuit eyes.

'In the harem of the Great Sultan Mulai Ismail you shall have everything any woman could possibly desire: power, pleasure, wealth . . .'

'The King of France himself laid all his power and all his wealth at my feet, and I refused them.'

Now she had truly astonished him at last. 'Is that possible?' he asked. 'Did you refuse your sovereign when he entreated you? Was it because you were being faithful to your husband?'

'No, I have had no husband for many long years.'

'It seems unlikely you could be a woman insensible to the joys of love.

You have a freedom of spirit and a feminine way about you that should make it easy for you to get along with men. You have the life urge, the boldness of looks and laughter that bespeak a true courtier. I know I am not wrong.'

'Perhaps so,' said Angélique, delighted to see him so concerned. 'I have deceived all my lovers and become a widow, and now I prefer to live in peace, free from the torments love affairs inevitably bring. My coldness was a source of despair to King Louis XIV, it is true, but what could I do about it? Soon enough I would have deceived him too and he would have made me pay dearly for it, since monarchs don't like to be spurned. Your Mulai Ismail will hardly thank you for bringing such an indifferent mistress to his bed.'

Osman Faraji rubbed his princely hands together in perplexity. It was hard for him to conceal the deep frustration her words had caused him. Here was a flaw indeed in the well-oiled machinery of his plans! What could be done about a slave of such breathtaking beauty who promised on the surface to satisfy every vagary of the sophisticated Mulai Ismail's temperament, yet would be undemonstrative in his arms? What a mess! Osman Faraji broke out in a cold sweat just thinking of the results. He could hear Mulai Ismail bellowing now.

He betrayed his dismay by exclaiming aloud in Arabic: 'What am I going to do with you?'

Angélique understood and took advantage of the occasion to gain time. 'You do not need to show me to Mulai Ismail. In his harem where you say there are almost eight hundred women I could slip off to one side and mix with the female slaves. I would avoid ever coming face to face with your sultan. I would always wear my veil and you could say that I was disfigured by some loathsome skin disease. . . .'

Osman Faraji put an end to her imagining with a gesture of impatience. He said he was going to think it over. Angélique watched him move away with no small satisfaction. Yet in the bottom of her heart she was sorry she had so disturbed him.

When they crossed the frontier into Morocco, a change in atmosphere was immediately noticeable. The bandits disappeared, and in their place rose fortresses of huge trimmed stones that Mulai Ismail had ordered his legions to build in every corner of his realm. From each one of these emerged a garrison of red-turbaned Negroes as soon as the approach of the caravan was discerned. They pitched their tents near Arab settlements whose chiefs brought them quantities of chicken, milk and lamb. After the caravan departed, these chiefs burned white reeds to purify the air that had been defiled by the Christian slaves. This was a sombre, extremely religious country.

They got news that Mulai Ismail was at war with one of his nephews, Abd el Malek, who had aroused certain tribes and barricaded himself in Fez. But already the Grand Sultan was victorious. A messenger brought Osman Ferradji the welcome of his sovereign, who was rejoicing at the return of his best friend and chief adviser. Fez had just fallen into his hands.

As they approached Fez, traces of the fighting which had taken place came into view. Dead horses and corpses lay where they had fallen in the hollows of the pinkish grey sand. A wheeling flight of vultures cast its shadow on the city. On the golden-coloured ramparts three thousand heads still dripped blood from the pikes on which they were set, and three rows of twenty wooden crosses each still held the mutilated bodies of Ismail's enemies. The stench of the corpses was such that Osman Faraji did not wish to enter the city and chose to camp on the outskirts.

The following day messengers arrived with news that the felonious nephew Abd el Malek had been captured and was being brought back alive by the janizaries. Mulai Ismail himself was leading him back in chains with two thousand footsoldiers, forty Christian slaves carrying a huge cauldron, a thousand pounds of pitch and an equal amount of tallow and oil. They were being followed by a cartload of wood and six woodchoppers, axes in hand.

As they drew near to Meknès the caravan separated, some taking the road into the city, others pitching camp. Osman Faraji took with him a squadron of cavalry, Mezzo-Morte's young soldiers on their horses, and three of the most beautiful women, whom he placed on a white, a grey and a roan camel respectively. The porters and the slaves followed, bearing some of the most sumptuous presents sent by the Admiral of Algiers.

The Grand Eunuch came up to Angélique, who was seated apart on her horse.

'Wrap yourself tightly in your woollen veil if you don't want to meet Mulai Ismail today,' he advised her drily.

Angélique did not need to be told that twice. She had hoped the Grand Eunuch would leave her in the encampment, but he insisted she be present with him. Nevertheless, three eunuchs, on whom their chief had enjoined complete silence, escorted her. They were instructed to keep the curious away from her. She was to see but not be seen.

As they came out onto a small rocky plateau, Angélique saw Mulai Ismail's cavalry in full array. Their wonderful horses seemed to be weightless as they sped through the fierce light and the riders seemed to be borne on the very wind that fluttered their burnouses behind them.

In contrast to this brilliantly coloured spectacle there emerged to her left a group of Christian slaves covered with sweat and dust, their hair and beards matted, their tattered garments hitched above their knees to reveal legs welted by the whip. They were carrying an enormous brass cauldron which looked as if it might have come from the kitchens of Hell. It had been destined for the rum distilleries of America, but had been plundered near Madeira by the pirates of Salé, who had presented it to their sovereign. The slaves had been carrying it for four leagues out of Meknès and were wondering in anguish whether they would have to go much farther.

They came to a crossroads where a few palm-trees grew beside a well. The cart with the wood and the woodcutters had just arrived there. Near them, seated cross-legged on a crimson platform, was a personage clad in yellow being fanned by two little Negroes. Osman Faraji dismounted and went toward him, bending his great height in many bows and finally prostrating himself with his head in the dust. The personage in yellow, doubtless some important chief, replied by touching his forehead and his shoulder with his hand and then laying it on Osman Faraji's head. Then he rose, and the Grand Eunuch did likewise.

Beside Osman Faraji every man seemed short. The chief, who was taller than average, barely reached to his shoulder. His garments were simple: a full robe, the cuffs of which were turned back to disclose his bare arms, and a burnous of a deeper yellow than the robe with a hood that ended in a black tuft. A voluminous turban of cream-coloured mousseline perched on his head. As he came near, Angélique could see that he was a young man with negroid features whose dark skin gleamed like polished wood over his cheekbones and forehead and the bridge of his nose. A short black beard decorated his well-shaped chin. He began to laugh merrily at seeing seven of Osman Faraji's caravan approach, each one holding by its bridle the splendid horses Mezzo-Morte was sending to the Sultan of Morocco. The Negroes prostrated themselves on the ground.

Angélique leaned down to one of the eunuchs, a fat mound of a creature named Rafai, and whispered to him in Arabic: 'Who is that man?'

The Negro's eyes opened wide in surprise. 'Why it's he . . . Mulai

Ismail our ruler.' Then he added, rolling his eyeballs like castanets: 'He is laughing, but we should be wary for he is wearing yellow, the colour of anger.'

Then the captives staggering under the weight of their burden set up a chorus of groans. 'What shall we do with the cauldron, lord? What shall we do with the cauldron?'

Mulai Ismail bade them set it on a big fire of wood that had just been kindled. Oil and fat were poured in to help melt the pitch. During the next few hours the gifts from Algiers were brought out and presented.

The pitch in the cauldron was beginning to smoke as a deafening din of tambourines, musket salvoes and piercing shouts announced the arrival of the vanquished rebel.

The Sultan's nephew, Abd el Malek, was of the same age as the uncle against whom he had been fighting, that is to say, quite young. He was on muleback, his wrists bound behind him. Following him came his lieutenant, Mohammed el Hamet, similarly bound on a mule, and all his chiefs pushed along by the janizaries who had overtaken them in their flight. The women were tearing their faces with their nails and wailing.

Mulai Ismail signalled for his black horse to be brought him, and leaped into the saddle. Suddenly he seemed transformed, greatly increased in size, and strangely inflated as his sun-coloured burnous billowed around him. He made his horse curvet several times. His face gleamed like bronze against the blue enamel of the sky, and glints like molten steel flickered in its shaded parts. Under the arches of his coal-black eyebrows his glance became penetrating and fearsome. He brandished his javelin and spurred his horse into a gallop briefly before reining it in short before his chained enemies.

Abd el Malek had dismounted from his mule and thrown himself prostrate on the ground. The King applied his lance to his stomach. The unlucky prince kept throwing glances at the cauldron in which the pitch was now seething, and at the woodcutters, and fear overcame him. He was not afraid of death itself, but Mulai Ismail was renowned for the tortures he inflicted on his foes.

Abd el Malek and Mulai Ismail had been brought up together in the same harem, and had been part of a band of descendants of a great prince who traced his line from Mohammed. They were a pack of cruel little wolves whom no one dared discipline and whose most harmless amusement consisted of blowing darts at Christian slaves as they toiled. The same day had seen them both mount a horse for the first time, they had speared their first lions at the same time, and together had participated in raids on Tafilalet. They had loved each other like brothers until the time the tribes of the south and of the Atlas Mountains had called Abd el Malek's attention to the fact that his rights to the throne of Morocco were quite as sound as those of a son of a Sudanese concubine. Abd el Malek, who was of pure Moorish blood and of Kabyle extraction, had answered the call of his people. At the beginning his chances surpassed those of his uncle, but Mulai Ismail's persistence, strategy and imperious ways had finally brought him victory.

'For the love of Allah,' Abd el Malek exclaimed, 'do not forget I am your relative.'

'You forgot it easily enough, dog!'

'Remember we were like brothers, Mulai Ismail!'

'I killed two of my brothers with my very hands, and had ten others put to death. What does a mere nephew matter to me!'

'For the love of the Prophet, forgive me.'

The King did not answer. He gave a signal to take the prince and force him into the cart. Two guards leaped upon him, one taking him by the right arm, the other by the left elbow to extend his hand over a chopping block.

The King summoned one of the woodcutters and ordered him to perform the butchery. The Moor hesitated, being one of those who had secretly desired victory for Abd el Malek. With the death of the young prince would vanish the eager hopes of the tribes he led for founding a noble dynasty. The humble woodcutter-executioner hid his feelings, but he knew Mulai Ismail's eye could pierce his secret thoughts. He began to climb into the cart, then stopped and took a step backward, declaring that he could never cut off the hand of a man of such noble birth, his sovereign's own nephew. He would rather have his own head cut off.

'So be it!' exclaimed Mulai Ismail. And drawing his scimitar, he decapitated the woodcutter with a single stroke that betrayed his long experience in such matters.

The man toppled to the ground, his head bouncing away from his trunk, his blood spurting over the burning sand.

Another woodcutter was selected and, somewhat intimidated by the fate of his predecessor, did mount the wagon. While he was climbing into it, the King ordered the children, the wives and the relatives of Abd el Malek to be brought close.

'Come hither,' he said to them, 'and see cut off the hand of that beast who dared to take arms against his King, and the foot cut off of him who dared march against him!'

Such howls of despair rose into the stifling air that they drowned the cry of the prince as the woodcutter chopped off his hand. Then he cut off one foot.

The Sultan came closer and said: 'Now do you acknowledge me to be your King? You did not so recognise me previously.'

Abd el Malek did not answer as he watched the blood drain from his veins. Mulai Ismail curveted back to his previous position, turning his fearsome face toward the sky in the throes of an excitement that froze with terror all those who beheld him. Suddenly he lifted his lance and with one thrust pierced the heart of the woodcutter.

Seeing that, his former rival, dripping with blood, shouted: 'See what a valiant man he is! He kills those who obey him and those who disobey him. All he does is vain. Allah alone is just. Allah alone is great!'

Mulai Ismail began roaring to drown the voice of his victim. He shouted that he had brought the cauldron so that the traitor could taste the supreme torture, but because he was great and magnanimous, the pitch designed for his execution would instead be used to save him. He had acted as an outraged King should act, but he would leave it to Allah to decide whether Abd el Malek should live or die. It could never be said that he had killed his brother, for too many things bound them one to the other, and he was experiencing now the greatest sorrow of his life. The woodcutter's axe had, as it were, sliced off his own hand and foot. Yet Abd el Malek was no more than a traitor who, if he had won, would have cut off his hand, he knew. Still he would show him grace.

He ordered his nephew's gory stumps to be dipped into the boiling pitch to stop their bleeding. Then he dismissed the assembly and ordered four chiefs on pain of their lives to bring his nephew alive to Meknès.

The officers knew what fate he was keeping in store for the lieutenant Mohammed el Hamet. Mulai Ismail delivered him to his game-beaters, little Negroes of twelve to fifteen years of age, who dragged the sheikh to the walls of the city. No one knew what they did to him, but when they brought him back at the end of the day, he was certainly dead, and none of his people could recognise him.

Mulai Ismail and his escort and the gaily-coloured caravan of Osman Faraji had reached Meknès at the hour of sunset, the time when banners were hoisted on the golden globes that tipped the minarets and the plaintive yet commanding summons of the muezzins drifted over the ivory-hued city and rose over its rocky crest into the glow of the scarlet sky.

The black jaws of the massive gate shut on the swarming figures, swallowed up its ration of footsoldiers and horsemen, slaves and princes, camels and donkeys, leaving the plain deserted at night. Within its ramparts the city absorbed all human sounds – cries and weeping, fever and passion.

As she passed through the gate Angélique turned her eyes away from a naked giant slave nailed to the arch above it by his hands, his blond head hanging down on his chest like a crucified Christ's.

CHAPTER EIGHTEEN

Angélique put her hands over her ears to shut out the hysterical screams of Abd el Malek's women shrilling throughout the palace in a crescendo punctuated with sobs. It had been going on for hours, and now an almost unbearable pain drilled her temples, and she shivered uncontrollably.

Fatima, who, although technically a free woman, had decided to follow Angélique into Morocco so that she might die by the side of one from her own land, tried in vain to get her to take some liquid, either hot or cold, and to eat some fruit cake. But the very sight of these glutinous, sickly sweet delicacies heaped in quantities to appease the fatigue of her journey, recalled to her all too vividly the frightful situation she was in now, shut up in the harem of the most cruel prince the universe had ever known.

'I'm afraid. I want to get out of here,' she kept repeating in the halting voice of a child.

The old Provençal woman could not understand why she should be taken with such a sudden fit of depression now that they had reached the end of their arduous journey during all of which Angélique had been a model of courage and forbearance. To Fatima-Mirelia's mind nothing could be better than this enormous establishment, where the iron hand of the Grand Eunuch kept everything calm and in order. In spite of the confusion caused by the recent events, traces of which still remained in the city, and the apprehension everyone felt as a result of Mulai Ismail's being defied by his own nephew, and in spite of the fact that the Grand Eunuch had been immediately called into conference by the King, the new arrivals in the harem and, for that matter, all the members of the caravan, had been given a lavish, joyous welcome.

This provisional seraglio of the Grand Eunuch's was perfectly appointed. Fatima rejoiced in it after all the hard years she had spent in the stinking casbah of Algiers, a poor rootless old woman with nothing to eat but a handful of figs and a swallow of water to wash them down. Here there were plenty of other old women full of experience and gossip, slaves raised to the rank of servants or housekeepers. Among them, too, were former concubines of the King and his predecessor who had not been granted the privilege of withdrawing to faraway harems like the favourites. These still carried on their love of intrigue, and spread their rancour among the household servants.

These were responsible for each of the present concubines or favourites – for their clothes, their jewels, their appearance. They were constantly busy painting their faces, plucking out their grey hairs, doing up their hair, giving them advice, gratifying their whims, and slipping them treasured prescriptions for keeping the love and favour of their lord and master. Fatima was completely at home. She had already heard of a member of the suite of Sultana Leïla Aisheh whom her mistress favoured and who, like Fatima herself, came from Marseilles. Furthermore the eunuchs were more polite here than in the average harem. Osman Faraji did not underestimate the influence of the old slaves on the new, and knew how to use them to their best advantage as jailors.

The more she thought about it, the more pleasant Fatima found this seraglio. She almost thought that not even the harem of the Grand Sultan in Constantinople could surpass it for opulence and elegance. The only flaw in the picture was Angélique's behaviour. She seemed on the point of weeping and howling and tearing her face with her nails like Abd el Malek's native women in the next room, or like the Circassian girl who would occupy the royal bed that very night and whom the eunuch had carried off screaming with terror through the winding corridors and courtyards. When women began to lose their self-control, and when there were more than a thousand of them together, anything was likely to happen. In Algiers Fatima had seen captives hurl themselves from balconies and split their skulls open on the tiles beneath. Sometimes, too, these wanderers succumbed to homesickness. Any one of these things could happen to Angélique.

Fatima did not know what to do. She would have to delegate her responsibility. She asked the advice of the second-in-command among the eunuchs, Rafai, Osman Faraji's right arm. He advised a soothing potion for her, such as had already been brewed for the Circassian girl.

Her head splitting, Angélique looked with haggard eyes upon them as if they were creatures of a frightful dream. She hated the sight of the old slaves, the popping eyes of the innocent Negro boys, and more than anything else the slinky Rafai with his hypocritical way of playing sympathetic nursemaid to her. He was the one who always ordered intractable women to be flogged, and he was never without his quirt. Oh, how she hated them all! The pungent odour of the cedar woodwork made her headache worse. The shrill screams, however far away, were suddenly less frightful to her than the continual feminine laughter that floated to her from a screened alcove along with the scent of mint and green tea.

She sank into a fitful sleep only to awake during the night and find another black face bending over her. At first she thought it was a eunuch, but from the way the face was veiled and from the blue emblem of Fatima, the daughter of Mohammed, on its forehead, she knew it to be a huge woman with mountainous breasts.

The Negress bent her thick-lipped, sharply inquisitive face over Angélique. The lamp she held cast a yellow glow over her features and made a golden halo around the pale pink, dawn-clear tints of her companion's flesh and the honey-coloured locks escaping from her filmy veil. The two women, one white, the other black, were whispering in Arabic.

'She is beautiful,' said the pink and white angel.

'Much too beautiful,' said the black demon.

'Do you think she will take his fancy?'

'She has everything it takes to do it. Damn Osman Bey, that sly tiger!'

'What are you going to do, Leila?'

'Wait. Perhaps she will not please the King. She may not be clever enough to captivate him.'

'And if she isn't?'

'I shall make her my puppet.'

'Suppose she remains Osman Faraji's?'

'There are spirits of nitre and acids that can spoil faces that are too beautiful, and silken cords to strangle voices too seductive.'

Angélique let out a piercing shriek like a Moslem in religious ecstasy. The angel and the demon vanished into the darkness.

Angélique got up, aflame with a fire that gave her the strength of a madwoman. She shrieked and shrieked.

Fatima was beside herself, as she and all the other women and the Negro boys ran in every direction, stumbling over the cushions, trying to light the lamps to see what the matter was.

Osman Faraji appeared, his huge shadow stretching over the tiled floor. Just the sight of him seemed to calm Angélique, he was so tall and serene, so supremely intelligent. Now she was no longer hemmed in by demons. She slipped to her knees and buried her face in the folds of his sage's garment as she sobbed over and over again: 'I'm so afraid, so afraid!'

The Grand Eunuch bent down to rest his hand on her hair. 'What are you afraid of, Firousi? You did not fear the anger of Mezzo-Morte.'

'I'm afraid of that bloodthirsty beast, Mulai Ismail. I'm afraid of his wives who came here and wanted to strangle me. . . .'

'You're burning with fever, Firousi. When you are well again, you won't be afraid.'

He ordered her to be put back to bed, kept well covered, and given broth to reduce her temperature.

Angélique was still panting as she lay back on her cushions. The weariness of the journey, the heat of the sun, the horror of all she had seen and the stench of the corpses had brought on another attack of the same Mediterranean fever that had smitten her on d'Escrainville's vessel.

The Grand Eunuch knelt beside her couch. She groaned.

'Osman Bey, why have you inflicted me with these trials?'

He did not ask what she meant. He was well aware that Angélique had been violently affected by the sight of Mulai Ismail rendering justice, for he had noticed that Christians of Western nations were much more inclined to be disturbed at the sight of blood than Moors or Christians of oriental origin. He had not yet made up his mind whether that was due to hypocrisy or whether it was a genuine revulsion. In every woman's heart sleeps a panther licking its chops as it revels in another's suffering. His charges, whether taciturn Russians or giggling little Negresses, preferred seeing a Christian martyred to any entertainment, be it dancing or feasting, that he could devise for their amusement. Even the English Daisy-Valina, ten years now a convert to Islam and much in love with the King, still drew her veil across her eyes or peeped through her fingers when certain spectacles became too bloody.

He would just have to possess his soul in patience. This one was intelligent enough to shed her sensitivity quickly.

'I thought it necessary,' he murmured, 'to let you see the full power and glory of the master I chose for you . . . whom you must enslave.'

Angélique started to laugh nervously, but it caused her such pain

235

that she put her hands to her throbbing head and stopped.

Enslave Mulai Ismail! She could still see him whirling in his yellow cloak, beside himself with rage and grief, as he cut off the head of the woodchopper.

'I wonder whether you understand the meaning of that word "enslave". Your Mulai Ismail does not seem to me made of the kind of stuff a woman can wrap around her little finger.'

'Mulai Ismail is a prince of astonishing strength. He can see things clearly and in perspective. He acts quickly and justly. But he is an insatiable bull. He needs women, and he is always in danger of falling under the influence of a crafty little mind. He needs a woman near him to gratify his whims . . . to appease the loneliness of his heart . . . to swell his dreams of conquest. Then he will be a great prince. He can aspire to the title of Emir el Muminin, the Commander of the Faithful.'

The Grand Eunuch spoke slowly and with a certain hesitancy. This woman he had searched for so long and at last had found, who would help him to bring about Mulai Ismail's true ambitions, still raised doubts in his mind. He saw her crushed before him, yet at the same time slipping through his hands and eluding him, though even now she was still clinging to his robe.

Women are strange and difficult beings. Their greatest weakness hides an implacable awareness.

Once more Osman Faraji, Grand Eunuch of the Seraglio of His Majesty the Sultan of Morocco, thanked the Most High that fate and the skilled hand of a Sudanese witch-doctor had set him apart ever since his youth from the slavery to a woman that can change a man of lofty mind into the silly plaything of a capricious doll.

'Didn't you find him young and handsome?' he asked softly.

'More burdened with crimes than he is with years, I dare say. Who can count the number of murders he has committed with his own hands?'

'But think of the attempts on his life he has escaped. As I reminded you before, all great empires are built on murder. Such is the law of this earth. In sha Allah! I should like you, Firousi – listen carefully, for such is my desire – I should like you to insinuate into Mulai Ismail that subtle poison you alone possess that turns men's hearts faint and makes them thirst after you as did that fool d'Escrainville, not to mention your own great sovereign the King of France, whom you hurt so cruelly. You know very well your King of France can never forget you. He let you escape him, and now he shall nevermore achieve anything good or great. Use your power on Mulai Ismail. Plunge into his heart the poisoned dart of your beauty. But,' he added in an even lower voice, 'I shall never let you escape me.'

Her eyes closed, Angélique listened to his clear, youthful voice as if it were a close friend's. When she opened her eyes she was astonished to find so black a face with such an austere expression so characteristic of the worldly wisdom of the great African peoples.

'Listen to me, Firousi. Reassure me too. I shall give you time for your fever to subside and for your reason to understand and for your body to quicken with desire. I shall bide my time to disclose you to my sovereign. He will not know of your existence until the day you agree to let me reveal you to him.'

Suddenly Angélique felt her pain diminish. She had won the first round. In this mixed crowd of odalisques she would be better hidden than a needle in a haystack, and she could put that time to good use to seek her freedom and escape.

'You won't deceive me, will you?' she asked. 'You won't accidentally let fall some remark that would disclose me to Mulai Ismail?'

'I shall give orders. My commands are supreme in the harem, even taking precedence over the King's. Everyone bows to them, including the Sultana Leïla Aïsheh. She will hold her tongue if she knows what is good for her, for it will not take her long to dread your power.'

'She has already wanted to disfigure me with acid and strangle me,' Angélique whispered. 'That's just the beginning.'

Osman dismissed such commonplace threats with a sweep of his hand. 'All women who court the favour of the same man hate one another and fight among themselves. Are the Christian women any different in that respect? Didn't you have any rivals at the Court of France?'

Angélique swallowed hard. 'Yes indeed,' she said, as the Montespan suddenly took shape before her eyes.

No matter where she was, her life was one long struggle, one dream after another shattered, one more illusion dispelled. She was tired to death of it all.

Osman Faraji noticed how pale her face was, how tense with fever. Far from seeing in this mask of exhaustion the first signs of her yielding, he saw only what Angélique's usual vivacity and her customarily pink plump cheeks often disguised: the well co-ordinated bone structure that betrayed an unbridled power of will, the strong foundations of an indomitable character. It was as if he were seeing her much later, in her old age. Her face would never sag, never grow jowled and puffy, but rather would become more ascetic as her skin tightened over the exquisitely powerful armature of her skull. She would age like ivory, turning more and more lovely with the years, like dedicated women of strong convictions who in the fullness of their age at last transcend the travesty their youth has made of them. For a long time yet she would still be beautiful, no matter how seamed with wrinkles or how crowned with hair of white. Her eyes would lose their lustre only when they closed in death. Pale they might in her twilight years, but still their sea-green depths would gleam like deep, clear water and always keep their loadstone power.

It was this woman he needed to set close to Mulai Ismail, for if she were willing, he would always call her back to him. Osman Faraji knew what doubts assail a tyrant. His fits of frenzy in which he would slice off heads with one stroke of his sword were no more than an outburst of impatience with the stupidity of the people he found around him, a release from thoughts of the immense things remaining for him to do and the knowledge of his own weakness and of all the snares set for him. At times like those he would be seized with a fiendish need to demonstrate his power to himself as well as to others.

If he were to find in a warm and loving woman a refuge from all that, he would never tire of her. She would be the springboard, the fulcrum from which he would launch himself to conquer the world under the green banner of the Prophet.

In Arabic he murmured: 'You, you can do anything. . . .'

Already half asleep, Angélique yet heard him. Many times before, she had given others this same impression of invincibility. Yet she herself felt now so weak and helpless. 'You can do anything,' old Savary had said to her once when he wanted her to get something for him from Louis XIV. And she had done it. How long ago that was! Did she miss it? Madame de Montespan had wanted to poison her, just like Leïla Aisheh and the English girl. . . .

'Would you like me to send you that old slave who knows so much about medicine, the one you like to talk to?' Osman Faraji asked her.

'Oh, yes! Oh, how I would like to see my old Savary again! Would you let him into the harem?'

'With my permission he may enter. His age, his knowledge and his skills will be sufficient justification. No one will be shocked at seeing him here, for he looks and acts just like a priest. If he were not a Christian, I would be tempted to take him for one of those beings we venerate as possessed of Allah. During the journey he seemed to be completely preoccupied with his researches into magic, for strange vapours issued from the cauldron in which he brewed his charms, and I saw two blacks go into trances just from inhaling them. Has he ever revealed to you the secrets of his magic?'

Angélique shook her head.

'I am only a woman,' she said, knowing this modest answer would raise Osman Faraji's esteem for the wisdom and knowledge Savary possessed.

Angélique had trouble recognising Savary. He had dyed his beard a reddish-brown, which gave him the appearance of a Moroccan hermit, and this was heightened by a sort of camel's hair robe of a russet colour much too big for his body. He seemed in good physical shape, thin though he was, and brown as a berry. She finally recognised him by the big spectacles behind which his eyes still danced.

'Everything is going fine,' he whispered as he crossed his legs to sit down near her. 'I could never have imagined events could take such a good turn for us. Allah – I mean God – has taken us by the hand.'

'Have you found us some accomplices and a means of escape?'

'Escape? Oh yes, yes, that will come all in due time, don't you fret. And meanwhile, look.'

Out of the folds of his mantle he drew a cloth pouch and, smiling from ear to ear, began to extract from it some pieces of black, dusty stuff.

Angélique's eyes were still drooping from her fever. She said languidly that she could not see what he was showing her.

'Well, if you can't see it, you can smell it,' said Savary, passing the mysterious substance under her nose.

The odour made Angélique start, and in spite of herself she could not help smiling.

'Oh, Savary! The maumie!'

'That's right,' said Savary gleefully. 'Mineral maumie exactly like what oozes from the sacred rocks in Persia, except it is now in a solid state.'

'But . . . how is this possible?'

'I am going to tell you everything,' said the old apothecary. And with many furtive glances about the room he described his discovery to her in Arabic. It had occurred during the long journey of the caravan as they were crossing the region of the salt pools near the border between Algeria and Morocco.

'You recall those long arid stretches that reflected the sunlight? There didn't seem to be a thing of value there, and yet guess what happened.'

'A miracle, I suppose,' said Angélique, touched by his credulity.

'You're right,' said Savary excitedly. 'If I were a fanatic, I would name it the "miracle of the camel". Listen, now . . .'

He had noticed, he said, a camel that looked like an old moss-covered rock, its hair almost completely gone in some places from the mange. When the caravan halted one evening this camel began to snuffle in the dirt. It wandered off and from time to time stopped to sniff at the dunes. Savary, who was not asleep, got up and went after the beast to bring it back to the driver in the hope that the man might reward him with an extra ration of meal. Or perhaps he was instigated by the finger of Allah – er – of God. The sentinels, who often mistook him for an Arab or a Jew, paid hardly any attention to him, most of them being asleep anyway, for there was no longer any fear of bandits and still less of any Christian slaves escaping in a region like that, where one could wander for days on end without finding a scrap of food or a drop of drinkable water.

The camel roamed for a long time, passing dune after dune in which Savary was almost buried alive by the shifting sand, making the ground firmer. The camel had begun to crack this crust with its feet and then tear pieces of the surface off with its teeth and dig a hole.

'A camel digging a hole with its feet when it can't bear to set them down on pebbles surprises me. I can see you don't believe me,' Savary said with a suspicious glance at Angélique.

'But if . . .'

'Do you think I was dreaming?'

'No indeed.'

'Well, out of the dry brown soil that beast was digging what you identified right away. Then he took his teeth and spread the pieces he had excavated along the edges of the hole like a mattress, and rolled himself around on it.'

'And so his mange was miraculously cured.'

'Cured it was, but you ought to know there was nothing miraculous about it,' Savary corrected her. 'You have already seen as well as I the wonderfully curative effect it has on skin diseases. The only thing was that when I picked up some of those clods I never noticed the analogy between them and the divine Persian liquid. I was only planning to use it as a salve for my own ailments. But this is what I did observe, and thereby made a remarkable scientific discovery.'

'Another one? What was it this time?'

'Why, that salt is an indication of the presence of mineral maumie. It's exactly the same in Persia. So now I don't have to go to Persia. Just by going back to southern Algeria perhaps I can find enormous deposits of that priceless substance, which at least has the advantage of not being the closely guarded private property of the Shah as the ones in Persia are. I shall be able to get there easily.'

Angélique sighed. 'Perhaps the deposits are not guarded as they are in Persia, but you are, my dear Savary, right in the middle of Morocco. Doesn't that make a slight difference in your plans?'

Then she was ashamed of having been so sceptical of her only friend, and warmly congratulated Savary, which was just what he wanted. Presently he suggested that they have a brazier of coals and a copper or earthenware dish brought them.

'Why, for heaven's sake?'

'Why, to distil some of this for you. Once I tried distilling it in a closed vessel and it exploded with a noise like a cannon.'

Angélique persuaded him not to repeat that experiment in the middle of the harem. Her headache was disappearing as a result of the broths the Grand Eunuch had made her drink, and she was sweating freely all over her body.

'The fever is leaving you,' Savary said, looking at her over his spectacles.

Angélique began to think more clearly. 'Do you think your maumie could again help us escape?'

'Why is your mind always so set on escaping?' Savary asked as he carefully dropped the pieces of oily sand back into their case.

'It's more set than ever,' Angélique said emphatically, sitting up in indignation.

But her strength failed her, and she fell back on her cushions, wondering in despair if her only friend were going to forsake her. She could see no alternative to escaping.

'I feel the same way,' Savary said. 'I don't mind telling you I can't wait to get back to Paris to devote myself to the researches this discovery of mine has opened up. It's only there that I have the proper apparatus for distilling and experimenting with this inflammable mineral which I feel in my bones will greatly advance civilisation.'

He could not resist picking up a little piece of it again and examining it through a small magnifying-glass framed in tortoise-shell and ebony. One of Savary's characteristics was to produce like a sleight-of-hand artist, no matter what clothes he might be wearing, all kinds of things that exactly suited the needs of the moment. Angélique asked him how he had come by that magnifying-glass.

'My son-in-law made me a present of it.'

'I never noticed it before.'

'I've only had it a few hours. When that nice son-in-law of mine saw me envying it, he gave it to me as a token of welcome.'

'And who is your son-in-law?' asked Angélique.

Savary folded the glass into its tortoise-shell case and stowed it in the folds of his garments.

'A Jew here in Meknès,' he said, 'a dealer in precious metals, as was his father before him. I haven't had a chance to tell you about all this, but I have put to good use the time that's elapsed since we arrived in this fine city of Meknès. It has changed a lot since the time of Mulai Archi. Mulai Ismail is building everywhere. There is as much scaffolding as there is at Versailles.'

'Go on about your son-in-law.'

'I'm getting there. I told you that I made two good friends in Morocco when I was a slave here before.'

'And two sons.'

'That's right, except that I didn't remember quite correctly. It seems that I had the joy of having a daughter by Rebecca Cayan, not a son. It's that daughter I found today, fully grown and married to Samuel Maimoran, who was kind enough to give me the magnifying-glass.'

'As a token of welcome! Oh, Savary,' said Angélique, unable to keep from laughing, 'you are so French it does my heart good just to listen to you. When I hear you say "Paris" or "Versailles" it seems to take me away from this stench of cedar and sandalwood and mint, and turn me back into the Marquise du Plessis-Bellière.'

'So you really want to be she once more? You really want to escape?'

'Haven't I said so over and over again?' Angélique exclaimed with some irritation. 'Do I have to tell you a hundred times before you'll believe me?'

'You have got to know what you are exposing yourself to. You could die fifty deaths before you even got outside the seraglio, twenty before you'd crossed the threshold of Mulai Ismail's palace, ten before you got out of Meknès, fifteen before you got to Ceuta or Agadir, and three before you got inside one or the other of these Christian strongholds.'

'So you give me only two chances of success out of a hundred?'

'That is correct.'

'I will succeed just the same, Maître Savary!'

The old apothecary shook his head anxiously. 'Sometimes I wonder whether you are not too stubborn. It's not healthy to tempt fate to such a degree.'

'Now you talk like Osman Faraji,' said Angélique.

'Sometimes I think that if this princely seraglio agreed with you . . . if the great Mulai Ismail's personality did not displease you too much . . . it would be simpler . . . oh, never mind,' he broke off, seeing Angélique's eyes fill with tears. 'Pretend I didn't say anything. Take a little comfort. . . .'

He patted her hand gently. He would not for all the world deliberately have made this great lady weep, for had she not been as friendly to him as if he were of her own station, always listened to his explanations courteously, done him many favours . . . ?

Why, he wondered, had not this woman, to whom nothing was impossible, become Louis XIV's mistress? Of course, there was that legend about her husband Mezzo-Morte had used as bait for his trap. He had been more clever than she thought.

'We shall escape,' he said indulgently. 'We shall escape. That's understood.'

He undertook to show her that the chances for escape from Meknès were even better than they might have been from Algiers. Some escapes from here had, indeed, been successful. Since the King owned all the captives, they could organise themselves into a sort of guild. They had elected a leader, a Norman from Saint-Valéry-en-Caux named Colin Paturel, who had been a slave for twelve years and who had gained considerable influence over his companions in misery. For the first time in the history of slavery Christians of different persuasions had stopped fighting among themselves, for he had set up a kind of parliament in which a Russian and a Cretan represented the Orthodox; an Englishman and a Dutchman the Protestants; a Spaniard and an Italian the Catholics. He, a Frenchman, healed their breaches and settled their rivalries justly.

He had been bold enough to go to Mulai Ismail, whom few men dared address directly for fear of their lives, and by some unknown power of persuasion had succeeded in making that tyrant listen to him. As a result he got the wretched state of the slaves considerably improved. A common fund made up of contributions from every slave served to pay for accomplices. Piccinino the Venetian, a former bank clerk, was made treasurer of this fund. Some Moors, always greedy for money, agreed to serve as guides for the escapees. Under their guidance six escapees had already succeeded within the past month. The king of the slaves, Colin Paturel, was deemed responsible and sentenced to be nailed by his hands above the gate of the city and left there till he died. Rebellion had smouldered among the captives after that sentence which deprived them of their leader. The black guards were using their clubs and lances to drive the slaves back into their prison, when suddenly Colin Paturel appeared before them and bade them quieten down.

His hands were torn to shreds after his twelve hours of torture, for he had fallen alive to the ground, and instead of escaping had voluntarily returned to the city and asked to speak to the King.

Mulai Ismail almost believed him to be under the protection of Allah. He began to fear and respect this Norman hero, and it amused him to talk with him.

'All of which goes to show, Madame, that it is far better to be a slave in Morocco than in the foul den of Algiers. Here life is intense, if you know what I mean.'

'And death is too.'

'It's all one and the same. A slave's chief strength, Madame, is his power to fight. And after a man has survived enough torments to be able to say to himself every night that he is glad still to be alive, he will stay in good health. The Sultan of Morocco has assembled an army of slaves to build his palaces, but soon that will become a thorn in his side. There's a rumour the Norman has just demanded that the King call back the Trinitarian Fathers to redeem the captives, as in other Berber states. I have just thought of something. If ever one of their missions comes to Meknès, you could send out a letter by one of the Fathers to the King of France informing him of your sad plight.'

Angélique blushed. She could feel the fever coming back, the blood pounding in her temples.

'Do you think the King of France would raise legions just to come to my aid?'

'It's quite possible Mulai Ismail would not ignore his demands. He pretends to admire that monarch greatly. He would like to copy him in every respect, especially as a builder.'

'I'm not so sure His Majesty would be any too eager to rescue me from this situation.'

'Who knows?'

Angélique knew the old man spoke with the voice of wisdom, but she would have preferred to die a thousand deaths rather than suffer the humiliation of the King's refusal of help. Her head was spinning. Savary's voice seemed to drift farther and farther away as she sank into a deep slumber just as a new day broke over Meknès.

CHAPTER NINETEEN

'We're going to the spectacle! We're going to the spectacle!' shrilled the harem women with a great jingling of their bracelets.

'Now, now, ladies, let's be a little calmer,' cautioned Osman Faraji soberly.

He walked up and down the rows of veiled figures, closely inspecting the costume and the ornaments of each one, and checking to see that the face veils were tightly fastened so as to reveal no more than a pair of dark eyes here, or light ones there, all sparkling in anticipation.

Once the women were ready for the parade to the spectacle, they all looked just alike – pear-shaped bundles of cloth balanced on tiny red or yellow slippers with curving toes. Only the first hundred favourites were to go, and Mulai Ismail would make his choice from amongst them by dropping his handkerchief before the one he had selected for his pleasure that day – or rather, that night. This, he had been told, was the way the Grand Sultan of Constantinople behaved in his seraglio.

When any woman had been passed over too many times, Osman Faraji took her out of the group and sent her elsewhere to put her to other work. Hence, it was the worst of all punishments to be banished from the 'presentation'. From then on all hope was gone of sharing the delights of the sultanate. It was the beginning of oblivion, of old age, of a cruel exile far from this luxurious abode. The Grand Eunuch was absolute master of these banishments or promotions, and he knew the effect of threatening restive captives with exile. When a woman was kept out of a presentation, she was also deprived of other pleasures, such as walks, spectacles, little excursions on which Osman Faraji did not hesitate to take the most interesting members of the harem.

On this particular day those left behind burst into sobs and wails when they heard the musket shots and the shouts of the crowd that indicated the festivities were beginning.

Osman Faraji himself came to bid them be quiet. The King was tired of hearing such groans in his seraglio. Did they want to happen to them what befell the wives and daughters of Abd el Malek? At the death of Abd el Malek, which occurred from gangrene a week after his hand and foot had been cut off, his women had renewed their lamentations, and the King had been obliged to threaten them with instant death if they did not stop. For several days while the King was in his palace, they had restrained their groans, but as soon as he went out, they began again. So the King had had four of them strangled before the eyes of the rest.

After this salutary rebuke those left behind stayed silent and began searching for some chink through which they might peep out over the terraces for a glimpse of the spectacle.

On his return the Grand Eunuch passed by Angélique's apartment, where her serving girls were swathing her in veils. She had no mind to weep and wail because she had been left behind, but the head of the harem continued his dangerous game of allowing the future favourite every chance to see her future master without being seen by him.

Consequently Angélique always had to mingle with the groups of women who accompanied the Sultan on his walks or on his public appearances. If he cast too inquisitive an eye on the mass of white and green cocoons that escorted him, three sharp-eyed eunuchs were instructed to conceal Angélique or ease her out of the way. It was Osman Faraji's policy to familiarise her with the nature and conduct of Mulai Ismail, the better to overcome her dislike and initiate her into her responsibilities. She could still be shocked by his violent explosions, but in time she would get used to them. He wanted her to accept without any reservations the master and the role he had planned for her.

So Angélique joined the group of women proceeding to the gardens. The English girl was there, unveiled, and holding by the hand two lovely little mulatto girls with yellow hair and amber skins – twins she had borne the Sultan. Their birth had cost her the title of Wife Number One, for Leïla Aisheh had borne him a son.

As an indication of her rank Leïla Aisheh came last in the procession. She, too, was unveiled, and she had joined the others by a private stairway leading from her own apartment. She had her own bodyguard of eunuchs, and a serving woman carried before her the sword that symbolised her power. Her imposing height was draped in red and striped scarves.

The exposed faces of the two favourites were enough to indicate that they did not feel bound to strict obedience to the commands of Osman Faraji. Leïla Aisheh had been plotting for a long time to raise the loyal chief of her bodyguards, Raminan, to the position of Grand Eunuch of the Seraglio. He was a coal-black eunuch whose forehead was tattooed in blue, indicating that he was of a different tribe from Osman Faraji, who was a Harrar. The feuds of the harem were merely an extension in miniature of the great tribal rivalries that existed in Africa.

Little Prince Zidan walked behind his mother. He owed his round chocolate-coloured face to his double Negro ancestry. He was dressed in a white turban and wore a robe of pistachio green and raspberry red. Angélique was much amused by him and nicknamed him Prince Bonbon, although there was nothing particularly sweet about his nature. From his six-year-old height he kept looking down at the real steel sword his father had just given him. Now at last he was finished with wooden swords and could cut off the heads of Mathieu and Jean Badiguet, the two French slaves who were his playmates. He was planning to try it today after the spectacle.

The two favourites drew their veils across their faces only as they went through the last gate leading to the palace gardens, where they ran the risk of meeting the male slaves building Mulai Ismaïl's mosque, baths and amphitheatre, and digging a pond there. But today the toolsheds were deserted. Ladders and cut stones lay beside the rude outlines of the structures under the silvery olive trees.

A distant rumble came to their ears from beyond the outer wall of the palace, where the slaves' encampment was, with a hut of adobe and wattles for each one, and each nation with its own section and its own leader and council.

The troop of women was taken under the protection of the King's horseguards and joined the royal procession which was forming. Mulai Ismaïl walked under a parasol held by two Negro boys. His principal tribal chiefs were around him, as well as his favourite advisers; Samuel Baidoran, a Jew; the renegade Spaniard, Juan di Alfero, known as Sidi Mushadi since his conversion; and another renegade, a Frenchman named Romain de Montfleur and now called Sidi Rodani, who was in charge of munitions.

The Sultan made a great show of welcome to Osman Faraji as he took his place among the dignitaries.

The Arabs were swarming in the stifling heat, and their shouts drowned the flourishes of the flutes and the jingling thump of the tambourines. But even louder cries were heard when the procession entered the central square of Meknès. As the throng of white burnouses opened a pathway for it, there was revealed on the esplanade a sad mass of tatters and white faces shrieking wildly. Like the damned in Hell the captives were stretching their hands toward Mulai Ismaïl, but were kept back by their guards, whips and clubs in hand. One name alone could be distinguished from the babel of cries in every language of Europe: 'The Norman! The Norman! Pardon for Colin the Norman!'

Mulai Ismaïl stopped the procession, a wan smile on his lips as if he regarded these supplications as shouts of acclamation. Then he mounted a small grandstand with the people in his suite. His women were settled in seats with a good view. It was then that Angélique saw what it was that separated the King and his entourage from the mass of slaves.

In the centre of the square was a rectangular hole about twenty feet deep and quite wide. The ground about its edges had been sprinkled with white sand. Rocks and some desert plants gave it the appearance of a small garden. The ammoniacal stench of wild beasts rose from the pit into the suffocatingly hot air. It was a den of lions!

Later Angélique noticed scattered carcasses in the corners, and in the bottom of the pit two wooden lattices which concealed the tunnels leading to the lions' cages.

Mulai Ismail raised his hand. One of the lattices was raised by some invisible means.

The slaves rushed forward with such force that those in front were almost hurled into the pit, and crawled to the edge, where on their hands and knees they peered into the gloomy chasm yawning below them.

Slowly a form emerged – a slave chained hand and foot. The lattice rattled down behind him. The slave blinked in the blinding sunlight. From the grandstand he appeared to be a man of unusual height and strength. The shirt and the short drawers he wore revealed his heavily muscled arms and legs, and his broad hairy chest on which shone a religious medal. Out of his light-coloured, matted hair and beard peeped sky-blue eyes. Closer to, his Viking's mop of hair and his beard would have revealed a few grey streaks, for he was at least forty years old and had been a slave for a dozen years.

A murmur rippled through the crowd until it reached the proportions of a mighty shout: 'Colin! Colin Paturel! Colin the Norman! '

A thin, red-headed boy leaned over to him and shouted in French: Colin, my friend, fight! Kill, murder, anything, but don't die. Do not die!'

The slave lifted his hands to quieten the mob. Angélique could see the bloody holes in the hollows of his palms, and recognised him as the man she had seen crucified above the gate as she entered the city. With measured steps he moved to the middle of the pit and raised his head toward Mulai Ismail.

'I greet you, my lord,' he said in Arabic in a firm voice. 'How do you do?'

'Better than you, dog,' replied the Sultan. 'Have you realised at last that the day has come for you to pay for the insolence you have made me swallow for years now? Even yesterday you dared anger me with your demand that I summon the Fathers into my kingdom so as to sell them my own slaves. I do not wish to sell my slaves. They belong to me. I am not in Algiers, or Tunis either, and I am of no mind to copy those corrupt traders who think only of their own welfare and forget what they owe to Allah. You have exhausted my patience, but not in the way you hoped. Did you think yesterday when I fell on your neck and made you promises that today you would be in the lion pit? Hahahah!'

'No, my lord,' said the Norman meekly.

'Yet you rejoiced, and boasted to your followers that you get from me all you wanted. Colin Paturel, you are going to die!'

'Yes, my lord.'

Mulai Ismail sat down again gloomily. The slaves began wailing and imploring again, until the guards levelled their muskets at them. The Sultan also looked in their direction, his face darkening.

'I take no pleasure in sentencing you to death, Colin Paturel. I forced myself to do it several times, then was glad to see you return safe and sound after the torture designed to destroy you. But this time, make no mistake, I shall give the demons no chance to save you. I shall not leave this spot until your last bone has been devoured. It does not please me, though, to watch you die, especially since you shall die in the dark night of your false beliefs and thus shall be eternally damned. I could still pardon you. All you need do is become a Moslem.'

'That is out of the question, my lord.'

'How is it impossible for any man who knows Arabic to pronounce these simple words: "There is no god but Allah, and Mohammed is his prophet"?' roared Mulai Ismail.

'If I were to say them I should become a Moslem. And then you would be in trouble, my lord. Why does it not please you to see me die, and why do you wish me to save my own life? Merely because I am the leader of your slaves here in Meknès and, because thanks to me, they work at your buildings with more zest and greater obedience, and because you need to keep me with them to finish your palaces and mosques. But if I were to become a Moslem, I would be a renegade, and then what influence would I have with these Christians? I could wear a turban, and go to your mosque, and never have to lift another trowel for you. As a renegade I am lost to you through your pardoning me; as a Christian I am lost to you through your lions.'

'Dog, your wily tongue has deceived me long enough. Die then!'

A breathless silence had fallen over the crowd, for while the slave was speaking, the lattice behind him had slowly risen. A magnificent Nubian lion had slowly slunk out of the dark passageway. It shook its massive, black-maned head and stalked forward with slow, cat-like stealth. Behind it came a lioness, and then a lion from the Atlas Mountains with a sandy pelt and a reddish mane. Silently they approached the slave, who did not flinch. The Nubian lion began to lash its tail, but what seemed to arouse him more than the motionless man beside him was the eager faces leaning over the edge of the pit. Growling, he moved his fearless eyes over the crowd, then roared a few times as he languidly stretched his hind legs.

Angélique muffled her face in her veil. Then she heard the crowd muttering, and looked anew. Completely disgusted with the obscene curiosity of which he was the object, the lion had gone to lie down in the shade of a rock, passing by the slave with total lack of interest except for rubbing up against his legs like a big house cat.

The crowd of Arabs began to scream hysterically out of frustration, and to throw stones and chunks of earth into the pit to arouse the lions. But the beasts merely roared in unison, and after making several circuits of the pit stretched out in front of the closed lattices as if they wanted nothing more than to continue their afternoon naps in peace.

Mulai Ismail's eyes were starting out of their sockets. 'He has a charm,' he muttered over and over again. Then he rose and went to the edge of the pit. 'Colin Paturel, the lions do not want to harm you. What is your power over them? Tell me, and I will spare your life.'

'Grant me my life first, and I will tell you afterward.'

'So be it! So be it!' said the King impatiently.

He motioned to the keepers to raise the lattices again. The lions yawned and loped back into the dark passageways. The lattices fell into place behind them.

A mighty shout burst from the throats of the slaves. The Christians threw their arms around one another and wept. Their leader had been saved!

'Speak! Speak!' shouted Mulai Ismail impatiently.

'One favour more, my lord. Allow the Fathers to come to Meknès to bargain for the repurchase of the slaves.'

'Bring me my musket. I will kill him with my own hands!'

'I shall take my secret with me.'

'So be it, then. Let your Fathers come. We shall wait and see what kind of gifts they bring me and then see what I may give them in return. Come forth, Colin Paturel.'

In spite of his heavy chains the mighty slave nimbly climbed up the stones that jutted out here and there on the sides of the pit. When he stepped out of it among the Arabs, none of them dared touch him, even though they felt ashamed and disappointed. He prostrated himself before the throne of Mulai Ismail, pressing his forehead to the earth.

A puzzled expression almost like a smile spread over the thick lips of the tyrant as he touched the curved toe of his slipper to the slave's thick neck.

'Rise, cursed dog!'

The Norman rose to his full height.

Angélique could not take her eyes from the sight of these two confronting each other. She was so near them she dared not move a muscle even to breathe. The passion seething in silent waves through the two men almost overcame her with its intensity. Osman Faraji had been right to force her into Mulai Ismail's presence. She could not escape the force of the man's character which emanated from him like heat from a red-hot stove. From a distance she would have judged him a dangerous puppet manipulated by sadistic whims. But he was not that. He was worse. If his rather handsome, gleaming bronze face inspired terror in chieftains heavy with years and accustomed to war, it was through some well-nigh supernatural power of his that he drew from them to himself their loyalty and their supreme efforts.

She remembered having felt the same way when she stood before Louis XIV. Weakness made Mulai Ismail see red and strike out at it, as if it were an insult to the life-force that smouldered within him like the fire in a volcano. He demanded an adversary of strength equal to his own, such as this barehanded slave. One had supreme power, the other was laden with chains, but each of them – king and slave, Moslem and Christian – knew only one enemy: Azrael, the angel of death.

But the black angel of death recoiled in dismay before creatures like these, and departed to scythe down lesser souls. Azrael would have to wait for another day to claim their lives – Mulai Ismail's in spite of the coat of mail he always wore beneath his burnous; Colin Paturel's in spite of his wiles. Still the battle each would offer the angel would be a furious one, and it would be many a long day before Azrael would finally triumph over them. One had only to look at them staring at each other to realise that.

'Speak!' said Mulai Ismail. 'What magic did you employ to stop the lions' jaws?'

'It is not a question of magic, my lord. When you decreed this punishment for me, you forgot that for a long time I had worked in the lions' cages and had often helped their keepers. The lions know me well, and I have often gone into their cages unharmed. Just yesterday I offered to take the place of the man who feeds them, and I gave them double rations. Double, did I say? Triple! The three animals you chose as the most ferocious came into the pit as stuffed with food as a cannon with wadding. Need I add that they were not in the least hungry? The very sight of a piece of flesh, alive or dead, would have turned their stomach, for I had mixed a soporific herb with their food.'

Mulai Ismail turned black with fury. 'Impudent dog! Do you dare tell me before my people that you have made a fool of me? I shall slice your head from your shoulders myself!'

He rose and drew his sword, but the leader of the captives protested.

'I have told you my secret. I have kept my promise. You have a reputation as a prince who keeps his word. You owe me my life and you have promised that the Fathers may come to redeem us.'

'Don't anger me with your words!' roared the tyrant, brandishing his scimitar. Then he sheathed it, muttering.

A line of servants bringing the King's repast in a huge copper bowl created a diversion. Mulai Ismail had given orders for his dinner to be served there, as he had thought the lions' appetite would increase his own.

The servants almost fell over backward at seeing the lions' meal standing before their master.

The King seated himself on a pile of cushions and motioned his suite to gather around him to share his meal.

Then he asked again: 'How did you guess I had planned to feed you to the lions? I never told a soul before dawn today. On the contrary, the rumour that I had heard you favourably had spread through the palace.'

The blue eyes of the captive narrowed. 'I know you, my lord. I know you.'

'Do you mean to say my plans are so obvious that I cannot deceive those who have access to me?'

'You are as sly as a fox, but I am a Norman.'

The Sultan laughed, his white teeth gleaming like a ray of light across his dark face. And his laughter released that of the slaves, who by now had learned the 'secret' of Colin Paturel.

'I like you Normans,' said Mulai Ismail warmly. 'I shall order the pirates to cruise the coasts of Normandy from Honfleur to Le Harve and bring me back vast numbers of them. There is only one thing about you I do not like, Colin Paturel. You are too big. You are taller than I, and that is something I cannot endure.'

'There are several means by which you can correct that, my lord. You could cut off my head, or you could ask me to sit beside you. Then you would be taller than I, what with your turban.'

'So be it,' said the Sultan after a moment's reflection during which he had apparently made up his mind not to take offence. 'Sit down.'

The slave folded his long legs and sank to the sumptuous cushions at the King's side. Mulai Ismail offered him a squab.

The chieftains and the other dignitaries of the entourage muttered in outrage, even Leïla Aisheh and Daisy-Valina. Mulai Ismail glared at them.

'What have you got to mutter about? Haven't you been served?'

One of the viziers, Sidi Ahmed, a renegade Spaniard, answered with a laugh: 'It's not lack of food we're worried about, my lord, but only to see a stinking slave sitting beside you.'

The King's eyes darted fire. 'And why do you think I am obliged to treat a stinking slave as an equal?' he asked. 'I shall tell you. Because none of my counsellors wished to sully his reputation by speaking for the slaves. If the slaves wish to ask something of me, they must speak to me directly, and that is the reason I am in the awkward position of punishing their insolence. Consequently I lose a slave every time because of your remissness. Shouldn't it be up to you to act as intermediary between them and me, especially you, Sidi Ahmed Mushadi, and you, Rodani, who once were Christians? Why did not you take it upon yourselves to ask me to let the Fathers come here? Have you no pity for your former brothers?'

As Mulai Ismail spoke, his fervour increased. The Spaniard did not worry, for he knew the strength of his position, having been the Sultan's chief officer in his campaigns against the rebel tribes. He replied to the bitter reproaches of the Sultan by casting a scornful look at the Christian slaves.

'I renounced their Lord and Master. I do not see why I should concern myself with his servants.'

'May I eat, my lord?' Colin Paturel asked meekly, still holding his squab in his fingers. At the moment he was suffering a torture worthy of Mulai Ismail's invention, for his stomach had been undernourished for years and had known no delicacy whatever.

The question threw the King into a new burst of fury. It called his attention to the fact that his chieftains had begun to eat without waiting for him, and he began to abuse them.

'Eat!' he roared at the Norman, 'and you other gluttons, stop stuffing yourselves as if you were slaves on a diet of bread and water instead of being filthy rich from all the money you have stolen from me.'

He ordered the servants to take away the food that had been served to the chiefs, and give it to the captives. The chieftains tried to keep their plates, saying that Christians were unworthy of eating from the same dish as the King, but Mulai Ismail made them give up the dishes just as they were, piled high with chicken and squabs and saffron rice.

The captives descended on the royal provender like a pack of starving dogs, and fought over the last scraps.

Still hidden in the throng, Angélique watched these poor creatures with pity, thinking how debased they had become as a result of their harsh and hopeless captivity. Among them were certainly to be found noble names, churchmen, people of quality, but misery had clad them all in the same grey uniform of rags. She noticed how thin they all were and thought of Savary, whose fingers had shrivelled to little more than matchsticks. The poor old man was, in fact, dying of starvation, and yet she had not even thought of offering him a wafer.

From her position she could hear the conversation between the King and the Norman, and get the drift of nearly everything they discussed. She observed that Mulai Ismail's violent, restless personality both allured her and revolted her. To master a man like that would be like trying to tame a wild animal, which would always remain wild and bloodthirsty.

The little Circassian girl from the Green Nile leaned against her shoulder, her eyes never leaving the Sultan. She had hesitantly confided in Arabic no more fluent than Angélique's that she thought him attractive.

'He is not so terrifying, you know. . . . He tried to make me laugh and forget my tears. . . . He gave me a bracelet. His hand was gentle when he touched me. His chest is like a buckler of silver. . . . I was not a woman before, but now I am. . . . And every night I discover new delights.'

'The Circassian pleases Mulai Ismail,' Osman Faraji had said. 'She amuses him and fascinates him like a kitten. That is all to the good. It gives me time to prepare him for the tigress.'

Angélique had shrugged rather rudely. She said nothing, but every day she found it harder to continue her passive resistance, plied as she was with candy and nuts, with beauty treatments and the titillating stories the women kept whispering to one another about their experiences in love. There was something about the harem that roused every sense and kept it sharp. Everything turned around the personality of Mulai Ismail, the all-powerful, the invisible. His spirit pervaded everything until it became an obsession. Angélique would wake up with a start in the middle of the night, certain she was seeing him take form in the shadows.

When she had the chance to see him in the flesh, as now, she preferred it to seeing him in her imagination. Now he had human dimensions, not the abstract, well-nigh divine qualities of a myth. She had never felt beyond her depth with a real man. She kept watching him, as the others did, and finally – found him to her liking.

'When will you let our Fathers come?' Colin Paturel asked as he crammed the food into his mouth.

'They can come when they want. Let them know that I will deal fairly with them.'

The Norman suggested that two letters be written to them, one from the King to Ali the son of Aballah, a chieftain in the Spanish city of Ceuta, so that he could start negotiations; the other to the Trinitarian Fathers themselves, to whom the French traders at Cadiz would forward it.

Mulai Ismail immediately called for his pen, and Colin Paturel summoned a scribe, the thin boy who just a few minutes before had cheered Colin with his shouts of 'Don't die! Kill!' He was nicknamed Jean-Jean, and he came from Paris – one of the very few slaves from that city.

Colin Paturel dictated a letter to him, addressed to the Reverend Trinitarian Fathers, beseeching them to equip a mission to repurchase the captives in Meknès who had up till now been abandoned there. He advised them to bring lavish presents to please the King, especially clocks with golden dials to symbolise the sun.

The Sultan's eyes gleamed. Suddenly he was in a hurry to dispatch his messengers.

Piccinino the Venetian, the captives' treasurer, drew four ducats out of the common till and gave them to the scribe who had written the letter to Ali. The letter was sanded, sealed, and slipped into a pouch which the messenger was to carry next to his skin in his armpit.

Mulai Ismail's face clouded. 'So you call them Trinitarian Fathers?'

'Yes, my lord. They are consecrated to religion, and they wander about the countryside collecting small donations from pious folk so as to get enough money to redeem penniless slaves.'

The Sultan's concern was of another variety, however. 'The Trinity?' he said. 'Isn't that the dogma you profess – that God is divided into three persons? There is no God but one God. I cannot allow in my realm infidels who hold to such a sacrilegious superstition.'

'Well, we can send the letter to the Redemptorist Fathers,' said the Norman simply, as he corrected the address.

Finally the messenger was off in a cloud of reddish dust, and Mulai Ismail continued his inquiries.

'You Christians say there is the Father, the Son and the Holy Ghost. You insult the nature of God. I believe that Jesus was the Word of God made flesh. I believe he was one of the greatest prophets, for the Koran says: "Every man born of woman is a child of Satan, except Jesus and His mother." But I do not believe that He was God in human form, for if I were to believe that . . . I would have to burn all the Jews in my kingdom.' He pointed his finger at Samuel Baidoran.

The Jewish counsellor hunched his back. Mulai Ismail's mind was a tangle of religious prejudices which kept him from thinking clearly. Most of his actions were inspired by his feeling that his god was frustrated and abased by the disbelief of the unbelievers, and that he, as Commander of the Faithful, had to make his god revered.

The Sultan sighed deeply. 'I would like to argue the Law with you, Colin Paturel. How can a sensible man find any comfort in a faith that preaches eternal damnation as punishment for sin?'

'I am no theologian,' replied Colin Paturel, crunching a squab's wing, 'but what do you call Good and Evil, my lord? For us the murder of one's fellow-being is a crime.'

'Fools! How can you be so stupid as to confuse worldly things with the eternal verities? Evil . . . the only unpardonable sin is to deny salvation, for that is denying the Truth. That is the crime you Christians commit every day of your life. You condemn yourselves, and so do the Jews, who were the first to receive the Word of God. Jews and Christians alike have corrupted our holy texts – the Books of Moses, the Psalms of David, the Gospels – and have made them say what they never did say. How can you live in such error? In such sin? Answer me, you bastard dog!'

'I cannot answer you. I am only a poor Norman sailor, born in Saint-Valéry-en-Caux. But I will recommend to you Renaud de Marmondin, a Knight of Malta, who is very learned in theology.'

'Where is this Knight of yours? Bring him to me.'

'He is not in Meknès. He left early this morning with the squad that went into the desert for gravel to make into mortar.'

His words suddenly distracted Mulai Ismail from his metaphysical inquiries. It didn't take his builder's soul long to realise that for three hours now his slaves had been resting.

'What are those dogs doing feasting on the scraps from my table?' he bellowed. 'I invited them to watch your death, not jeer at the humiliation you have caused me. Out of my sight, you swine! I pardoned you today, but tomorrow . . . beware of tomorrow!'

And he had all the French captives beaten with a hundred lashes each for having wasted the morning to watch Colin Paturel die.

CHAPTER TWENTY

The gardens of Meknès were a thing of wonder. Angélique went to them often, either with some of the other women or alone in a two-wheeled chaise drawn by mules, whose curtained sides hid her from view but allowed her to enjoy the beauty of the flowers and trees, and relax in the warm sunlight. But on these little excursions she was often fearful that the Grand Eunuch's strategy might have prearranged an encounter between her and her master at the turning of some garden path.

For Mulai Ismail had a certain fondness for walking in his gardens in which he resembled his fellow-monarch Louis XIV. He, too, liked to see the progress of his works in person. It was always a good time to catch him in his best mood, especially if he happened to be dandling one of his latest children or fondling one of his cats as he strolled along the shaded walks followed by several dignitaries of his Court. Every one knew this was the time to ask him for a particular favour, for Mulai Ismail never got angry then for fear of disturbing the little brown infant he held to his bosom or the sleek cat he was petting. Toward babies and animals he had a love and gentleness which impressed all who had access to him as much as his brutality toward his equals.

The gardens and palaces were full of rare animals. All kinds of cats wandered everywhere – under the flowers, in the trees, in the patios – and required a veritable army of servants to care for their grey, white, black or spotted fur. As one walked along the paths one could feel their bluish, golden-pupilled eyes like velvety invisible presences haunting the garden like local divinities, giving it a dreamy, mystical atmosphere.

Here cats were not trained to guard the slaves or the treasure rooms as in the Orient. They were loved for themselves, and that made them gentle and tame. All Mulai Ismail's animals were well cared for. His horses, which next to his cats he loved best, were kept in magnificent stables made of marble with fountains and troughs of green and blue mosaic.

At the edge of one pond pink flamingos, ibises and pelicans preened and strutted without the slightest timidity.

In spots the plantings were so thick, and the alignment of the olive-

257

trees and tall eucalyptus trees so cleverly arranged, that it seemed like a vast forest which made one forget one was actually in a prison, hemmed in by crenellated walls.

Generally eunuchs accompanied the women on these outings, for in spite of the high walls there were many people coming and going within them in connection with the continuous building schemes. Only the little patios with their tiny fountains and oleander bushes were freely accessible to the women.

One morning Angélique wanted to pay a visit to the dwarf elephant, hoping thus to encounter Savary, who was the head veterinary of this valuable animal. The Circassian girl and two other of Mulai Ismail's concubines joined her – one a big, cheerful Ethiopian named Muira, and the other a Nigerian with an impassive face the colour of lemon-wood.

They proceeded toward the menagerie under a guard of three eunuchs, one of whom was Raminan, the chief of the Queen's bodyguard, who was carrying Prince Zidan in his arms. The Prince had heard about the elephant and had screamed and cried until someone consented to take him to see it.

Angélique's prognostications were correct. There was Savary, administering an enema to his patient with a huge leaden syringe and the help of two other slaves. The elephant had eaten too many guavas. The Prince immediately wanted to feed him another. The veterinary gave in to his whim rather than risk the wrath of the royal piccaninny. Another guava more or less would not make the elephant feel any worse.

Angélique took advantage of this diversion to slip Savary a couple of loaves of bread which she had hidden under her scarves. Fat old Rafai saw her, but said nothing, for he had very strict orders not to antagonise her with nagging discipline.

'Have you been able to map out any plan for our escape?' she whispered.

The apothecary looked around him warily before he said between his teeth: 'My son-in-law Samuel Maimoran, that splendid fellow, is ready to lend me a sizable sum to pay guides. Colin Paturel knows some who have already helped others to escape.'

'Are they dependable?'

'He swears they are.'

'Then why hasn't he escaped himself?'

'He is always kept in chains. His escape would be as difficult to manoeuvre as yours. He says a woman has never tried to escape that he knows of. My advice is to wait for the Redemptorist Fathers to come and then ask the aid of the King of France.'

Angélique was about to make a spirited answer, but a growl from Rafai gave her to understand that their secret conversation, of which he could not understand a word, had gone on long enough.

Presently the guards told the women it was time for them to leave, but they had considerable difficulty persuading Prince Bonbon. Raminan had to pick him up bodily. His tantrum subsided only when they rounded a corner and came upon an old, white-haired slave named Jean-Baptiste Caloens, a Fleming, who was picking up fallen leaves. The child screamed that he wanted to cut off his head because he was hoary and not good for anything any longer. Nothing could distract him from this desire, so the eunuchs told the old man to fall down as soon as he felt the blow. The Prince raised his tiny scimitar and struck the slave with all his might. The old man dropped to the ground and played dead. Nonetheless he got a cut on his arm that bled copiously, at the sight of which the little darling was all smiles and quite content to go on with his walk.

They passed by a sunken garden full of clover for the palace horses. A little farther on was a little forest of orange and rose trees, the most charming spot of all. It had been designed by a Spaniard who had blended the blue-green foliage studded with golden globes with the banks of roses at their roots so that the fragrance of the two made an intoxicating perfume. Two slaves were working there.

As she passed, Angélique heard them speaking French. She turned back to look at them more closely. One of them was young and had such a sophisticated light touch about him that it was easy for her to imagine him dressed in a periwig and a lace jabot like any Court dandy. He winked at her, for a Frenchman would have had to be utterly bent to the yoke of slavery not to have an eye for a mysterious veiled beauty passing so close to him.

Suddenly the Circassian girl exclaimed: 'I want that lovely orange growing way up there. Tell the slaves to pick it for me.'

Actually she, too, had noticed the handsome youth and wanted to stop and look at him a little longer. Her experiences in the arms of Mulai Ismail had turned this innocent child into a woman eager to try her charms on other males, and these, in spite of their emaciated bodies and wretched rags, were the first she had encountered except the King since he had disclosed to her the basic rules of the subtle yet violent game that since the world began had made every Eve and every Adam look upon each other in a different light.

Her wondering eyes devoured through the thin veil these white-skinned, round-muscled slaves. And the young man with the fetching smile was blond and silky-haired. What would it be like to be folded in his arms? How did Christians make love? She had heard they weren't even circumcised. . . .

'I want that lovely orange up there,' she insisted.

Fat old Rafai told her severely that she had no right to ask for the fruit, all of which belonged to the King and to no one else. The girl grew angry and replied that what belonged to the King was hers as well, for from henceforth he was her slave, and so he had assured her, and she would compain to him about the eunuchs' insolence, and they would be punished.

The two slaves watched the argument out of the corners of their eyes. The young blond, who was the Marquis de Vaucluse and had been in captivity for only a few months, grinned with pleasure at hearing a demanding feminine voice. But his companion, a Breton named Yan le Goën, was an old hand, having spent twenty years in slavery in Morocco. He advised the Marquis in a low voice to look away and seem to be absorbed in his work, for slaves were forbidden under pain of death to stare at the King's women. The Marquis shrugged. How sweet that little one was, so far as he could guess, and just what he wanted!

'She wants that orange,' the Breton translated.

'How could anyone refuse such a pretty girl?' said the Marquis de Vaucluse. He laid down his pruning knife and straightened his elegant body to reach into the tree. He picked the fruit and, bowing before the Circassian girl as if she were Madame de Montespan, handed it to her.

What then descended upon him came with the speed of a whirlwind. Something whistled in the air, and a javelin pierced young Vaucluse's chest up to the hilt. He crumpled to the ground.

At the end of a grassy path appeared Mulai Ismail on his white horse, his face convulsed with rage. Spurring his horse, he galloped to the fallen slave, pulled the lance from his body and turned toward the other slave as if to transfix him also. But the Breton darted forward and threw himself under the forefeet of the horse, crying piteously in Arabic: 'Pardon, my lord, pardon for the sake of your sacred horse which has been to Mecca.'

Mulai Ismail tried to reach him under the horse's belly, but the slave, at the risk of being trampled by the restless hooves of the horse, never left his refuge. Some of Mulai Ismail's horses did have the reputation of being sacred, especially those that had been to Mecca. Yan le Goën had recognised this one in time as one of the most admired and best loved of the Sultan. Mulai Ismail relented out of his love for the horse, whose name was Lanilor.

'Well,' he said to the slave, 'at least you know our holy ways. But get out of my sight, foul vermin, and let me never hear of you again!'

The Breton crawled out from under the horse, stepped over the dead body of his companion and fled at top speed through the fragrant little forest.

Mulai Ismail turned around, his lance still poised, looking over his eunuchs for one to be punished first for such carelessness. But Raminan found a way to turn his wrath aside, merely by holding up Prince Zidan, who had loved every minute of the scene.

'For the sake of your son, my lord, for the sake of your son. . . .'

With a great flow of words the eunuch explained that the Circassian girl had boasted she would have them all punished by him, the master of all, who had always relied on his eunuchs to tame the intractable. She wanted an orange. She pretended that what belonged to the King belonged to her as well.

Mulai Ismail's face grew dark as night. Then a sardonic smile spread over his lips and revealed his gleaming teeth.

'Everything here belongs to me and to me alone. You will learn that to your cost, Marrianti,' he said in a deep voice.

Then whirling his horse around he galloped away.

The women were taken back to the harem. All that day an atmosphere of anguish hung over the apartments and the courtyards where the odalisques languidly sipped their tea and talked in whispers.

The little Circassian was white as a sheet. Her huge eyes kept wandering over the faces of her fellow-concubines to try to read in them what her fate would be. Mulai Ismail was going to punish her horribly, there was no doubt about that.

When Raminan told her of the incident, Leïla Aisheh herself brewed over a brazier a concoction of herbs known to her alone, and had two servants summoned to take it to the Circassian. The child was to drink it at once. Then she would drowse painlessly into death and escape the hideous tortures the master himself would devise as punishment for her boldness.

When it dawned on the Circassian what was prescribed for her, she let out a scream of horror and overturned the bowl, spilling the potion. Leïla Aisheh made a face like a frustrated monkey. She had acted out of kindness, she said, but now what difference did it make? Let destiny take its course.

One of the cats lapped at the spilled potion and died on the spot. The terrified women buried it secretly. All they needed now was for the King to learn of the death of one of his beloved pets.

The Circassian girl took refuge in Angélique's arms. She was weeping no longer, but trembling like an animal with a pack of hounds on its heels. Everything was deathly still in the harem. The fragrance of the flowers pervaded the room as evening turned the sky jade green. Still the soul of the invisible cruel hunter on the track of his prey seemed to wander in the shadows, and the helpless creatures cowered.

Angélique stroked Marrianti's night-blue hair, and tried to piece together a few words of Arabic to soothe her.

'For just an orange . . . it's not possible he will punish you too cruelly . . . perhaps he'll just have you whipped . . . but he would already have ordered that, and nothing has happened . . . so pull yourself together. . . .'

But she herself felt far from reassured as she felt the unlucky girl's heart skip a beat.

Suddenly the Circassian let out a scream. The eunuchs were moving toward them from the end of the room, Osman Faraji at their head, their arms crossed over their scarlet satin vests. They wore no turbans but exposed their shaven skulls, naked except for a braided lock hanging from the top. They made no sound, and their fat faces were devoid of any expression whatever.

The women fled. They had recognised the costume as that of an executioner.

The girl whirled around like a frightened animal seeking some escape, then threw herself again on Angélique's lap and clung to her with all her strength. She was not screaming now, but her piteous face pleaded desperately for help.

Osman Faraji himself pried loose her feeble fingers.

'What is to be done to her?' Angélique asked hesitantly in French. 'It can't be they would harm her for just an orange.'

The Grand Eunuch did not deign to answer her. He delivered the victim to two of his guards, who dragged her off. Now she began to cry out in her native tongue, calling on her father and her mother whom the Turks had killed, and praying to the holy icon of the Blessed Virgin of Tiflis, her patron saint, to save her.

Terror had robbed her of the strength to stand, and she had to be dragged over the tiles. Thus had they taken her to meet her lover. Thus they were taking her to meet her death.

Angélique was alone, her nerves strained to the snapping point. She was living a nightmare, and the soft murmur of the water in the fountain was as horrid to her as a monstrous image in her unconscious mind. She looked up to see the Ethiopian girl beckoning to her from the balcony, and joined the group of women leaning over the balustrade.

'We can hear everything from here.'

One long piercing shriek rose in the darkness, then another, then more.

Angélique stopped her ears and stole away as from a temptation. For these screeches of agony and inhuman pain a sadistic tyrant was wringing from the body of a little slave guilty only of having picked an orange worked on her a sort of horrible fascination, something she had not experienced since she was a very little girl. She could see the burning eyes of her Moorish nurse telling her and her sisters of the tortures that Gilles de Rais inflicted on children whose souls he was delivering to Satan.

She wandered the length of the balcony. 'Something has to be done! They must not be allowed to do this!'

But she was only a slave in a harem, whose life was in equal jeopardy.

She caught sight of a woman straining her ears toward the King's apartments. Her golden hair hung over her shoulders. It was Daisy, the English girl. Angélique approached her, feeling one with her among these dark Orientals, Spaniards and Italians. She was the only other blonde except for the poor Icelander who was no good to anyone and would die soon.

They had not yet spoken to each other, but when she approached, the English girl put her arm around Angélique's shoulder. Her touch was cold as ice.

They could hear from there too.

At an even more inhuman groan, Angélique moaned in sympathy. The English girl shushed her. She whispered in French: 'Oh, why didn't she drink the potion Leïla Aisheh made for her? I can't ever get used to these things.'

She spoke French with a heavy accent but fluently enough, for she studied languages to amuse herself as she had not yet succumbed to the laziness that beset the other concubines. For a long time Osman Faraji had had his eye on this northerner, but Leïla Aisheh had got there before him.

Her eyes sought Angélique's face. 'You are afraid of him, aren't you? But you are as hard as steel. When Leïla Aisheh looks at you she says you have daggers in your eyes. The Circassian girl took the place

Osman Faraji was saving for you, and yet you are trembling at the way she is being punished.'

'What are they doing to her, for heaven's sake?'

'Oh, the master's imagination is quite sufficient for the invention of exquisite tortures. Have you heard how he put Nina Varadoff to death? She was a lovely Russian who spoke impertinently to him. He cut off her breasts by shutting the lid of a trunk upon them and then weighing it down with the two executioners. She is not the only woman he has tortured like that. Look at my legs.'

She lifted the hem of her skirt to reveal feet and ankles swollen with frightful burns and angry red in colour.

'They stuck my feet into boiling oil to make me renounce my religion. I was only fifteen years old. I gave in. They said my resistance made him love me twice as much. I have known heavenly delights in his arms.'

'Are you speaking of that monster?'

'He has a compulsion to make others suffer. It's a form of pleasure for him. Shh! Leïla Aisheh is watching us.'

The tall Negress was standing in a doorway.

'She is the one and only woman he really loves,' Daisy whispered in a tone of admiration not unmixed with bitterness. 'He has to be with her. So nothing terrible will happen to you. But beware of the Grand Eunuch, that gentle, implacable tiger. . . .'

Angélique wandered off, the eyes of the two women following her, and took refuge in her own apartment. Fatima and the serving girls offered her cakes and coffee, but she would not touch them. She kept sending them for news of the Circassian.

No, they reported, the girl was not dead. Mulai Ismail was not yet satiated, and extreme precautions were being taken that death might not come too quickly.

'I wish lightning from Heaven would smite those fiends!' said Angélique.

'Why?' said the astonished servants. 'She was not your daughter or your sister, was she?'

She finally collapsed on her divan, her hands over her ears, and the cushions piled on top of her head. When she stuck her head out again, the moon had risen. Everything was still. She thought she saw the Grand Eunuch making his rounds on the balcony, and leaped up to go to him.

'She is dead, isn't she?' she exclaimed. 'Oh, for the love of heaven, tell me she is dead!'

Osman Faraji was perplexed to see her clasped hands and her face so twisted with anguish.

'Yes, she is dead,' he replied. 'She has just breathed her last.'

A sigh of relief escaped Angélique. It sounded like a sob.

'For an orange! All for just an orange! And is that the fate you are keeping in store for me, too, Osman Bey? You want me to become his favourite so that he can kill me with torture like that for the least offence.'

'No, that will not happen to you. I will protect you.'

'Why didn't you stop him killing her so horribly?'

A pained astonishment spread over the features of the Grand Eunuch. 'Why . . . she was not of enough interest, Firousi. She was not very bright. True enough, she had a delectable body and an instinctive, even perverse, knowledge of the ways of love. That was the only thing that made Mulai Ismail take a fancy to her. But he had already begun to lose his taste for her, and he knew it, and disliked her for it. His anger is often his best adviser. The executioner has rid him of a passion that was lowering his stature . . . and left a place vacant for you to fill!'

Angélique recoiled from him, her hand over her mouth. *A gentle, implacable tiger!* The words of the English girl kept ringing in her ears.

'You are a monster,' she murmured. 'You are all the monsters in the world rolled into one. You fill me with loathing.'

She fell back on her cushions, shaken with convulsive trembling.

A little later Fatima-Mirelia came with a bowl of soothing herb tea that the Grand Eunuch had commanded her to bring Angélique. When she had fetched the broth from the kitchens she had picked up fresh details about the various tortures the Circassian girl had undergone, and she was dying to tell her mistress about them. But the first words were scarcely out of her mouth before Angélique struck her and went into a fit of hysterics from which the old Provençal woman had difficulty in restoring her.

She lay there listening to the night sounds. The noise of the harem had ceased, for each of the women had withdrawn into her own apartment. Free though they were during the daytime to wander from one patio to another and visit each other, at night they stayed alone under the guard of a eunuch and their serving girls. No one would have dared break that rule. Any woman so rash as to try to slip past her guards would have risked finding herself face to face with a panther trained to leap upon such wanderers.

Quite a few of the little serving girls, sent by their mistresses to the kitchens for some dainty they wanted at once, had been killed that way. In the mornings the two eunuchs who had trained the beast roamed through the palace looking for it. When it was caught again, the cry went up: 'Alchadi is tied up.' Only then did everyone breathe easier and the harem come to life again.

The only woman not afraid of the panther was Leïla Aisheh, the sorceress. She had no fear of wild beasts or of the King or of her rivals – only of Osman Faraji, the Grand Eunuch. In vain she murmured spells against him and manufactured charms for his undoing. The Grand Eunuch escaped them all, for he, too, had knowledge of the invisible world.

Angélique looked over the railing of her balcony at the dark flames of the cypress trees against the white walls of the inner courtyard which they filled with a bitter scent that mingled with the fragrance of the roses. The fountain splashed in the centre. This was the extent of her world. The blind walls shut out the life of freedom just beyond them. Prison walls! She had come to envy the slaves, hungry and toilworn though they were, just because they could come and go on the other side of those walls. Yet they complained of how impossible it was for them to leave Meknès and flee into the desert.

To Angélique it seemed that even if she could get past the tight walls of the harem, the rest of her flight would be no easy matter. There was, first of all, the impossibility of getting accomplices for her escape. It was a miracle that, through the quiet calculated intervention of the Grand Eunuch, she was able to say a few words to Savary from time to time. She had thought Savary could organise her escape once she was outside the walls, yet even his inventive mind had failed him in this respect. There were too many hidden obstacles.

At night there was the panther. Day and night, the eunuchs, immune to any appeal, patrolled the gates and the terraces with their lances and their whips.

What about the serving girls? Angélique asked herself. Old Fatima loved her and was completely loyal to her. But her loyalty did not extend to helping her mistress in an undertaking for which she would pay with her own life if Angélique succeeded. She thought it a stupid idea anyway. Angélique had once asked her to slip a note to Savary, but the old woman had refused. If anyone caught her with a message from one of the King's concubines addressed to a Christian slave, she would be tossed into the nearest fire like any stick of wood. That would be the least that could befall her. And who could imagine what would happen to the Christian slave? Out of fear for Savary's welfare, Angélique did not press the matter.

She did not know what else she could try. Sometimes, to rekindle her courage, she thought of her two little boys so far away, Florimond and Charles-Henri, but that seldom rallied her determination. She could not surmount so many obstacles to join them.

She sniffed the ravishing fragrance of the roses and listened to a Moorish servant-girl plucking the string of a gittern to lull her mistress to sleep. Why struggle so? Tomorrow she could have that flaky pastry again stuffed with minced squab flavoured with pepper, sugar and cinnamon. And she had a craving for a cup of coffee. She knew she had only to clap her hands and the old Provençal woman or the Negress who helped her would fan the coals in the brazier to boil the water always ready in the shiny kettle. The aroma of that brew might dispel her sorrow and bring back to her like a sweet dream the memory of a strange evening in Candia. Angélique folded her arms behind her head and lay back to recapture it. . . .

Over the blue sea sped a white ship like a gull before the wind. . . . A man who had paid for her the price of a whole ship and its crew! That man who had so madly desired her, where was he now? Did he still remember the lovely captive who had eluded him? Why had she fled, she often wondered now in her despair. Of course he was a pirate, but he was also a man of her own kind. A disturbing man, possibly with a hideous face beneath his mask, still he had not awaked the slightest fear within her. . . . From the moment that his dark, magnetic eyes had gazed into hers she knew he had come not to enslave her but to free her – from her rash folly, she realised now. How absurd she had been to think a woman alone could escape the fate awaiting her in the Mediterranean! Now she was not free even to choose her own master. By refusing him, she had fallen into the hands of another, much more implacable owner.

Bitter tears stole down her cheeks and she comprehended how heavily weighed upon her soul her double slavery as a woman and as a captive of Mulai Ismail.

'Drink your coffee,' whispered the old Provençal woman. 'Things will go better soon. Tomorrow I'll bring you a nice hot pigeon pie. They're already making the pastry in the kitchens. . . .'

Above the black spires of the cypresses the sky was turning green. From the peaks of the minarets came on the wings of the morning the voices of the muezzins calling the faithful to prayer, and through the corridors of the seraglio ran the eunuchs seeking Alchadi the panther.

CHAPTER TWENTY-ONE

One day, quite near her own apartment but hidden in a corner of the wall, Angélique found a chink through which she could glimpse the outside world. It was like a keyhole, too narrow for her to lean out of, and too high for her to call through. It opened on a broad square where people passed to and fro.

Thereafter she would spend many long hours peeping through it at the slaves toiling at the endless building schemes of Mulai Ismail. He was always building, building, building – for no other purpose, so far as she could tell, than the pleasure of destroying what he had constructed and building it over again.

The sight of the workmen, whom she could see in only one corner of the square, so narrow was her chink, became familiar to her. Often she saw Mulai Ismail among the slave-drivers with their clubs always ready to descend upon the back of some captive, riding his snow-white horse or walking under his parasol and accompanied by his retinue. Then the dreary scene came to life. Angélique yielded to the curiosity her forced idleness had fostered. Mulai Ismail came into her range of vision. Colin Paturel approached him to ask that the next day be one of rest in honour of Easter. The Sultan ordered a hundred lashes for him on the spot. With his own musket he shot a slave he caught resting a moment, unaware that the Sultan was present, and toppled him from a thirty-foot wall. He sliced off the heads of a few Negro guards because he thought them responsible for the slow progress of the work.

She could not hear any voices or distinguish any words. The proscenium of her little chink revealed to her only dumb-shows, short scenes of death so tragic as to appear parodies of themselves. Nothing but puppets falling, fleeing, entreating, scrambling up the long ladders of the scaffoldings, stopping only when the shadows lengthened and the evening came.

Then the dazzling white square filled with the faithful prostrating themselves in the dust, their heads toward Mecca, where the Prophet lay entombed. The slaves would return to their quarters or their subterranean dungeons.

Some of them Angélique could identify by nationality if not by name. The French, because they only grinned when they were beaten, having learned to argue with their black jailers until the keepers were so exhausted finding answers that they let the slaves do what they wanted, even to taking a little rest to smoke a pipe or two in the shade of the walls. The Italians knew how to sing at their work in spite of the choking chalk-dust that blew into their open mouths. She could tell they were singing because their fellow-labourers would stop to listen to them. The Italians also took the anger of the Negroes lightly, thinking only of living as long as possible. The Spaniards were identified by the condescension with which they handled their trowels; they never complained of the hot sun or of hunger or thirst. On the other hand, the Dutch were painstaking about their work, and never got involved in quarrels. Their strict self-discipline revealed their Protestant training. The Catholics and the Orthodox, however, hated one another cordially and got into fights like mad dogs which could be broken up only by the clubs of the guards, who often had to send for Colin Paturel to put an end to these antagonisms.

The Norman was always laden with chains, and often his arms and his back were covered with bleeding wounds from the lashings and beatings his boldness brought upon him. These never prevented him, however, from loading heavy sacks of mortar on his herculean back and climbing up the ladders to the very top of the scaffolding in spite of the heavy fetters that encumbered his ankles. He took care of the weak, and no one dared say anything to him. One day with his wrist-chains gathered into a loop he killed one of the guards who had been beating up puny Jean-Jean from Paris. The guards ran up, sword in hand, but withdrew when they saw Colin the Norman had done it. Only the King had the right to punish him.

When Mulai Ismail came to inspect the work of the slaves, as he did every evening, he pointed his lance against the slave's chest. Angélique could hear the fateful words: 'Become a Moslem!'

Colin Paturel shook his head. Would this be the last moment for this blond giant who had endured so many years of persecution during which he had come close to death a hundred times? Was Azrael at last about to seize him?

Angélique bit her knuckles. She wanted to shout to him in French to renounce his faith. She could not understand his stubbornness in the face of his executioner, waiting lance in hand.

At last Mulai Ismail threw his lance aside in rage. Later Angélique learned he had said: 'The dog wants to be damned!' Colin Paturel's preference for burning in Hell instead of gaining the Paradise of True Believers caused the Sultan of Morocco a disappointment akin to grief.

Angélique sighed with relief and went for a cup of coffee to restore her nerves. She kept wondering at these thousands of slaves, most of them ordinary folk from every land, who could still find courage to brave death or more long years of captivity rather than forsake a God they had seldom thought of when they were at liberty. If any one of these wretched, starving, tortured, desperate animals were only to deny his religion, he would at once have plenty to eat, a comfortable life, an honourable position in society, and as many wives as Mohammed allowed his faithful followers. There were certainly plenty of apostates in Meknès and in the whole of Barbary. Still these were few in contrast to the hundreds of thousands of captives who had passed through the hands of the Sultans from generation to generation. What made Angélique brood as she watched from the height of her chink was how a man could get so much out of his poor tortured body. They kept on working, kept on suffering, kept on hoping. . . .

From her window Angélique saw a troop of new captives that had been sent the King by the pirates of the coast. They had not eaten for a week. Their ragged, salt-stained garments had not yet become so dilapidated as the slaves', and she could still pick out the gold embroidery on some nobleman's coat and the stripes on some sailor's vest. Soon they would be fellow-Christian captives in Barbary, brothers all. Some of them must have had to carry the heads of comrades who had died on the long march lest their guards be accused of selling these off for their own benefit.

In the middle of the square, where the fiery sun cast deep blue shadows, Angélique noticed an astonishing personage one morning. He was so incongruous that she could not take her eyes off him, for he was wearing a complete suit and a wig, and his high heels and buckled shoes showed no effects of a long trek. Even the lace at his cuffs was clean. A chieftain had to come up to the man and bow three times before she could believe she was not having an hallucination, for the dazzling light of the square often provoked mirages.

Then she rushed inside the building to send a serving girl out to inquire what was going on. But she realised that by doing so she would only betray her observation post. She would have to wait until the news spread of its own accord . . . as it soon did.

The extraordinary ambassador in the wig was none other than a French trader from Salé, Maître Bertrand, an old inhabitant of the Moroccan coast who had taken it upon himself to come to Meknès to announce the arrival of the longed-for Redemptorist Fathers. A good Christian and eager to come to the aid of his unlucky brethren, he had put his familiarity with Morocco at the service of the Redemptorists, who for the first time had landed in the jealously protected realm of

Mulai Ismail. The Fathers with their presents and their credentials were following him on donkeys by easy stages.

At once there was great and enthusiastic excitement among the captives. The seafaring people amongst them, some of whom had endured many different captivities in Algiers or Tunis and had escaped only through the intervention of these Fathers, loved them dearly, and called them the Mathurins, meaning 'Brothers-on-donkeys', for they were used to seeing them bravely penetrate deep into the interior of these countries to redeem slaves. But for fifteen years Morocco had been barred to them. Colin Paturel had gained no easy victory in bending the King's will on this matter.

At last they arrived. Old Caloens, the doyen of the slaves, seventy years old, twenty of which had been spent in slavery, fell on his knees and gave thanks to God. At last he was to know freedom again! This astonished his fellows, for Caloens, who tended the gardens of the Sultan and seemed to take great joy in his work, had always seemed quite content with his lot. He confessed he would not leave Morocco without shedding a few tears, but he would have to go because he was growing bald and the Sultan did not like bald men and whenever he saw one would split his skull with a blow from the copper head of his walking-stick. Caloens was too old, he said, to die that way.

The King allowed the slaves to welcome the Fathers with palms in their hands.

Angélique could not stand it any longer. For the first time she asked the Grand Eunuch to grant her a favour and let her attend the reception Mulai Ismail would give the Fathers. Osman Faraji half closed his catlike eyes as he pondered what lay behind her request, then granted it.

She had to wait quite a while. The Mission had been lodged in the Jewish quarter, where it remained shut up for a week under the pretext that the Fathers could not be allowed to visit anyone until they had been given audience by the King. The chieftains, the ministers and the high-placed renegades went there to inspect the gifts the Fathers had brought and see if there was any money in the visit for themselves.

Finally one morning Angélique was told to get ready for an excursion. Osman Faraji led her to her curtained chaise, which was to be closely guarded. At the gate which opened on the esplanade the Grand Eunuch made the vehicle stop. Angélique peeped out through the joins of the curtains.

The King was already in his place, seated cross-legged on the ground, his feet encased in yellow slippers with turned-up points. Today his garments and his turban were green, a sign of good humour with him. He kept covering his mouth with a fold of his burnous, which lent intensity to his eyes. He, too, was eager to see these Christian priests close to, and to feast his eyes on the gifts they had brought him. Rodani, the renegade, had already assured him these included two clocks. But Mulai Ismail was really interested in making an assault on the faith of these high priests of the Christian religion. What a triumph that would be for Allah! He had prepared his address to them carefully, and was burning with the intensity of his convictions.

He had brought a bodyguard of only thirty blacks armed with long, silver-stocked muskets. Behind him stood two Negro boys, one fanning him, the other holding the parasol above his head. Around him the chiefs and renegades, in full Court dress with aigrettes in their turbans and brocaded robes, squatted on their heels.

The Redemptorist Fathers appeared at the far end of the square, followed by a dozen slaves bearing their gifts. They were presented to the Sultan by the French renegade Rodani, the Jew Zacharias and the chieftain bin Messaud.

The Fathers had carefully chosen their representatives for the extraordinary mission which they had tried so many years to arrange. These were six in number, three of whom could speak Arabic, and all of whom knew Spanish. Each had been on at least three similar missions to Algiers and Tunis and were renowned for their acquaintance with the customs of the Moslem world. Their Superior was the Reverend Father de Valombreuze, the younger son of a prominent family from Berry, and a professor at the Sorbonne, who brought to diplomatic conferences the crafty common sense of a peasant and the dignity of a noble lord. No one was better equipped than he to deal with Mulai Ismail.

The King was much impressed with the habits of the Fathers – white robes with a red cross in front – and with their beards. They looked like the pious hermits of Islam so revered by the Moslems.

The Sultan was the first to speak. He welcomed the Fathers and praised their zeal and charity in coming so far to rescue their brethren. Then he paid tribute to the great King of France. Father de Valombreuze, who had often been at the Court of Versailles, gave a worthy reply to this tribute, and told the Sultan that Louis XIV, through the valour of his deeds and the magnificence of his way of life, was the greatest king in Christendom.

Mulai Ismail showed he approved, then continued with a long eulogy of the Great Prophet of Islam and His Law.

Angélique was too far away to follow this lengthy disquisition, but she noticed that Mulai Ismail grew more and more excited as he progressed. His face shone like thunder-clouds tinged with sunlight behind them. His fists were tightly clenched as he adjured his guests to acknowledge their errors and see that the faith of Mohammed was the only true, the only pure belief, handed down and defined by prophets since the days of Adam. He did not urge them to renounce their creed because they came as ambassadors rather than as slaves, but merely lest they have to answer before God for their failure to do so. It was painful for him to have in his realm human beings so plunged in such confining error. Happy were those who did not subscribe to the blasphemous doctrine of the Trinity which dared hypothesise three gods, not one!

'Yes, God indeed is one God, far above such human weakness as having a son. Jesus was like unto Adam, whom He created from the dust of the ground. He was only the envoy of God and His Word, a part of His Spirit implanted in the Virgin Mary, the daughter of Amram. Neither He nor she had been the child of sin. Believe, therefore, in God and His Prophet. Say no more that God exists in three persons, and you shall find yourselves. . . .'

The brave Redemptorists endured with patience this long oration which accused them of having inflicted their false beliefs on others. They refrained from calling the attention of the Sultan to the fact that they were in truth 'Fathers of the Trinity' and that Redemptorists was merely their familiar title. In his letter Colin Paturel had clearly indicated they should be known by this nickname, and now they understood why.

They thanked the King for the concern he had shown for their souls and assured him they indeed wished to die in a state of holiness. But in obedience to the teachings of Christianity they had come all this distance to redeem their brethren, and in spite of their earnest desire to please him, they could not renounce their faith after undertaking so perilous a journey for no other purpose than to redeem slaves who had remained Christians.

The King yielded to their reasons and made an effort not to show his disappointment.

The slaves by now had untied the ropes that bound the cases containing the gifts, and opened the lids of the chests. The Fathers offered the King many bolts of sumptuous material wrapped in cloth of gold. Then they unpacked three rings and three necklaces, which they offered next. Mulai Ismail slipped the rings on his fingers and laid the necklaces on the ground near him; from time to time he would take up one or another of them and inspect it carefully. Finally they unpacked the cloaks, which had not suffered much damage during the journey. The largest had a dial of gold representing the sun, with numerals of blue and gold cloisonné.

The sight of them made Mulai Ismail as happy as a child. He assured the Fathers he would hear their requests favourably, and released two hundred slaves to them. No one had even dared hope for such a large number.

That night, to show their joy and their gratitude to the Sultan, the slaves produced a great show of fireworks along the banks of the moat surrounding the castle. The Moors had never seen anything like it – a galley of flame, a tree that sprang from the earth, a bird that whirled above them emitting flames of varicoloured lights from its beak.

Mulai Ismail watched the display from the roof of his palace, much impressed. He said only his slaves truly loved him, for whenever he granted his own people a favour, instead of thanking him they just asked for more of the same, whereas the Christian captives delighted him with their gratitude. That same day he had a robe made for himself out of the precious stuff the Fathers had brought from Brittany. He thought it particularly handsome.

From a distance Angélique and her companions were also watching the fireworks. After much hesitation, seeing that things were in her favour, she asked the Grand Eunuch to let her talk with these mission Fathers. She needed the comforts of her religion, she said. Osman Faraji thought he ought not to refuse her this request.

Two eunuchs were sent to the ghetto, where the Fathers were awaiting the results of their conferences and receiving an endless string of visits from the captives, each of whom begged to be included among the two hundred French slaves to be redeemed.

Father de Valombreuze was asked to follow the black guards, as one of Mulai Ismail's wives wished to talk with him. At the entrance to the harem he was blindfolded, and when the scarf was removed from his eyes he found himself before an iron grille behind which was a heavily veiled woman who, much to his surprise, spoke to him in French.

'I hope you are pleased with the success of your mission, Father,' said Angélique.

The Father prudently remarked that not everything had been accomplished yet. The King's humour might change. The stories the captives told him every hour were not entirely reassuring. How speedily he wished to return to Cadiz with these poor slaves whose souls were in such danger under the rule of such a sanguinary king!

'And since you were once a Christian yourself, Madame – as I suspect you were from your language – I entreat you to intercede with your master not to alter his kindly feelings for us.'

'I am no renegade,' said Angélique, 'but a Christian.'

Father de Valombreuze stroked his long beard in embarrassment. He had heard all the wives and concubines of the Sultan were considered Moslems and had to openly profess the religion of Mohammed. There was a special mosque for them in the interior of the palace.

'I was captured,' said Angélique. 'I am not here of my own accord.'

'I do not doubt that, my child,' said the priest.

'My soul is in great peril,' said Angélique clutching the grille in her despair, 'but that means nothing to you. No one will try to rescue me, no one will try to ransom me. Because I am only a woman. . . .'

She could not bring herself to say that she feared even more than torture the temptations of the gilded sensuality that pervaded the harem, the slow disintegration of her soul that the poisonous weeds of leisure and cruelty and pleasure were accomplishing. This was what Osman Faraji wanted. He knew her everlasting femininity was but sleeping. He would wait until it woke.

The priest heard the woman weeping. He nodded his head compassionately. 'Bear your lot in patience, my daughter. At least you are not suffering from hunger and exhaustion as your brethren are.'

Even in the eyes of the good Father the loss of a woman's soul seemed less important than that of a man. Less through scorn than because he thought her woman's nature and lack of responsibility would earn her some indulgence on the part of God.

Angélique pulled herself together. From her finger she took one of her rings, a huge diamond whose gold band bore the name and device of Plessis-Bellière engraved inside it. She hesitated, fearful of the presence of the Grand Eunuch watching her. She had thought this over carefully. The time had come, she knew, for Osman Faraji to have her taken to Mulai Ismail's apartments. He had made it clear to her that she should follow his instructions. She would lose her influence if she deceived him, would alienate the king by defying him, would perish by torture.

She had begun to wonder with terror whether she was not eager for the hour of her surrender to strike rather than go on living in such false hope. Nothing could help her, either within or without. Work as hard as he might, Savary was only a poor old slave who had used up his strength. Even if the Christian slaves did attempt one of their futile mass escapes, as some of the more hotheaded were planning, they would not want to be bothered with a woman. *One never escapes from the harem.* At least she could try not to end her days there. She saw but one single being who could stand up to Mulai Ismail and compel him to surrender one of his prizes.

She poked the jewel through one of the openings in the grille. 'Father, I beseech you . . . I implore you to go to Versailles when you return to France. Ask an audience of the King and give him this ring. He will see my name on it. Then tell him everything you have seen. Tell him I have been captured, that I am a prisoner, that I . . .' Her voice failed her, and she could only gasp out: 'Tell him that I ask his forgiveness and appeal to him for help.'

Unfortunately the negotiations were not completed when Mulai Ismail learned from a renegade Frenchman that Redemptorist was only another name for the Order of Fathers of the Holy Trinity. His wrath was terrible to behold.

'You have tricked me again with your forked tongue, you crafty Norman,' he said to Colin Paturel. 'But this time you have not had time to play your joke out.'

He had the Norman's beard and nose and ears filled with gunpowder, intending to light it, but then changed his mind. He would not put Colin Paturel to death yet. He would be satisfied merely to bind him to a cross and expose him naked in the burning sun of the square, guarded by two armed Negroes to shoot the vultures that gathered to tear out his eyes. One of the guards aimed poorly and wounded the slave in the shoulder. The King cut off his head with one stroke of his sword. Her eye glued to the chink in the wall, Angélique could not tear herself away from the sight of that horrible gibbet. Sometimes she could see the muscles of the slave striving to loosen the bonds that were causing his limbs to swell. His great blond head fell forward on his chest, but he immediately raised it and turned from right to left to look at the sky. He was continually moving his body to keep the blood flowing in his tortured limbs.

His tremendous will triumphed over the punishment. When they unbound him that evening, not only was he still alive, but after the King had made him drink a bowl of spiced broth, he stood erect. His companions, who were already lamenting him, saw him come to them, his head held high in spite of the blood that poured from his wounds.

The news spread quickly, and everyone existed in a state of unbearable tension. In his rage the King had spat upon the gifts the Fathers had brought. He had given the necklaces and the rings to his Negro boys. He had ripped the new robe to shreds. But he had not gone so far as to smash the clocks.

The Fathers, who had been ordered to leave Meknès at once under pain of being burned alive in their residence, were in a state of consternation. They conferred on what they should do. With great courage two merchants from the coast, Bertrand and Chappe-de-Laine, who had not been ordered to leave, said they would demand an audience with the King and get some explanation of this change of mind, while the Fathers settled their affairs and got on their donkeys.

But Colin Paturel, foreseeing these obstacles, had devised a remedy for this lamentable state of affairs. In the days before the Fathers' arrival he had gone to see all the Moorish families with relatives who were galley-slaves on French vessels, and had raised their hopes that an exchange could be negotiated permitting their relatives to return to them.

Now that they saw the negotiations broken off because of the King's anger, the Moors rushed in droves to the palace, abusing the King and begging him not to lose this chance – the first they had ever had – of having the captive Moslems restored to them.

Mulai Ismail was obliged to give in to them. His guards galloped after the Fathers and commanded them to return to Meknès under pain of decapitation.

The conferences were stormy, and lasted three weeks. Finally the Redemptorists obtained a dozen captives instead of the two hundred that had been promised. Each one was to be exchanged for three Moors and three hundred piastres. The Fathers were to take them to Ceuta, where they were to wait until the exchange was made.

The King himself chose the twelve slaves from among the oldest and feeblest. He made them all march before him in review. Naturally they all put on as piteous an air as they could. Mulai Ismail rubbed his hands together and said with satisfaction: 'Indeed they are all poor and wretched.'

The keeper agreed. 'You have spoken truly, my lord.'

They were being registered when a lame slave called attention to the fact that old Caloens was not French, for he had been captured under the English flag. The affair was twenty years ago and there was hardly time to check on it now, so Caloens was hauled away from the gate, and a lame man was substituted for him.

The Fathers hastened their departure as they could see that every day brought them some new outrage. Jealousy and anger made the captives ill-humoured and they complained bitterly. They had to pay all the chieftains and renegade officials who pretended to assist them, and load them with presents. They left Meknès under a hail of stones and insults from Christian and Moslem alike.

Old Caloens kept wailing: 'Oh, when will the Brothers-on-donkeys return? I am forsaken!'

He thought he felt the King's walking-stick on his bald head already, and ran into the palm garden to hang himself, but Colin Paturel arrived in time to cut him down.

'Don't give up hope, old man,' he said. 'We all tried to better your lot. Now only one thing remains – flight. I must leave. My days are numbered. Renaud de Marmondin, the Knight of Malta, can take my place. If you don't think you are too old, you can come with us.'

It was not without good reason that Colin the Norman had insisted the Fathers bring clocks with them. At the end of two weeks they did not run any longer. A Genevan watchmaker, Martin Camisart, offered to repair them, but he needed a great number of little tools which were collected by some means or other. By the time the clocks were ticking again, the Genevan had enough tools to knock off the chains that fettered Colin and free him.

He also broke off those of Jean-Jean, the scribe of the captives. These two were joined by Piccinino the Venetian; the Marquis de Kermoer, a nobleman from Brittany; Francis Bargus from Arles, a native of Martigues; Jean d'Harrosteguy, a Basque from Hendaye; and Camisart the Protestant. All were willing to risk their lives to regain Christian lands. Old Caloens also joined them, and so did the apothecary Savary, who had proposed idea after idea for outwitting the bloodthirsty Mulai Ismail, and had finally convinced them that the impossible could become the possible.

CHAPTER TWENTY-TWO

Angélique felt the trap closing on her. Mulai Ismail could not be kept for ever from inquiring about her, and when she was strolling along the garden paths she could not help pondering the nature of the master who had created these pleasant places, a being who ran from one extreme to the other. He could throw slaves to the lions, he invented tortures so frightful that suicide was a sweet alternative to them, still he loved flowers, the murmur of running water, birds and animals, and he believed with all his soul in the mercies of Allah. A descendant of the Prophet, whose limitless courage he had inherited, he could admit with Mohammed: 'I have always loved women, prayer and perfumes. But only prayer can satisfy my soul. . . .'

Around her the concubines were whispering and day-dreaming and intriguing as usual. All these females had abandoned themselves to the sensual passions of their lovely bodies consecrated to love. Soft and smooth, perfumed, anointed, their flowing curves were made for the embraces of a royal master. They had no other reason for existing, and they lived in the expectation of the rapture he would give them. Their inactivity and their forced continence annoyed them, for far too seldom was there one of these hundreds of women who received the royal favours.

These fervent houris reserved for the pleasure of one man alone turned their frustration into plotting. They were insanely jealous of Daisy and Leïla Aisheh, the only ones who seemed able to discover and retain the secrets of his strange heart. They served him at mealtime. He sometimes asked their advice. But none of them forgot that the Koran authorised a true believer to have only four wives. Who would be the third?

Old Fatima was annoyed that her mistress, whom she beautified every day, had not yet been presented to the Sultan and had not yet become his favourite. She could not fail but be that. The King had only to see her. There was no one in the harem more lovely than Angélique. Her complexion, thanks to the dim light of the apartments, had become even clearer, and against her rosy flesh her green eyes shone with an almost supernatural brilliance. Fatima had darkened her eyelids with blue henna mixed with milk, which gave them the softness of dark velvet. On the other hand she had bleached her abundant hair with baths of special herbs, and each lock was as smooth and shiny as silk. Her skin had taken on an iridescent quality, thanks to baths of almond milk and water-lily juice.

She was ready, thought Fatima. What could they be waiting for?

She told Angélique of her doubts and her impatience, and how she felt like an artist whose masterpiece is ignored. What good was all her beauty doing her? The moment was propitious for presenting her to the tyrant so that he could make her his Number Three Wife. From then on she would no longer have to fear old age, or being relegated to the depths of some distant seraglio, or, worse, sent to the kitchens to lead the life of a menial till the end of her days.

The Grand Eunuch ignored their impatience, which perhaps suited his designs and at any rate was not unforeseen. He was doing more than just watching the days pass by. Once again he thought he detected a sign and considered, dreamer that he was, the new odalisque he had created, lovely as the sinful pictures of the Italian painters. He nodded his head slowly. 'I have read it in the stars . . .' he murmured. What he had seen but would not tell made him indecisive.

He spent whole nights on the top of a square tower sweeping the sky with his telescopes, of which he possessed the best there were. The Grand Eunuch had all the failings of a collector. In addition to optical instruments, for which he had gone to Venice and Verona as well as Saxony, where the glass works were acquiring a reputation for the precision of their lenses, he also collected Persian pencil cases of mother of pearl and cloisonné, and owned many rare examples. He loved tortoises also, and raised all kinds of them in the gardens of the mountain villas where Mulai Ismail banished his discarded concubines. Not only were these poor women banished for ever from Meknès, but they had to end their days with no other companions but these monsters which brought them many a visit from the Grand Eunuch.

For he seemed to have the gift of ubiquity. He was always where he was least wanted and least expected. Mulai Ismail always found him beside him when a sudden notion made him seek the advice of his Grand Eunuch. He frequently visited every minister of state, received daily reports from his many spies, went on numerous journeys, and still seemed to pass his days in meditation on the perfection of his Persian enamels and his nights with his eyes riveted on the stars. Nor did any of this keep him from prostrating himself five times a day in the rituals of Moslem prayer.

'The Prophet said: "Do the work of this world as if you were always going to inhabit it, and that of the other world as if you were going there tomorrow",' he was fond of saying.

His thoughts seemed to communicate themselves invisibly to the men and women under his jurisdiction. Like a waiting spider he snared them by silken cords from which they could never escape.

'Aren't you pining, Firousi,' he said to her once, 'for the delights of the flesh? It has been a long time since you have known a man.'

Angélique turned her eyes away. She would rather have been hacked to pieces than admit the fever that disturbed her rest and woke her in exasperation, muttering to herself: *A man! I don't care what one!*

Osman Faraji pressed the point. 'Your woman's body which fears no man, which longs for a man and does not dread his ways as so many inexperienced girls do, doesn't it burn to have one again? Mulai Ismail will satisfy you. Forget your thoughts and think only of the pleasures in store for you. Do you want me to present you to him at last?'

He was seated near her on a low stool. Angélique felt inexplicably drawn to him. She contemplated him dreamily, this great exile from the realms of love. He inspired in her mixed feelings of revulsion and admiration, and she could not help feeling a strange sadness when she discerned in this man the signs of his state – the heavy curve of his chin, the smooth, too shapely arms, and beneath his vest the shape of his breasts which were approaching the fullness of all old eunuchs'.

'Osman Bey,' she said on the spur of the moment, 'how can you say such things? Do you never miss not having the right to talk of love?'

Osman Faraji raised his eyebrows and smiled almost humorously. 'No one ever misses what he never had, Firousi. Do you envy the lunatic who laughs at the phantoms of his crazed mind? He is happy in his own way. His visions satisfy him. Still you do not want to share his fate and you thank Allah that you are not like him. So appears to me the behaviour that the imperious commands of lust impose on one to such degree that a man of sound mind can become a braying old buck leaping after the most stupid of his does. I thank Allah I have never known such humiliating servitude. Yet I admit no less the strength of that power and I labour to direct it toward the ends I desire, which is the magnification of the power of Morocco and the purification of all Islam.'

Angélique raised herself on her elbow, enthralled by the ambition of this man to remould the world according to his wishes.

'Osman Faraji, they say you steered Mulai Ismail to power and showed him whom to kill or have killed in order to achieve it. But there is yet one murder you have not perpetrated – his own! Why do you keep this sadistic madman on the throne of Morocco? Wouldn't you be a better ruler than he? Without you he would be only an adventurer at the mercy of his foes. You are his strategy, his wisdom, his hidden protector. Why do you not take his place? You could do it. Haven't eunuchs been crowned emperors of Byzantium?'

The Grand Eunuch was still smiling. 'I am much obliged to you, Firousi, for the high opinion you have of me. But I will not murder Mulai Ismail. He is secure on the throne of Morocco. He has just the madness every conqueror needs. How can one rule without the vigour of fertility? The blood of Mulai Ismail is like molten lava. Mine is like the water of a shaded spring. Such is the will of God. I have passed on to him my wisdom and my stratagems. I have trained him and taught him since he was no more than a princeling lost among the hundred and fifty sons of Mulai Archi, who took scarcely any pains about their education. He was concerned only with Mulai Hamet and Abd el Ahmed. But I was concerned with Mulai Ismail, and, see, he has triumphed over the other two. Mulai Ismail is my son far more than he was ever Mulai Archi's. How can I destroy him then? He is not a sadistic madman as you think in the narrow terms of your Christian judgement. He is the sword of God! Haven't you heard how God rained down fire and brimstone on the wicked cities of Sodom and Gomorrah? Mulai Ismail has suppressed the shameful vices of many Algerians and Tunisians. He has never taken a wife who had a living husband, for adultery is forbidden by the Law, and he has prolonged the fast of Ramadan an entire month. When you become his third wife you can appease the excesses of his exalted nature. My work will then have been finished. Do you wish me to present you to Mulai Ismail?'

'No,' Angélique said firmly. 'No, not yet.'

'Let destiny take its course then.'

The blade of destiny fell one cool morning when Angélique had had her curtained chaise brought into the palm garden. She had received a note from Savary, which Fatima had delivered reticently, in which he told her to go to the palm garden near the hut reserved for the gardeners. The wife of one of them, a French slave named Badiguet, would point out to her where she could meet her old friend.

Under the transparent canopy of the palm leaves shone the amber clusters of the ripe dates, which the slaves were gathering. From the gardeners' hut came Dame Badiguet toward the chaise, the curtains of which Angélique stealthily opened a little way. The woman cast a furtive look around and then whispered that old Savary was working not far from the palm garden, gathering fallen dates which he made into a kind of sour bread for the slaves. The third path on the left. . . . Could she depend on the eunuchs guarding her chaise? Yes. Luckily they were two young guards who knew only that Osman Faraji had instructed them not to oppose the Frenchwoman's wishes.

So she had her chair driven into the designated path, where she soon saw Savary picking up his provender like a little brown gnome. The place was deserted, and the only sound was the incessant buzzing of the flies around the piles of oozing dates.

When Savary came up to her, the eunuchs tried to intervene.

'Out of my way, my fat babies,' the old man said to them humorously. 'Let me pay my respects to this lady.'

'He is my father,' said Angélique. 'You know perfectly well Osman Bey lets me meet him from time to time.'

They did not object.

'Everything is going well,' whispered Savary, his eyes dancing behind his spectacles.

'Have you found another deposit of maumie?' asked Angélique with a wry smile.

She watched him tenderly. He was looking more and more like the wicked little goblins that came and danced around the stone tables in the fields of Poitou. She liked to imagine Savary as one of those old bearded sprites for whom she had waited for hours, lying in the dewy grass, expecting them to appear and follow her faithfully ever after.

'Six slaves are going to try to escape. Their plan is perfect. They aren't going to use any guides, for they often betray the Christians they are pretending to lead to safety. They've got instructions from slaves who did escape but were recaptured. They have the route all planned to get to Ceuta, the roads they should follow and those they should shun. The right time for the flight will come in a month or two. Then it will be the season of the equinox, when the Moors come in from the country since they no longer have to tend their wheat crop or their fruits. We will travel by night only. I have persuaded them to take a woman, though they did not want to. No one has ever known a woman to make good her escape. I told them your very presence would serve as a protection for them, for if anyone saw a woman in the group he would think they were traders and not fugitive slaves.'

Angélique wrung his hand warmly. 'Oh, my dear Savary! And to think I was accusing you of forsaking me to my sad fate!'

'I have laid my plans,' said the old apothecary, 'but they are not finished yet. You still have to get yourself out of the fortress. I have been studying all the exits from the harem to the palace as a whole. There is a little door, not always guarded, on the north side in one of the walls that faces a manure pile not far from the Jewish cemetery. I learned this from the servants. It opens on a courtyard called "the secret court" a few feet away from the stairs to the harem. That's the way for you to take. One of the band will wait for you outside. Furthermore you must remember that this door can be opened from the outside only, and just two persons have a key to it – the Grand Eunuch and Leïla Aisheh – so that they can use it for quick returns after they have been to some public display. You'll have to sneak that key away and get it out to one of us so that he can come and open it for you. . . .'

'Savary,' sighed Angélique, 'you are so used to moving mountains that everything seems simple to you. How am I going to sneak a key away from the Grand Eunuch, avoid the panther . . .'

'Don't you have a servant you can depend on?'

'Yes . . . I mean, I don't know. . . .'

Savary laid a finger to his lips and slunk away like a ferret with his basket of dates under his arm.

Angélique heard a horse galloping up. Mulai Ismail emerged from a path, his burnous streaming behind him, and followed by two chieftains. He stopped as he saw the red-curtained chaise under the trees.

Savary spilled his basket in the middle of the path and began to utter great lamentations. This turned the Sultan's attention to him, and he prodded his horse into a slow walk. The awkwardness and the pretended terror of the old slave aroused the Sultan's desire to torment someone.

'Why, isn't that Osman Faraji's little Christian hermit? I've heard fantastic stories about you, you old sorcerer. You have taken wonderful care of my elephant and my giraffe.'

'I am grateful for your kindness, my lord,' Savary said in a tremulous voice as he prostrated himself before the Sultan.

'Rise,' said the King. 'It is not fitting for a hermit, a holy person through whom God speaks to men, to be in such a humiliating posture.'

Savary got to his feet and picked up his basket.

'Wait! I do not like people to call you "hermit" when you persist in your infamous beliefs. If you possess a secret magic, then you have learned it from Satan. Become a Moor and I will attach you to my retinue to interpret my dreams.'

'I shall think about it, my lord,' Savary assured him.

Mulai Ismail was in a bad humour. He raised his lance and drew back his arm, ready to let fly.

'Become a Moor,' he repeated threateningly. 'A Moor! . . . A Moor!'

The slave pretended not to hear him. The King struck him a first time. Old Savary half fell to the ground, putting his hand to his side where the blood was spurting. With his other hand he straightened his spectacles and turned on the Sultan a look of anger.

'I a Moor? A man like me? What do you take me for, my lord?'

'You blaspheme the religion of Allah!' roared Mulai Ismail, plunging the head of his lance into the old man's stomach.

Savary pulled it out and started to get to his feet to run away, but he could stagger only a few steps. Mulai Ismail spurred his horse after him, shouting: 'Moor! Moor!' and sticking his lance into him with each repetition of the word.

The old man fell to the ground again.

Angélique was watching the frightful scene from between the curtains of her chaise, biting her knuckles to stop herself from screaming. No, she could not let him slaughter her old friend. She jumped out of the chaise and knelt by Mulai Ismail's saddle-bow.

'Stop, my lord, stop!' she pleaded in Arabic. 'Have pity! He is my father.'

The Sultan paused with his lance held high, ready to throw. The appearance of this magnificent woman whom he had never seen before astonished him. Her hair had come undone and spread around her like rays of the sun. He kissed her arm.

Angélique ran to Savary and lifted him up enough so that she could drag him to the shade of a tree and prop him against it. He was so thin she could easily manage his weight. His old garment was sticky with blood, and his spectacles were broken. Gently she took them off his nose. The red blots kept spreading over his threadbare robe, and she saw with horror that his face was turning pale as suet under his henna-dyed beard.

'Oh, Savary!' she moaned, 'oh, my poor old Savary, do not die, please do not die.'

Dame Badiguet, who had been watching the scene from a distance, ran into her hut for medicines. Savary was groping in the folds of his garment trying to find a little piece of the black, oily sod. He squinted his eyes and recognised Angélique.

'The maumie!' he gasped. 'Alas, Madame, now no one will ever learn the greatest secret of the earth. No one but me ever knew it . . and now I am dying . . . dying.' His eyelids were turning grey.

The gardener's wife ran up with a broth of tamarisk seeds flavoured with cinnamon and pepper. Angélique raised it to the old man's lips. A smile spread over his countenance.

'Ah, the spices!' he murmured. 'The odour of wondrous voyages . . . Jesus, Mary, receive my soul. . . .'

And with these words the old apothecary breathed his last.

Angélique kept holding his hand until it grew cold.

'It's not possible,' she kept saying over and over again, 'not possible . . .'

The nimble, invincible Savary was no more. Instead there lay before her merely a piteous broken doll. It was all a bad dream she was having here in the green light of the palm garden. This was but one of his tricks. In a moment he would leap up and shyly whisper in her ear: 'Everything is going well, Madame.'

Finally she had to face the fact that, no, he was dead. She felt an unbearable weight descend upon her, the weight of eyes staring down at her. Then she saw near her in the sand the print of a horse's hoof, and raised her head. The shadow of Mulai Ismail was over her.

CHAPTER TWENTY-THREE

Osman Faraji entered the bath where the serving girls were helping Angélique up the mosaic-covered steps that led from the bottom of the marble pool to its edge. Blue and gold mosaic in arabesque patterns covered the ceiling also, in imitation of the Turkish Baths of Constantinople. An Orthodox Christian who had worked in Turkey had built this delicate treasure for the comfort of Mulai Ismail's women. The steam, perfumed with benzoin and roses, eddied around the gold-encrusted columns, giving the place a dreamlike quality like some palace out of an Arabian Nights fairytale.

When she saw the Grand Eunuch, Angélique looked around quickly for a veil to cover her nakedness. She had never got used to the eunuchs sharing the intimate details of a woman's toilet, and she could bear still less the presence of the supervisor of the seraglio.

Osman Faraji's expression was inscrutable. Two young, chubby-cheeked eunuchs were with him, carrying an array of iridescent rosy mousseline delicately embroidered with silver threads. Osman Faraji told the serving girls to open these one by one.

'Are there seven veils there?'

'Yes, master.'

He surveyed Angélique's well-proportioned body with the eye of a connoisseur. This was the only time in her life she was ashamed of being a woman and a beautiful one to boot. She could not help thinking of herself as merely a work of art being inspected by some critical collector pondering its material values only. She felt as if she had been robbed of her soul.

Old Fatima fastened the first veil around her hips. It fell to her ankles. Its semi-transparency hinted at the porcelain-smooth glow of the flesh of her flowing limbs, her full round hips, the subtle swell of her abdomen. Two other veils shrouded her bosom in the same provocative way. A still wider one was draped over her arms. Then her hair was shrouded in the fullest veil of all. Finally Fatima pinned the face-veil over her features, leaving only her green eyes visible, gleaming strangely owing to her highly emotional state.

Angélique was led back to her own apartment, where Osman Faraji soon joined her. His skin seemed to have acquired a slate-blue quality. She herself was deathly white under the layer of cosmetics which coloured her face.

She looked him in the eye. 'What sacrificial rite are you preparing me for, Osman Bey?' she asked tensely.

'You know very well, Firousi. I am going to present you to Mulai Ismail in a short while.'

'No!' said Angélique. 'That shall never be!'

Her delicate nostrils were quivering as she proudly raised her head to stare into his face. The Grand Eunuch's pupils contracted until they were as shiny sharp as a needle's point.

'You have shown yourself to him, Firousi. He has seen you! I have had some trouble explaining to him why I have kept you concealed from him so long. He wanted to know why. Now he has seen your beauty and it has dazzled him.' His voice grew lower and seemed to come from far away. 'You have never been so lovely, Firousi! Have no fear, you will ravish him. He will think of nothing but his lust for you. You possess everything to delight his soul – your golden hair, your pearly skin, your eyes. It is not alone your pride that will impress him, used as he is to insipidity in women. Nor is it your modesty, so strange for a woman who has already known what love can be, which will move and soften his heart. I know him well. I know the thirst that consumes him. For him you can be as a spring of living water. It is you who can make him know the meaning of sadness and of fear. His destiny can be within your dainty fingers. You can do anything, Firousi!'

Angélique sank back on her divan. 'No!' she said. 'No! This shall never be!' She assumed as graceful an attitude as her cocoon of veils permitted her. 'You have never had a Frenchwoman before in your collection, have you, Osman Bey? Now you are going to learn to your cost what stuff they are made of.'

Osman Faraji put his hands to his head and began to moan and sway like a grief-stricken woman. 'Oh! Oh! Oh! What could I have done so to offend Allah that I should have to cope with such wilfulness!'

'What ails you?'

'You poor thing, you cannot understand that there can be no question of your refusing Mulai Ismail. Pout a little at first, if you want . . . a little resistance won't displease him. But you will have to take him as your master, else he will cause you to perish with hideous tortures.'

'Then, so much the worse. I shall die. I shall perish from his tortures.'

The Grand Eunuch lifted his arms to heaven. Then he changed his tactics and leaned down to her.

'Firousi, why are you not eager for the arms of a man to encircle your lovely body? The heat of passion is tormenting you. Do you not know that Mulai Ismail is an extraordinary male? He was made for love as he was made for the hunt and for war, because there is Negro blood in his veins. He can satisfy a woman seven times within a single night. I shall cause him to drink potions to exalt his feverish passions. You shall know delights that will make you yearn till you go mad waiting for them to occur again.'

Her face aflame, Angélique pushed him away from her. She got to her feet and strode toward the far end of the balcony. He followed her like a patient cat, curious to learn why she was heading for a little chink in the wall that looked out on the square where the slaves were toiling. He wondered what she saw to turn her tormented expression peaceful.

'Every day I have been in Meknès,' murmured Angélique, 'some Christian slave has died as a martyr to his religion. Rather than forsake their faith they have borne heavy labour, hunger, blows and torture. Still by far the greater part of them are only simple souls, seafarers, crude and uneducated. Yet I, Angélique de Sancé de Monteloup, descended from a line of kings and crusaders, cannot be so constant as they. True, no one yet has pointed a lance at my throat and shouted "Moor?" at me, but I have been told, on the other hand, "You shall give your self to Mulai Ismail, the torturer of Christians, the murderer of my dear old Savary!" Which is just the same as demanding that I deny my faith. I shall not forsake my religion, Osman Faraji!'

'You shall perish in the most hideous of tortures.'

'So much the worse, then. God and my ancestors will aid me.'

Osman Faraji sighed. For the moment he had come to the end of his arguments. He knew he would have to give in. Still, when she had been shown the instruments of torture and heard descriptions of the punishments Mulai Ismail reserved for his women, perhaps her glowing faith would weaken. But time was moving on, and the Sultan was waiting impatiently.

'Listen to me,' he said in French. 'Have I not proved to you I am your friend? I have never broken my word to you, and if you had not been so careless, Mulai Ismail would not now be demanding you. Can't you, out of consideration for me, merely agree to be presented to Mulai Ismail now? He is waiting for us. I can find no more excuses for keeping you from him. He could cut off my head too, you know. Just being presented to him will not involve you in anything. Who knows, perhaps he will not like you after all?'

That was a little hard for Angélique to swallow, but she began to think perhaps it would be the best solution after all.

'I have warned the Sultan you are a wild thing. I know how I can make him be patient a little while longer to gain you time.'

'Time for what? To yield to fear? To weaken? Or,' thought Angélique, 'perhaps to escape. . . .'

'For your sake, then, I agree,' she said.

Still she angrily refused the escort of ten eunuchs he had provided.

'I shall not be led in like a prisoner, or like a sheep to the slaughter.'

Osman Faraji gave in to her. At this point he was ready to do anything to humour her. He alone would accompany her, with only one eunuch to hold her veils as he himself removed them one by one.

Mulai Ismail was waiting in a narrow room where he liked to withdraw to meditate. Copper censers were burning perfume.

Angélique felt as if she were seeing him for the first time. Now the barrier of his ignorance of her existence had been removed.

Mulai Ismail straightened as they entered. The Grand Eunuch and his acolyte fell on their faces before him. Then Osman Faraji rose and stepped behind Angélique to take her by the shoulders and gently push her toward the Sultan.

The King leaned forward ardently. His golden eyes met her emerald ones. She lowered her eyelids. For the first time in months a man was looking at her as a woman to be desired. As the Grand Eunuch revealed her face, she knew that his would manifest the surprised enchantment the sight of her perfect features, her full lips and her serious yet mocking expression had awakened in so many other men. She knew Mulai Ismail's broad nostrils would quiver at the sight of her extraordinary head of hair tumbling like golden silk over her shoulders.

Osman Faraji's hands were smoothing it, but she did not see or wish to see the motions of his long black fingers with their scarlet nails and their diamond and ruby rings. She kept her eyes lowered. Still, it was a funny thing, but she had never noticed before how pink the palms of his hands were, almost as if they had been stained with ashes of roses.

She forced herself to think of something else to endure the torture of being stripped naked before the master for whom she was fated. Still she could not keep from shivering when she perceived that now her arms had been unveiled. Osman Faraji's hands moved swiftly over her body, recalling her danger to her. Now his hand was on the sixth veil which would bare her bosom and reveal the delicacy of her waist and her long, supple back like that of a young girl.

She heard the voice of the King speaking in Arabic. 'Stop there. Do not embarrass her. I can guess how lovely she is.'

He rose from his divan and came near to her.

'Woman,' he said in French. 'Woman . . . show me . . . your eyes!'

In spite of his hoarse voice which could roar so bestially, he spoke now in a tone she could not refuse. She raised her eyes to his fearful countenance. She could see a tattoo mark near his lips, and the curiously yellow-black pores of his skin.

A smile spread slowly over his thick lips. 'Eyes such as I have never seen before!' he said in Arabic to Osman Faraji. 'There can be none like them in the world.'

'Thou hast spoken, lord,' agreed the Grand Eunuch.

He draped Angélique again in her numerous veils, whispering to her in French by way of advice: 'Bow to the King and he will be satisfied for the present.'

Angélique did not move. Mulai Ismail, though he knew only the rudiments of French, was quick enough to guess what the Grand Eunuch had said. He smiled again, and his eyes gleamed with a light of wild glee. Toward this woman so unexpectedly and surprisingly wonderful, whom the Grand Eunuch had been keeping in store for him, he already felt full of patience and interest. She contained within herself such promises of joy that he did not want to be too hasty in demanding them all at once. She was like an undiscovered country of which he yet could see only the horizon. She was an enemy land to be conquered, a hostile territory to be explored, a walled city in whose bastions he must find a chink. He would have to question the Grand Eunuch about her, for Osman Faraji would know her well. Was she sensitive, did she like gifts, did she prefer gentleness or roughness, did she like lovemaking? Yes. The clear liquid quality of her eyes confessed her frustration and the warmth of her passion hidden now under a body as white and cold as snow. It was not fear alone that was making her tremble, for she was of a race unused to fear. Still under the gaze of the King the face she was trying to hide was already taking on that expression of exhaustion and surrender that it must wear after a bout with love. She was at the end of her rope now. She wanted to escape subjugation and like a bird hypnotised by a serpent was casting her eyes about for any way out.

Mulai Ismail smiled again. . . .

Angélique had been taken back to another apartment, larger and more sumptuous than the one she had been occupying.

'Why don't you let me go to my own apartment?'

The eunuchs and the serving girls did not answer her. Fatima, stony-faced to hide her satisfaction, served her dinner, but Angélique could not eat a morsel. She was waiting anxiously for Osman Faraji to appear so that she might talk to him.

When he did not come and did not come, she sent for him. A eunuch told her the Grand Eunuch was on his way, but hours went by and he did not appear. She complained that the penetrating odours of the precious woods with which the apartment was wainscoted were giving her a headache. Fatima was burning incense and the odour of that became even more suffocating. Nimbly she perceived the evening closing in on her. In the light of the oil-lamps the face of the old woman seemed like that of old Melusine, the witch in the forest of Nieul, who used to brew herbs to summon up the devil. Melusine was one of those women of Poitou to whom a drop of Arab blood had given wild dark eyes. Long, long ago that region, too, had known the wave of short-sabred conquerors under a green banner.

Angélique buried her face in her cushions, tormented by the shame she had felt since Mulai Ismail's eyes had awakened in her the call of sex. He had held her with his gaze as he would hold her in his arms, waiting perhaps in a kind of suspended animation until she gave herself to him. She would not be able to resist the touch of his demanding body.

'I am not strong enough,' she thought. 'I am only a woman. What can I do? What can I do?'

She cried herself to sleep like a child, but it was a restless slumber, in which the heat of her desire still troubled her. She kept hearing Mulai Ismail's voice repeating 'Woman! . . . Woman!' Was it an invocation . . . a prayer . . . ?

Then he was with her, leaning over her in the clouds of incense, his lips like those of an African idol and his eyes as huge and unfathomable as the desert. She felt the soft touch of his lips on her shoulder and the weight of his body on hers. She experienced the delicious mastery of his grasp as he raised her and welded her to his smooth, hard chest. Then, weakening, she threw her arms around the body that was emerging from her dream as a concrete reality.

Her hands slipped along his amber skin, perfumed with musk, stroking the hard thighs that were squeezing her body in a grip of steel. Then her fingers touched a firm, cold object – the hilt of a dagger. Her hand closed around it. It was like a souvenir from the depths of a life that had long since passed away. Marquise of the Angels! Marquise of the Angels! Do you remember the dagger of Rodogone the Egyptian that you held in your hand when you cut the throat of the Great Coesre

291

in Paris? Do you recall how you held that dagger then?

Now she was holding it. Her own fingers were grasping it. The feel of its cold metal sent a thrill through her. With all her strength she drew it forth and struck.

It was Mulai Ismail's steely muscles that saved him. The rebound he made as he felt the blade pierce his throat was as lightning-swift as a tiger. But he remained leaning forward, his huge eyes staring even wider in his utter disbelief. Then he perceived the blood gushing on to his chest and realised that a second later and his artery would have been punctured.

Without taking his eyes off her – though now she could do nothing more – he strode to the gong and struck it.

Osman Faraji, who was not far away, burst into the room, and took in the scene with a glance. He signalled, and four Negroes rushed in to seize Angélique by the wrists, drag her off her couch, throw her at the feet of the Sultan, banging her forehead on the tiles.

The King was roaring like a wounded bull. Without the protection of Allah he now would lie dead, his throat cut by a cursed Christian who had stabbed him with his own dagger. He would put her to death with frightful tortures. And at once! At once! Let all the other slaves be brought to witness it, especially those stubborn French! They would see the torture of a woman of their own race and nation! They would see how perish those bold enough to dare raise a hand against the sacred person of the Commander of the Faithful!

The floodgates had been opened, and everything was moving at top speed. There were no questions asked. Angélique's wrists were bound and tied above her head to one of the columns in the room.

Her back was stripped naked. She felt the lashes of the whip like flames along her spine. How often, she thought, have I seen this pictured in my book of Holy Martyrs. But now it was she who was tied to the stake. Her back smarted more and more, and she could feel the warm blood trickling down her legs. Then she thought: 'This is not so bad. . . .'

But what would come next? . . . What difference did it make! She could not stop the flood that had been unleashed. She was only a pebble now, rolled along in the mighty current. She remembered the streams plunging down the Pyrenees at the time of her first marriage. She began to have a terrible thirst, and her eyes clouded.

The blows of the whip ceased, and in the moment's pause she felt her flesh burning till she could bear it no more.

They unbound her wrists, but only to turn her around so that her face was toward the room. Then they tied her to the pillar again.

Through the mist that swam before her eyes she could see the executioner with his brazier of glowing coals and the frightful instruments he was arranging on a board. He was an obscenely fat eunuch with the face of a gorilla. Other eunuchs stood around him, but they had not had time to don their official costumes for an execution and had merely removed their turbans.

Mulai Ismail sat to the left. He had refused to have his wound dressed, saying it was only a scratch. He wanted everyone to see his blood, which was hardening already, and take note of the sacrilege that had been done.

In the rear of the room some twenty French slaves had been assembled. Colin Paturel was among them, chained again, and Jean-Jean of Paris, the Marquis de Kermoeur, and others. Their faces were puffy with shock as they stared open-mouthed at the torture of this half-naked woman with such milk-white skin. Guards kept them in order, whips and swords in hand.

Osman Faraji bent toward Angélique, speaking slowly in Arabic: 'Listen to me, the Great Sultan of Morocco is ready to pardon your insane act. Consent to obey him and he will pardon you. Do you consent?'

Osman Faraji's black face wavered before her eyes. She kept thinking it would probably be the last face she would ever see in this world. It was good that way. Osman Faraji was so great a soul! And all the others were so little, so petty. Then there came into her vision the rough blond face of Colin Paturel beside that of the Grand Eunuch.

'My poor little girl. . . . He is asking me to beg you to consent. . . . Not to let yourself be destroyed like this. . . . My poor little girl. . . .'

'Why did you let yourself be crucified, Colin Paturel?' she wanted to ask him. But her lips could form only a single word: NO!

'They will rip off your breasts. They will mutilate you with red hot pincers,' said Osman Faraji.

Angélique closed her eyes. If only they would leave her to herself and her pain. The other beings seemed to drift away . . . to be already far away . . . How long would it last? She could hear the slaves groaning at the far end of the room. What could the executioner be preparing next . . . ?

There was an interminable delay. Then her hands were freed and she slipped down the pillar for a long . . . long . . . long way.

When she recovered consciousness, her cheek was resting on a silken cushion. She was lying on her side, and Osman Faraji's hands seemed to be resting not far from her. Angélique remembered. In her delirium she had clutched those patrician hands with fingernails as red as the rubies in his rings. She turned a little. Suddenly her memory returned to her completely, and she was filled with the peculiar joy a mother feels at the moment her child is born. She understood that now her pain was over and she had accomplished something wonderful.

'Is it over?' she asked. 'Have I been martyred? Did I resist bravely?'

'Am I dead?' Osman Faraji mimicked her with a grin. 'Foolish little rebel! Allah showed me no mercy when he put you in my way. Well, you still have your life, and no harm has been done you except that your back is a little raw from the whip. That is because I told Mulai Ismail you had consented. But since you were in no state to demonstrate your obedience then and there, he agreed to let you be taken care of and cured. For three days now you have been raving with fever, and it will be at least a month before you are presentable again.'

Angélique's eyes filled with tears. 'So, everything is going to start all over again? Oh, why have you done this, Osman Faraji? Why didn't you let me die? I haven't the courage to go through it again.'

'So you will give up?'

'No, you know I will not.'

'Well, don't cry, little Firousi. You have till the new moon to prepare yourself for another martyrdom,' said the Grand Eunuch ironically.

He returned to her that evening. She had rallied her strength and could sit up a little on her cushions. Her back was covered with bandages.

'You have robbed me of my death, Osman Faraji! But you will get nothing by waiting. I shall never be the third wife, nor the favourite, of Mulai Ismail. I shall tell him so to his face the next time you present me to him. Then . . . everything will begin again. I am not afraid. It is true that God sheds His grace upon His martyrs. After all, that whipping was not so bad.'

The Grand Eunuch leaned back his head and laughed, something he rarely did.

'I don't doubt it,' he said. 'Just keep in mind, you little fool, that there are many kinds of whipping. Some strokes of the whip can tear off a long ribbon of flesh every time. And there are others that hardly damage the skin enough for blood to flow. Then there are whips whose tips have been steeped in painkilling drugs, and these numb the pain. So it wasn't so bad, eh? Well, that's because I gave orders. . . .'

Angélique experienced many different feelings before she realised with a certain vexation she had been duped.

'Why did you do this for me, Osman Bey?' she asked in all serious-
ness. 'I had deceived you. Did you hope I would change my mind? No,
that I will never do. I will never give in. You know perfectly well such
is impossible!'

'Yes, I know that well,' said the Grand Eunuch bitterly. His priestlike features fell, and there crossed his face that fleeting look of a sad
monkey that Negroes crushed by fate so often get. 'I have tested your
strength of character. It is hard as a diamond. Nothing will ever break
your will.'

'Then, why? . . . Why don't you abandon me to my wretched fate?'

He shook his head. 'I cannot. I can never allow Mulai Ismail to destroy
you, the loveliest and greatest of women. Allah has never created anything like you before. You are Woman herself! At last I have found it
after searching through all the slave markets of the world. I will never
let Mulai Ismail destroy you!'

Angélique bit her lips. She was perplexed, for this was the greatest
surprise she had experienced yet. She wondered how she should take
this sudden avowal.

Osman Faraji saw her gaze wander. 'Coming from me, these words
sound strange to you, don't they?' he said with a smile. 'I cannot desire
you physically, but I can admire you. Perhaps, too, you have moved my
heart.'

A heart? When it had not cost him a moment's anxiety to torture the
Circassian to death?

He himself was astonished, too, at the breaches the Frenchwoman
had made in his defences of pure reason. He began to speak in a slow
meditative fashion.

'I love the blending of your beauty and your character. . . . The
perfect way your body mirrors your soul. You are a fantastically noble
creature. . . . You have all the tricks of a woman, her cruelty, her
sharp nails, and yet you have not lost the tenderness of a mother. . . .
You are as changeable as the weather, yet as fixed as the sun. . . . You
seem capable of adjusting to any situation, yet you cling with your Latin
naïveté to whatever you have set your mind upon. . . . You are like
every other woman, but you resemble no one of them. . . . I love to
think of the life that lies beyond you, the promises of your old age. . . .
I love the poison that oozes from your smiles and from your tears. . . .
I love the fact that you crave the love of Mulai Ismail, that you are as
shameless as Jezebel, and that you dared to kill him as Judith did
Holofernes. You are the treasure-chest into which the Creator of us all

poured every jewel of womanhood. . . .' He paused a moment, then finished: 'I cannot let you be destroyed. God would punish me if I did.'

Angélique had listened to him with a rather ironic smile on her pale lips. 'If anyone should ever ask me,' she thought, 'what was the most beautiful declaration of love I had ever received, I would answer that it was the one of the Grand Eunuch Osman Faraji, guardian of the harem of His Majesty the Sultan of Morocco.' Great hope dawned in her. She was on the point of asking him to help her escape, but an instinctive reticence kept her from it. She had learned the implacable laws of the seraglio well enough to know assistance from the Grand Eunuch was but a dream of perfection. He would have to be 'naïvely Latin', as he said, to envisage such a thing.

'Well, what is going to happen?' she asked.

The eunuch's eyes were looking at her distantly. 'There are still three weeks before the new moon.'

'What can happen before the new moon?'

'How impatient you are! A thousand thousand things can happen in three weeks. Allah may decide to destroy the world just a moment after we stop talking. Firousi, would it please you to breathe the cool night air from the top of the Mazagreb Tower. Yes? Then follow me. I am going to show you the stars.'

The Grand Eunuch's observatory was on the summit of the Mazagreb Tower, not so high as the minarets, but higher than the ramparts. Between the pointed battlements gleamed the expanse of desert, spotted near the city by dark tufts of olive-trees, but beyond bare and stony in the moonlight.

The powerful telescope, the sextant, the compasses, the globes and all the other measuring instruments reflected in their copper and highly varnished mountings the light of the great star of the night and of the lesser stars themselves, especially brilliant in the dry clear air.

A Turkish scholar whom Osman Faraji had brought back from Constantinople, a frail little old man sinking under the weight of his turban, was his assistant. When he practised astrology Osman Faraji liked to put on his Sudanese cloak and his turban of gold brocade. Seeming even taller in them, he displayed himself under the great vault of the limpid firmament, only a silvery line distinguishing his profile from the darkness. He became a being almost without substance.

Timidly Angélique took her seat some distance apart. The top of the tower seemed a sanctuary of the soul. 'No woman should ever have come here,' she thought. But the Grand Eunuch did not scorn women's intelligence as real men did. With his maimed senses he judged them for what they were, dismissing the stupid but encouraging those who stimulated him. Angélique had taught him a great deal about the character of westerners and especially about her great king Louis XIV. All her information would be valuable to him for instructing the embassy Mulai Ismail planned to send to the master of Versailles.

It would have been too easy to say that Osman Faraji had once and for all given up his intention of making Angélique the third wife of Mulai Ismail. The project had only been postponed; it still hovered in space like a comet perceived only once in a lifetime, yet always present and exerting its influence on human fate. To the eyes of a Latin the situation could have only a tragic ending, but Osman Faraji was waiting. The stars had revealed to him that he was heading for disaster, for the destiny of Angélique would touch but briefly that of Mulai Ismail. She would depart like a shooting star, but whether through death or not remained yet undisclosed. The omens had sent a shiver along his spine and depressed him like the passing of the dark angel of death, to such a degree that his fingers could no longer grasp the cold metal of the telescope. Tonight, when he wanted to wring the deepest secrets from the heavens, he had brought along the very woman whose destiny he was inquiring.

The invisible strength Angélique possessed was of a peculiar nature. He had underestimated its power at first, but now he admitted that she was one of those rare beings whose essence he had not known how to judge. It had been a serious mistake on his part, and he could explain it only by the mystery of her femininity that disguised her unconquerable soul. He had to bow before the fact that her worldly beauty concealed an unexpected character and an extraordinary destiny of which she herself was unaware.

As he adjusted the mechanism of his observatory instruments, he wondered whether he had not wandered into a trap.

Angélique was looking at the stars. She liked them better as tiny pinpoints of twinkling light than as dazzling jewels set on a black velvet background, as they appeared through the telescope. What could Osman Faraji be seeking in this vast panoply of worlds?

Angélique did not think her own mind equal to so lofty and mysterious a science. And because being on the top of a tower like this under a starry sky reminded her of long distant nights in Toulouse, she remembered how her husband, the scholarly Comte de Peyrac, had sometimes brought her into his laboratory and taken the trouble to explain certain of his experiments. Doubtless he had found her stupid.

It would have been better if he had not done so.

Her soul was tired and so cruelly disenchanted. Life had reduced her to the common level from which it was vain for her to rise. She was only a simple woman – a woman who had no other choice than to yield to Mulai Ismail, or die because of her stubbornness. No other choice than to give herself to the King of France or be banished. To sell herself so as not to be sold. To strike so as not to be crushed. Was there any purpose in going on living? Living! She tilted her head back and gazed at the limitless freedom of the heavens. Living, oh Lord! Not being always caught between degradation and death!

If only the captives would help her escape! Now that Savary was no more, they were not likely to encumber themselves with a woman. Still if she could only lay her hands on the key to that little door and get out of the harem itself, Colin Paturel would probably not refuse to take her with them. She would kneel to him and entreat him to.

But how could she get hold of that key which only the Grand Eunuch and Leïla Aisheh possessed . . . ?

'Why did you escape?'

Angélique shuddered. She had forgotten the presence of the Grand Eunuch and his disturbing ability to read one's mind. She opened her mouth, but no words came, for he was not looking at her. He had spoken, as it were, to himself, keeping his eyes on the stars.

'Why did you escape from Candia?' He rested his chin in his hands, and closed his eyes. 'Why did you desert that Christian pirate who bought you?'

His voice was so strange, so troubled, that Angélique was too astonished to answer.

'Tell me, why did you flee? Did you not feel your destiny and Rescator's were linked together? Answer me, didn't you feel it?'

Now he was looking at her again and his voice was imperious. She stammered meekly: 'Yes, I did feel it.'

'Oh, Firousi,' he exclaimed almost sadly, 'remember what I told you: "One can never force fate, and when the signs warn you, you must not ignore them"? That man's peculiar sign has crossed your path and . . . I can't foresee everything, Firousi. I would have to make endless calculations to read in the stars the extraordinary story I think I glimpse in them. What I do know is that that man is of the same race as you.'

'Do you mean he is French?' she asked timidly. 'They said he was a Spaniard, or perhaps a Moroccan.'

'I do not know. . . . I mean . . . he is of a race not yet created . . . like you.' His hands traced a mysterious design in the air. 'An independent spiral . . . joining another which . . .' He began to speak rapidly in Arabic. The old Turk wrote down what he said.

Angélique was at her wits' end trying to catch the drift of their talk and to read on their faces and in the movement of the compasses they were manipulating and the globes they kept consulting the meaning of the verdict on which hung her life.

Recently her thoughts had drifted far from Rescator, an image already blurred, which the violence of her struggle against Mulai Ismail had pushed away to the back of her mind. But now all of a sudden the memory of that figure in the black mask gripped her.

Seeing Osman Faraji train his telescope on the heavens again, she dared to interrupt by asking: 'Did you know him, Osman Bey? Was he a sorcerer like you?'

He shook his head slowly. 'Perhaps. But his magic was of another source than mine. But I did meet him, as a matter of fact. Although a Christian, he spoke Arabic and several other languages, but we had trouble exchanging our ideas. I was like a man from the past facing a man from the future laden with provender for times to come.'

'But wasn't he only a common pirate?' she exclaimed angrily. 'A low smuggler of silver. . . .'

'He was seeking his way through a world that had cast him out. He will go on like that until the day he either is destroyed or finds his proper place. Can't you understand that, you who have lived through so many vicissitudes and now are seeking in vain to find your own true nature?'

Angélique began to tremble from her head to her feet. No, that was not true! The Grand Eunuch could not possibly know! He could not have read that in the stars. In fright, she scrutinised the dark sky. The night was clear and sweet. The wind from the desert had become imbued with the fragrance of the gardens of Meknès. It was a night like any other night, but on the top of the Mazagreb Tower she felt that it was full of disturbing currents. Angélique would have liked to flee and leave this black sage there, among his strange instruments and with his spectacled scribe scratching cabbalistic signs like a busy insect.

She wished to know no more. She was too tired for that. Still she stood motionless, unable to take her eyes from the slow movement of the telescope that pointed toward the heavens.

Osman Faraji's lore was raising a corner of the curtain that veiled the invisible. What would he tell her next? She thought she saw stealing into his face that slaty colour which was his way of turning pale, and suddenly he fixed her with an almost horrified stare as if he were seeing at her feet a disaster that he had set in motion.

'Osman Bey,' she exclaimed, 'what have you read in the stars?'

There was a long silence. The Grand Eunuch lowered his eyes and assumed his inscrutable expression.

'Why did you flee from Rescator?' he murmured at last. 'He would have been the only man strong enough for you . . . except, perhaps, Mulai Ismail . . . I do not know now whether the risk would not have been worse. You bring death to the men who attach themselves to you. There it is!'

She let out a cry of agony and besought him with folded hands: 'No, Osman Bey, no! Don't say that!'

It was as if he had accused her of killing with her own hands the husband she had so dearly loved. She hung her head like a guilty person and shut her eyes to rid her of the sight of other faces looming from her past.

'Yes, you bring them either death or disaster, or such pain as to spoil their taste for living. A man would need exceptional powers to escape a fate like that. And all because you insist on going where no one can follow you. Those who prove too feeble you leave by the side of the road. The strength the Creator has given you will not permit you to stop before you reach the place you want to go.'

'What is that place, Osman Bey?'

'I do not know. But inasmuch as you have not yet reached it, you will destroy everything on your way, including your own life. I wanted to tame that strength and I was trapped by it instead, for it is not the kind to be subdued. Even you yourself are largely unaware of it.'

Angélique began to weep. 'Oh, Osman Bey, I can see now you are sorry you did not leave me to die under the torture of Mulai Ismail. Oh, why did you have to look at the stars tonight? Why? You were my friend, yet now you tell me such terrible things!'

The voice of the Grand Eunuch softened, but she remained weak and plunged in worry.

'Do not weep, Firousi. It is not your fault. It all comes from beyond you. You don't bring bad luck, only unhappiness. But there are some people too weak to support the burden of riches. So much the worse for them! Alas! Yes, I am still your friend. So much the worse for me! It is not without hazard that one can take the responsibility of your death. In preventing it I wanted also to spare Mulai Ismail unforeseen woes. But now I shall have to accomplish something superhuman – a struggle against what is written, a struggle against fate – so that you may not prove too strong for me.'

Doves were fluttering about the patio as the group of women passed through it. A slave repairing the fountain looked up and whispered: 'Are you the Frenchwoman?'

Angélique heard him and slowed her steps, letting her companions proceed without her. Since this was a patio within the harem itself, there were no eunuchs guarding them. But how could a French slave be working there? If a eunuch had seen him, he would have cut the captive's throat.

As he bent over the pipe he was unscrewing he repeated his question in a whisper.

'Yes,' said Angélique. 'But be careful. Men are forbidden here.'

'That doesn't apply to me,' he muttered. 'I have a right to go where I want in the harem. Pretend you're looking at the doves while I talk to you. Colin Paturel sent me.'

'Oh?'

'Are you still determined to escape?'

'Yes.'

'Did Mulai Ismail pardon you because you yielded?'

Angélique had no time to explain the Grand Eunuch's deception. 'I did not yield to him. I will never yield to him. I want to escape. Help me!'

'We will help you for old Savary's sake. He was determined to get you out of here. He was your father, wasn't he? We can't leave you behind, although we are taking an extra risk in having a woman with us. Well, here's the plan. Some night – the date has not yet been set – Colin Paturel or someone else will be waiting for you at the little door in the north wall by the manure pile. If there is any watchman there, our man will kill him. He will open the door with the key, since it can be opened only from the outside. You will be by it, and he will guide you. Your job is to get that key.'

'The only persons who have one are the Grand Eunuch and Leïla Aisheh.'

'That's no help. Well, without that key, there's no other way. Try to think of a way to get it. You can bribe some servant girl, can't you? Once you get it, slip it to me. I am always prowling around here, for I have been given the job of repairing all the fountains in the harem. Tomorrow I'll be working on the one in the Sultana Abechi's patio.

She's a nice, likeable woman who knows me well, and she'll let us talk without reporting us.'

'How am I going to get that key?'

'That's for you to work out, dear lady! You have several days to work at it. We're waiting for a moonless night for our escape. Good luck! When you want me, ask for Esprit Cavaillac, from Frontignan, His Majesty's plumber.'

He gathered up his tools and bowed to her with an encouraging little smile. Later she was to learn his history from the Sultana Abechi, who was quite a gossip. To make him renounce his faith, Mulai Ismail had inflicted an especially loathsome torture upon him. He had tied one end of a rope to his private parts and the other to a horse, which he proceeded to lash into a mad gallop. Esprit Cavaillac had been cared for by his companions and had survived, and now, thanks to his amputations, he had free access to the harem and thus could serve as a messenger between Angélique and the band on the outside.

Meeting him restored her courage. She was not utterly forgotten after all. Someone was still thinking of her. They were even planning her escape. Hadn't Osman Faraji said her strength was like that of a volcano? Then she was sick and weak, and her back was raw, and his words had seemed like a bad joke. But now she thought of all she had done in the few years of her lifetime, and she could not see why she should not succeed in this mad attempt to escape from a harem.

Quickly she circled the patio and left by a long balcony. She crossed a garden where two fig-trees were spreading their biblical shadow over a pool of water, and from there entered another patio from which she proceeded to the arcade leading to the shaded balconies of the apartments. There Raminan, the chief of Leïla Aisheh's bodyguards suddenly appeared before her.

'I should like to see your mistress,' said Angélique.

The Negro surveyed her coldly without replying. What could this troublesome rival of his mistress be wanting? She was the Grand Eunuch's creature, and Leïla Aisheh and Daisy-Valina had been brewing charms against her all the past week. The manner in which Angélique had been whipped did not fool the imperious Sudanese Sultana. By showing resistance to him, she had taken the surest way of alluring Mulai Ismail. The dagger she had plunged into his throat had only whetted his desire for her. He was taking his time to tame this tigress and make her as gentle as a dove. He had even gone so far as to confide this to Leïla Aisheh herself, saying that this Frenchwoman could not resist his love. If he had not been so careless as to be wearing this dagger,

Angélique would have swooned in his arms. He was being very clever to keep her tortured by desire. He would lull her fiery spirit and take possession of her body. For the first time in his life Mulai Ismail really wanted a woman and would do anything to make her smile at him.

The perceptive Negress was quite aware of this change in him. It made her both angry and fearful, for inexpert as the Frenchwoman might be, she yet had the tyrant inescapably in her power, and was leading him on a leash like a tame cheetah just as Leïla Aisheh did the panther Alchadi.

Osman Faraji was using her as his pawn in a fiendish intrigue. He had circulated the rumour that the Frenchwoman was dying. The Sultan had been asking for news of her incessantly, and wanted to go to see her, but the Grand Eunuch would not let him. The sick woman was still terrified by him, and the sight of her lord and master would only bring on her fever again. Nonetheless she had smiled to see the gift Mulai Ismail had sent her, a necklace of emeralds plundered from an Italian galley. So the Frenchwoman liked jewels! At once the Sultan summoned all the goldsmiths of the city and inspected their finest pieces under a magnifying glass.

All this worried Leïla Aisheh and Daisy. They had carefully considered many solutions to this problem. The simplest appeared to be to help along with appropriate medicines what had already been so nicely started. But the serving girls they sent with their 'restorative' drinks always seemed to get stopped, no matter how adroit they were, by the freshly alerted guards of Osman Faraji.

Now the Frenchwoman was in excellent health again, so it seemed, and had come to ask for an interview with the woman who had been trying to destroy her. After quite a bit of reflection Raminan asked her to wait. Prince Bonbon, in his raspberry-coloured turban and his sugar-white robe, was not far away, playing at cutting off heads with his wooden sword. They had taken his steel sword away from him after he had caused too much damage with it.

When the eunuch returned he motioned Angélique into a room where the huge Negress was enthroned amid a jumble of braziers, chafing dishes and copper pots in which aromatic herbs were steeping. Daisy-Valina was with her. Decanters of Bohemian glass stood on two low tables, as well as a great number of dishes containing mint-flavoured tea, tobacco and sweetmeats.

The first wife of Mulai Ismail took her long pipe from her mouth and puffed a cloud of smoke toward the cedar beams of the ceiling. This was her secret vice, for the Sultan disapproved as heartily of smoking as he did of drinking, which was forbidden by Mohammed. He himself drank nothing but water, and his lips had never touched the mouthpiece of a narghile, as did the impious Turks who enjoyed the pleasures of this world and gave little thought to God. Leïla Aisheh got her tobacco and brandy from Christian slaves, who were the only ones permitted to buy it and use it.

Angélique knelt reverently on the thick carpet, where she remained with lowered head while the two women looked at her in silence. Then she took from her finger the turquoise ring the Persian Ambassador Bakhtiari Bey had given her, and laid it before Leïla Aisheh.

'Pray accept this gift,' she said in Arabic. 'I have nothing finer to offer you, for this is all I have.'

The Negress's eyes began to smoulder. 'I will not accept your present. You are lying. You have an emerald necklace the Sultan gave you.'

Angélique shook her head, and said in French to the Englishwoman: 'I would not accept the emerald necklace. I do not wish to be Mulai Ismail's favourite, and I will never be . . . if you will help me.'

The Englishwoman translated, and the Negress leaned forward toward Angélique intently.

'What do you mean?'

'I mean that there are better ways for you to get rid of me than by poison or acid. Help me to escape instead.'

The two women whispered together for a long time. Angélique had turned to her own good the hatred her rivals bore her. After all, what did they have to lose in the process? If Angélique succeeded in escaping, they would never see her again in their lives. If she did not, she would be recaptured and really put to death in a horrible fashion this time. How could the two chief wives of the Sultan ever be implicated in her disappearance, whereas they might be if she were found dead of poison. They were not responsible for guarding the harem, and the flight of one concubine would never be laid at their door.

'No woman has ever escaped from the harem,' said Leïla Aisheh. 'The Grand Eunuch would have his head cut off if one did.' Then her bloodshot, yellowish eyes began to burn with red fire. 'Now I understand it all. Everything is as it should be. My astrologer read the stars correctly. They told him you would be the cause of Osman Faraji's death.'

A shiver ran the entire length of Angélique's spine. *He, too, would have read the same fate in the stars,* she thought. *That is why he looked at me so strangely.* 'Now I shall have to struggle against fate, Firousi, so that you will not prove too strong for me.'

The anguish she had experienced on the top of the Mazagreb Tower swept over her again. The smell of the herbs and the tobacco were stifling her, and she felt perspiration break out on her forehead. With relentless persistence she proceeded to wheedle the key away from Leïla Aisheh. Finally the Sultana gave it to her. She had delayed only because she liked to do nothing except after a long discussion. In fact, from Angélique's first words, she had silently consented to the plan. It would rid her of a dangerous rival and at the same time work the destruction of her enemy, the Grand Eunuch, by putting him in the way of Mulai Ismail's wrath, for the King would never forgive him for depriving him of his latest passion.

She also plotted to learn from Angélique the plans of the fugitives so as to have them caught. This would add to her prestige and increase her reputation for seeing the future. It was agreed that on the night of the escape Leïla Aisheh in person would guide Angélique through the harem to the staircase that led to the courtyard where the secret door was. Thus she would not fall prey to the panther, which might be lurking in some corner along the way. Leïla Aisheh could talk to the animal, and she would also bring along some delicacy to appease it. The guards would let the Sultana pass, for they feared the power of her evil eye.

'The Grand Eunuch is the only one we have to be wary of,' said Daisy. 'He alone is to be feared. What are you going to tell him if he asks you why you paid us a visit?'

'I will tell him I heard how you hated me and wanted to get into your good graces.'

The two women nodded their heads in approval. 'Perhaps he will believe you. Yes, since it is you, he probably will believe it.'

That afternoon Angélique paid a call upon the Sultana Abechi, a fat Moor of Spanish extraction, to whom the Sultan still showed considerable attention, and whom he had almost made his Wife Number Three. Esprit Cavaillac was there, and she slipped him the key.

'So soon!' he said in astonishment. 'You certainly didn't let the grass grow under your feet. Old Savary was right about your being brave and shrewd, and that we could depend on you as if you were a man. Well, at least we won't be taking along a liability. Now all you have to do is wait. I will let you know what day we decide on.'

The waiting was what Angélique knew would be the most agonising part of the whole scheme, and in addition to keeping herself under control, she would be at the mercy of two insidiously deadly women, and under the eye of the Grand Eunuch.

Her back healed, for she obediently submitted to the treatment old Fatima relentlessly applied in hopes that her mistress would end her stubbornness. All the trouble she had endured, not to mention her bruised and torn skin, should have proved to her once and for all that she was not the stronger. So why be so stubborn?

Then the rumour spread that the Grand Eunuch was going on a journey to see his tortoises and the old sultanas. His absence would not last more than a month, but when she heard of it Angélique heaved a great sigh of relief. It was absolutely necessary that she take advantage of his absence to make her escape. Things would be much easier that way, and if the Grand Eunuch were absent at the time, he would not get his head cut off. She did not like to think of that eventuality, and she trusted that the Grand Eunuch stood too high in Mulai Ismail's estimation to draw his anger upon him, even for allowing a slave to escape. Still she could not forget the predictions of Leïla Aisheh's astrologer: 'He has read in the stars that you will be the cause of Osman Faraji's death . . .' She must avoid that at any cost. His own departure would be the means.

The Grand Eunuch came to say good-bye to her and warned her to be very careful. He had continued to give out that she was still very sick and still in terror of Mulai Ismail, and the Sultan was being patient. That was a miracle! He warned her not to spoil her luck by becoming too friendly with Leïla Aisheh, who was only looking for a way to injure her. In a month he would be back, and then things would all work out, she could trust him to see that they did.

'I do trust you, Osman Bey,' she said.

Once he was gone, she undertook to make the captives decide on their day of flight, using Esprit Cavaillac as her go-between. Colin Paturel sent word to her that they must wait for a moonless night. But by the time that came, the Grand Eunuch might be back again. She gnawed her knuckles in frustration. If she could only make these Christians understand that she had set her mind against inexorable destiny! It was a superhuman struggle against the oracle that she would be the cause of Osman Faraji's death, a titanic struggle against the stars in their courses. In her nightmares the star-studded sky seemed to whirl and crash down upon her, crushing her beneath it.

At last Esprit Cavaillac told her the leader of the slaves had yielded to her arguments, as it would be much better for her to escape while the Grand Eunuch was away. The light of the moon might be an additional hazard for the others, but that could not be helped. Freed from his chains, Colin Paturel would make a tour of the palace and kill the watchmen at the first ring of walls and again at the second. He would have to cross the little grove of orange trees and a courtyard that led to the secret door. There was nothing to do but pray it would be a cloudy night to hide even the wan light of the moon, already in its last quarter. The date was set.

That evening Leïla Aisheh sent her some powders to slip into the drink of the servant girls guarding her.

Angélique offered coffee to Rafai, who had come to inquire after her health, for in the absence of the Grand Eunuch he was responsible for the harem. The fat old monster liked to imitate the half-familiar ways of the Grand Eunuch with his charges, but they did not suit Rafai. All he got for his pains was guffaws of laughter. So he liked to be with Angélique, who treated him as an equal, and he drank the coffee she gave him to the last drop. Then he retired to mingle his snores with those of the reclining serving girls.

Angélique waited for what seemed an eternity. When she heard an owl hoot, she stole down into the patio. Leïla Aisheh was already there with Daisy, who was carrying an oil-lamp. Alas, it was not needed, for the moon was shining like a white sail on the night's dark ocean, and there was not a cloud in the sky.

The three women crossed the little garden and proceeded under the shelter of a long arcade. From time to time Leïla Aisheh heaved a strange sort of hoarse rattle from her chest, her way of speaking to the panther.

They reached the end of the arcade without accident, and followed another that enclosed a garden redolent with the fragrance of roses. Suddenly the Negress stopped.

'There it is!' whispered Daisy, clutching Angélique's arm.

The animal leaped out of the bushes, its nose to the ground like a huge cat ready to pounce on a mouse.

The Sultana held out a squab to it, still making the strange rattling sound in her throat. The panther seemed to relax. It came to her, and Leïla Aisheh fastened a chain to its collar.

'Stay a couple of steps behind me,' she said to the two white women.

They resumed their progress. Angélique was surprised that they did not encounter any eunuchs, but Leïla Aisheh had chosen to go through the old concubines' quarter, where the rejected women were not very carefully guarded. Furthermore the usual strict discipline had been somewhat relaxed in the absence of the Grand Eunuch. The other eunuchs preferred their own company to making eternal rounds checking on the harem.

A few sleepy-eyed serving girls saw them pass, and bowed to the Sultana of Sultanas.

Now they were climbing a stairway leading to the ramparts. This was the most difficult part of the trip. Beneath them yawned on one side the dark gardens surrounding the mosque, its green-tiled cupola glistening in the moonlight, and on the other a deserted square where the palace market was held. Mulai Ismail had built himself a fortress like a walled town, capable of holding out for months against a besieging army from the city that surrounded it.

At the end of this stretch a guard was leaning over the battlements, staring down at the market-place. His back was towards them, his lance pointed skyward. The women slipped into the shadow of the merlons as they drew near him. When they were just a few steps away, Leïla Aisheh threw in his direction the squab she had not yet given the panther. The animal darted after it. The guard turned, saw the beast almost upon him, and let out a scream of terror as he hurled himself over the edge. They could hear the dull thud as his body hit the ground far below.

The women held their breaths and waited to see whether his cry would draw other guards to the place. Nothing stirred.

Leïla Aisheh calmed the panther down, and took its chain in her hand. They descended to a lower level which had been abandoned and was about to be demolished to make room for another building. The Sultana led Angélique to the top of a crude stairway which descended into a pit as dark and deep as a well.

'This is the place,' said the Negress. 'Go down. When you are at the bottom you will see that the door is open. If it is not, wait. Your accomplice will not be long. Tell him to put the key in a little crack in the wall to the right of the door. I will send Raminan to get it tomorrow. Now, go!'

Angélique began her descent of the narrow steps. Then she turned, thinking she ought at least to say 'Thank you.' She thought she had never seen anything stranger than these two women side by side, leaning over the stairwell to watch her go – the blonde Englishwoman lifting her oil-lamp high, and the dark Negress holding the panther Alchadi by the collar.

As she kept going down the stairs, the light from the lamp grew fainter and fainter. She stumbled a little on the last steps, but she quickly perceived the outlines of the door. It was open! The slave had got there early.

Hesitantly Angélique groped her way to it, trembling so much in spite of herself that she could hardly take the last few steps that lay between her and freedom.

Softly she called in French: 'Is it you?'

A human form stooped to squeeze through the opening, blocking the moonlight that shone through the crack so that Angélique could not tell who it was. She did not recognise the form until it rose again, and a ray of moonlight silvered its high turban of cloth-of-gold.

The Grand Eunuch Osman Faraji stood before her.

'Where are you going, Firousi?' he asked softly.

Angélique pressed herself against the wall as if trying to melt into it. She was not sure she was not dreaming or having an hallucination.

'Where are you going, Firousi?'

She had to admit it was he. She began to shake. Her strength gave way.

'Why are you there?' she said. 'Oh, why are you there? You were away on a journey.'

'I came back two days ago, but I did not think it necessary to announce my return.'

How diabolical he was, that Osman Faraji! A gentle, implacable tiger! He kept on standing between her and the door that meant liberty to her. She clasped her hands and wrung them in her despair.

'Let me go, Osman Bey,' she begged breathlessly. 'Oh, let me go! You alone can let me. You are all powerful. Let me go!'

The Grand Eunuch's face took on an expression of outrage, as if she had blasphemed.

'Never has a woman escaped from a harem I guarded,' he said fiercely.

'Then do not tell me you are trying to save me,' Angélique exclaimed in anger. 'Never say you are my friend. You know that from now on my only fate is death.'

'Did I not ask you to trust me? Oh, Firousi, why do you always tempt fate? Listen, my little rebel, I did not go to see my tortoises, but to try to join your former master.'

'My former master?' said Angélique uncomprehendingly.

'Rescator, the Christian pirate who bought you for thirty-five thousand piastres in Candia.'

Everything around her began to whirl. Every time she heard that name she felt the same mixture of hope and longing and could not order her thoughts.

'I went aboard one of his galleys at anchor at Agadir. The captain told me where he was. I sent him a message by carrier pigeon. He is coming. He is coming for you.'

'Coming for me?' she asked incredulously.

Little by little the weight on her heart grew lighter. He was coming for her . . .

Of course, he was a pirate, but all the same he was a man of her own kind. Perhaps he bore a hideous face beneath his mask, but he had not inspired her with fear the time before. He would only have to appear, black and slender, and lay his hand on her head, so humbled now, for all the warmth of life to flood back into her. She would follow him and ask him: 'Why did you pay thirty-five thousand piastres for me in Candia? Do you find me that beautiful, or did you read in the stars, like Osman Faraji, that we were fated to meet again?

What would he answer her? She remembered how hoarse his voice was, how it had made her shiver. Yet he was unknown to her. Still she could see herself weeping on his breast as he took her far, far away. Who could he be? He was the traveller from the future laden with provender for times to come. He would take her away . . .

'It's impossible, Osman Bey. That is madness on your part! How could Mulai Ismail ever agree to that? He is not the kind of wild beast that gives up its prey easily. Would Rescator have to redeem me for the price of a ship again?'

The Grand Eunuch shook his head. He began to smile, and in his eyes appeared a look of utter serenity and kindness.

'Don't ask so many questions, Madame Turquoise,' he said humorously. 'Know only that the stars do not lie. Mulai Ismail will have more reasons than one to consent to Rescator's request. They know each other and owe each other many debts. The treasure of the realm could not do without this Christian pirate to bring silver in exchange for the protection of the Moroccan flag. But there are other reasons too. Our Sultan, who holds the Law in such high regard, could not do otherwise than consent. For this is where the hand of Allah intervenes, Firousi. Listen to me. That man was once . . .'

He broke off with a kind of hiccup.

Angèlique saw his eyes grow large and fill with the same expression of horrified surprise she had seen in them that night on the top of the tower. He hiccuped again. Suddenly a stream of blood gushed from his mouth, spraying Angèlique's robe. He fell at her feet in a heap, his arms flung out, his face in the dust.

His fall revealed a blond bearded giant clad in rags, his hand still holding the dagger with which he had stabbed the Grand Eunuch.

'Are you ready?' asked Colin Paturel.

PART FOUR

Flight

CHAPTER TWENTY-FIVE

Whimpering, Angélique stepped over the body of the Grand Eunuch, and squeezed through the door which Colin Paturel closed behind them as carefully as if he were its guardian. For a moment they stood motionless in the shadow of the wall. The white expanse of the square they had to cross loomed before them ominously.

Colin Paturel seized Angélique's arm and they plunged into the bare, exposed area as if they were diving into water. A few steps, and they were on the other side, sheltered again by dark shadows. They waited to see if they were being followed, but nothing stirred. The only guard who could have seen them was the one who had thrown himself from the rampart a few minutes previously.

As they passed through the arched gateway, Angélique bumped against something soft – the corpse of another sentinel whom Colin had stabbed in order to get inside the walls. A sickening stench assailed their nostrils as they passed the manure pile near the palace wall. Angélique had to cling to her guide.

'Nothing better to throw them off our trail,' muttered the man, 'if they decide to set their hounds on us tomorrow.'

Angélique asked for no explanations. In deciding to escape she had also decided in advance to take whatever came her way.

Colin Paturel wallowed in the slimy gutter where running water was supposed to carry off the drainage from the waste but failed to do so. Trying not to look at the stinking mess, they splashed through it, almost choked with its vile stench. Angélique slipped and clutched at the slave's tattered garment to save herself from falling. He helped her back to her feet. When he lifted her up, she felt as light as a straw. Then she recalled that the leader's strength was legendary. Some of the harem women had once seen him twist the neck of a bull in a single combat in which Mulai Ismail had made him face the animal barehanded.

'There it is, I think,' he whispered, disappearing into the darkness and leaving her alone.

'Where are you?' she called.

'Up here. Give me your hand.'

Angélique raised her arm and felt herself being lifted into the air and perched on the branch of a thick tree.

'Another good way to throw them off the scent, eh? Now, pay attention!'

He executed a difficult manoeuvre in which he lifted Angélique like a bundle to the top of a high wall and shoved her onto its flat surface. Then he pushed her off on to a mound of cool grass. Colin Paturel jumped down beside her.

'Not bad, eh, little girl?'

'No. Where are we?'

'In Sidi Rodani's garden.'

'Is he one of your accomplices?'

'By no means. But I know this place. I built his house. Those lights you can see through the trees are on his terrace. If we can get through the garden we won't have to cross about half the city.'

The stench of the sewer clung to Angélique's garments and made her retch. On tiptoe they glided under the olive trees planted along the wall at the end of the garden. Suddenly loud barking came from the direction of the house. Colin Paturel stopped. The barking doubled in volume. The dogs had scented the intruders and were in a great state of excitement. The leafy branches prevented them from seeing what activity the barking dogs might have aroused inside the house, but they could see servants running about outside with torches, and they could hear voices calling to them in Arabic.

'It looks . . . it looks as if they are organising a hunt right here in the garden,' whispered Angélique.

'That was to be expected.'

'What are we going to do?'

'Don't be afraid.'

It was then that Angélique realised how Colin the Norman had become the leader of the thousands of slaves of every nation and origin that had filled the barracks at Meknès for the last twelve years. It was his slow, persuasive voice, with its somewhat rough inflections, a voice that feared nothing and typified the kind of man he was – one who had never known what panic is.

There was nothing in his make-up of that inner tension that can cramp the bowels and twist the nerves. He never had to get control of himself, for he did not know what it was to waver. Never did his heart-beats vary from their normal rhythm, and seldom did his blood run faster. There was such an extraordinary balance between his body and his modest, brave soul that death itself stood in awe of him. Angélique kept comparing him to a rock that no chisel could hew.

But the situation was becoming desperate. Some servants had leashed the two black hounds and, followed by the head of the household and several other servants with torches, were searching up and down the garden paths. The dogs were leading them right to the spot where the fugitives were hiding. They could hear the voices drawing nearer and the crackling of the pitch torches showering the leaves with sparks.

'We're finished,' whispered Angélique.

'Don't be afraid, little girl. Draw your veil across your face and say nothing, no matter what happens. Do what I say!'

He lifted her in his arms and with gentle firmness laid her down on the mossy earth. His body blotted out the light the torches suddenly beamed into the depths of the shrubbery. The sensation of his muscular chest pressing upon her, and the feel of his beard against her face, surmounted her other emotions. Colin Paturel grasped her ever tighter. In his brawny arms she was like a bird whose breath he could squeeze out with ease. She tilted her head back to try to catch her breath and could not repress a groan.

All around them they could hear the master of the house swearing in Arabic, and the servants chuckling. The master began to kick at Colin Paturel, who decided to get to his feet.

'Why, Joseph Gaillard,' he said mischievously in French, 'can't you let a couple of poor lovers alone? Lord knows, I haven't got ten wives the way you have.'

Sidi Rodani, who was none other than Joseph Gaillard, the renegade Frenchman in charge of munitions, turned every colour of the rainbow.

'You foul-minded Christian,' he shouted, shaking his fist, 'I'll teach you to do your fornicating in my garden! I'll make you pay for your infernal indecency, Colin Paturel. Don't forget you are only a slave, a . . .'

'I am a man like any other, and I am a Frenchman, too, like you,' said the Norman humorously. 'Come, come, old man, don't take it out on me just on account of a little wench to satisfy my hunger, poor slave that I am!'

'I will complain to the King tomorrow.'

'So you want my guards to have their heads cut off? The King will let me off with twenty lashes. He knows me. He gives me a few privileges like this, and when I have done a good day's work for him, he knows the best way to reward me is to send me one of his Moorish girls. Why should I refuse? Or don't you agree with me?'

'But why in my garden?' said Sidi Rodani, still outraged.

'The grass is so soft here, and my comrades won't get jealous.'

The renegade shrugged his shoulders. 'Your comrades! Are you trying to make me believe any of those half-starved, worn-out fellows still want women? It's just your way of having a lark.'

'That's right, old man. The priest in my village warned me about just that before I was sixteen. "Colin," he said, "fooling around with women will be the death of you." Don't you remember, Gaillard, when we tacked as we put into port at Cadiz and . . .'

'No, I don't remember,' shouted the renegade, 'and I want to see you take yourself out of here. How did you get into my garden anyway?'

'By the little door at the end. After all, I made the lock for it, so I know something about opening it.'

'Housebreaker! I'll have that lock changed the first thing in the morning.'

Under a hail of blows from the servants' sticks, Colin Paturel and Angélique were hustled to the door at the end of the garden. It was locked, but the servants, annoyed at this exposure of their carelessness, did not try to solve that mystery. They opened the door and shoved the captives out unceremoniously.

Colin Paturel led the way along the dark streets, Angélique just a step or two behind him. They threaded their way through an endless labyrinth of streets through which Colin proceeded as if he knew them all well.

'When are we going to get out of the city?' Angélique whispered.

'We are not going out of the city.'

He stopped and knocked at a door near a red-latticed window behind which a lantern was burning. After he said a few words through the peephole, the door opened to reveal a man in a long black coat. His velvety eyes peered out at them from under his black skullcap.

'This is Samuel Maimoran, old Savary's son-in-law,' said Colin Paturel. 'We are in the ghetto. Here we can take refuge.'

The other fugitives were waiting in the next room, where the curious tinted glass globes of the Venetian lamps cast a weird light on their pale faces and scraggly beards. Here were Piccinino the Venetian, the Marquis de Kermoeur, Francis Bargus from Arles, Jean d'Harrosteguy, old Caloens and Jean-Jean from Paris. They all looked to Angélique like the last dregs of humanity, and it was hard for her to conceive that they were all French. She leaned against the door to rest while the Norman introduced her to her future companions on this expedition. They all laughed uproariously at his tale of what had happened in Sidi Rodani's garden.

'When they find out you were in the process of abducting the favourite-to-be of Mulai Ismail . . . !'

Then they turned toward Angélique and their faces froze.

316

'Whew!' whistled Jean-Jean. 'Something's gone wrong already. The little girl is wounded.'

'No, that's the blood of that big devil I stabbed in the back.'

Angélique looked at herself all covered with filth and blood. Then a young Jewess entered and led her by the hand into the next room, where a kettle of water was steaming. Angélique began to take off her clothes. The woman offered to help her, but Angélique declined her assistance. Her hands clasped the blood-stained cloth and pressed it to her bosom. 'Don't ask so many questions, Madame Turquoise. Know only that the stars do not lie. . . .' Her nerves gave way and she burst into sobs, her tears streaming down her cheeks as she washed from her veil the blood of the Grand Eunuch Osman Faraji.

There in the ghetto the seven Christians were protected by strict barriers centuries of hatred and fierce rivalry had erected. It was not wise for a Jew to be found after nightfall in the Arab part of the city, or for an Arab to linger too long after dusk in the ghetto. But at that particular time the Jews of Meknès were a powerful segment of the population, as once or twice in a century they managed to be, for Mulai Ismail was bound to them by many obligations. They had reached a degree of prestige sufficient for them to believe they could get away with almost anything, even sheltering escaped slaves. This gave the important Zacharias Maimoran considerable inner satisfaction, especially when he went to the palace and prostrated himself before the King, who was foaming at the mouth with rage and raving about the loss of Colin Paturel and his other slaves, swearing he would bring them back in chains and execute them with atrocious tortures.

Maimoran had stroked his long beard and nodded. 'You will do right, my lord. I sympathise with your anger.'

Mulai Ismail had a piercing eye and was almost clairvoyant, but he knew he could never read the thoughts of this Jew, who had made the fortunes of his father Mulai Archi. It was a source of resentment to him, which made his anger work within him like yeast that would some day swell it into an outburst of destruction. 'Some day,' he promised himself with a glance toward the walls of the ghetto. 'Some day . . . ?'

Colin Paturel's scheme had been the boldest ever attempted by a fugitive. While the Sultan's guards directed their pursuit to the north and the west, the band remained hidden in the depths of the ghetto for three days, only a few feet from their pursuers. Later they would head south.

But the three days passed with incredible slowness for the refugees in the house of Samuel Maimoran, Zacharias's son. In the evening of the second day there was a commotion outside, as a band of cavalry dashed through the narrow street. Samuel's wife Rachel stood on tiptoe to peer out of the lattice.

'They are the Sultan's guards,' she said in a mixture of French and Arabic. 'They're going to the house of Jacob and Aaron, the embalmers.'

The guards had come to warn these skilled craftsmen to get their pickling vats ready. In his rage at the escape of the slaves the King had cut off the heads of more than twenty guards with his own hand, and had stopped only when his arm got tired. The heads had been exposed at intersections of the city streets after having been pickled by Jacob and Aaron or one of their associates. It was a sordid occupation, practised by Jews alone. Because of it the Arabs called the ghetto the *mellah*, from the Arab word for salt, *mel*.

A neighbour reported the news in whispers. The soldiers sent after the fugitives had not returned yet, and were petrified at the thought of coming back empty-handed. So far as anyone could tell, nothing was known about the escape of a slave from the harem or the murder of the Grand Eunuch. How far would the King's wrath go then! There was a lot of work in store for Aaron and Jacob.

Angélique sat among these gossiping Jewesses, decked out like images in a shrine with jewels of pure gold encrusted with gems, and apple-green, red, orange, and lemon-coloured satins, their black eyes and their amber complexions gleaming richly through their striped veils. Beside the men who slunk along on cat feet in long black coats, they were lavish and gaudy, and so were the wondrously handsome children who were also dressed in bright colours.

Angélique was sharing their wafers of unleavened bread, their saffron rice, their salt fish and pickled cucumbers, when her attention was diverted to the shouts in the street and the grinding wheels of the cart that was bringing more heads to be soaked in brine.

'Hurry up. Move along. Go faster!'

The guards did not like to stay long in the ghetto. After a while they departed, only to return the next day with more heads.

Rachel laid a reassuring hand on Angélique's and smiled at her. Why, Angélique wondered, should these men and women take such a risk? The sword dangling above their heads would fall on other Jews as well.

'Everything is going well,' Rachel was saying. These were almost the only French words she knew, and when she uttered them, the cheerful look in her eyes and her delicate smile suddenly recalled to Angélique that this woman was old Savary's daughter. She had not had time to mourn for Savary; in fact, she could not get over the feeling that she was still waiting for him to appear. She could not imagine herself on the road again without him jogging along tirelessly beside her and giving her advice and sniffing in the wind 'the odour of wondrous journeys'.

'Damn Mulai Ismail!' she exclaimed in Arabic.

'Damn Mulai Ismail a thousand times!' answered the women as if they were chanting a litany.

The second evening brought Cavaillac and another slave, a Knight of Malta named de Marmondin. They reported that all Meknès lived in apprehension of the storm that would surely break soon. At last the frightful scandal of the escape of a slave from the harem had come to light. The body of the murdered Grand Eunuch had been found. What would Mulai Ismail do? What would he say? He had not moved from the ground on which he had prostrated himself when he heard the news.

'I had only two true friends in this world,' he kept repeating. 'Osman Faraji and Colin the Norman. And in one day I have lost both of them!'

He did not mention the woman out of his native Arab modesty. But everyone knew that when he felt this new pain, the effects would be terrible. What massacres could possibly relieve him of the ache in his strange heart?

'We shall have to stay here another day,' said Colin Paturel.

Sweat broke out on the foreheads of the others. They could not bear another day of waiting in the silence of the ghetto. Mulai Ismail would feel their presence through the walls.

'One day more!' the Norman said in a voice that invited no argument.

They accepted his decision calmly. His strength could confound their seditious tendencies, much as Maimoran's coolness and extraordinary self-control deflated the extravagant conceits of his bloodthirsty master, who was searching for them on all the desert roads that led to Mazagan on the coast. He was also sending messengers to warn the sheikhs that if the fugitives were not brought to him at once, they would have to answer with their heads.

Subsequently Angélique heard Colin talking with the Knight of Malta, de Marmondin, a man of about fifty who, after Colin Paturel's escape, had been continuing his work of maintaining order, handing down justice, and adjusting differences among the captives.

'You can count on someone like that,' Colin Paturel was saying, 'but beware of the other one. Never leave an Orthodox alone with a Catholic. . . .'

Then Cavaillac and de Marmondin departed to return to the slaves' encampment before their prolonged absence attracted attention. They promised to bring the news again on the day set for the fugitives to leave.

Another day limped by. The following morning, when Angélique was alone in the women's room, one of her future comrades, the Marquis de Kermoeur, came to ask for a bowl of hot water from the samovar. He was taking advantage of his enforced leisure to shave, something he had been able to do but rarely during his six years' captivity except with fragments of broken bottles.

'How lucky you are, my dear, not to be bothered with such things, he said as he tickled her cheek with his finger. 'Lord, but your skin is soft!'

Angélique cautioned him to hold his bowl in both hands so as not to be scalded when she poured the water. The Breton looked at her with fascination.

'What a joy it is after all this time to see such a captivating French girl! Ah, my beauty, you don't know how embarrassed I am to appear before you in this sorry state. But be patient! As soon as we get to Paris, I am going to have red satin small-clothes made for me. I've been dreaming of them ever since I've been in captivity.'

Angélique burst into laughter. 'It's been a long time since anyone in style wore small-clothes, sir.'

'Oh? What are they wearing now?'

'Trousers that come to just below the knee and a wide-skirted coat of the same length.'

'Tell me more,' begged the Marquis, taking a seat beside her on the pile of cushions.

She gave him many details of Court fashions. With a periwig, it occurred to her, he would look rather like the Duc de Lauzun.

'Let me hold your hand, my dear,' he said suddenly.

She gave it to him and he kissed it. Then he looked at her in astonishment.

'So you really lived at Court?' he said as if he could hardly believe it. 'I'd have to kiss a thousand hands in the Grande Galerie at Versailles, I suppose, to be able to do it completely to your satisfaction. I'll guarantee you have even been presented to the King, haven't you?'

'What difference does it make, sir?'

'What is your name, you mysterious beauty? What strange chance caused you to fall into the hands of pirates?'

'What about yourself, sir?'

'Marquis!' Colin Paturel's voice interrupted them. The giant was standing in the doorway.

'Yes, Majesty!' answered Kermoeur.

The title was not ironic. All the captives had got into the habit of calling him that during the years in which he had brought order into their confused and troubled existence. It even had a tone of affection with those who admired him, and of awe with those who feared him. They needed to feel they had someone in authority, and certainly Colin Paturel had been a bold spokesman for them. He had got them a hospital and doctors to tend the sick; better rations, including wine and brandy and tobacco; the right to celebrate the great Christian feast days; and the Redemptorist Fathers. This final act had not turned out so well in the long run, but it had paved the way for future negotiations.

The Marquis de Kermoeur sincerely admired Colin Paturel and obeyed him gladly, for he recognised him as an intelligent leader, such as he had never known during his career in the royal navy, where he had been a twenty-two-year-old ensign until he was captured. He served the king of the captives as a bodyguard, for he was the best swordsman among them, and Colin had obtained permission for him to wear a sword.

When he learned his chief was for the third time planning to escape, he joined with him. Colin the Norman had, in fact, taken all his staff with him – the 'mules' as Mulai Ismail called them. Now he turned toward the other room and called to them: 'Comrades, come this way!

The captives filed in and stood in line before him. Kermoeur joined their ranks.

'Comrades, tomorrow evening we will set out. Later I will give you final instructions, but first I have something to say to you. We are seven fugitives – six men and one woman. This woman is something of a liability, but she has well deserved what help we can give her in her fight for freedom. Now hear this: if we expect to reach our goal, we must stick together. We are going to know hunger, thirst, exhaustion, the burning desert sun, and fear. But we shall know no hatred amongst ourselves. None of that hatred that festers among persons who have to live together and who all want the same thing. You know, I believe, what I am thinking of. None of that, friends, or we are lost! This woman over there,' he said, pointing to Angélique, 'is not for any of us. She belongs to no one. She is taking as great a risk as any of you. In our eyes she is not a woman, but a comrade. The first man who takes the liberty of flirting with her or shows her anything but the deepest respect, will have to answer to me, and you know how.' He doubled his sinewy fists. 'And if he repeats the offence, we will judge him according to our own law, and he can serve as fodder for the carrion birds of the desert.'

'How well he speaks and how stern he is!' thought Angélique, struck with the tone of his voice.

She had watched Colin Paturel so many times from her chink that she knew him better than he knew her. He was very familiar to her, yet now that she saw him close to, he gave her gooseflesh, and she was in awe of the scars of his martyrdoms – the deep black furrows of the burns on his arms and legs, the imperfectly healed wounds on his wrists and ankles from the chains, and especially the holes that still marked the palms and backs of his hands which had been ripped by the nails that fastened him above the gate to the city. He was not yet forty, but there was grey at his temples, the only indication of weakness in his otherwise rock-like nature.

'Are you agreed?' he asked after giving them time to think over what he had said.

'Agreed!' they answered together.

The Marquis suggested one qualification: 'Until we stand on Christian ground again.'

'That's up to you, you old rascal,' said Colin, laughing and clapping him on the shoulder. 'After that, long live liberty! All kinds of liberty! Ah, my friends, what a time we shall have!'

'I'm going to eat for three whole days,' said Jean-Jean, his eyes popping.

They went out talking of what they were going to do just as soon as they were within the walls of Portuguese Mazagan or Spanish Ceuta. Colin, however, remained in the room with Angélique.

'You heard what I said. Are you in agreement also?'

'Indeed I am. I am grateful to you, sir.'

'I was talking not only for your sake, but for ours too. If there is any discord in an undertaking like ours, it spells our doom. And who has held the apple of discord since the world began? A woman! As my old village priest used to say: "Woman is a flame, man is tinder, the devil is the wind." I did not want to take you with us. We took you only for old Savary's sake. The Jews would not help us, even for money, unless we took you. They are hard to get to know, but once they have adopted

someone, they treat him as one of their own people. That was their
attitude toward Savary; they had made him one of their own. The one
thing he wanted was to get you out of the harem, and so we had to
fulfil his greatest wish for him. I do so gladly, for I was fond of him.
What a wonderful old party he was! And how much he knew! A
hundred – no a thousand – times more than all of us put together. So
we are taking you along. But I must ask you to keep your place. You
are a woman who has lived and you are accustomed to men, but don't
forget these fellows have been deprived of women for many long years.
It won't be hard for them to recall what they have been missing. Stay
by yourself, and keep your veil over your face like a Moorish woman.
It's never foolish to be in the fashion, if you know what I mean.'

Angélique was annoyed. Although she knew he was fundamentally
right, the tone in which he had warned her did not please her much.
Did he think she could find much of interest in these pale, hairy, stinking Christians? She could not have been paid to have any of them.
She was ready to make an effort to be nice to them, but now she had
been told to keep her distance, she would do so only too gladly.

'Yes, Majesty,' she answered a little sarcastically.

The Norman wrinkled his eyes. 'You don't have to call me that, my
dear. I have laid down my crown. I am just Colin Paturel from Saint-
Valéry-en-Caux. What is your name?'

'Angélique.'

A smile lit up his hairy face and he looked at her attentively. 'Good!
Stay that way – angelic!'

The Knight of Malta, de Marmondin, returned. 'I believe the time
is right for you,' he said. 'They have somehow got word the fugitives
are on the Santa-Cruz road. That's the one being watched. Now is the
time!'

Colin Paturel ran his hand through his tousled blond hair, and an
expression of panic twisted his rough face.

'Suddenly I am wondering if I ought to do it,' he said. 'Oh, sir, when
I think of all those poor souls I am leaving behind in bondage . . .'

'Don't reproach yourself, brother,' the Knight said softly. 'The time
has come for you to leave. If you don't go, death will take you from
your comrades.'

'When I get to a Christian country,' Colin Paturel said, 'I will let the
Knights of Malta know of your fate so that they can undertake to
ransom you.'

'No, that's useless.'

'Why?'

'I do not want to leave Meknès. I am a monk and a priest, and I know my place is here as a captive of the infidels.'

'You'll end up at the stake.'

'Perhaps. But our Order teaches us that martyrdom is the only death worthy of a Knight of Malta. And now, farewell, my dear, dear brother.'

'Farewell, Sir Knight.'

The two men laid their hands on each other's shoulders. Then de Marmondin took his leave of each of the six other slaves in the same fashion, naming them one by one, as if to engrave their names on his heart. He looked at them in sorrow, for he knew that in the last ten years no one had heard of a man who had succeeded in escaping from the kingdom of Morocco.

He bowed silently to Angélique, then went out into the dark narrow street.

CHAPTER TWENTY-SIX

The Christians had pulled the hoods of their burnouses down over their faces. They were entirely clothed in Moorish garments, and their faces were shaved and stained with walnut juice to darken them. Jean-Jean, however, wore a Jew's long black coat. Angélique was swathed in as many veils as she could get on, with an opaque one tied just under her lower eyelids. How she blessed the jealousy of the Moors which permitted her this disguise!

'Keep looking at the ground as much as you can,' Colin Paturel had advised her. 'Moors with eyes your colour turn up but once in a blue moon.'

He did not tell her Mulai Ismail had issued a special command to bring back the woman with the green eyes. He himself was handicapped enough by his own blue eyes and his broad shoulders. In all Morocco there were said to be only two men of such an imposing height as his six feet two inches – and one of them he had murdered.

Consequently he had decided to pass as a merchant travelling with his goods so as to be able to ride a camel and disguise his height. Angélique, in the role of his wife, followed him on a mule. The others were to be his servants, and Jean-Jean his Jewish business manager. These went on foot, armed with javelins and bows and arrows to guard the caravan, for muskets were hard to come by and were reserved for the King and his army.

In the pitch dark, by the light of a single lantern, they fell into line.

Maimoran muttered his last instructions: his brother, a Rabbi, would be waiting for them at Fez near the well of Cebon. He would let them rest at his house and guide them as far as Xauen, when they would be turned over to another trustworthy guide, a trader, whose business allowed him frequent entry into Ceuta. He would make it possible for them to get through the lines of the Moors besieging the city, would hide among the rocks and would go ahead to inform the governor of the city, who would send a squadron of soldiers to find them. He advised them once more to watch their behaviour, not to forget to prostrate themselves twenty times toward Mecca, and especially not to make water standing, for that alone would be enough for even people at a distance to tell they were Christians. All these little details were extremely important. Luckily all the fugitives spoke Arabic fluently and knew these customs. Since a Moorish woman was supposed to keep silent, all Angélique needed to do was keep her mouth shut.

The camel lurched to its feet, and they set off through the narrow tunnel of streets in a silence as heavy as the night. 'If only the night would last forever!' thought Angélique.

A gust of cooler air wafted the acrid odour of smoke to them. She noticed that the blind walls of the ghetto had yielded to huts of bamboo and reeds. Their open doors showed the flickering embers of fires the smoke from which was escaping through the dry leaves that formed the roofs of these dwellings. She could see the occupants huddled around their hearths. The dogs began to bark at the fugitives. She realised they were passing through the two or three thousand huts of the King's guard, a quarter of its own and a kind of suburb of the city.

Hoarse voices announced the arrival of some Negroes who could find their way easily in the dark. Jean-Jean explained to them that his master, Mohammed Raki, a trader from Fez, was going home and was travelling at night to avoid the heat of the sun. He imitated the peculiar accent of the Jews so well that the Negroes were completely deceived.

The camel went at an exasperatingly slow speed. The dogs kept snapping at its feet, and barking. More and more huts! The penetrating odour of cow-dung fires and dried fish frying in oil. . . .

At last the first danger was past and they were on a fairly well-defined road on which they continued the remainder of the night. As dawn broke, Angélique apprehensively watched the sky grow light and take on gorgeous pearly tints of pink and green. They were passing through a region of olive groves, beyond which the countryside looked quite barren.

She did not dare ask for information, yet it increased her anxiety not to know where she was and what dangers or advantages awaited them. Active by nature, she fretted at being reduced to the status of a bolt of cloth strapped on a mule's back. Whether death or disaster awaited her, she wanted at least to know about it. Were they far from Fez, where a Jew was to give them a guide? The caravan proceeded. Had Colin Paturel seen that inn they passed at the last bend in the road? When an Arab had come out of it, Angélique had almost screamed. But as the man came to meet them, the leader made his camel kneel and got down from it.

'Get down, my girl,' said Caloens to Angélique.

She dismounted. The sacks of provisions were distributed among them. Angélique's was as heavy as any of the others. The Marquis de Kermoeur could not help protesting.

'Load a woman like that! I am shocked, Majesty.'

'There's nothing more suspicious to a Moslem than a woman walking without a load behind soldiers laden like donkeys,' replied Colin Paturel. 'They never permit any foolishness of that kind. Don't forget, we can still be detected.'

He himself loaded the sack on to Angélique's back. 'You'll have to excuse us, my girl. But we are not going far. We will hide during the day and proceed by night.'

The Arab had taken the camel and the mule by their bridles and led them into the inn. Piccinino counted him out a sum of money, and the fugitives resumed their march over a stony path. Soon behind a sand dune appeared a wide stretch of reeds along the bank of a river.

'We are going to hide all day in that marsh,' Colin Paturel explained. 'Everyone will find a spot for himself away from the others so that we won't reveal our presence by too great a mass of flattened reeds. At nightfall I will give the call of the ringdove as a signal and we will get together again on the edge of the woods over there. Everyone has a little water and food. So, till tonight . . .

They scattered among the tall smooth rushes with sharp edges that slashed their legs. The ground beneath them was either spongy or so dry it cracked in the sun. Angélique found a nook where the earth was mossy and stretched herself out on this soft carpet.

The day seemed endless. The heat in the marsh was stifling and the flies and mosquitoes buzzed and hummed around her incessantly. Fortunately her layers of veils protected her from their stings. She drank a little water and ate a wheaten cake. Above her the sky glowed like molten steel. The rushes cast pointed shadows of jet black over her. She dozed off.

When she awoke she heard voices and thought her comrades were looking for her, but it was not yet evening. The sky was still as blinding as a blast furnace. Suddenly she saw a form wrapped in an Arab robe rise out of the reeds not two feet away from her, but its face was turned away and she could not identify it.

Was it the Arlesian or the Venetian? she wondered.

The man turned around, and she could see that his dark complexion owed nothing to walnut juice. He was a Moor! Her heart stopped beating. But the Moor had not seen her. He was talking to a companion she could not see.

'These reeds here aren't good for much,' he was saying. 'They all seem to have been flattened by some animal. Let's go over to the other shore and if we don't find any better ones there, we can come back here again.'

She listened to them swish away through the rushes, hardly daring to believe her luck. Suddenly her hair stood on end, as another voice sounded not far from her. But immediately she recognised it as Francis the Arlesian's. He was starting to sing.

'The fool!' she thought angrily. 'He is going to tip off the Moors and they'll turn in their tracks.' Still she didn't dare go to him to shut him up, or call to him. But when after a while nothing stirred, she decided to slip over to him.

'Who goes there?' he asked. 'Oh, it's you, charming Angélique!'

She was trembling with anger and nerves. 'You must be crazy to sing that way! There are Moors in the marsh cutting rushes. It's a miracle they didn't hear you.'

The carefree young Provençal turned pale. 'Good lord, I never thought of that! I was just so happy at being free for the first time in eight years that I kept thinking of the old songs of my country. Do you think they heard me?'

'Let's hope not. But don't move an inch.'

'But, if they were only two . . .' He unsheathed his knife and tested its blade. Keeping it in his hand, he began to daydream again. 'I had a girl back in Arles. Do you think she'll still be waiting for me?'

'It would surprise me if she was,' Angélique said flatly. 'Eight years is a long time. She probably has a whole flock of children by now – by another man.'

'Do you really think so?' he said disillusionedly.

At least, now he wouldn't be singing out of joy any more. They sat in silence listening to the rustle of the rushes. Angélique raised her eyes and sighed in relief. At last the sky was reddening in the west. Soon it would be evening, and the night would come to their aid to guide them by its stars.

'What direction are we heading?' she asked.

'Southward.'

'Why, for heaven's sake?'

'It's the only direction Mulai Ismail's soldiers have not combed looking for us. What slaves would escape into the desert to the south? Later we will turn in a diagonal toward the east and then go straight north, swinging wide of Meknès and Fez and continuing with a guide toward Ceuta or Melilla. This will make the journey twice as long, but only half as risky. The mouse is playing tricks on the big old cat. While Mulai Ismail is waiting for us to turn up in either the north or the west, we are actually in the south and the east. We can only hope that by the time we finally take the right direction he will have got tired of waiting. At any rate, those who took a straight route never got where they wanted. We can at least try it the opposite way. Don't forget the local chieftains pay with their heads for letting escaped Christians pass through their territory. And don't think they're not on the lookout. All their hounds are trained to follow the trail of a Christian.'

'Shh!' she said. 'Didn't you hear the signal?'

The violet, misty shadows were lengthening as the soft call of the ringdove rose again and again from the swamp. With the greatest of care the fugitives stole out of their hiding places to reassemble silently to be counted and resume their trek.

They walked all night, half in the woods and half in vast open spaces so littered with rocks that it was hard to follow the trail. Above all they wanted to avoid the natives, and relied on the crowing of cocks and the barking of dogs to warn them when to give dwelling places a wide berth. The nights were cool, but there were still a good many Moors sleeping out in the fields to guard their unharvested crops. Piccinino's keen nose would detect the odour of smoke, and the Marquis de Kermoeur's sharp ears the slightest sound. Frequently he would lay his ear to the ground. They had to hide in a briar patch while two horsemen went by, fortunately not followed by their dogs.

In the morning they hid in some woods, where they spent another day of nerve-racking waiting. They were beginning to feel the tortures of thirst, for their supply of water was exhausted. They searched through the woods for a spring until they heard the croak of a frog and discovered a pond of stagnant water full of insects. They strained the water through a cloth and drank it just the same. Angélique chose a nook for herself not far from the men, and slept, only to dream of the

Sultanas' bath with its clear, perfumed water and all the serving girls to sprinkle rose-water over her as she emerged from it. If only she could take a bath now! Anything to get rid of the sweat-stained garments sticking to her. How she loathed Colin Paturel for insisting she wear such a heavy veil over her face all the time!

Angélique succumbed to profound meditations on the sad fate of Moslem women of poor estate. At last she could understand how the soft life of the harem was the fulfilment of their dreams, as it was for poor old Fatima-Mirelia. She was frightfully hungry too. Her stomach had grown so accustomed to being stuffed with pastry and candy that it rebelled against the daily ration of one wheat cake a day, which was all each of them was allowed.

The former slaves suffered less than she, for their daily fare was not much different from what they had had in captivity, and they knew how to survive on far less. They had acquired from their Arab masters the blessing of restraint, and were satisfied with a little barley flour and a few dates.

Angélique listened to them chatting among themselves.

'Remember the day,' the Basque Jean d'Harrosteguy was saying, 'you made Pasha Ibrahim eat a piece of our mouldy bread when he came on a visit from the coast? He put on a great show of protesting about it to Mulai Ismail. What a conference they must have had about that!'

'A war almost broke out between the Sublime Porte and Morocco because of the slaves.'

'If it had, the Turks would have lost,' said Colin Paturel. 'In spite of their huge empire, they have come to fear Mulai Ismail. He is such a fanatic, who knows whether he's not threatening Constantinople now?'

'That didn't stop you getting couscous for us, not to mention wine and brandy.'

'I explained that Christians can't work on a diet of water alone. So, since he wanted to see his mosque finished as rapidly as possible, he . . .'

Angélique heard them laughing. 'I wonder,' she thought, 'whether these fellows will ever have anything more exciting to talk about than their captivity in Barbary.'

When evening fell again, they started their march once more. The moon was shining now like a golden sickle among the stars. Toward the middle of the night they came to a settlement where the dogs started barking. Colin Paturel called a halt.

'We'll have to go that way or get lost,' he said.

'Why not go by the woods over there on the left?' suggested the Marquis de Kermoeur.

After some discussion they entered the woods, but it was so thick that after they had gone about half a league through the thorny under-brush, which scratched their hands bloody and tore their clothing, they had to turn back on to the road. Angélique had lost one of her sandals, but she did not dare mention it. The captives emerged on the outskirts of the settlement. A decision had to be made.

'Let's proceed,' said Colin Paturel, 'and trust in God!'

As swiftly as they could, and as noiselessly as ghosts, they darted through the narrow streets between the mud huts. Dogs were roaming about, but no human being appeared until they got to the last house, from which a man emerged and started to shout at them. Colin Paturel answered him without stopping, and told him they were on their way to the famous hermit Adur Smali, who worked miracles only a little way from there, and they were in a hurry because they had been told to arrive before sunrise to get the full benefit of his magic spells. The Moor did not protest.

Once past that hazard, they continued on their way without stop-ping, taking a side road in case the inhabitants of the settlement should change their minds and follow them. But the people of that region were not used to seeing escaped slaves heading south, and their dogs were not trained for pursuit.

At the first streaks of dawn, they could come to a halt at last. Angélique sank to the ground exhausted. Her fear had kept her walking in a semi-conscious state. Now she noticed that her bare foot was cut to ribbons by the sharp stones in the road and was beginning to pain her terribly.

'Something wrong, little girl?' asked Colin Paturel.

'I have lost one of my sandals,' she replied, on the verge of tears.

The Norman did not seem to show any sympathy. He set his sack on the ground and took out of it another pair of women's sandals.

'I asked Rachel, Samuel Maimoran's wife, to put in an extra pair for you, as I thought something like this might happen. If we men have to, we can walk barefoot, but we have to look out for you.'

He knelt before her and poured some ointment from a bottle he had on to a piece of linen, with which he anointed her sore foot.

'Why didn't you tell me about this sooner,' he asked, 'instead of letting your foot get into such a state?'

'We had to get past the settlement. I was so frightened I didn't feel anything.'

In the Norman's huge hand her foot seemed fragile and delicate. He kept stroking the ointment over it with the linen rag and looking at her intently out of his blue eyes. 'You were afraid, but you kept on

330

walking just the same, eh? Good for you! You are a fine comrade!'

It was clear to her now why they called him king; it was because of his ability to command their respect and be tender and mild to them at the same time. She had the deep conviction that Colin Paturel could never be vanquished. Under his protection she would surely reach a Christian land, see the end of her long journey at last, whatever hardships she might have to endure in getting there. Gone from her mind were her dread of this savage countryside and the fiercely hostile people who infested it, and the caution with which they took every step like tightrope walkers across a yawning abyss. She went to sleep hidden by the burning rocks around her, her face pressed to the earth in search of a mite of coolness.

The desert trails wound across vast stretches broken only by an occasional palm-tree, but they came upon no watercourse or pool. Thick deposits of snow-white saltpetre sparkled in the low places at the foot of the barren sand dunes. Colin Paturel gathered several chunks of it and stowed them in his sack in preparation for the game they hoped to catch when they turned northward. They could kill plenty of gazelles and wild boars, rub them with salt and thyme and wild pepper, roast them over a roaring fire, and wash them down with fresh water from the waterholes.

Good lord, where was that fresh water? Their tongues clove to the roof of their mouths.

It was thirst that woke Angélique. Her cheek was burning from the sun that had been broiling it where her veil had slipped down. Her skin was the colour of a boiled lobster, and was so sensitive she could not even touch it. From behind the rock that concealed her came a succession of dull blows. Colin Paturel was taking advantage of the halt to get some exercise. Thirst and fatigue affected him not at all. He had uprooted a tree stump, and shaped it into a huge club which he was testing by swinging it against the rock.

'There's a weapon just as good as Kermoeur's sword,' he boasted. 'Perhaps it's not so efficient for pricking a belly, but it will pound some sense into any Moor's head.'

The sun was setting in streamers of flame. The fugitives cast a weary eye on the hills disappearing into the velvety blueness which streaked their sides like the rivers they so longed to see.

'We're thirsty, Colin. . . .'

'Be patient, friends! The mountains we are going to cross have deep gullies where the shade will have kept the springs from drying up. Before tomorrow night we will have found something to wet our throats.

To the thirst-crazed band this seemed a long way off, yet they had no choice but to wait for his prediction to come true. Colin gave each of them a piece of a nut that grows in the heart of Africa and that the Negro guards of Mulai Ismail liked to chew when they were on long marches. It had a bitter flavour, and it had to be kept in the mouth as long as possible, but it renewed strength and dulled the pangs of hunger and thirst.

As soon as night fell, they resumed their march. All too soon they were scrambling up cliffs well nigh impossible to scale in the daylight, and worse in the darkness. The moonlight was not bright enough to show them the easiest routes. Sometimes they had to haul themselves up hand over hand to reach a level spot, and then repeat the process. They made very slow progress. Their feet dislodged bits of stone which went rolling down the precipices till they hit the bottom with a resounding crash that echoed through the silent night. The air grew colder and colder. It dried their sweat, but it made them shiver in their soaking garments. Several times Colin, who led the way, had to stop and strike a flint to see where he was, dangerous though that might be. The Arabs on the plain could see the flame in such an unlikely place as these cliffs and would guess there were people up there.

As Angélique proceeded, she was surprised at her own powers of endurance, which she attributed to the kola-nut she was chewing. She could keep the white burnouses of her comrades in sight, and saw to it she did not fall too far behind. Suddenly she heard a sound like an avalanche. Something rolled past her and was swallowed up in the darkness. Then an unearthly scream and the echo of a dull thud rose from the depths. She clutched at a jutting rock, not daring to go forward or back.

She heard the voice of the Basque shouting: 'Colin, someone has fallen!'

'Who?'

'I don't know.'

'The girl?'

Angélique's teeth were chattering so she couldn't make a sound.

'Angélique!' shouted the leader, convinced that the inexperienced girl had fallen to her death. How stupid of him not to have put her with Caloens, who was as sure-footed as a mountain goat. They had left her to fend for herself, and now . . .

'Angélique!' he roared, as if the echoes of his voice could remedy the fatal catastrophe.

Then, as if by a miracle, she could find her voice. 'I'm here.'

'Good. Don't make a move. Jean?'

'Present!'

'Jean-Jean?'

'Present!'

'Francis?'

No one answered.

'Francis of Arles? Piccinino?'

'Present!'

'Marquis? Caloens?'

'Present! Present!'

'It must be the Arlesian,' said Colin Paturel, descending to them cautiously.

They gathered to discuss how the accident might have happened. The Arlesian must have been a little above Angélique. She reported she had heard him slip on the pebbles, and then after a hoarse scream and an instant of silence, the dull crash of a body dashed to pieces in the abyss.

'We shall have to wait till daylight,' the Norman decided.

They waited, shivering with cold, and numb from crouching in the hollows of the cliffs. Dawn was clear and bright. Around the reddish mountain a lone eagle was soaring in the lemon-coloured sky. Against the rising sun the bird seemed as beautiful as the great bronze emblem of the Holy Roman Empire. Gracefully he wheeled in ever-narrowing circles above the ravine.

The Norman followed its flight. 'He must be down there,' he muttered.

As soon as it had grown light enough to see, they inspected every one of the group, hoping against hope to find the black eyes and the curly beard of the Arlesian still amongst them, but the light-hearted Provençal was gone. Eventually they could see him lying at the foot of the precipice, a white spot against the jagged black rocks.

'Perhaps he is only hurt. . . .'

'Hand me the rope, Kermoeur.'

Colin Paturel anchored it firmly to a rock and passed the other end around his waist with the skill of a sailor accustomed to handling and knotting rope all his life. Then at the moment he was about to descend into the gulf, he changed his mind, and with a glance at the wheeling eagle said: 'Hand me my club.'

He tied it to his waist. Its weight and bulk made his descent harder, but still he managed expertly.

His comrades leaned over the brink, watching him breathlessly. They saw him set his foot on the ledge where the body was lying, and bend over it. Then he straightened up. They saw him lay his fingers on the man's eyelids and make the sign of the cross.

'Oh, the poor Arlesian!' moaned Jean-Jean.

All of them knew what had gone with him – deathless memories of toil and torture, hope and laughter, and the songs he sang under the starry skies of Africa while cool breezes murmured in the palm fronds above the wretched world of the slaves and soothed their longings. Angélique sensed their common grief, there was suddenly so much of all suffering humanity written on their dark, care-lined faces.

'Colin! Look out for the eagle!' shouted the Marquis de Kermoeur.

The bird had soared up into the sky as if it had given up its prey, but now it was darting down with the speed of lightning. They could hear its wings beating, blotting Colin Paturel from their view. For a few moments they could not follow the progress of the battle that was raging between the man and the bird. Then at last they saw their leader again, swinging his mighty club like the sails of a fearful windmill.

It was hard for him to keep his balance on the narrow ledge, but he was fighting with as much vigour and deliberation as if he had no need of a retreat. He had taken his stance on the very edge of the cliff rather than against the rocky wall, which might hinder his movements. The slightest careless step or badly calculated lunge could topple him into the void. He was smiting his antagonist without pausing for breath, and the eagle could not reply in kind. Several times the bird withdrew, one of its wings hanging limp where Colin had smitten it, but it kept returning to the attack, its eyes flaming and its talons forward.

Finally Colin Paturel managed to get it by the neck. Dropping his club, he pulled out his knife and slit its throat before hurling it into the depths.

'Blessed Mother of God!' murmured old Caloens.

Everyone was deathly white, and the sweat was streaming from their foreheads.

'Well, fellows, are you going to give me a lift?' came the leader's voice. 'What are you waiting for up there?'

'Right away, Majesty!'

Colin Paturel had slung the body of the Arlesian across his mighty shoulders, and the double weight made the ascent long and tortuous. Once back on the higher ledge, he rested a moment on one knee to catch his breath. Blood from the wounds the bird had inflicted on him was running down his chest and staining his white burnous.

'I was going to leave the Arlesian there,' he said, 'but I couldn't find the heart to let him be picked at by the carrion birds.'

'You are right, Colin. We'll give him a Christian burial.'

While they cleared the rocks to make a space where they could scratch out a shallow grave with their knives, Angélique went to Colin Paturel, who was seated on a stone.

'Let me tend your wounds the way you tended mine yesterday, Colin.'

'How can I refuse, my dear? That bird hurt me sorely. Get the bottle of brandy out of my knapsack and pour it on freely.'

He did not wince once as she swabbed the deep gashes the eagle had torn in his chest. As she touched him, Angélique could not help feeling her respect for him increase. Such a man was a tribute to his Maker.

But Colin Paturel was no longer thinking of his battle with the eagle. His thoughts were on Francis the Arlesian, and he was sick at heart with a pain far more grievous than the wounds in his chest.

CHAPTER TWENTY-SEVEN

For three days they wandered among the barren, scorching rocks, tormented by thirst, proceeding no more by night so as to avoid another accident in the darkness. There were few inhabitants in the region, but on the second day two Moorish shepherds pasturing their flocks on the grassy slopes of a ravine hailed them, looking with suspicion upon this tattered band which numbered a woman and a Jew in a long black coat.

Colin Paturel shouted to them that they were going to Meljani, which brought astonished exclamations from the shepherds. Why would they be going to Meljani over the mountains when the shortest way was through the valley, where the trail was well marked ever since Mulai Ismail had cleared it with his black slaves? Were they strangers who had lost their way, or bandits, or – for heavens' sake – escaped Christian slaves? The two shepherds laughed at that last suggestion, but suddenly their expressions changed and they whispered to each other without taking their eyes off the travellers on the other side of the ravine.

'Hand me your bow, Jean d'Harrosteguy,' said Colin Paturel, 'and you, Piccinino, stand in front of me so they can't see what I'm doing.'

Suddenly the Moors began to yelp, and took to their heels. But the Norman's arrows hit them in the back, and they rolled down the steep bank while their sheep panicked and dashed into the ravine, where most of them landed with broken legs.

'They had only to sound an alarm, and we would have found all the villagers waiting for us at the mouth of this valley.'

They remained on the alert. They saw the road the shepherds had mentioned, but there was no question of their taking it. Their torn clothing and their exhausted, anxious looks would betray them to the first person they encountered. They had to continue through the cruel cliffs under a searing sun and a deep blue sky which made the rocks look like dried bones. Their tongues were swollen with thirst, and their feet were bleeding. Toward evening they saw a sheet of water glistening at the foot of a precipice, and in spite of the steepness of the cliffside decided to climb down to it as the one thing to save them. Then, as they drew near it, they heard growls and roars which the echoes swelled in volume.

'Lions!'

They hugged the sides of the cliff while the beasts, aroused by the stones the fugitives dislodged, kept up their roaring. Angélique could see the tawny beasts pacing just a few feet below her, as she clung to a tuft of a juniper which she feared would come up by the roots.

The Norman, a little above her, saw how white she was and how full of terror were her eyes. 'Angélique!' he called.

Whenever he gave an order his slow, calm voice took on a different tone, deep and curt, to which no one could fail to respond.

'Angélique, don't look down! Don't stir! Reach me your hand!'

He lifted her as if she were a feather, and she clung to him, pressing her face against his massive shoulder to blot out the gruesome scene below her. He waited patiently until she had stopped shaking, then taking advantage of a moment of silence between the deafening roars of the lions, he shouted: 'Back to the top, fellows! There's no point in forcing the issue.'

'But what about the water?' groaned Jean-Jean.

'Go and get it if you've got the courage.'

That evening Angélique sat apart from the rest while they set up their little encampment around the tiny fire which was all they dared kindle so that they might roast in its embers the wild potatoes they had found. She leaned her head against a rock and dreamed of sherbets and iced beverages and water shimmering in the palm-tree shade.

'A bath!' she moaned. 'Something to drink! I can't go on.'

She felt a hand on her head, a hand so large it could belong only to the Norman. She hadn't the strength to move, but he tugged gently at her hair to make her lift her head and see the leathern bottle he was offering her, a scant cupful of water in its bottom. She raised her eyes questioningly.

'It's for you,' he said. 'It has been kept for you. Everyone has contributed the last drop of his own supply.'

The warm water tasted like nectar to her, and the thought that these crude fellows had robbed themselves for her gave her courage.

'Thank you. Things will be better tomorrow,' she said, trying to spread her cracked lips into a smile.

'Of course! If any of us can still go on, you will be one of them,' he replied with such conviction that she believed him implicitly.

'Then men think me stronger than I am,' she thought as, somewhat reassured, she stretched out on her bed of stone.

She felt terribly alone in her exhaustion and her misery and her fear, as if she were in a deep mine completely isolated from the rest of the world. Was this what Dante felt when he descended into Hell and heard the baying of the three-tongued Cerberus. Was Hell like this? Yes, this was Hell save for the charity of a comrade offering her his last cup of water. Without hope! But now hope was flickering. 'Some day we will see the steeples of a Christian town against the starry sky, some day we will breathe freely once more, we shall drink . . .'

The next day they descended to the plain. The lions were devouring the remains of a horse, which indicated they could not be far from a settlement. Presently they heard dogs barking and veered toward the mountain again, but the sight of a well brought them back toward the dangerous outskirts of the inhabited district. Luckily no one was about. A rope was hastily tied around the thinnest of them all, Jean-Jean, and he was lowered into the well with two gourds. They heard him splashing around and then he let out a screech and they yanked him up again.

The poor fellow kept vomiting as if he would heave up his very soul. He had felt an animal's carcase under his feet blocking the bottom of the well. He had not been able to keep from bending over to get a drink, but the water he had gulped was so poisoned by the decaying flesh that he thought he would die on the spot. All the rest of the day he was tortured by cramps and could scarcely drag himself along.

That was another terrible day, and it was not till evening that relief appeared in the form of blue water on the floor of a little valley shaded by fig-trees and pomegranates with date-palms towering above them. Scarcely believing it could be anything but a mirage, they descended the slope. Caloens was the first to reach the bottom. He was running over the white gravel till he was only a few feet from the marvellous water when a lioness sprang from the ground and leaped upon the old man.

Colin dashed to the scene and struck the beast with furious blows from

337

his club, beating its head and smashing its back. The lioness rolled over in agonised convulsions.

The Marquis de Kermoeur's shout was almost drowned by a fierce roar. 'Watch out, Colin!'

With his sword drawn he flung himself between the Norman, whose back was turned, and a brown-maned lion, just as it leaped from a thicket. His sword pierced the animal in the region of its heart, but before it expired, its claws had ripped open the Breton's abdomen and spilled his guts on the sand.

The bewitching oasis had in these few moments turned into a scene of carnage where the blood of man and beast mingled in a stream that was polluting the clear water.

Colin Paturel stood, club in hand, waiting for another visitation from the beasts, but the spot had regained its rustic tranquillity. The fugitives had disturbed a pair in the mating season.

'Post a guard in each direction with lances ready!' Then Colin Paturel leaned over the Marquis de Kermoeur. 'Comrade, you saved my life!'

The Marquis's eyes were already glassy. 'Yes, Majesty,' he gasped. His vision clouded as old memories returned to him. 'Your Majesty . . . at Versailles . . . Versailles . . .' And with the name of that glorious, distant spot on his lips he breathed his last.

Caloens was still alive, but the flesh of his shoulder was ripped to the bone.

'Water,' he moaned. 'Water!'

Colin dipped a gourd in the water they had won at such cost and held it to his lips. Such was his power over his comrades that in spite of their torments of thirst, none had even thought of approaching the water-hole, but had stood by in stupefaction.

'Go on and drink, you idiots!' he yelled at them angrily.

This was the second time he had had to close in death the eyes of one of the comrades he had sworn to lead to liberty. He had the feeling that there would be yet another for whom he would have to perform this sad ritual.

They discovered the lair of the lions under a tangle of vines where they had dragged the half-eaten remains of a gazelle. They carried the wounded man here and laid him on a litter of dried grass. Colin swabbed his wounds with the last of his brandy, and bandaged them as best he could. No matter what happened, he would have to wait to see how the old man responded to treatment. He was strong enough to recover, and perhaps he would. But how much time could they waste in this region, where the fresh water would attract both beasts and men?

The leader counted on his fingers the number of days that remained before they could hope to reach the oasis of Cebon. Even if they set out that night, they would be two days late, and that was impossible for them even to consider with Caloens in such a perilous condition. He decided to spend the night there. They would have to bury the Marquis de Kermoeur, and think over what to do next. Everyone needed a rest anyway, and the next day they could make up their minds.

When night fell, Angélique slipped out of the lions' cave. Neither fear of wild beasts nor the anguish the old man's stertorous breathing caused her could still her craving to plunge into the water. One after another the fugitives had tasted the delights of a bath, but all that time she had remained by the wounded man's bed.

Caloens kept calling to her with the demanding tone of a strong man who in pain turns to a woman, seeking her motherly tenderness which can understand and listen to complaining with sympathy.

'Hold my hand, little girl. Don't go away and leave me, little girl.'

'I'm right here, old man.'

'Give me a little more of that delicious water.'

She would bathe his face and try to make him as comfortable as possible on his bed of straw. With every passing moment his suffering grew worse.

Colin Paturel distributed the last of the wheat cakes. All that was left of their provisions now was beans, but the leader forbade them to build a fire.

Now Angélique was moving through the sheltering darkness, for the moon had not yet risen above the trees whose fronds it was spangling with flecks of silver. Before her the pool was a mirror, its surface marred only by the ripples around the tinkling cascade that filled it. The occasional croak of a frog and the hum of the locusts were all that disturbed the silence.

She stripped off her dust-caked, sweat-stained garments, and sighed with delight as she slipped into the cool water. Never had she felt so exquisite a sensation. After she had soaked herself to the full, she washed her clothes, except for the burnous which she wrapped around her to protect herself from the cool night air until the breeze had dried her other garments. Meanwhile she washed her hair free of sand and felt it come unmatted in her fingers.

The moon emerged from behind a palm and revealed the long silver stream flowing down the black cliff from the spring beyond. Angélique climbed to a stone beneath it and let its icy shower flow over her. Water was surely the loveliest of all God's creations! She remembered how the water-vendors used to cry through the streets of Paris: 'Who'll buy good clean water? . . . One of the four elements. . . .'

Raising her head, she looked lovingly at the stars winking through the fan-like fronds of the palms. The water trickled over her naked body, and in the moonlight she could see her reflection in the pool, glimmering like marble amid the dark wavelets.

'*I am alive*,' she murmured to herself. '*Alive!*'

Every passing moment erased another memory of the exhausting struggle she had been through, and she remained standing there until a crackling in the dry underbrush put her on the alert.

Only then did her fear return to her. She remembered the wild beasts lying in wait, and the malignant Moors. The peaceful scene once more became the fearful battlefield on which they had striven so many endless days. She slipped back into the water to get to the other side of the pool, sure that something was spying on her from the depths of the thicket. Living like a hunted animal had aroused her instinct of self-preservation, and she could sense danger afar off. She flung her burnous about her and began to run barefoot across the tangle of vines and sharp, spiny cactus. She bumped into the solid obstacle of a human form and let out a faint cry as she tried to run backward, crazed with fear. Then in a ray of moonlight she recognised the blond beard of Colin Paturel, his eyes sparkling in their deep sockets.

'Are you out of your mind?' he said in a level voice. 'Were you bathing all by yourself? Don't you know the lions will come to drink here, and leopards too, not to mention some wandering Moor?'

Angélique wanted to cling to his powerful chest to calm her fright, all the greater after the few moments of relaxation she had enjoyed. She would never forget her almost supernatural bliss under the waterfall in that heavenly oasis. Truly Paradise itself must be like that.

But now she was back in the world of men and of perils, where she had to fight to keep herself alive.

'Moors?' she said in a shaky voice. 'I think they're there. Something was peering at me a minute ago, I'm sure.'

'It was I. I set out to look for you when I noticed you had been gone unusually long. Now, come with me, and don't do anything foolish like that again, or, so sure as my name is Paturel, I will strangle you with my own hands.'

There was a touch of irony in his voice, but he was not joking. She believed he really might strangle her, or at least beat the independence out of her.

Colin Paturel's blood had run cold when he observed their female comrade had stolen away and not come back. Another crisis, he had thought, and another grave to dig! Oh righteous God, have you forsaken your children! Noiselessly he had followed the shore of the pool like a slave used to prowling through the night. And there she had been revealed to him under the silver stream that flowed from the spring, her shoulders veiled by her hair like a sea nymph's, her snow-white body mirrored in the dark surface of the glassy pool.

As Angélique followed him, it distressed her to realise he must have seen her at her bath. Then she wondered what difference it could possibly make. He was a man without breeding and with no other feelings for her than the scorn the strong have for the weak, regarding her only as an additional burden he had assumed against his will. It was hard for her not to feel a certain resentment at his attitude, for he was responsible for the quarantine she had so faithfully maintained towards the other fugitives, associating with them only to tend the hurt. Her sense that she was alone and unwanted had made all her other hardships even more difficult to bear. Perhaps he had not been wrong in imposing it, but he was so severe and authoritative that he still awed her to the point of craven fear of him. His perfect balance of physical and moral prowess seemed a reproach to her own wavering courage, her feminine weakness and fragility, her nerves and her emotions. His piercing blue eyes never failed to perceive her fright or her weariness or her carelessness, and he seemed to despise her for them. 'He has the same scorn for me as a sheep dog for a silly ewe,' she thought.

She took her seat again beside Caloens's pallet, but she could not take her eyes from the bushy profile of their leader outlined by the feeble lamplight. Colin Paturel was drawing in the sand a map of the route they were to follow, and explaining it to the Venetian, Jean-Jean and the Basque as they leaned over his shoulder .

'You will stop at the edge of the woods. If you see a red handkerchief on a branch of the second cork tree, advance and hoot like an owl. Then the Rabbi will come out of the bushes . . .'

'Are you there, little girl?' came the weak voice of Caloens. 'Give me your hand. I used to have a little daughter. She was ten years old when I went to sea twenty years ago. She must look like you now. Her name was Mariejke.'

'You'll soon see her again, grandfather.'

'No, I don't think so. Death will claim me first. It will be better that way. What would Mariejke do with an old fisherman father like me, coming back from twenty years of slavery to dirty up the pretty tiles of her kitchen floor and bore her with tales of a sunny land? It's better this way. I am glad to sleep forever in Moroccan soil. I keep thinking how my gardens back at Meknès must miss me, and that nevermore will I see Mulai Ismail galloping like the wrath of God. I should have waited till he split my skull with his walking-stick. . . .'

The Parisian, the Venetian and the Basque prepared to leave at dawn. Colin Paturel beckoned Angélique over to him.

'I am going to stay with the old man,' he said. 'We can't take him with us, and we can't leave him behind. I'll have to wait here. The others must go ahead so as not to miss the rendezvous with Rabbi Maimoran. After they have met him they will know what is best to do. Do you want to go with them or follow after them?'

'I shall do what you order me to do.'

'I think it's better for you to stay here, then. The others can go faster than you can, and time is short.'

Angélique nodded her head and started to move back to the sick man's bedside, but Colin Paturel restrained her as if he were sorry for his unfriendly manner.

'Besides, I think old Caloens needs you with him so that he can die in peace. But if you would rather go . . .'

'I will stay!'

They divided the provisions and the remaining arrows. Colin Paturel kept a bow, a quiver, his club, a compass, and the Marquis de Kermoeur's sword.

The three men departed after pausing for a moment by the grave of the Breton nobleman. No one told old Caloens, who was gradually growing weaker. He kept raving in Flemish and clutching Angélique's hand with the weird strength of the dying. Then his failing powers returned to him in a flood as, after struggling all through the night, he sat up on the following morning. It took all Colin Paturel's strength to restrain the old man fighting him with as fierce an energy as if he were combating death itself.

'You shall not get me!' he kept shouting. 'You shan't take me!'

Suddenly he seemed to recognise the face before him.

'Ah, Colin, my boy,' he said in a feeble voice, 'it's time to move on, don't you think?'

'Yes, old friend, it is time indeed. Go!' he commanded in his steady voice.

Then as trustingly as a child old Caloens expired in the arms of his friend.

His death agonies had upset Angélique, and now she began to weep as she looked at the bare bald head reposing on his comrade's chest as if on his own son's. Colin Paturel closed the old man's eyes and crossed his hands on his breast.

'Help me carry him,' he said to Angélique. 'His grave is already dug. We must hurry. Then we too shall leave.'

They laid him beside the Marquis de Kermoeur, and covered him hastily with dirt. Angélique wanted to erect two crosses, but the Norman forbade her.

'The Moors who pass by here will know Christians have been recently buried, and dash after us.'

And so they began marching again across the countryside streaked with the silvery rays of the moon. Rested by her two days in the oasis, Angélique resolved that Colin Paturel would not be able to blame her for falling behind, but she tried in vain to keep up with his long strides and had to see him stop and turn back to her, standing like a statue of Hercules with his club on his shoulder. She was eager to catch up with the others, who at least walked like ordinary human beings, not like heroes of legend far superior to any earthly weariness.

Doesn't that fiend ever get tired? she thought. Isn't he ever afraid of anything? Doesn't he ever feel anything in body or soul?

She had already decided he was a brute at heart, and now this march with him alone for company confirmed her opinion. But they made so much progress that by evening of the next day they had come to the edge of the cork woods where the rendezvous with the Rabbi was to have taken place. The crossroads where the roots of the trees ridged the sand appeared before them.

Colin Paturel called a halt. His eyes narrowed and she was surprised to see him staring at the sun, which was suddenly darkened by a flight of vultures rising slowly from the trees. The newcomers must have disturbed them. After wheeling around the woods a few times they headed back toward earth, stretching out their hairy necks, and settling down around a thick cork tree that branched over the crossroad. Then Angélique caught sight of what had allured them.

'Look at those two corpses hanging there,' she said in a choked voice.

The man had already seen them. 'They are two Jews. I can tell from their long black coats. Stay here. I'm going to creep closer to reconnoitre. No matter what happens, don't stir from here!'

She suffered agonies as she waited. The vultures kept beating their wings and by their frequent flights and piercing cries betrayed the approach of trouble, but she could not see what it might be. Suddenly Colin Paturel appeared behind her.

'Well?'

'One is a Jew I don't know, probably Rabbi Maimoran. The other is . . . Jean-Jean.'

'Oh God!' she moaned, hiding her face in her hands.

This was too much. The total failure of their escape now seemed inevitable. The Christians had fallen into a trap set for them at this meeting place.

'I noticed a settlement on our right, the village of the Moors who hanged them. Perhaps the Venetian and Jean d'Harrosteguy are still there, in chains. I'm going to it.'

'That's madness!'

'I've got to try everything. I found a cave a little way up the mountain. You hide there and wait for me.'

She had never dared argue with his orders, but she knew this was utter folly. This was the end of everything. The cave, the access to which was hidden by clumps of broom, would be her prison. She would be only waiting in vain for the return of her comrades.

Colin Paturel left what remained of the provisions with her, including the last bottle of water. He even left her his club, keeping with him only the dagger in his belt. He took off her sandals to rest her feet. He divided his tinder and flints. If a wild beast appeared she need only light a fire of dry grass to frighten it away. Then without another word he slipped out of the cave and disappeared.

She began her long wait. Night came and with it the howls of wild beasts foraging in the undergrowth, their rustling and scratching seeming to fill the entire cave. From time to time, when she thought she couldn't stand the uncertainty a moment longer, she struck a light and waved the tinderbox around her. She was relieved to see only the rocky walls, but eventually she noticed curious little black velvet sacks hanging close to one another from the roof of the rave, and realised these bats had been the cause of the strange squeaking and rustling that had so startled her.

Keeping her eyes open, but trying not to think, she managed to endure the maddeningly slow passage of the hours. A snapping of twigs outside filled her with hope. Had the Norman returned already, bringing Piccinino and Jean d'Harrosteguy with him? How good it would be to see them again! But at once a mournful howling began quite near her. A hyena was prowling outside.

She went back down to the crossroads where the body of Jean-Jean of Paris was swinging in the breeze. He was dead, the happy little clerk, the favourite of Colin Paturel, who had made him his scribe. The carrion birds had already plucked out his laughing eyes. He was dead, and dead too were the Arlesian, the Breton nobleman and the old Flemish fisherman. One after another they all were going to die. The kingdom of Morocco would not give up its captives. Mulai Ismail was winning another victory.

What would become of her if no one returned? She did not even know where she was. What would befall her when hunger and thirst drove her out of her refuge? She could expect no help from the Moors, much less from their submissive, frightened women. She would be discovered and brought back to the Sultan. And Osman Faraji would not be there to protect her.

'Oh, Osman Faraji, if your noble soul is wandering in the Paradise of Mohammed . . .'

The screeching of the vultures as they wheeled again around the dangling corpses told her dawn had come. The cave was full of a milky mist. Angélique tried to move her stiff, numb limbs thinking that at least she had survived the worst experience of her life. To be so helpless, so inactive, to be so incapable of achieving anything by herself! But still she did not stir, for Colin Paturel had commanded her not to. The sun rose higher into the heavens.

The captives did not come back. They would never come back.

Still she waited, taking hope in the thought that their fate was not wholly inescapable. She was despairing when the massive form of Colin Paturel loomed at the mouth of the cave. Her immediate sense of deliverance and of boundless joy made her throw her arms around him to make certain he was truly there.

'You came back! Oh, you have returned to me!'

He seemed neither to see nor hear her, or even to feel her fingers digging into the flesh of his arms. His strange silence alarmed her.

'Did you find the others?' she asked.

'Yes, I found them. But no longer in human form. They must have suffered every known torture before finally they were impaled at the base of the fort. I do not know, and I shall never learn, who betrayed us, but Mulai Ismail has been informed of every move we have made. He has unleashed his wrath on Meknès. The ghetto is nothing but a smouldering ruin. All the Jews have been massacred. They were forewarned here. They used the Rabbi as bait. Then they ordered all the Jews to be hanged and the Christians executed without delay. They hanged Jean-Jean because they thought he was a Jew. I have just cut him down as I passed by and have brought him here – that is, as much of him as the vultures have left. I am going to bury his remains.'

He sat down and looked about him in astonishment at the red-veined rocks purpling in the morning light.

'All my comrades are dead,' he said dully.

He rested his chin on his hand for a long moment, then with an effort he got to his feet and went outside the cave. Angélique could hear the sound of his knife grating against the stones as he scratched out a grave, and went to help him.

But he shouted to her rudely: 'Get back. Don't come any nearer. This is no work for you. Go away. It's not pleasant to look at.'

She froze with horror and remained apart from him. She clasped her hands but, much as she wanted to, she could not pray.

With the sweeping strokes of a man used to working hard soil, Colin was pursuing his task of digging. When he finished heaping the earth into a little mound, she saw him, as if by a sudden decision, break off two sticks and fashion a cross from them. This he stuck into the mound with a defiant gesture.

'This time, I shall erect a cross!' he said.

Then he returned to sit once more inside the cave in the same pose of sombre meditation. Angélique tried to talk to him but he paid her no heed. Toward noon she spread a handful of dates on a fig leaf and laid it beside him.

Colin Paturel raised his head. His rough fingers had brought white ridges to his brown forehead. He stared at the woman bending over him and she could see the bitterness and disillusionment in his eyes as he seemed to say: 'My God, is she still here!'

He ate in silence. Ever since she had seen that strange look in his eyes, Angélique had felt paralysed, invaded by a new fear she could not identify. He was still on guard, his eyes wide open, but she could no longer resist the fatigue that made her own eyelids droop. She had walked for a whole day and a night with scarcely a break and had not closed her eyes once the whole of the preceding night. She finally went to sleep rolled up into a ball in a corner of the cave.

When she awoke she was alone. She had become accustomed to such solitary awakenings, for she always slept apart from the rest of the fugitives, but this time the silence seemed unusual to her. As she looked around, gradually the truth dawned on her. The last wheaten cake, the store of lentils, and the water bottle were carefully set out on a stone beside a javelin and a knife. But the bow, the arrows and Colin the Norman's club had disappeared. So he had abandoned her!

She was at a total loss as to what to do, and for a long time just sat with her head in her hands, weeping.

'How could you have done this?' she kept saying in a grief-stricken murmur. 'God will punish you!'

But she was none too sure that God would not be on Colin Paturel's side, for he had been crucified in His name, whereas she was only a woman, guilty of the first sin and responsible for all the woes of mankind, an object of scorn to be taken or left behind.

'Well, what's going on, my girl? Feeling sad?'

The voice of the Norman echoed in the cave like thunder. He was standing before her, a young wild boar across his shoulders with blood still dripping from its throat.

'I . . . I thought you had gone and left me,' she stammered.

'Gone? Well, hardly. I said to myself I needed something to sink my teeth into and I was lucky enough to run across this wild piglet. When I got back, you were in tears. . . .'

'I thought you had forsaken me,' she confessed.

His eyes widened and he raised his eyebrows as if he had just heard the most astonishing thing in his whole life.

'So that's it!' he said. 'Do you take me for a scoundrel? I forsake you? You, whom I . . .' His colour darkened as his emotions rose. 'I, who would have died for you,' he growled with a fierce intensity.

He threw his booty on the ground and went to pick up some sticks of wood which he piled in the centre of the cave, all his actions showing the anger seething within him. His tinder refused to light, and he swore like a Templar.

Angélique knelt beside him and put her hand on his. 'Forgive me, Colin. I am a fool. I should have remembered the many times you have risked your life for your brethren. But I was not one of them, only a woman.'

'All the more reason,' he muttered.

He did, however, lift his eyes to hers, and his expression softened as he took her by the chin.

'Listen to me closely, little girl, and let this be understood once and for all time. You were a Christian in Barbary like us. You were bound to a column and flogged, yet you did not renounce your faith. You have borne thirst and fear without ever complaining. I have never met as brave a woman as you in all my tossing about from one port to another over all the world. You are worth all the rest of the band put together, and if they marched as comrades should, without losing heart, it was because of your valiant spirit. They did not want to flag

347

before you. Now only you and I are left, bound to each other for life or death. Together we will find freedom. But if you should die, then I shall die beside you. I have taken an oath on it!'

'You don't have to say that,' she murmured. 'Alone, Colin, you would have much greater chances of succeeding.'

'You too, my dear. You are made of fine steel, as well tempered as poor Kermoeur's sword. I think I know you pretty thoroughly by now.'

The light in his deep-set blue eyes clouded with feelings he could not put into words, and his forehead wrinkled with the effort to define and express what was in his thoughts.

'You and I together . . . nothing can vanquish us!'

Angélique shuddered. Who else had said that to her? Another king – Louis XIV! And the light in his eyes had shone on her in just the same way. There were many similarities, now that she thought of it, between the Norman and the great ruler of France. People recognised that the two of them were meant to rule, and even in his servitude Colin had shown himself a king of the old school by his magnanimity, his wisdom and his physical strength.

Angélique smiled at him. 'You have restored my confidence, Colin, in you and in myself. I believe now that we are going to be saved.' A thrill ran through her. 'It has to be so. I would never have the courage to endure torture again. I will take whatever comes my way. . . .'

'Nonsense, you could do it. You always will have the courage for a second or third time, trusting that every time it is for the best. Believe me!' He looked at his scarred hands ironically. 'It's a grand thing this not wanting to die, providing you have no fear of death. To us who love life so, death is always at our side, and I have long thought it a good companion on our way. Life holds one of our hands, death the other. Each has a claim upon us. Neither has to be a bugbear. The whole point of the game is never to rest along the way. Well, that's enough talking, little girl. We're about to have a regular Belshazzar's feast. Just the sight of that splendid fire warms my heart. It's the first we've seen for a good long while.'

'Isn't it dangerous? What if the Moors see the smoke?'

'They are resting on their laurels. They think we are all dead. Those brave fellows, the Venetian and the Basque, had the presence of mind to tell them we had been slain by lions and they were the only survivors. When they asked what had happened to the woman, our comrades said she had been bitten by a venomous snake in the mountains and had died there. That was the report sent to Mulai Ismail. So now

348

everything is accounted for. So much the worse. Let's build the fire up a little to help our morale, eh?'

'Things are going better already,' she said, looking at him affectionately.

Colin Paturel's opinion of her invigorated her. It was the best reward for constancy she had ever had till now.

'Now I know you are my friend, I shall be afraid no more. Life is so simple for you, Colin Paturel.'

'Yes,' he said, suddenly growing serious, 'many times I have thought I had not yet seen the worst. It doesn't do any good to think of the future.'

They roasted the boar after rubbing it with saltpetre and thyme and sprigs of juniper, and turned it on a spit made from the poor Marquis's sword. For an hour all they thought of was getting the banquet ready. The wonderful savour of roasting meat drove them crazy with impatience and they wolfed down the first mouthfuls with great sighs of satisfaction.

'A fine time to preach a sermon on eternity,' said the Norman jokingly. 'Never was a time when the stomach didn't speak first. Blessed piglet! I could lick my fingers all the way to my elbows.'

'I never tasted anything so good in my whole life,' Angélique said in complete sincerity.

'Why, I thought Sultanas ate nothing but ortolans. What does one get to eat in a harem? Tell me just to fill out our menu here.'

'No. I don't want to remember the harem.'

They fell silent. Restored and refreshed by the clear water of a mountain stream with which Colin had filled his bottle as he returned from hunting, they let the bliss of rest enfold them.

'Colin, where did you learn so much deep wisdom? What you say opens the door to profound meditation, I have often noticed. Who taught you?'

'The sea. And the desert. And slavery. Little girl, everything you encounter is as good a teacher as any book. I don't see why what you have stored up here,' he tapped his head, 'isn't enough to reflect on from time to time.'

Suddenly he began to laugh. 'Profound meditation!' he repeated. 'Because I said that life and death walk hand in hand with us? Hasn't that ever occurred to you? How else would you get along?'

'I don't know,' said Angélique, shaking her head. 'I think I must be very silly and superficial. I have never truly thought much about anything.'

She broke off. Her eyes widened and she saw on his face the same expression of anxiety. He seized her wrist. They waited, holding their breath. The noise that had alarmed them began again. A horse was whinnying outside. . . .

The man got to his feet and stole to the entrance to the cave. Angélique followed him. At the foot of the hill four Arab horsemen had stopped and were looking up at the cliff from which they had seen smoke drifting.

Their pointed helmets gleamed above spotless white burnouses, proclaiming them to be soldiers of the Riff army assigned to the siege of the Spanish towns along the coast. One of them had a musket; the others were armed with lances.

Three of them dismounted and began to climb the hill in the direction of the cave, while the Arab with the musket remained in his saddle to stand guard over the horses.

'Hand me my bow,' said Colin Paturel. 'How many arrows are left in the quiver?'

'Three.'

'There are four of them! So much the worse! We'll have to manage somehow.'

Keeping his eye on the advancing Moors, he took the bow, braced his foot on a rock before him to steady his aim, and fitted the arrow to the string. His movements were even more deliberate than usual.

He loosed the arrow. The horseman with the musket fell across his saddle-bow, his dying scream drowned by the neighing of the frightened horses. The Arabs climbing up the cliff did not at once grasp what had happened.

A second arrow found the heart of one of them. The two others dashed forward.

Colin Paturel notched the third arrow and sank it almost up to its feathers in the chest of the Moor in front. The other hesitated. Suddenly he turned his back and dashed down the hill toward the horses.

The Norman had thrown his bow to the ground. Seizing his club, he leaped after his adversary who drew his scimitar and turned to face him. They circled round each other, watching each other's movements like wild animals on the point of leaping at each other's throats. Then Colin Paturel's club swung into action.

In a few moments the Arab's face was smashed, in spite of his helmet, and his neck was broken. The Norman bent over him to make sure he was dead. Then he inspected the man with the musket. He too was dead. Every one of the three arrows had found its mark.

'That was the only weapon I had when I hunted in the forests of Normandy when I was young,' he said laughingly to Angélique, who had joined him and was calming the horses.

The horror of murder had become so much of their normal existence that they wasted no time brooding over his action. Even Angélique gave only a passing glance to the four bodies lying among the tufts of juniper. 'We are going to take their horses. We will ride two, and each of us will lead one. We will hide the bodies in the cave, and that will del y any searching parties. There will be no riderless horses returning to the fort, and so no one will notice their absence until much later.'

They put on the pointed helmets of the soldiers and wrapped their burnouses around them, then after removing all signs of slaughter set out along the road at full gallop.

The inhabitants of the settlement had to tell the soldiers who came three days later in search of their missing comrades that they had seen two horsemen pass through their village as swiftly as swallows, each one leading a spare horse. They had not hailed them or stopped them. How could just a poor country farmer dare do that to such noble warriors?

The horses were recovered at the foot of the Riff mountains. The bandits that infested the region were blamed, and punitive expeditions were sent into their fastnesses.

CHAPTER TWENTY-EIGHT

Colin Paturel and Angélique abandoned the horses in the foothills of the mountains, over which only donkeys could travel. This was the last stage of their journey, but the hardest. Once over the barren barrier of the Riff mountains they would see the sea. Furthermore the Norman had stayed two years, when he had first been captured, in the mysterious and holy city of Xauen, and he knew the region which they had to traverse. He knew its dangers and hardships, but he also knew the shortest routes and that the higher they climbed the safer they would be from dangerous encounters. Their only enemies would be the mountains themselves, the cold at night, the scorching sun by day, hunger and thirst. Men would leave them in peace, and there were not many lions. Wild boars had to be watched for, but there was nothing to fear from the monkeys, the gazelles and the porcupines, which would be a source of food for them.

He had kept the musket and some ammunition, as well as the soldiers' rations he had found in their saddlebags, and the thick warm burnouses which would protect them.

'Just a few more days and then we will see Ceuta.'

'How many days?' asked Angélique.

The Norman was too cautious to name any exact number. Who could tell? With luck, fifteen; with none . . .

Bad luck befell them one afternoon as they were crossing the burning rocks. Angélique had taken advantage of a turn in the road which hid her from her companion to sit down on a stone. She did not want him to see her weaken, for he had often repeated to her that he thought her indefatigable. But she was far from matching his endurance. He never was tired. Without her, he surely could have tramped a day and night without stopping for more than an hour.

Angélique was catching her breath when she felt a sharp pain in her leg and looked down to see a serpent slithering like lightning among the stones.

'I have been bitten by a snake.'

The memory of a half-forgotten phrase returned to her mind. 'The woman was bitten by a snake and died,' the Venetian and the Basque had said before their death. The past had anticipated the present, but time did not exist, and what was written was written!

She instinctively untied her belt and bound it below her knee and remained there as if frozen, her thoughts rambling.

'What will Colin Paturel say? He will never forgive me for this. I can't walk any farther. I am going to die. . . .'

The tall form of her companion reappeared. Not having seen her behind him, he had turned back.

'What's the matter?'

Angélique tried to smile. 'I hope it isn't serious, but I think . . . I think I've been bitten by a snake.'

He knelt down to examine the wound which had begun to swell and darken. Then he pulled out his knife and, after testing the keenness of its edge, lit a few dry twigs and heated the blade red hot.

'What are you going to do?' asked Angélique in terror.

He did not reply, but grasped her ankle firmly and cut out the flesh around the wound, at the same time cauterising it with the hot knife. Angélique let out a cry of pain and fainted.

When she recovered consciousness, evening was falling over the mountain. She was stretched out on her burnous and Colin Paturel was making her drink a cup of strong, hot mint tea.

'You'll feel better now, little girl. The worst is over.' Then when she could rally herself, he said: 'I had to spoil your pretty leg. What a pity! You won't be able to lift your skirts any more to dance a bourrée under the elm-trees, my dear. But it had to be done. Otherwise you wouldn't have lived an hour.'

'I am grateful to you,' she said feebly.

She could feel her wound smarting. He had bandaged it with a poultice of medicinal leaves. 'The prettiest legs in Versailles . . .' She, too, like all the rest, would carry the marks of her captivity in Barbary – glorious scars she would sometime grow nostalgic about as she drew on her silken stockings and fastened her golden garters. Sometime! He saw her smile at the thought.

'Good for you! Your courage is still there. We're going to move on now.'

She looked at him a little fearfully, but already was ready to obey him.

'Do you think I can walk?'

'No doubt about it. But you should not set your foot on the ground for at least a week in case your wound becomes infected. Don't worry. I'm going to carry you.'

Thus they continued their slow climb into the mountains. The herculean Norman hardly stooped under his new burden and proceeded at the same even pace. He had had to leave his club behind as too much of an encumbrance, but he kept the musket and the sack of provisions slung over one shoulder. Angélique rode on his back, her arms around his neck, smelling the perfume of his hair and, when she grew tired, nestling her forehead in the neck of her giant bearer.

This very day she had once more escaped death. Her blood sang the song of victory: 'I am alive. Alive!'

She must have dropped off to sleep while Colin Paturel was carrying her on his back, which had borne far greater weights during his captivity, for suddenly the sky had turned pink before her. Colin was proceeding at the same steady pace. Angélique felt a wave of tenderness for him and almost kissed the hard skin so near her lips.

'Colin!' she pleaded, 'Oh, please stop and rest. You'll exhaust yourself.'

He obeyed her in silence, letting her slip to the ground, and went to sit down, his head on his knees. She saw him twist his huge shoulders to stretch them. 'It's too much,' she thought. 'Even a man with his powers of endurance cannot accomplish a feat like this.'

If only she could walk a little! She felt rested and full of enthusiasm. But as soon as she put her foot on the ground, shooting pains made her understand she was risking opening the wound and increasing her disability. She dragged herself over to the sack of provisions and got a handful of dates and figs which she brought to Colin Paturel with the waterbag.

The Norman lifted his head, revealing the fatigue in his face. He looked at the food without seeming to see it.

'Leave it there,' he said rudely. 'Don't bother.'

'You are exhausted, Colin, and it is all my fault. I'm so terribly sorry.'

'Stop it,' he said almost savagely. He shook his Viking head like an enraged lion. 'Don't bother. An hour of sleep and I'll be all right.'

He dropped his head again on his knees. She left him there and lay down eating some of the dried fruit. The air was cool. No matter in which direction she looked, she could see no trace of any living being. It was astonishing and wonderful!

For want of anything better to do, she went to sleep again. When she opened her eyes, Colin was returning from hunting, a fawn across his shoulders.

'Colin, you're crazy!' Angélique exclaimed. 'You should have been resting and restoring your strength.'

The Norman shrugged his shoulders. 'What do you take me for, little girl? Some puny thing like you?'

He was in a sullen mood and did not seem to want to talk to her or even look at her. Angélique began to worry that he was concealing some new danger from her.

'Could the Moors take us by surprise here, Colin?'

'I don't think so. For the sake of safety, we will light our fire down in that ravine, though.'

Angélique's leg was so much better that she could limp down to the stream. It was there they encountered their last wild beast, which they saw too late on the other side of the brook – a lioness squatting like a huge cat on watch. It took her only one mighty leap to reach them.

Colin Paturel stood rooted to the spot like a statue of stone. He never took his eyes off the lioness, but began to talk to it slowly. After a few moments the animal squatted down again in perplexity. They could see its eyes gleaming in the brush, then the bushes move as it took its retreat.

The Norman heaved a sigh powerful enough to turn all the windmills in Holland. His arm encircled Angélique and pressed her to him.

'Heaven must be watching over us. Whatever could have got into the head of that beast to leave us in peace?'

'You were speaking in Arabic. What did you say?'

'How do I know? I did not even heed what language I was using. I just thought I would try to communicate with the lioness to see if there was any way we could understand each other. It would have been impossible with a Moor.' He tossed his head. 'I got on well with the lions at Meknès.'

'I remember,' said Angélique, trying to laugh. 'They did not want to eat you.'

The man lowered his eyes to her. 'You never uttered a sound or made a single move. Good for you, my dear.'

The colour returned to Angélique's cheeks. Colin Paturel's arm was a bulwark, and his grasp a source of strength. Raising her eyes, she smiled at him with assurance.

'When I am with you, I can know no fear.'

The Norman clenched his teeth and his face darkened. 'Let's not stay here,' he said. 'There's no point in tempting fate. Let's go farther on.'

They filled their water-bottles from the stream and searched for a crevice in the cliffs along its bank in which to light a fire. But their meal brought them no satisfaction other than to appease their hunger. The atmosphere was heavy, and Colin Paturel said little. Angélique tried to start a conversation, but ended by falling prey to an insidious anxiety that made her nervous. Why was Colin Paturel so sober and worried? Was he angry with her for having slowed their progress because of her wound? What danger did he foresee, and what was the meaning of the sidelong glances he kept casting?

The evening breeze fanned them like a velvet wing. The fading light powdered the mountains with soft pastel shades of dark blue. In the gathering dusk she turned her pale and troubled face to him.

'I . . . think I could walk a little tonight,' she said.

He shook his head. 'No, little girl, you cannot. Don't worry, I will carry you.' There was a touch of sadness in his voice.

'Oh, Colin,' she had to exclaim tearfully, 'what's the matter? Are we both going to die?'

Even when she was on his back with her arms around his neck she was not at ease as on the previous night. His breathing corresponded to the heavy beating of her heart and recalled to her the confessions of love so many men had made within her frail arms. It was she who seemed to be carrying them then, yet here she was dozing off with her head against the damp, sinewy neck of her crude companion. She felt as if she were weighing him down with the burden of her eternal femininity.

The wind from the mountains blew upon them its icy breath laden with pungent odours of a rich and mysterious fragrance that called up visions of sumptuous luxury.

The rising sun showed them a mountainside covered with cedars whose long, swooping branches seemed like sombre tents. In their shade was a grassy meadow speckled with white flowers.

Colin Paturel crossed a tumbling brook, scrambled up the steep bank opposite and discovered the mouth of a little cave with a floor of white sand.

'Let's stop here,' he said. 'Apparently it's not a wild beast's lair. We can light a fire here safely.'

He was speaking between his teeth, and his voice was hoarse. Was this due to exhaustion? Angélique watched him anxiously. There was something so strange about him, and she could not endure not knowing what it was. Perhaps he was sick of some grievous malady that might afflict her too. How terrible that would be! But she would not forsake him. She would nurse him back to health as he had tended her.

He turned his head away from her questioning look and said curtly: 'I am going to sleep.'

He went out. Angélique sighed. The cave was a pleasant place. Unless they stumbled into some hidden trap, what could hinder them from now on?

She set out on a flat stone the remains of the fawn they had cooked the previous night, and some dried figs. Without too much difficulty she worked her way down to the mountain brook, but not without the precaution of keeping her eyes alert for any danger. Only a few twittering birds were on its banks. She filled the bottles, and then washed herself carefully in the icy water which made her blood race. As she bent over a still pool among the rocks she saw herself as in a mirror. She almost let out a shriek of surprise.

The face reflected there seemed to be only twenty years old. The delicate features, the violet-tinted eyelids framing her large eyes so accustomed to scanning the horizon, the curve of her chapped and blackened lips, were no longer those of a woman who had been through such bitter experiences, but those of a young, simple girl who yet knew nothing of the world and needed no artificial beauty. The dry winds, the ruthless sun, the neglect of her appearance in the incidents that had befallen her, had restored to her face a sort of virginity and innocent adolescence. Her skin was as brown as a gipsy's, of course, but her hair was like a ray of moonlight on the white sand. Her thin, frail body lost in the folds of her burnous, her unkempt hair and her bare feet were those of a barbarian.

She untied the bandage round her leg. The wound had closed, but the scar was ugly indeed. So much the worse! She replaced the bandage philosophically. As she was bathing she had perceived how thin her waist still was, how graceful her legs now that they had lost all the fat she had put on in the harem. She had come through rather well, all things considered. Once more she leaned over the mirroring pool and smiled to herself.

'I think I am still presentable,' she said to the birds.

As she was climbing back up the slope she burst into song. Suddenly she stopped, as she noticed Colin Paturel stretched on the grass among the white flowers. One arm was under his head, and he did not stir. The anxiety she had felt about him returned, and she tiptoed up to look at him more closely.

The Norman was asleep, his slow, regular breathing heaving his broad, hairy chest beneath the open burnous. No, he could not be sick. His colour was good, and the serenity of his closed lips and his relaxed position were those of a man in good health merely restoring his strength after heavy labour. As she looked at him lying there under the cedars she thought of Adam, there was so much primitive perfection in his huge, vigorous body, and he was such a simple man – a wandering hunter, a law-giver, the shepherd of his flock. She knelt down beside him and brushed a fly from his creased forehead.

Colin Paturel opened his eyes and fixed her with a strange and frightening stare. She drew back instinctively. The Norman seemed to find it hard to rally his wits.

'What's going on?' he stammered in his hoarse voice. 'Moors?'

'No, everything is calm. I was just watching you sleep. Oh, Colin, don't stare at me like that!' she exclaimed all of a sudden. 'You frighten me. What's been the matter with you these last few days? What's happened? If you think we're in danger, tell me so. I can share your cares, but I cannot suffer your . . . yes, that's it, your bitterness towards me. Sometimes I have thought you must truly hate me, that you are terribly angry with me. For what? Was it because I got bitten by a snake and slowed your progress? I can think of no other reason. Colin, for the love of God, if you blame me for anything, tell me what it is. I can't endure this not knowing. If you have come to hate me, what will become of me?'

Tears were spilling out of her eyes. To lose her last and only friend seemed the worst thing that could possibly happen.

He had got to his feet and was looking at her so impassively she began to think he might not have even heard her. His gaze was so overpowering that she thought of the wretched captives in Meknès brought before him for judgement, and how they must have suffered.

'Why should I blame you?' he said at last. 'For being what you are – a woman?' His lids narrowed over his eyes till all she could see was their dark, forbidding pupils. 'I am no saint, my beauty. You would be wrong to think I was. I am a child of the sea, a former pirate. My life has consisted of killing, plundering, tossing in storms, running after girls in port. Even in captivity I did not change my tastes. I have always had to have women. I caught those I could. It wasn't hard. When Mulai Ismail wanted to reward me, he would send me one of his black women. But that happened seldom. For twelve years I lived a life of fasting and abstinence. When at the end of those twelve years I began to exist side by side with a woman . . .' He was speaking rapidly as if to hide his embarrassment under a cloak of anger. 'Can't you understand? Didn't you ever live before you were sold to Mulai Ismail? Your eye is too bold for anyone to suspect the contrary. Did you never ask yourself how it was possible for a fellow like me to exist day after day and night after night with a woman . . . and what a woman!' His eyelids closed, and ecstasy illumined his countenance. 'The most beautiful woman I have ever seen!'

He went on in a low voice, as if to himself.

'Your eyes like the depths of the sea . . . looking at me, beseeching me . . . your hand on mine, the fragrance of your body, your smile. I don't know how you are put together. But I have seen you . . . lashed to the column when those black devils were thrusting the red-hot tongs at you. . . . I saw you the other night when you were bathing under the waterfall. . . . And now I have to carry you on my back. . . .'

His fury broke out again.

'No, I can't stand it. . . . What Saint Anthony endured is nothing beside this. There have been days when I would rather have been . . . bound to a cross again with the vultures snapping at me . . . or nailed above the gate to the city. . . . And now you ask what is plaguing me!'

He raised his fist to call heaven to witness his torment. Then with an oath he turned away and strode off toward the cave.

His confession left Angélique dumbfounded, but after a while, re-assured. 'Oh, was that all it was?' she thought.

A smile spread over her lips. The gentle wind stirred the branches of the cedars and wafted their fragrance to her. Her hair blew against her cheek and her half-naked shoulders from which the burnous had slipped. A few minutes earlier she had seen in the mirroring pool what Colin Paturel now saw in her. She recalled how she had yearned to plant her mouth upon his neck, and when the tortured nights of this savage land had fallen around them, how she had craved to find refuge against his mighty chest – all these inarticulate indications of a still deeper desire that had slumbered within her and that she had not wanted to arouse.

Now that he had spoken, the eternal life-force expanded within her like a bird spreading its wings. She felt the lifeblood throbbing. Life! She plucked a frail white flower, so perfect, so fragile.

Her chest swelled as she took several deep breaths. Whatever there was of fear lying in wait for her had retreated beyond the horizon. The heavens were clear, the air clean and sweet. The whole world was deserted.

Angélique rose to her feet and ran barefoot back to the cave also.

Colin Paturel was at the entrance, leaning against its rocky frame with his arms folded. He was contemplating the distant yellow and pale-green glow at the foot of the mountains, but his thoughts were running in a different direction, as she could tell from his back, which was that of an extremely embarrassed man wondering how he could extricate himself from the scrape he had got himself into.

He had not heard her coming, and she stopped to look at him tenderly. Dear Colin! Dear valiant heart! Invincible and modest! How tall and broad he was! Her arms would never go all the way around him . . .

She slipped to his side, but he did not notice her until she laid her cheek on his arm. He shuddered violently and pulled away.

'So you did understand what I just said to you?' he said mischievously.

'Yes, I think I understood,' she murmured.

Her hands reached softly over his chest to his broad shoulders. He withdrew again, turning scarlet.

'Ah, no!' he gasped. 'It's not that. No, you have not understood. I wanted nothing of you. My poor little girl, what are you going to think of me?'

He took her hands in his to lead her aside. If she but touched him, if he felt once more her caress upon his skin, he would succumb and lose his head.

'What will you think of me, who suffered such pain so that you would suspect nothing? I should never have opened my mouth, and you would never have known if you had not taken me by surprise . . . when I was just waking up . . . from a sleep filled with dreams of you. Forget what I said. I hate myself. Go! I know . . . I doubt myself, you poor little girl! You have known what slavery is for a woman and that it is less than for a man. It is enough for you to have been sold and passed from one master to another. It cannot be said that I am such a scoundrel as to have forced you . . .'

Angélique's eyes were filled with light. Colin Paturel's hands transferred their warmth to her, and she found his peasant face very moving as it twisted with his emotion. She had never noticed how cool and full his lips were. Of course, he was strong enough to keep away from her, but he did not know the power of her eyes. She flung herself again upon his chest and groped with her white hands.

'Go away, little girl,' he murmured, 'go away . . . I am only a man.

'And I,' she said with a shaky laugh, 'am only a woman. . . . Oh, Colin, dear Colin, haven't we enough to endure . . . I know what can comfort us both.'

She laid her forehead against his chest, as she had so often longed to do during their toilsome journey. His vigour intoxicated her, his male scent that at last she now dared savour as she touched her lips timidly to his hard flesh.

At her silent confession the Norman was like a tree struck by lightning. A shudder tingled through his mighty frame. He bent over her. A boundless thrill shot through him. This creature, a little too proud and a little too intelligent for him, as he had sometimes thought, whom fate had given him as a comrade during this cruel odyssey, he was now discovering to be a woman like any other, wheedling and subtly demanding, like the girls in port who run after big, blond-bearded fellows.

As she clung to him she could not ignore the mad desire that took possession of her, and she responded to it with a slight movement of her tense body, modestly shy yet already its slave, calling to him in silence with a ripple in her throat like that of an enormous dove.

Distracted, he lifted her to him to look into her face. 'Is it possible?' he murmured.

For reply she grasped his shoulder. Then, trembling, he lifted her in his arms and carried her to the rear of the cave as if he were afraid to see her dazzling bliss in the light. The shadows were deep there, and the sand soft and cool.

The world's most basic passion in the blood of Colin Paturel was as intense and violent as a torrent, destroying everything in its path including the defences his sensitive soul and his magnanimous heart had so long raised against the force of his desires. Now these were unleashed, he could do nothing but abandon himself to them, drunk with the power they had given him. He was devouring her like a famished beast, unsatisfied with her smooth bare body, with feeling her close to him, with touching her woman's skin and her flowing hair, with the intoxicating tenderness of her breasts beneath his hands. He was so greedy for her and so impatient after his secret torments that he almost violated her as he demanded that she yield to him. Then he collapsed upon her and remained there in silence, his arms clutching her to him like the most precious of treasures.

The light had thickened when Angélique opened her eyes again. Outside the twilight was almost gone. She stirred a bit, overwhelmed by these iron bands that clamped her to Colin Paturel.

'Are you asleep?'

'I have been asleep.'

'You're not angry with me?'

'You know I'm not.'

'I am a brute, aren't I, my beauty? Why don't you say so? Go ahead and tell me so.'

'No. Didn't you feel you made me happy?'

'Really? Then you must treat me as a close friend.'

'If you wish me to. Colin, don't you think it is dark enough for us to move on?'

'Yes, my lamb.'

They walked in happiness over the stony path. He was carrying her, and she was laying her head against his firm neck. Nothing would come between them ever again. They had signed and sealed an alliance between two lives so greatly in jeopardy, and all danger or suffering would in future be shared.

Colin Paturel's nerves were no longer tense with torments like those of a soul in hell as his spirit wrestled with his fear of betraying her trust. Angélique no more would have to bear his evil looks and his rudeness, no longer bewail her loneliness. Now, whenever she wanted to, she could touch her lips to his neck ridged with scars from months of wearing an iron collar studded with spikes.

'Softly, my darling,' he said laughing, 'take it easy. We still have a journey to make.'

He was dying to pull her to him and press his lips on hers, to lie with her on the sand in the moonlight and experience again the intoxication of being close to her. But he mastered his desires, for they still had a long way to go, and the girl was tired. He could not forget that she was suffering from hunger and that she had been bitten by a horned viper. For a moment he had almost forgotten it himself, brute that he was! He had never taken much thought about treating a woman with kindness, but he would learn for her sake.

If only he could have given her everything she wanted, and kept her from all pain and sorrow! If only he could have set before her a table spread with dainty dishes, or offered her the repose of 'a big square bed with white sheets and bunches of daffodils at each post', as the old song went! At Ceuta they would drink from the spring whose water Odysseus sipped when for seven years he languished with Calypso, the daughter of old Atlas – or so the sailors said.

Daydreaming thus, he kept on walking and felt no fatigue, though Angélique slumbered on his back. His burden was all the joy in the world.

At dawn they halted and stretched out in a field of short grass. They no longer searched for shelter, for they were sure of being unmolested from now on. Their eyes met in a question. This time he was not afraid of her. He wanted to know her completely, study the blissful relaxation of her face pillowed on her golden hair. He was in an ecstasy of marvelling at her.

'How you like to make love!' he said. 'I would not have thought it.'

'I love you too, Colin.'

'Shh! You don't have to say that now. Are you all right?'

'Yes.'

'Did I give you any pleasure?'

'Oh, great pleasure!'

'Then go to sleep, my lamb.'

They revelled in their love as if they had been starved of affection. The force which brought them together was as strong as the instinct that drove them to seek out fresh water that they might survive. In their embraces they forgot their grief and pain and all desire for revenge on fate. They drank of the living water of hope and tasted on each other's lips the sublime discovery that love was born to comfort the first man and the first woman and to give them courage to endure their earthly pilgrimage.

Never before had Angélique been in the arms of so tall and physically powerful a man. She loved to sit on his knees and press herself close to his massive frame while his strong hands caressed her.

'Do you remember the orders I gave our poor comrades?' he whispered. "She is not for any of you, and she belongs to no one"? Now I have taken you for myself, and you are my treasure. What a scoundrel I am!'

'It was I who wanted you to.'

'I did that to protect myself from you. I had already held you in my arms in Rodani's garden, and my blood was hot. That's why I issued the ban. I said to myself: 'Colin, you will be forced to face the music. . . ." '

'You seemed so stern, so rude.'

'But you never said a word. You bore it all meekly, as if you were asking pardon just for being there. I know how many times you were afraid and at the end of your rope. I would have liked to carry you then, but I had made a pact with our comrades.'

'It was better that way. It was you who were right, Majesty.'

'Sometimes when I looked at you, you were smiling. It's your smile I love the most of everything about you. You smiled at me after the snake had bitten you and you were waiting for me by the path. It was as if you feared me more than you feared death. You don't know how I suffered when I thought you were lost. If you had died, I would have lain down by your side and never got up again.'

'Don't love me so much, Colin. But kiss me once again.'

CHAPTER TWENTY-NINE

Step by step and pebble by pebble they drove their way onward. The mountains had changed. Gone now were the cedar trees and the green grass of the slopes. The game had become scarce, and the springs few and far between. Hunger and thirst had begun to harass them again. but Angélique's leg had healed and she had finally convinced her companion that she could walk. They progressed slowly, walking both day and night in easy stages, clambering up the passes and ravines among sombre cliffs and grey underbrush.

Angélique did not dare inquire whether they were still far from their destination, which seemed to recede with every ridge of the mountains. Nothing but walking, walking, and still more walking.

Angélique stopped. 'This time I really am going to die,' she thought. Her faintness increased. Her ears were ringing as if all the bells of a steeple were jingling inside her head, and she was filled with dismay. *Yes, surely this time death was at hand.* She sank to her knees with a feeble cry. Colin Paturel, who was already almost on the top of the cliff they were scaling, returned to her side. He knelt and raised her to him. She was sobbing, but no tears would come.

'What is it, my sweet? Come on, just a little courage . . .'

He stroked her cheek and kissed her dry lips as if to infuse her with his own inexhaustible strength.

'Get up. I'm going to carry you for a while.'

But she shook her head despondently. 'Oh no, Colin. This time it's too late. I am going to die. I can hear the church bells ringing my knell.

'What nonsense! Courage! Just beyond this peak . . .'

He broke off, staring before him intently.

'What is it, Colin? Moors?'

'No, but I too hear something . . .' He stood up and shouted: 'I hear church bells!'

Like a madman he dashed to the summit of the cliff. She could see him waving his arms, and heard him yelling something she could not understand. Forgetting her exhaustion and heedless of the sharp stones that cut her feet, she hurried after him.

'The sea!'

That was what the Norman was shouting. When she caught up with him, he pulled her to him and hugged her frantically. They could not believe their eyes. Before them spread the shimmering ocean rippling with golden waves, and to their left was a walled city bristling with church towers.

Ceuta! Ceuta the Catholic! The bells of the cathedral of San Angelo were ringing the Angelus. This is what the two had heard and thought was only an hallucination.

'Ceuta!' murmured the Norman. 'Ceuta!'

Then he calmed down and began to think things out carefully. Ceuta was being besieged by the Moors. They could hear a cannon boom, and see a wisp of smoke drift from the ramparts into the peaceful twilight.

'Let's go this way,' said Colin Paturel as he led Angélique into the shelter of the cliffs. While she was resting, he crept along the top of the ridge.

When he returned he had spied out the thousand tents of the Moorish camp, each flying a green banner, at the base of the cliff. They had almost tumbled right on top of the sentinels.

Now they would have to wait till nightfall. He outlined a plan. Before the moon rose, they would get down the mountainside and make for the beach. Jumping from rock to rock, they would try to reach the isthmus on which the city was built. Then they would creep to the base of the walls and hope the Spanish sentinels would recognise them.

When it was fully dark, they abandoned their weapons and sacks and stole down the cliffside, holding their breath and freezing with terror whenever they dislodged even a pebble. As they were nearing the beach, three Arabs galloped by on their way back to the camp. For a wonder their fierce hounds were not with them.

As soon as they had passed, Colin Paturel and Angélique dashed across the beach and hid among the rocks on the shore. Through water up to their waists they groped their way in a winding, twisting line. The sharp shells cut and slashed them. From time to time they stumbled into a hole under the water. They had to take great pains not to stand upright, for the moon was rising higher and higher and spreading its light over the surface of the sea around them. Closer and closer drew the city, its curling battlements silver in the moonlight, its domes and towers rising into the starry sky. The sight of what they had dreamed of for so long doubled their fortitude.

Now they were not far from the first tower of the outer fortifications. Then the sound of Arab voices mingled with the swish of the waves, and froze them in their tracks. They clung to the slimy rocks, trying to blend into them. A squad of Moorish cavalry appeared, their pointed helmets glistening in the moonlight. These alighted on the beach and proceeded to light a bonfire.

Hardly a few feet away from the fugitives, still clinging to the rocks and soaked with brine, the Arabs settled down to watch. Colin Paturel could hear them talking together. They did not like, they were saying, this duty of having to stand guard right under the ramparts of Ceuta. It was a good way to get an arrow in the heart from one of those damned Spanish archers just as soon as dawn broke. But their chief had said the place must be guarded at night because that was the route by which the guides escorted escaping Christian slaves.

'They will leave at daybreak,' the Norman whispered to Angélique. 'We'll have to wait till then.'

Wait! With the cold water almost up to their necks, its salt smarting their sores, buffeted by the tide, struggling against sleep and exhaustion, not daring to relax a finger of their grip. . . .

Finally a little before dawn the Moors washed themselves, saddled their horses, and as soon as the sun peeped over the horizon, leaped into their saddles and galloped off toward the camp.

Colin Paturel and Angélique dragged themselves up out of the water and got to their knees, dizzy from exhaustion. But just as they were catching their breath, another squadron of Moorish cavalry appeared from behind the mountain and caught sight of them. They let out a string of raucous shouts and spurred their horses in their direction.

'Come on!' Colin told Angélique.

The distance between them and the city seemed as endless as the whole desert. Hand in hand they ran, practically flew, over it, paying no heed to the stones and shells that gashed their bare feet, sustained by one thought alone: Run! Run! Get to the gate!

The Arabs pursuing them were armed with muskets, a weapon hard to discharge while galloping on horseback. A crossbow could not have missed them, so fully exposed were they, but the bullets merely hit the sand around them.

Suddenly Angélique thought she saw two other horsemen rise up before her.

'This is the very end. . . . We are hemmed in.'

Her heart gave out and she stumbled and fell under the hooves of the horses. The weight of the Norman descended upon her and she swooned as she heard her own voice rasp out: 'Christians! . . . Christian slaves! . . . In the name of Christ, *amigos*! . . . In the name of Christ!'

'Why did you put so much pepper in the chocolate, David? I have told you a hundred times, less pepper and less cinnamon. You don't have to make that horrible Spanish mess . . .'

Angélique was writhing. She couldn't see why she had to start all over again breaking her back to serve chocolate to the Parisians. She knew she would never get anywhere in business so long as that stupid David kept adding so much pepper and cinnamon, which made the chocolate spicy enough to revive a corpse. She pushed the cup away in disgust and felt the hot liquid burn her. Then she heard a little cry of dismay.

With an effort she opened her eyes. She was in a bed with white sheets stained with the horrible black chocolate she had just upset. A woman with a pretty dark face framed by a mantilla was trying to wipe up the mess.

'I am terribly sorry,' said Angélique.

The woman seemed delighted. She began to speak rapidly in Spanish, and wrung Angélique's hands effusively. Then she fell on her knees before a statue of the Virgin clad in gold and crowned with diamonds which stood in a little oratory under an oil-lamp.

Angélique gathered she was giving thanks to the Blessed Virgin for restoring her to health. For three days she had been delirious with fever. Then the Spanish woman called a Moorish maidservant and the two of them quickly changed the sheets, replacing them with spotless ones embroidered with flowers and scented with lavender.

It seemed strange to find herself between cool sheets once more, under the canopy of a huge bed with posts of gilded wood. Angélique turned her head cautiously. Her neck was stiff and pained her. Her eyes, unaccustomed to the gloom, ached. A few rays of golden sunlight were trickling through wrought-iron arabesques which shielded the room from the blinding light outside. But the rest of the room, which was full of Spanish furniture and ornaments, and contained only two little black dogs and a thick-lipped dwarf dressed as a page, was as dim as the harem. From time to time the house shook with explosions that came from the citadel. Angélique suddenly remembered where she was. Those were the cannons of Ceuta!

Ceuta, the last outpost of Spain, perched on a scorching rock, transmitting over the whole land of Mohammed the voice of its cathedral bells, chipped and cracked by bullets a hundred times and more, pealing above the dull roar of the artillery.

As she knelt in her oratory the Spanish woman recited the prayers of the Angelus and crossed herself. For her it was all peaceful enough, for the noise of the cannons had become a commonplace thing. Her son had been born in Ceuta, and now at the age of six was up on the ramparts with all the other children of the garrison, helping the soldiers destroy the Moors. Hatred of the Moors ran in the blood of every Spaniard, whose soul yearned toward Africa much more than toward Europe. The Andalusian had many causes to remember the Arab oppressor who had bequeathed him his dark skin and white teeth. Guerrilla warfare was natural to both of these races that flourished under a fierce sky. The boldness of the besieged Spaniards had often incited them to sally forth from their walls to harass the Moorish legions.

A squadron of Spanish cavalry in black steel helmets and brandishing long lances were returning from a nocturnal expedition against the Moors when they saw the two Christian slaves running toward the citadel. They had ridden between them and the pursuing Moors, and Colin Paturel and Angélique had been trampled by their horses. A violent skirmish had taken place, and the squadron had finally withdrawn into the citadel dragging the rescued fugitives with them.

Angélique knew enough Spanish to understand the drift of the Spanish woman's long explanation of what had happened. Her memory was coming back to her, and she was growing more and more conscious of the pains in her body. She could feel the blisters and cuts smarting on her feet, the dry skin peeling off her face, the thinness of her body, and the broken nails of her fingers on hands as brown as a spice cake.

'Holy Mother!' murmured the Spanish woman, raising her eyes toward heaven. 'What a state she had been in, the poor woman! Her clothing drenched, her pretty feet streaming blood, her hair full of sand and sea water. It was so unusual a thing for them to rescue a fugitive slave that they sent at once for Monsieur de Breteuil, the Ambassador of the King of France.'

Angélique shuddered. Monsieur de Breteuil? That was a not unfamiliar name to her. She had met the diplomat at Versailles. Doña Inez de Los Cobos y Perrandez helped her remember with loud cries of *'Si! Si!'* Monsieur de Breteuil was indeed in Ceuta on a special embassy. He had just arrived on the *Royale* to bring aid from Louis XIV to a noble lady who had fallen into the hands of Mulai Ismail in the course of a perilous voyage.

Angélique closed her eyes. Her exhausted heart began to beat faster. So, the message she had entrusted to Father de Valombreuze had reached its destination! The sovereign had heard the call of the deserter. Monsieur de Breteuil, laden with gifts to soften the heart of the Berber monarch, was trying to reach Meknès to negotiate, with the authority of the French King, the liberation of the rash Marquise.

The news that a half-dead woman had escaped from the Moroccan harem and was in Ceuta, had been brought to the French Ambassador, who immediately went to the little convent of the Redemptorist Fathers, where she had been taken. He had hesitated to recognise her, so he said, so altered was she by the last stages of exhaustion and deprivation.

Angélique's hand roamed around her on the sheets. She was searching for another hand, a calloused one, to enfold her own. Where was her comrade? What had happened to him? Worry lay on her heart like a stone she could not lift off. She dared not ask any questions, for she had hardly the strength to utter a word. All she could recall was that he had fallen with her under the hooves of the Spaniards' horses.

Then Monsieur de Breteuil was standing beside her bed. The curls of his periwig had been carefully arranged over his gold-embroidered silk coat. Carrying his hat in the crook of his arm, he bowed to her, his toes pointed outward, his red heels carefully set.

'Madame, I have received good news of your state of health, and have made haste to call upon you.'

'Thank you, sir,' said Angélique.

She must have gone to sleep while the Spanish woman was talking to her at such length. Unless it was still yesterday. . . . She felt well rested. She looked around for Doña Inez, but she had withdrawn in disapproval of a man's visiting a woman's private apartment. These French were so casual about things like that!

Monsieur de Breteuil took a seat on an ebony footstool. He took a box of candy out of his coat-tail pocket, offered some to Angélique, and began sucking the sweetmeats. He was delighted, he said, that his mission had met with such early and complete success, thanks – he acknowledged – to the valour of Madame du Plessis-Bellière, who had herself escaped from the captivity into which her shameless audacity and her disregard of the King's commands had dispatched her.

He kept on talking with scornful superiority like any other nobody. Lord knows, the King's anger had been fearful to behold when he discovered the unprecedented conduct of the widow of a Marshal of France. Monsieur de la Reynie, who had been made responsible for her remaining in Paris, had been publicly reprimanded and had almost been removed from his office for carelessness. The Court – and the police – had been questioned at great length about the means the lovely lady had used to escape from Paris. It was said she had seduced a high-ranking police official, who let her get out disguised as a jailer. But the funniest thing had been the innocent satisfaction of the Duc de Vivonne, who had boasted to the King of meeting Madame du Plessis-Bellière in Marseilles and taking her aboard his galley. He could not understand why he had been treated so coolly.

Monsieur de Breteuil coughed into his cuffs. His inquisitive eyes – as stupid as a rooster's, she thought – never strayed from her as she lay in bed before him. He was licking his lips in advance at the thought of the secrets she would tell him, which he would be the first to hear. She seemed very tired still, and rather absentminded, but soon she would recover her spirits without a doubt. Already she looked quite different from the pitiful waif he had found a few days before. He told her how he had first seen her, half-naked in her dripping rags, her feet bleeding, her face waxen, her eyes closed and circled with deep purple rings. She was lying in the arms of a kind of hairy giant who was trying to force between her lips the rum-spiked tea the doctor of the Order had prepared. How captivity among these cruel barbarians could reduce civilised human beings!

Good lord, was it possible? Was this truly the haughty Marquise he had seen dancing at Versailles, whom the King had escorted the entire length of the *tapis vert*?

He could not believe his eyes. No, it could not be the same woman for whom His Majesty had equipped a vessel and called upon all his skill as a diplomat to go to Mulai Ismail. But there had been something about this pitiful creature – perhaps her hair and the delicacy of her joints – that had made him hesitate.

Then, upon being questioned, the slave with her had said he did not know her full name, but her first name was Angélique. So it was really she! Angélique du Plessis-Bellière! The beloved of King Louis XIV.

369

The widow of the great Marshal who had died in battle! The rival of Madame de Montespan and the jewel of Versailles!

At once she had been taken to the Governor of the City, Don de Los Cobos y Perrandez, whose wife had been instructed to give her the best possible care.

Angélique swallowed hard. Hunger and thirst had made her react strangely. The sight of anything whatever to eat, even a few pieces of candy, made her faint, and yet as soon as she had eaten them, she felt her pains return.

'What has become of my comrade? 'she asked.

Monsieur de Breteuil did not know. The Redemptorist Fathers must have taken care of him, given him something to eat and some decent clothing. He rose and took his leave. He expressed the hope that Madame du Plessis would soon be herself again. She could easily understand that he did not wish to remain in this besieged city any longer than necessary. Just that very morning a stone cannon-ball had landed at his feet as he was taking the air on the ramparts. Actually the place was untenable. There was nothing to eat in it except a few beans and some salt codfish. Only these damned Spaniards would continue to hold out this way. They were as fierce and fanatical as the Moors themselves. He sighed, waved the plumes of his hat back and forth as he bowed, and kissed her hand.

After he had left, Angélique could not help thinking she had seen a wicked gleam in his eye, the reason for which she could not grasp.

In the evening Doña Inez helped her rise and take a few steps. The next day she dressed herself in the French gowns Monsieur de Breteuil had brought in his luggage. The Spanish lady, cramped into a farthingale and enormous panniers that were the Spanish Court style, looked with admiration on the soft flowing satins that swathed the slim waist of this French noblewoman. Angélique asked her for face-creams to bleach her skin. For a long time she sat before a looking-glass framed with carved cherubs, combing her hair and thinking of the shadowy pool under the waterfall. As then, she saw now her hair had been bleached almost white by the sun, but it still framed the innocent face of a young girl. A sharp line on her bosom separated the tanned skin from the white. Yes, she was scarred all right, yet she had not grown old looking. She was another being! She fastened a gold necklace about her throat to conceal the unsightly line.

She found the brace of her tight corset not unpleasant, but she still instinctively reached for a burnous to gather about her bare shoulders. Lastly, she examined her apartment, in which the dark tapestries with which the walls were hung did not entirely conceal the masonry of a fortress. A balcony outside her window gave her a chance to see the comings and goings in the narrow street below her that led to the harbour, where many masts and spars were visible. The sea was very blue, and in the distance she could glimpse the rosy coasts of Spain.

She was leaning over the balustrade, her fan in her hand, gazing at the shores of Europe, when she saw two sailors walking toward the harbour. They were barefoot, with red woollen bonnets on their heads and fat sacks on their shoulders. One of them was wearing gold ear-rings. The other's figure seemed familiar to Angélique, but it was not until he passed beneath the arch at the top of the steps that led down to the waterfront that the dimmer light revealed his tall shape and broad shoulders. Then she recognised him.

'Colin! Colin Paturel!'

The man turned. It was indeed he. His blond beard had been trimmed and he was tightly laced into his new clothes of heavy linen which had replaced the tattered shirt and trousers of slavery.

She waved to him vigorously. Her throat was so tight she could not call out to him. He hesitated a moment, then retraced his steps, his eye fixed on the great lady in sumptuous attire who was leaning over the balcony. Finally she found her voice.

'The door is open. Come up quickly!'

The hands that held her fan were icy cold. When she had returned to the room, he was already in the doorway. He was so different from the image of him she had cherished that she had to look at his hands for the ugly scars that would truly identify him for her. Something had come to an end. She did not know what it was, but she could no longer address him so familiarly.

'How are you, Colin?' she asked softly.

'Well. And you also, I see.'

His blue eyes were staring at her with that incisive look she had come to know so well. Colin Paturel, king of the captives!

He saw her with a golden chain about her throat, her hair exquisitely done, her wide skirts floating around her, a fan in her hand.

'Where were you going with that sack on your shoulder?' she asked to break the silence.

'Down to the harbour. I'm sailing today on the *Bonaventure*, a merchant ship bound for the East Indies.'

Angélique felt herself go white to the lips.

'You were going away . . . without saying good-bye to me?'

Colin Paturel sighed deeply, and his eyes grew colder.

'I am Colin Paturel from Saint-Valéry-en-Caux,' he said. 'And you are a noble lady, a Marquise, it appears, the widow of a Marshal of France. And the King of France has sent a ship to search for you. Isn't that true?'

'Yes, it is true,' she stammered, 'but it is no reason for you to go without saying good-bye to me.'

'At times it could be a very good reason,' he said soberly. 'At times, when you were asleep,' he murmured, 'I would look at you and say: "This little girl I know nothing about, and she knows hardly more about me. The fact that we were both Christian captives in Barbary is the only thing that has brought us together. But . . . I feel that she is like me. She has suffered, been humiliated, soiled. . . . Yet she still can carry her head high. She has been tossed about by life, and seen much of the world and its works. I feel that she is of my kind . . . !" And because of that, I used to say to myself: "Some day, when we get out of this hell and land in some port that is home to us . . . under a grey sky and in drizzling rain . . . then I shall try to make her tell me about herself. . . And if she is alone in the world . . . and if she consents, then I will take her to my cottage in Saint-Valéry-en-Caux." Nothing very big, but nice . . . with a thatched roof and three apple-trees. I have a little hoard hidden away there under one of the stones of the hearth. Perhaps if she likes it there, I'll give up going to sea . . . she will keep me from wandering . . . we will buy a couple of cows . . ."

He broke off, his jaw set, and rising to his full height he turned on her that proud, terrible look with which he had faced the bloodthirsty Mulai Ismail.

'But . . . you are not for me! That's all.'

His anger surged and he growled: 'I would have forgiven you anything. I would have accepted your past. But not that! If I had known, I would have let them tear you with the red-hot tongs. People of high degree I cannot bear.'

Angélique let out a cry of indignation. 'Colin, that is not true! You are lying to me. What about the Knight de Marmondin and the Marquis de Kermoeur?'

He stole a look toward the windows as if he were seeing in the ramparts of Ceuta the Catholic the lofty walls of Meknès.

'There it was different. We were all Christians. We were all poor slaves.'

He bent his head as if once more he were laden with the heavy sacks of stone the slave-drivers of Mulai Ismail had loaded on his back.

'I could have forgotten the tortures,' he said. 'I could have forgotten the cross. But that I could never forget. You have given me a burden to bear, Madame, a heavy burden.'

And she, too, knew how she had laden his heart and that he would carry the burden with him for ever more.

The corners of Angélique's mouth began to tremble, and the tall form of Colin Paturel seemed to vanish behind the screen of her tears.

He stooped to pick up his sack and throw it over his shoulder. Then he took off his red bonnet, murmuring: 'Good-bye, Madame. *Bon voyage!*'

He went out of the door.

She dashed into the hallway and leaned over the stairwell, but he had already reached the bottom. If he raised his eyes, could he see the tears on her cheeks? Did he remember them, and would they be some balm for his wounded heart? She would never know. She stood there weeping, her breast heaving with painful sobs.

Unable to stay shut up any longer, she went out to walk on the battlements. She needed the clean sea air to rid her of depression. The cannons on the waterfront were protecting the departure of the ships. One of them was already far out to sea, its chalk-white sails spread against the azure sky. Was it the one bearing Colin Paturel, the king of the captives away from her forever? 'How stupid life is,' thought Angélique, crying softly.

Oh, Mediterranean! Our sea! Our mother!

Our mother! Blue cradle, broad salty bosom of humanity, bearing every race, nurturing every dream! Sorcerer's cauldron, brewing every passion!

It seemed to her she had undertaken this journey only to clear the image of her husband from her mind, to discover that till then her memory of him had vanished into unreality. On these shores which had seen so many empires crumble, everything turned to dust. Now she was tired. She thought she had sacrificed enough to an impossible goal, a cruel fantasy. As little Cantor had called 'My father! My father!' before he disappeared beneath the waves, so she had cried 'My love!' But nothing had answered her.

Her fantasies, her dreams of bliss, were vanishing in the slow movement of the white sails on the horizon, in the odour of black coffee and the name of exciting, mysterious cities – Candia of the pirates; Meknès, where slaves breathed their last in gardens worthy of Paradise; Fez, which means 'gold'. . . .

Now she was weeping less for the failure of her plans and her disillusionment than for the deathless memories of Osman Faraji, the

Grand Eunuch; Colin Paturel, the crucified; even the weird Mulai Ismail, to whom prayer and desire were of equal rank; and finally of that thin, sombre personage Rescator, of whom the Grand Eunuch had said: 'Why did you flee? The stars record your history and his, the most extraordinary tale that ever was.'

In the distance the mad voice of d'Escrainville shouting: 'It's for you she wears her lover's face, damned sorcerer of the Mediterranean!'

But not even that was true. Once again the deceptive wind had confused all their destinies, and her lover's face she had shown only to a poor sailor who had carried her like a stolen treasure in the most incredible of adventures.

Everything was confused, everything put to the question. But Angélique was beginning to see one truth in the chaos. The woman she had studied in the pool, the one she had bathed in the oasis and who had stood in the moonlight as a young woman, had nothing whatever in common with the woman who less than a year earlier had spurned Madame de Montespan under the blazing chandeliers of Versailles.

Then she had been a woman already touched with corruption, calculating, dissipated, loving intrigue, navigating with ease in the troubled waters of the worst possible associations. Her spirit had been obscured because of her dealing with so many repulsive people.

At the recollection of just that phase of her life she felt so sick she wanted to vomit. Never, she said to herself, never would she go back to *them*! She had been bathed and purified by breathing air perfumed with cedar-trees. The sun of the desert had burned the poisons out of her.

Now she would always see 'them' for what they were. No more could she endure the vain stupidity written all over the face of a de Breteuil, or make the effort even to answer him politely.

Of course, she would go in search of Florimond and Charles-Henri, but then she would go away again. Yes, she would go away!

Where would she go?

Good lord, couldn't there be some place on this wide earth where a Breteuil had no right to scorn a Colin Paturel, or a Colin Paturel would not feel humiliated by his love for a noble lady of the Court . . . ?

A *new world* where those possessed of kindness and good will, courage and intelligence, would be in command, and where those who lacked those qualities would always be inferior.

Couldn't she find some virgin land where men of good will would be welcomed?

Oh Lord . . . where?

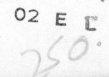